USA TODAY BESTSELLING AUTHOR

LYNSAY SANDS

In Her Highlander's Bed

*"Have fun picking your
favorite brother from the bunch!"*
—Fresh Fiction

*Be sure to read the entire
Highland Brides series!*

THE HIGHLANDER'S PROMISE

SURRENDER TO A HIGHLANDER

FALLING FOR THE HIGHLANDER

THE HIGHLANDER TAKES A BRIDE

ISBN 978-0-06-313531-4

9 780063 135314

50999

EAN

Praise for Lynsay Sands

By Lynsay Sands

In Her Highlander's Bed
Highland Wolf
Highland Treasure
Hunting for a Highlander
The Wrong Highlander
The Highlander's Promise
Surrender to the Highlander
Falling for the Highlander
The Highlander Takes a Bride
To Marry a Scottish Laird
An English Bride in Scotland
The Husband Hunt
The Heiress • The Countess
The Hellion and the Highlander
Taming the Highland Bride
Devil of the Highlands

What She Wants
Love Is Blind
My Favorite Things
A Lady in Disguise
Bliss • Lady Pirate • Always
Sweet Revenge • The Switch
The Key • The Deed

The Loving Daylights

LYNSAY SANDS

In Her Highlander's Bed

AVONBOOKS

An Imprint of HarperCollinsPublishers

Excerpt from *The Perfect Wife* copyright © 2005 by Lynsay Sands.

IN HER HIGHLANDER'S BED. Copyright © 2023 by Lynsay Sands. All rights reserved. Printed in the United States of America. No part of this book may be used or reproduced in any manner whatsoever without written permission except in the case of brief quotations embodied in critical articles and reviews. For information, address HarperCollins Publishers, 195 Broadway, New York, NY 10007.

First Avon Books mass market printing: January 2023
First Avon Books hardcover printing: January 2023

Print Edition ISBN: 978-0-06-313531-4
Digital Edition ISBN: 978-0-06-313532-1

Cover design by Nadine Badalaty
Cover art by Alan Ayers
Cover images © Shutterstock (head/hair)

Avon, Avon & logo, and Avon Books & logo are registered trademarks of HarperCollins Publishers in the United States of America and other countries.

HarperCollins is a registered trademark of HarperCollins Publishers in the United States of America and other countries.

FIRST EDITION

23 24 25 26 27 BVGM 10 9 8 7 6 5 4 3 2 1

In Her Highlander's Bed

Prologue

"*Allie?*"

Allissaid MacFarlane glanced up from the tunic she was darning as her younger sister Annis suddenly dropped into the chair next to hers in front of the fire in the great hall. Eyebrows rising slightly at her sister's troubled expression, Allissaid asked, "What is it, love?"

Annis hesitated briefly, but then queried, "Now that Claray has married and moved to Deagh Fhortan with her husband, will you be taking over the running of MacFarlane?"

Allissaid stared at Annis blankly for a moment, her mind slow to comprehend what she was suggesting. But then, she'd been having trouble coming to grips with the sudden change in their lives since waking that morning to learn that their eldest sister, Claray, had married her betrothed, Bryson MacDonald, and left for her new husband's home.

Apparently, it had all taken place while Allissaid and the rest of her siblings had slept. Claray, who had been off visiting their cousins the Kerrs, had been brought home by her betrothed after the castle had settled down for the night. The servants had been woken for the wedding and celebration that followed, but Allissaid and her brother and sisters had not. They'd simply woken to the news that their sister had returned home, married and left at the break of dawn without seeing any of them.

There had been a bit of an uproar as Allissaid and the others burst into question, which shouldn't have been surprising. They'd been told their whole lives that Claray's betrothed had been murdered along with his parents, almost before the ink was dry on the betrothal contract between the pair. But her father had not answered most of the questions they'd shot at him. He'd merely explained that the tale of Bryson's death had been a lie to protect the boy from his parents' murderer while growing up. But MacNaughton's antics had forced the situation.

Allissaid sighed at the thought of MacNaughton. The man was their neighbor, and was causing them no end of troubles. It had started a couple of years ago with his petitioning to marry Claray, the only daughter of the house who had appeared to be without a betrothed. Of course, Allissaid understood now why her parents had refused the offered marriage contract. But at the time, she had thought it terribly unfair of them to refuse it and leave Claray unmarried. Until Allissaid had met MacNaughton on one of his visits. The man wasn't more than ten years older than Claray, and was handsome as could be. He was even polite and somewhat charming in his address, but . . .

Allissaid even now couldn't put her finger on what it had been about him that had troubled her. But she hadn't liked him at all, and had sensed that he was dangerous and should be avoided at all costs. His persistence in trying to get her father to agree to the marriage by using everything from bribery to threats had only confirmed those instincts. But it appeared he'd given up on gaining his permission and moved on to trying to force the issue. It was his following Claray to Kerr and convincing their uncle to aid him in forcing a marriage on Claray that had moved Bryson MacDonald to give up the lie that he was dead and claim her to wife.

Their father had admitted that this morning. He'd also said there was even more to MacNaughton's plan. That he had intended to force the marriage and then kill the rest of them all and claim Mac-Farlane as part of MacNaughton. MacFarlane was apparently all he was really after. He wanted the extra land, soldiers and power. Marrying any of the daughters would help him achieve that so long as the rest of the family died and couldn't lay claim to it. MacNaughton had planned to bring about those deaths the moment he had Claray to wife.

Her father, Gannon MacFarlane, had explained all of this as briefly as he could before announcing that none of them were to leave the keep until the matter was resolved. MacNaughton was too much of a threat to risk one of them being taken by the man and forced into marriage. Their father had followed that up by assuring them that he was looking into ways to handle this problem, but he needed them all to remain safely in the keep until he had taken care of it.

Allissaid had spent the hours since learning this news trying to come to grips with the threat they were under, but Annis's question now brought up the other changes Claray's marriage had brought about. The main one being that she'd probably now be expected to take over the running of MacFarlane. A large undertaking she wasn't sure she was ready for. Claray had always managed that.

"Ooh! Aye! But no' fer long!"

Allissaid barely got her sewing out of the way before her younger sister Cairstane suddenly dropped into her lap to hug her excitedly. As usual, they hadn't even heard the girl approach. But Cairstane was sneaky like that. She'd probably followed Annis to her and lurked about behind them to listen to her question.

Now, the fifteen-year-old hugged Allissaid happily and crowed, "Aye, ye'll run MacFarlane until father can arrange yer marriage, and Annis and Arabella's too. Then once the three o' ye are off and married, I'll be runnin' the keep and Cristane, Islay and I'll each have our own bedchamber instead of havin' to share one!"

Allissaid pushed her sister's clinging arms away with exasperation. "Nice to ken ye're so eager to see us go. But I'd no' get too excited if I was you.

Ye ken me marrying is no' likely to happen any-time soon. Nor Annis and Arabella either. Da has been putting off me betrothed fer years now, and he sent Annis's betrothed away just two months ago. He's no' likely to—"

"He's sent messengers out to all three men to come take ye three away to be their wives," Cairstane interrupted her to announce.

"What?" Allissaid asked with shock.

"Aye, what?" Annis echoed, her eyes wide.

Cairstane nodded. "'Tis true. I heard him talking about it to our cousins Aulay and Alick. He sent the messengers last night just ere the wedding. Since Graham is so close, he expects your betrothed to arrive this afternoon, Allissaid," she said and then turned to Annis to add, "but he thinks the MacLaren and the MacLean should be no' more than a day or two behind if they travel quickly as he requested."

Allissaid stared at Cairstane blankly, her mind having trouble absorbing this news. Alban Graham, her betrothed since she was a wee child, had been trying to claim her to wife for more than three years, but her father had always refused to allow the wedding until he saw Claray married. It was something her father had continued to insist on even after their mother, Lady MacFarlane, had died four years ago. But since Claray's betrothed was, as far as they'd known, dead, and her father hadn't seemed to be trying to arrange another, Allissaid had begun to think there might be something wrong with Alban Graham, and her father was trying to back out of the contract. She'd worried that, like Claray, she might never marry. Only that didn't appear to be the case. It seemed she would be marrying him after all. And quite soon too.

"Are ye sure?" Annis asked, looking more concerned than excited at this news. Something Allissaid completely understood. It wasn't that she didn't want to marry and start having children of her own and a home to run, but this was all so sudden and—it was quite taking her breath away. She didn't know how to think or feel and was sure Annis must be feeling much the same way.

"Aye," Cairstane assured them. "I told ye. I heard them talking about it. Aulay was saying as how he thought it a good idea to get the three o' ye married and away. 'Twould hamper the MacNaughton further, and might save everyone without the need to wage war against the 'bastard MacNaughton.'"

"Well," Annis frowned, her gaze dropping to the floor as expression after expression flickered across her face, and then she muttered, "It would ha'e been nice did he bother to tell *us* this news."

"Aye," Allissaid agreed on a sigh, and then stood abruptly, nearly dumping her younger sister on the floor. Fortunately, Cairstane had always been as quick on her feet as she was quiet and managed to save herself from landing in the rushes.

"Where are ye going?" Annis asked, standing as well.

"To pack," Allissaid said grimly, heading for the stairs.

Much to her relief, Annis didn't follow and neither did Cairstane. Instead, she heard the murmur of their voices as she started up the steps. No doubt they were discussing what Cairstane had heard, but she didn't want to have to talk about any of it. She needed time alone to think. Everything was happening so swiftly. First Claray was married and gone which had been more than a shock. Allissaid and her older sister had been close, and she knew Claray had yearned to have a husband, a home and children of her own as all girls expected to do. She also knew Claray had resigned herself to never gaining any of that after all these years of their parents not arranging another betrothal for her, and that it had troubled her terribly. So Allissaid was happy that her older sister was now married with her own home and the chance to have children. But that didn't change the fact that she would miss her terribly. And now she herself was to marry? When? Would it happen as soon as Alban arrived? Another rushed wedding like Claray's had been? Or would they—

"Oh, m'lady, thank goodness!"

Allissaid pulled herself from her thoughts, and forced a smile for the maid rushing toward her.

Smile fading as she noted the anxiety clear on the girl's face, Allissaid asked with concern, "What is it, Moire?"

"It's yer brother, m'lady," Moire gasped, stopping before her and grasping her hands anxiously. "I fear Eachann— Well, I caught him trying to sneak out o' the keep. He was wantin' to go to the river. O' course, I reminded him that 'twas no' allowed, and he said he understood and was going to his room. But I just checked and he's no' there and I fear he may ha'e . . ."

"Snuck out and gone anyway," Allissaid finished grimly. Her brother had a tendency to take off to the river every chance he got, but even he should have known better than to go out right now. Their father had been most clear on the danger they were all in at the moment. But he was still young at eleven, and impetuous at the best of times.

"Aye," the servant said unhappily, drawing her from her thoughts. "And 'tis all me fault. I should ha'e kept a closer eye on him, or told yer father then. But if he finds out now, he might blame me for no' telling him what Eachann was up to at the time, and—"

"Da will no' find out. I'll go fetch Eachann back," Allissaid interrupted soothingly, thinking she'd drag her brother back by the ear to get the point across that leaving the castle was off limits.

"Truly?" Moire asked with relief.

"Aye," Allissaid murmured, turning to the door to the room she shared with Annis. "Go wait below. I'll bring him down to the great hall with me the minute we return."

"Aye, m'lady. Thank ye, m'lady," Moire murmured, backing away as Allissaid slid into her room.

Allissaid closed the door softly, and then moved quickly to the fireplace. With the twist of one stone and a push of another, she opened the entrance to the secret passage and took a step inside, only to stop and turn back for a candle. She then stepped briefly into the hall to light it from one of the torches there before returning to her room and heading into the passage again.

Nose wrinkling at the stale air, Allissaid let the entrance close behind her and started forward. While Eachann loved the secret tunnels and passages and had used them regularly since he'd been told about them at ten, she had never much cared for them herself. The dark, the smell, the spiderwebs, and the skitter of little creatures that she was quite sure would make her scream if she could see them were all enough to put her off the dark corridors and make her move swiftly. But none of it was enough to distract her from her irritation with her brother. Her father had been quite clear on the matter of leaving the castle and Eachann wouldn't normally disobey him like this, but her brother had been difficult of late. Most boys would have been sent off to train by now. Unfortunately, their mother's illness and then death had delayed that and after . . . Well, life simply hadn't gone back to normal since. It had been hard on them all, but Eachann appeared to be taking it the hardest if his acting out was anything to go by.

Allissaid sighed at the thought of how life at MacFarlane had changed since her mother's death and how it was continuing to change. She then pushed those thoughts away and grabbed up her skirts with her free hand to lift them slightly as she started down the stairs hewn into the stone. They were steep and long, leading all the way down to a tunnel that ran under the bailey and outside the curtain wall.

Despite not liking the passages, Allissaid had used them on several occasions, usually chasing after her brother. Eachann liked to use them as a shortcut to the river where he went to swim and fish or just paddle about on most of the warmer days. He shouldn't be using it now though with the threat of MacNaughton hanging over them. Something she fully intended to blister her brother's ears over once she found him.

What she would say to him kept her nicely distracted for the walk through the tunnel. There were several exits from it, but she took the passage all the way to the end and the set of steps that led up to a trapdoor. Pushing it open, she scrambled up the last few stairs and out, then let the wooden door ease back into place in the ground, and turned to survey the bushes surrounding her. They were tall and dense and had to be cut back twice a year to ensure they didn't cover the trapdoor.

After a quick peek through the bushes to be sure the area was clear, Allissaid pushed her way through them and into the woods beyond. She paused there to brush down her skirts to remove the few leaves that had caught on the cloth, and then headed for the river. It was a short walk, and Allissaid reached the clearing quickly, only to find it empty. No Eachann.

Clucking her tongue with irritation, she turned to start searching some of his other favorite places, only to freeze as several men slid out of the woods to surround her. Their sudden appearance was such a shock that it took a moment for her to recognize the man at the front of the group. Her eyes widened with alarm when she did, but before she could say anything, pain exploded in the back of her head.

Chapter 1

"BLOODY MACNAUGHTON. ONE O' THESE days the bastard'll go too far and get his comeuppance."

Calan Campbell grunted in agreement with his cousin's irritated words, and then shifted in his saddle to glance briefly back the way they'd come. He then scanned the woods on either side of them too, but there was nothing to see. The prickling of hair at the back of his neck that made him think they were being watched must just be a result of weariness after being roused from his bed in the middle of the night. What he needed was a dip in the loch to wake himself up and wash away his exhaustion, Calan thought as he settled in the saddle again.

"Did he really think we'd believe his men's lies about crossing onto Campbell land in search o' his *lost* bride?" Gille growled with disgust. "He should ken we'd have our ear to the ground and ha'e heard about his attempt to force the eldest MacFarlane daughter into marriage," he said, and then added heavily, "And that he failed."

"Hmm," Calan muttered, mouth tightening at the thought of that mess. It was bad enough that Mac-Naughton had made the attempt, but that the lass's uncle, Gilchrist Kerr, had conspired with the bastard to get the deed done just made it all that much worse. He'd been glad to hear that the lass had been rescued and returned home.

"Especially with the Wolf involved," Gille added now. "His intervention was enough to ensure all of Scotland heard o' the debacle ere MacFarlane's daughter was even returned home to him."

"Aye," Calan agreed solemnly. While they hadn't heard the particulars, they had learned that the renowned mercenary called the Wolf had got the lass away from Kerr, returning her to her father, Gannon MacFarlane, just the day before last . . . and all without the necessity of battle. It was something Calan suspected few could have managed. But the Wolf's reputation would be enough to scare most men into submission. Her uncle would not have wanted the Wolf and his warriors laying siege to Kerr Castle. The mercenary was not known for being merciful to his enemy. And he never lost.

"Ye ken that lost bride business was all lies to cover for the fact that he and his men were intending on running more raids on Campbell land," Gille said with anger, and before Calan could respond, added, "I can no' believe the bastard's up to his old tricks. I thought we'd taught him a lesson the last time he tried this nonsense. He certainly came sniveling to Kilcairn afterward." He snorted. "Though that business o' tryin' to convince ye to let him marry Inghinn was a surprise. The man certainly has some huge bollocks on him. I would no' doubt yer refusal is the reason he went after Claray Mac-Farlane afterward."

"Most like," Calan said grimly.

"Aye. Which makes it surprising he'd try raiding again."

Calan didn't bother to respond, and wasn't surprised when Gille smiled grimly and continued, "But we sent the bastard and his men packing. His men'll think twice ere crossing onto Campbell land again."

"Aye," Calan murmured. Gregor, his first, had woken him in the middle of the night with the news that a party of six MacNaughton soldiers had crossed onto Campbell land and had been confronted by a group of his own men patrolling the border. He'd dressed and headed out at once with Gille, Gregor and two dozen warriors to ride to where the battle was taking place. But by the time they'd arrived, it was over. Two MacNaughtons were dead, three seriously injured, and one was on his knees with several swords at his throat when Calan had entered the clearing where the confrontation had occurred.

He'd taken a moment to check on his own men, none of whom had more than a paltry wound here or there. Even so, Calan had sent his wounded soldiers back to the castle for tending because even paltry wounds could kill a man if they got infected. He'd then questioned the last MacNaughton capable of answering. The man had insisted they weren't there to raid, but to find their laird's new wife who had "got lost." He'd said that men had been sent in all directions to try to find her. Most, he'd said, had gone east, but his party had been sent north to Campbell in case she'd "wandered" that way.

Calan hadn't believed a word of it, especially when the men had refused to give the name of this supposed bride. Still, he hadn't seen any reason to keep the men. They'd paid dearly for their trespass. While only two were dead, the three who were wounded had taken injuries so severe they weren't likely to survive. He'd escorted the group back to the border with a warning to pass on to MacNaughton. That if he valued the lives of his men, he'd not send them onto Campbell land again without first dispatching a messenger to ask permission. For the next time a group of armed MacNaughtons crossed the border unexpectedly, no one would be alive to return their dead.

Calan and his men had then watched the uninjured man lead the horses carrying his injured and dead comrades back into MacNaughton territory.

He supposed he could have returned to the castle and his bed then to indulge in at least a couple more hours of sleep. But his blood had been up after the abrupt waking and confrontation, and Calan had known sleep was unlikely in that state. He'd decided to stay with his men and joined them on patrol for the last couple of hours of night. But once the sky began to lighten, a prelude to the sun's rising, he'd decided to head back to the keep. Calan hadn't been surprised when Gille had opted to join him.

"If we hurry, we might yet get in a short nap ere everyone wakes up," Gille said suddenly, stifling a yawn that tried to claim him at the end of this suggestion.

Calan had to fight a sudden urge to yawn himself, but shook his head and reined in as they broke from the trees into a clearing along the loch. "Nay. I've a full day planned. A nap would do little but make me grumpy at this point. You go ahead and find yer bed though, do ye wish."

Gille drew his own mount to a halt and turned in the saddle to frown at him as he asked, "Ye're no' going to swim, are ye?"

Calan glanced around the small, secluded bay they were stopped in. "'Twill wake me up to face the day."

Gille shook his head. "Ye're a mad bastard, cousin. The loch is bitter cold fer swimming."

"Aye, 'tis," Calan agreed mildly. "But I'll no' go out deep or stay long. Just a quick dip and I'll follow ye back."

Gille did not look reassured. "Mayhap I should join ye fer the swim. Just in case ye—"

"Nay," Calan interrupted with a snap, and then took a deep breath to regain control of his sudden temper. Letting it out slowly, he forced a smile. "I appreciate yer concern, cousin, but I'm fine. And I'd rather ye stop fussing o'er me."

"I'm no' fussing," Gille argued at once.

"Aye, ye are," Calan countered dryly. "Ye're worse than me mother in playing the nursemaid. Next ye'll be trying to shove a teat in me mouth."

"Well since I do no' have teats, that's unlikely," Gille snapped, and then sighed and said solemnly, "Ye can hardly blame us fer worrying, cousin. We near to lost ye just two weeks past. Ye're still recovering and are no' the sort to rest and allow yer body to heal like ye should. And frankly ye could do with a nursemaid," he added, getting testy now as well. "A big mean one who'll make ye stay abed so ye can recuperate properly."

"Ye'd ha'e better luck keeping me abed did ye find a sweet young thing with lots o' curves," Cal told him with amusement. "And if ye're looking, keep in mind I prefer blondes."

"A fat lot o' rest ye'd get that way," Gille groused, and then shook his head with resignation. "Fine, go swimming then. But do no' blame me if yer wound becomes infected and ye end up abed with a fever."

"I promise to no' blame ye," Calan said mildly. "Now ride back and when me mother rises, let her ken all is well and I'm fine so she does no' send a search party to hunt me down."

"'Tis no' a joke. She'll probably do exactly that if she gets up and finds ye absent," Gille said sharply. "What am I supposed to say when she asks where ye are?"

"If she rises before I get there, just tell her no' to worry and I should be back directly."

Gille scowled at the words, but then huffed out a breath and said, "Fine. But ye ken as well as I do that if ye get yerself drown in this godforsaken loch, yer mother'll blame me. She'll make me life a misery. And if that happens, I shall curse ye every day to hell fer it."

"Understood," Calan said dryly.

Giving a "harrumph," Gille shook his head, tightened his hands on his horse's reins, and finally rode out of the clearing.

Calan watched until the other man was swallowed up by the trees, and then turned to survey the shoreline. Finally, he dismounted, tied the reins of his horse to the branch of the nearest tree, and ran his hand down the beast's side before walking toward the water. Once on the sand and shingle beach, he stripped off his plaid and shirt, let both drop to the ground, and then waded, naked, into the water.

It was warmer in the shallows, retaining the last bits of heat from the sunny day before. But the shallows didn't last long. Calan waded out until the water reached his thighs and then with the next step it was like walking off a cliff. If he hadn't grown up here and known this loch, he might have been in trouble. But he was prepared for the sudden drop and was fanning his arms through the water to stay at the surface even as it happened. He was also ready for the bone-deep cold that enveloped him.

Loch Awe was approximately twenty-five miles long, little more than half a mile wide, but one hundred to three hundred feet deep depending where you were in the lake. It made for very cold water. Drop too deep in this loch and the sudden plummet in temperature could be enough of a shock to the body that it could be fatal. Over the years, Calan had seen more than one or two corpses float up after such an encounter. But he wouldn't be one himself.

He swam briefly in the deeper, colder section, allowing the brisk water to wash his exhaustion away, and then struck out again back toward the shallows. He'd just reached it and stood upright when movement onshore caught his attention. Stopping, he glanced around and spotted a pale figure racing away into the woods in the gray morning light. Calan stared blankly at the naked lad until he recognized the dark patch of cloth hanging over his shoulder as his own plaid, and then he began to move.

The water slowed him down as Calan waded out, but once free of the hampering liquid, he burst into a run. He quickly closed the distance between himself and the young thief, taking no more than a dozen long strides into the woods before he was able to tackle the smaller figure to the ground. The thief went down with a squawk of alarm that turned into a groan, followed by silence.

Realizing the body beneath him had gone limp, Calan pushed himself up, and then shifted to kneel beside the thief and turn him over. Unfortunately, there wasn't much light reaching them in the trees, just enough for him to make out their basic size and shape and guess that he was dealing with a lad of twelve or thereabouts. But the fact that there was any light at all told him the sun must have risen a bit more than when he'd first stopped to take his swim. It made him worry about how much time had passed since he'd gone into the water. Calan hadn't thought he'd been in the loch long, but he often lost track of time when swimming. The last thing he needed was for Gille or his mother to come searching for him like an errant child.

Sighing, he picked up his plaid, dropped it on the unconscious thief, and then scooped him up—or tried to. Pain shooting through his chest as he started to lift made him stop. Recalled to the injury he'd taken just two weeks earlier, he looked down at himself, but the poor light in the trees didn't reveal much. Shaking his head, he shifted his gaze to the unconscious thief, considering just taking his plaid and going, but even he wasn't heartless enough to leave an unconscious lad in the woods for wolves or some other animal to find. Thief or not.

Gritting his teeth, he tried again to lift the boy, this time ignoring the pain. He managed to get upright with his burden, and moved quickly back out of the trees to the clearing.

As Calan had suspected, the sun had made more of a showing in the time since he and Gille had stopped here. Rather than black, the sky was now a dark cerulean that lightened to a soft pastel blue as it neared the horizon where ribbons of yellow, orange, and red were creeping upward. It wasn't full daylight, but was bright enough for him to see the would-be thief he was carrying.

Calan's feet halted when his gaze slid over a heart-shaped face, bee-stung, bow-shaped lips, long dark hair, and a chest that wasn't flat as it had seemed in the glimpse he'd got, but had two small mounds. His gaze shot instinctively to the groin, but his plaid had gathered there and was covering what would have been the ultimate proof that he was carrying a female. He didn't really need it though. The breasts were small, but there. His would-be thief was a young lass.

His gaze moved over her face again, and a frown began to pull at his lips as he took in not only the bleeding wound on her forehead, but dark red bruising both under one eye and on her jaw. The head wound he could believe she'd gained when he'd tackled her. His guess would be her head slammed into a rock or branch in the woods as she went down, but the bruises were too dark a red to be new. They weren't old either though. He'd guess they were caused no more than a handful of hours ago. So were the ones on her neck, he noted, his gaze moving downward. It looked like someone had choked her. There was red bruising on her upper arms and breasts too, and one on her calf, he realized, his gaze skipping over the woolen cloth covering her lower stomach and groin, to find her legs.

Cursing, Calan knelt and laid her on the ground, then removed his plaid so that he could examine her more fully. He winced when he saw the dark red bruising forming on her stomach. Someone had beat the hell out of her, and the finger-shaped red marks on her thighs made him suspect that she'd been raped too.

His gaze slid back up her body to her face and he sat back on his haunches with a sigh and then stiffened as his gaze landed on a ring on one of her fingers. Leaning forward, he took her hand in his and raised it to examine the ring. It was fine gold with an amethyst gem. Something a lady would wear. Frowning, he slid it off and examined the pale indent left on her finger where it had rested. She'd obviously worn that ring for years. It was hers, not something she'd stolen.

Mouth tightening, Calan replaced the ring and then took a moment to consider what he should do. Finally, he stood and walked down to the beach to retrieve his shirt from where he'd left it when he'd stripped to swim. He carried it back and laid it over the lass, and then quickly laid out and pleated his plaid. Once he'd donned it, he turned his attention to dressing the lass in his shirt.

Calan had never tried to dress an unconscious woman before, and decided there and then that it wasn't something he wanted to do again. The lass was as limp as an asparagus stalk that had been boiled too long. It made it hard to maneuver her into his shirt. Trying to get the material over her head one-handed while holding her in a seated position with the other was damn near impossible. But only damn near. He did eventually accomplish it, but was sweating with the effort as he reached inside the shirt to shove her hands and arms into the sleeves.

Once that was done, Calan tugged the shirt down to cover her breasts, stomach, and back before easing her to lie on the ground as he lifted her bottom and tugged the shirt down to cover her lower body as much as possible too. A shirt, even a shirt that belonged to a big man like him, was not the same as a gown, however, and he scowled when he saw that it barely reached halfway down her thighs, leaving a lot of leg on display. Unfortunately, there was nothing he could do about that. It wasn't like he carried women's dresses around with him in case he ran into naked ladies in need.

Shaking his head at the very thought, Calan now tried to pick her up again, intending to carry her to his horse, but he'd barely started the effort when a bellow made him pause and glance around with surprise to see his cousin, Gille, dismounting almost right beside him.

"What the devil are ye doing, Cal? Ye're in no shape to be picking up— Who the hell is this?" Gille interrupted himself to ask as he reached Calan's side and stared at the woman on the ground. "Where did ye find her? And what the devil did ye do to her?" he snapped, walking around to the other side of the lass and dropping to his haunches to examine her head wound and the bruises on her face.

"I did nothing to her," Calan growled, exhausted and more than a little insulted that his own cousin would think he'd hurt a wee lass. Mouth twisting guiltily, he admitted, "Well, I think she hit her head when I tackled her, so I may be responsible fer the head wound."

"Which one?" Gille asked grimly.

"What?" Calan barked with surprise.

Gille turned her face toward Calan so he could see the opposite side of her head. He then brushed some hair out of the way so that a second head wound in the hairline at her temple was more visible.

"Damn," Calan breathed.

Gille sat back and arched an eyebrow at him. "Ye say ye tackled her?"

"Aye," he said, sinking wearily onto his haunches again. "She tried to steal me plaid while I was swimming. I chased after her and tackled her to get it back. As I said, I think she hit her head when she went down, but all the other marks on her were there when I examined her. They can no' be more than a couple or six hours old."

"Hmm." Gille nodded and let his gaze slide over the lass, then tugged the collar of the shirt aside to get a better look at the bruising around her throat. His mouth tightened, and then he glanced at Calan, his mouth opening, but stiffened suddenly and cursed. "Goddammit, Cal, ye've opened yer wound again."

Calan looked down at his chest. Without his shirt on and slumping as he was, the strip of plaid that he'd pulled up to pin at his shoulder was sagging, leaving the two-inch wound next to his heart plainly visible. As was the blood trailing down from it. He'd burst a stitch picking up the lass.

Grimacing, Calan straightened so that the sag went away and the strip of plaid across his chest covered the wound again. He then stood up, muttering, "Then 'tis good ye're here and can lift the lass up to me once I'm in the saddle."

Ignoring his cousin's curses, Calan crossed the clearing to his horse, growling, "What are ye doing here anyway? I sent ye back to the castle."

"Yer mother was up when I got back and threat-ened to raise a search party when I returned without ye." Gille's words ended on a grunt as he picked up the lass. Following Calan to the horses, he added, "I had to promise I'd fetch ye back to prevent it."

Calan sighed at this news as he pulled himself up into the saddle, but didn't comment. Much as he hated to admit it, he was actually glad his cousin had returned. He wasn't at all sure he could have got the lass onto his horse on his own. At least not without popping several more stitches and losing even more blood than he had. He was not one to suffer injury or illness well. Calan knew he'd left his sickbed sooner than he should have, but he hated lying about like some pathetic—

"Here."

Tearing himself from his thoughts, Calan leaned down to take the lass when Gille lifted her toward him. But his cousin didn't release her at once and let him take her full weight. Instead, Gille shifted her onto his lap for him, so that Calan didn't pull any more stitches.

"Thank ye," Calan muttered, closing his arms around the lass, and taking the reins when Gille gathered them for him and held them out.

His cousin nodded, and walked to his own horse, muttering, "Yer mother is going to be fair froth when she sees yer wound."

Calan peered at the lass in his arms. He knew Gille was right. His mother would be froth at his reopening his wound . . . and she'd probably blame the lass for it. His gaze slid over the slip of a girl in only his shirt and he frowned as he considered how his mother would react to her arrival in this state. And how everyone else would react too. A lass's reputation could be ruined by something like this.

"Ready?"

Calan lifted his gaze from the girl to consider his cousin and then said, "We're using the tunnels to return."

Gille's eyebrows rose. "Is there a reason?"

Rather than explain, Calan took the girl's hand in his and held it up for his cousin to see.

Gille urged his horse closer and leaned to the side to examine the ring on her finger. A low whistle slid from his lips. "A lady then," he commented, and then straightened and nodded. "'Tis probably fer the best to take the tunnels."

Relaxing, Calan lowered her hand back to lie in her lap and gestured for his cousin to lead the way. He then urged his horse to follow Gille's out of the clearing.

Many castles had secret passages for the females in the family to use to escape in the event of an attack or siege. His home, Kilcairn Castle, had one too. It ran along the outer bedrooms on the upper floor, with an entrance to it from each room. It ended at a set of stairs that twisted around and down the tower, leading to a tunnel that ran under the bailey, the curtain wall, and out to a hidden cave a mile away from the castle itself. It was to that cave that Gille led him now.

"Ye'll ha'e to take the horses back," Calan said as he reined in his mount just inside the mouth of the cave.

"Aye." Gille dismounted and tied both horses to a

metal ring that had long ago been affixed to the cave wall. Moving to his side, he then reached up to lift the lass out of Calan's arms. "As soon as I carry the lass up to yer chamber."

"I can—"

"Burst more stitches?" he suggested grimly and shook his head. "I'll carry her up and come back fer the horses."

Calan scowled, not liking to admit that he needed the help, but then simply gave a short nod and dismounted to lead the way.

Chapter 2

"PUT HER IN THE BED," CALAN INSTRUCTED
as he opened the entrance to his room from the secret passage. He then rushed ahead of Gille and
pulled the linens and furs out of the way for him to
lay the lass down.

Both men then straightened and stared at her.

"Her head's still bleeding," Gille pointed out after a moment.

"Aye." Calan hesitated and then moved to the
chest that held his clothes and retrieved a clean
shirt. Returning to the bed, he balled up the cloth
and pressed it to her forehead.

"I suspect 'twill have to be stitched closed," Gille
murmured.

Calan grunted in response. He had already realized that and was trying to sort out how to manage it. He could clean the wound and stitch it up
himself if necessary, but getting the items needed
to do so might be something of a problem. Tending
the wounded was usually his mother or sister's area

of expertise. They were the ones with the weeds, needle and thread. How was he to get those items from them without raising their suspicions?

"You need sewing up too. Again," Gille added, sounding testy. "How many times ha'e ye split yer stitches now? Five? Six?"

Calan shrugged and muttered, "I'll tend it after I see to the lass."

Obviously irritated, Gille turned to head for the open passage entrance. "I'd best go fetch the horses back. And you'd best go down and let yer mother ken ye're here and safe so she does no' have hysterics when I return with yer riderless horse."

Calan shook his head with a small frown. "I do no' want to leave the lass alone here. What if she wakes up?"

"Fine," he said with a sigh, changing direction to head for the door. "I'll just run down before I go get the horses. I'll explain that we came back through the tunnels, and that ye're up here in yer room."

"Nay," Calan said at once. "She'll come up to be sure I'm really here."

"And find ye alone with a *lady* of unknown origin, naked in yer bed," he said dryly, and then smiled with sudden amusement. "O' course, that way she could stitch up both yer wounds."

Calan glowered at him for finding amusement in this situation, and walked quickly around the bed toward the door. "Go get the horses. I'll take care o' me mother."

Shrugging, Gille headed for the entrance to the secret passage again. He was still smiling, and Calan understood why when he said agreeably, "Good. Then she'll see yer chest, and knowing Lady Fiona, she'll insist on stitchin' ye up so ye stop dripping blood on her rushes."

Calan stopped abruptly and looked down to see that while he wasn't dripping on the rushes, his plaid had shifted aside and his wound was on display again. He was also still shirtless.

"Just go," he snapped, shaking out the shirt he held crumpled in his hand. He heard the passage entrance close as he quickly shifted his plaid out of the way and donned the shirt, tucking it under the material. He then straightened his plaid over it, glanced toward the lass in his bed to be sure she hadn't yet regained consciousness, and headed out of his room to go see his mother.

As expected, he found her at the table in the great hall. There was food and a beverage before her, but she wasn't eating or drinking. Instead, she sat with her hands under the table and her serene gaze trained on the doors to the bailey. Despite her expression, Calan wasn't fooled. It was the fact that her hands were under the table. She always did that when she was wringing them, to try to hide that she was. He had no doubt she was fretting over him, and the knowledge pinched at his conscience, which in turn irritated him. He loved his mother dearly, but he was a powerful warrior, laird of the Kilcairn Campbells and he was sure that her fretting over him as she did was disrespectful. Not that he'd ever say as much to her. She was his mother after all.

Straightening his shoulders, Calan stopped behind

Lady Fiona and bent to press a kiss to her cheek. "Good morn, Mother. I hope ye slept well."

"Calan!" She jerked around in surprise as he straightened, her wide eyes moving over him with concern. "I did no' see ye come in. And I have been watching the door," she added with a frown. "I thought ye were down by the loch. Gille said ye'd stopped to watch the sun rise."

"I did," he lied smoothly, appreciating that his cousin hadn't mentioned his plan to swim in the loch. "But I returned earlier and went straight to me room fer a bit."

"Oh, dear," she murmured, her gaze sliding to the doors again. "We did no' realize it and thought ye still out. I made Gille go look fer ye."

Calan shrugged and then had to hide a grimace as the action caused pain in his chest around his newly reopened wound. Forcing a smile, he said, "I'm sure he'll be back shortly."

"Why are ye grimacing?" she asked, eyes narrowing. "Are ye in pain?"

"I'm no' grimacing. I'm smiling," he said, smiling harder.

"Nay. Ye're grimacing," Lady Fiona countered sharply. "And there's blood on yer shirt."

Calan stiffened, thinking she meant his chest, that perhaps he'd bled through the shirt, but his mother grabbed his arm and turned it slightly. He scowled when he saw the blood there. It must have been from when he'd placed the crumpled-up shirt on the lass's head to soak up the blood from her wound. He'd forgotten about that when he'd pulled it on.

"Have ye hurt yerself again?" Lady Fiona asked with dismay. Standing, she tugged up the sleeve of his shirt to get a look at his arm.

"Nay, I ha'e no' hurt meself again," he said with irritation, very aware of the fact that every man and woman at the table was witnessing this. He was laird here, yet Lady Fiona still treated him like a bairn. Mothers could be so embarrassing. Scowling now, he tried to pull the sleeve back down as he said, "And I did no' hurt meself the first time either. I was shot with an arrow, Mother. I did no' fall into one."

"Well, I ken that," Lady Fiona said with some irritation of her own as she pushed his hand away and examined his arm. Finding it injury-free, she let the sleeve drop back into place and then plucked at the obviously fresh bloodstain. "But ye—" She stopped abruptly as her gaze moved up toward his face and halted on his chest. "Ye've reopened yer chest wound," she snapped suddenly, reaching up to jerk the strip of plaid aside to reveal the growing stain on his chest.

"One stitch," Calan said soothingly.

"Well, we'd best put in another then," she said, taking his arm to try to turn him toward the stairs.

"Nay," Calan said sharply, knowing she'd want to do it in his room. Forcing another smile, he urged her back toward the table. "Ye needs must wait fer Gille and assure him I'm here and fine when he returns."

"But yer wound needs restitching," she argued, trying to tug her arm free of his hold. "And ye're grimacing again, obviously in pain."

Calan gave up smiling at that and forced himself to remain patient. "I'm no' in pain," he assured her. "And 'tis better if ye stay to tell Gille I'm here and fine when he returns. Otherwise, he might arrange a search party to look for me," he pointed out, and when she opened her mouth to argue further, added, "I'll ha'e Inghinn tend me chest while ye wait fer him."

Fortunately, that argument seemed to work, and she stopped resisting his efforts to usher her back to the table. Settling back in her seat, she sighed, "Oh, very well. Inghinn can tend it then."

"What can I tend?"

Calan stiffened when his younger sister's voice sounded behind him. Turning slowly, he forced a smile for her.

"Why are ye grimacing?" Inghinn asked.

Calan dropped the smile and scowled instead, but it was his mother who answered.

"Calan's burst his stitches again and needs them put back in," Lady Fiona announced. "Can ye do it, love? I need to wait for Gille to return else he'll raise a search party to look fer yer brother."

"Oh. Aye, o' course," Inghinn said at once, and turned to head back toward the stairs. "Come along, brother. There's no sense putting the lasses all in a flutter by making ye take yer shirt off down here."

Calan hesitated, but then followed his sister up the stairs, trying to think of a way to convince her to let him tend his own injuries. He needed her needle and thread and medicinals anyway for the lass in his room. He just had to think of a way to talk her out of them. He was still working on that when they reached the upper hall and he realized she was heading for his room rather than her own.

"Where are ye going?" he asked with alarm. "Do ye no' want to fetch what ye'll need?"

Inghinn didn't even slow down, she merely patted the bag he hadn't noticed hanging from her belt and said, "I have me medicinals right here. I planned on going down to the village to check on the innkeeper's wife after I broke me fast."

Calan knew the innkeeper's wife had burned her arm quite badly the week past and that Inghinn had been taking care of her, but was more concerned with the fact that his sister was even now opening the door to his room. Cursing under his breath, he rushed forward, but it was too late. He knew that when she stopped dead just before he could catch her arm to stop her from entering the room.

"What—?" Her question ended on an "oomph" of surprise as Calan pushed her into the room, followed and closed the door behind them.

He turned from closing the door in time to catch her scowling expression before she swung away to walk up to the bed and look down at the lass in it.

"Who is she?" Inghinn asked as Calan joined her at the bedside.

"I do no' ken," he said wearily, rubbing at the wound on his chest and grimacing at the pain just touching it caused. The damned thing was itching, but hurt to be scratched.

"What do ye mean ye do no' ken?" Inghinn asked with disbelief, settling on the side of the bed, and brushing the hair away from the lass's face to get a better look at her wounded forehead. "She's in yer bed, brother."

"Well, I ken that," he snapped irritably.

"And yet ye do no' ken her name?" Inghinn asked more than a little shortly herself.

"She's in me bed because I had Gille put her there after he carried her up here," he explained. "And I do no' ken her name because she knocked herself out ere I could ask."

"She *knocked herself* out?" Inghinn turned a dubious expression his way.

"Well, I may ha'e helped," Calan admitted with a grimace, and then rolled his eyes at her expression and explained. "I was swimming in the loch and saw what I thought was a lad making off with me plaid. I got out to give chase, tackled the lad, and it turned out to be a lass. I think she hit her head as she fell."

Much to his relief, his sister stopped looking at him like he was some madman who ran about attacking wee lasses who wandered into his path. Her shoulders even relaxed. Briefly. The stiffness returned a moment later as she examined the lass though, and slipped a hand under her head to tip it this way and that. Finally, she set her head back on the bed and turned to glare at him as she asked grimly, "Just how many times did ye tackle her?"

"Once," he assured her. "I think she got the wound on her forehead when I did. She must ha'e already had the one on her temple before that."

"And the one on the back o' her head?" Inghinn asked sharply.

Calan gave a start at the question and moved around the bed to approach from the other side.

"I felt a bump on the back o' her head when I lifted it," Inghinn told him when he turned the lass's head on the bed again, trying to see what she'd found.

Frowning, Calan slid his own hand under the lass's head and stiffened when he felt the large knot there. It felt huge. But he didn't feel dry blood or any kind of open wound. This blow hadn't broken the skin. He eased her head back down and straightened. "She must ha'e got that ere I encountered her. The other bruises ye see too," he added when she ran her fingers gently over the bruise under the girl's eye, and then over the one on her jaw before drawing the linens and furs down to expose the bruising around her throat.

"Someone choked her," Inghinn said grimly, and then drew the linens and furs further down, exposing his shirt. Her eyebrows rose, but she didn't comment except to say, "I need to examine her. Help me sit her up so I can remove yer shirt."

Calan didn't ask how she knew it was his. She'd made it and probably recognized the stitching or something, so he simply set to work helping her get the shirt off the unconscious lass. It was easier taking it off with the two of them working than it had been for him to get it on, and the lass was soon lying flat again, her bruised upper arms and breasts on display.

Calan saw his sister's mouth tighten, but remained silent as she drew the furs down farther, revealing the rest of the lass's battered body.

Inghinn examined the lass's stomach, pressing gently where the bruising was, then moved on to examine her legs and feet.

"Nothing appears to be broken," she announced and then hesitated and met his gaze. "I need to check if she was raped."

"Why?" Calan asked with surprise. "She can tell ye that when she wakes up."

Inghinn hesitated, and then explained, "If she was raped as violently as it appears, there could be damage . . . internal bleeding and tearing that might need stitching. If so, 'tis better to do that while she sleeps."

While Inghinn blushed as she said that, Calan felt himself pale at the words. He'd never thought of his cock as a weapon, but what his sister was saying suggested it could be one. Horrified at the thought of the slip of a lass in his bed being torn up inside by some ham-fisted bastard, Calan nodded stiffly, and turned his back, then strode over to the fireplace to give her privacy to examine the chit.

He stared at the dying embers from the fire he'd lit before bed the night before, and then threw a couple more logs in and grabbed the poker to move the coals about to bring the fire back to life. All the while he was doing his best to ignore the rustling sounds behind him as his sister did what she had to. As he waited, he began to regret not having suggested their mother come up and take over the examination at that point. He knew that she had taught Inghinn much about healing, had even let her attend and help with several births over these last years.

But he was very aware that his sister was an unwed lass, innocent of the marriage bed and all it entailed. This kind of examination did not seem suitable for an innocent young lass to conduct and he—

"She was no' raped."

Calan turned sharply to see Inghinn drawing the linens and furs back up over the lass to her neck. Walking back, he asked uncertainly, "Are ye sure?"

"Aye," she assured him.

Calan frowned, his gaze moving over the lass. She might be covered now, but in his mind's eye he could still see the bruising on her breasts and thighs.

"From the bruises she has, it looks as if someone tried," Inghinn said as if her thoughts were following the same path as his own. "But they did no' succeed. Her maiden's veil is intact."

Calan didn't know how he felt about that. He was glad for the lass, but it seemed to him that what had been done to her was at least as bad, or bad enough.

"What's this?"

Blinking his thoughts away, Calan glanced to where Inghinn was now examining the ring on the lass's finger. Before he could respond, Inghinn turned a dismayed face his way.

"She's a lady?"

"It would seem so," Calan acknowledged. No servant could afford a ring like the one the lass wore.

"But then how did this happen?" Inghinn asked with horror. "Where is her escort?"

Calan shook his head. "She was alone when I encountered her."

"And her gown? Her slippers? Where are her clothes?" Inghinn asked now, turning back to the girl.

"She did no' ha'e any when I came upon her," he told his sister. "I presume that's why she was trying to make off with me plaid."

"I suppose," Inghinn sighed the words and set the lass's hand back on the bed. "I need to look at her back. Help me turn her over. But do no' look," she added sternly.

"How am I to help ye without looking?" Calan asked dryly as he moved around to the other side of the bed to help turn the lass onto her stomach. "And why can I no' look now? Ye did no' mind when her front was showing."

"I did no' ken she was an unmarried lady then," Inghinn pointed out. "Just close yer eyes and help me turn her."

Rolling his eyes with exasperation, Calan placed his hands on the girl's shoulder and hip, and then closed his eyes before shifting the lass onto her stomach. He then straightened and waited for his sister to finish examining the girl's back.

"Give me yer hands," Inghinn said a moment later.

Calan almost opened his eyes, but caught himself at the last moment and held his hands out. His sister then took them and placed them on the girl's body, before saying, "Now help me turn her again."

"How's her back?" Calan asked as he pulled on what he was sure was the lass's shoulder and hip, to turn her in the bed once more.

"Better than her front. At least her bruising there

is no' as bad as 'tis on her wrists and some other places," Inghinn said quietly and he heard the rustle of material being moved. "Ye can open yer eyes now."

Calan did and found the lass was again covered all the way to her neck.

"Her hair's wet," she commented.

"Aye. She was wet all o'er when I tackled her," he recalled.

When Inghinn remained silent, he eyed her with curiosity, noting her thoughtful expression. "What are ye thinkin'?"

Inghinn hesitated and then said, "I think she must ha'e fallen into the loch, back first and from some height."

Calan felt his eyebrows rise at the suggestion. "Why do ye think that?"

"Because her back is dark red from her shoulders to the tops of her thighs," she explained. "Just like yer stomach was that time ye went belly first into the loch from that oak tree in the bay."

Calan considered the lass in his bed with a small frown. If what Inghinn suggested was true, the lass's back would be terribly tender. "Should we turn her onto her stomach then, so it does no' pain her when she wakes?"

Inghinn hesitated and then shook her head. "Lying on her stomach would probably pain her more with the bruising she has there." Her mouth compressed briefly, and then she said, "Someone has mistreated her horribly."

"Aye," he agreed solemnly.

Sighing, Inghinn offered, "I'll clean both o' her bleeding head wounds and see if one or both need stitching."

"Thank ye," Calan said quietly. "I was going to try to do it meself, but ye're better at this kind o' thing."

Inghinn nodded absently, her troubled gaze still on the girl, but after a moment she straightened her shoulders and stood. "I'll need to fetch fresh water and clean linens to clean the wound."

"Inghinn, ye can no' tell anyone she's here," Calan said firmly as she started away.

Pausing at the door, his sister turned back with surprise. "Why?"

"We do no' ken what kind o' trouble she encountered ere I came across her. It could be dangerous fer anyone to ken we ha'e the lass here," he pointed out. "Besides, she's a lady, and according to you an untried one. Her reputation would be ruined if it was discovered I found her naked in the woods."

"Oh, aye," Inghinn said with a frown.

"So, tell no one. No' e'en mother," he persisted and when she opened her mouth in what he suspected would be an argument, he pointed out, "Mother would insist on her being moved to another room, and I do no' want to risk anyone seeing her being moved and word getting out."

Inghinn narrowed her eyes. "Do ye plan to sleep elsewhere?"

"Nay," he admitted. "She's under me protection. I'll be guarding her here." When he saw her eyes narrow, he added, "Hopefully with help from both you and Gille." Calan had hoped that would sway her, but still she hesitated to agree, so he said stiffly, "I'd no' take advantage o' a wounded lass, sister. Her virtue is safe with me. I'll be sleeping on a pallet by the door until we find out who she is and what trouble she is in."

Much to his relief, Inghinn nodded then, if a little reluctantly. "All right. But we need to tell mother as soon as 'tis safe to do so."

"O' course," he said, relaxing.

Nodding again, Inghinn turned to slip out of the room. This time Calan didn't stop her. As the door closed, he moved to the bed and stared at the lass in it. Nothing had really changed, she was still terribly pale, and the wound on her forehead was yet bleeding. But her hair was beginning to dry, and he could see that it was a pretty chestnut brown. He suspected she would be a lovely lass without the bruising on her face.

Calan wished he knew her name and who her clan was. Someone must be worried about her, and they should be. She may not have been raped, but from the bruises she carried, it was only because she'd put up one hell of a fight. He hoped that was a sign of her character, that she was a fighter and he wouldn't have a panicky, emotional female on his hands when she regained consciousness.

The door of his room opened and Calan turned sharply to see Gille sliding inside. Relaxing, Calan turned back to the bed as Gille approached.

"Has she woken up?" his cousin asked, stopping next to him.

Calan shook his head.

"I thought ye were going to clean and stitch her wound."

"Inghinn is going to do it," Calan explained. "She's gone to fetch clean linens and water to mix her medicinals in."

"Oh," Gille said with a nod. "So ye told yer mother and Inghinn about the lass?"

"Nay. Inghinn walked in and saw her," he admitted. "I asked her no' to tell anyone else."

"Good thing I did no' mention her to yer mother when I got back then," Gille said with a wry smile.

"Aye," Calan agreed, and then told him, "I'm thinkin' it may be better to keep her presence here a secret until we find out who she is and what happened to her."

"Mayhap," Gille said with a shrug, and then stifled a yawn.

"Ye're dead on yer feet. I'm surprised ye came back here rather than heading straight to yer bed," Calan commented, fighting a yawn of his own now. The damned things were contagious. He hadn't felt the least bit sleepy before Gille had started in yawning. But now he was becoming aware of his own weariness.

Gille grimaced. "I planned to head to bed when I got back, but stopped in the kitchen first to grab something to eat. A mistake," he said dryly. "Cook immediately started in talking to me about how Kilcairn needs a bigger kitchen to serve the growing clan and insisting I talk to ye about it." Gille grimaced. "Ye ken how he gets once he's on that subject."

"Aye," Calan said sympathetically. He'd been cornered himself more than a time or two by Cook wanting to harp on the subject.

"Ye ken this great need fer a larger kitchen is purely because our cousin at Ardchonnel down the loch just enlarged his," Gille pointed out. "Cook's nose is out o' joint."

"Aye," Calan agreed, and when Gille yawned again, said, "Well, ye've done as he asked and talked to me on it. Why do ye no' go rest fer a while now?"

"I think I will," Gille announced, and turned to head for the door. "Call me if ye need me, cousin."

Calan didn't respond. He didn't see any reason he might need his cousin. He planned on staying right where he was until the lass in his bed woke up.

Chapter 3

A SHARP PAIN IN HER FOREHEAD WOKE Allissaid. She came out of sleep fighting, or trying to. She couldn't move. Opening her eyes, she stared in horror at the man on top of her. He was sitting with his knees on either side of her hips, and his upper body leaning over her as he held her arms down. He had her pinned to the bed, and she was beginning to panic despite the fact that he wasn't the MacNaughton.

"'Tis all right, lass. I ken it hurts, but yer wound needs to be cleaned and sewn up."

Allissaid blinked in confusion, and then movement drew her gaze to a young blonde woman kneeling at her side with a bloody cloth in hand.

"I'm almost done," she assured her sympathetically. "But then I'll have to stitch ye. Yer wound does no' want to stop bleeding," she added with concern, and asked, "How long ago did it happen?"

"I—I'm no' sure," Allissaid admitted slowly. It was the truth. She wasn't even sure what day it was, and wondered anxiously how long she'd been unconscious.

"What's the last thing ye recall?" the woman asked, worry clear on her face.

Allissaid bit her lip and considered what she should say. The problem was she had no idea who these people were . . . or where she was. Perhaps these were MacNaughton's people, and—

"What's yer name?" the man asked.

Her gaze slid to him now, her eyes widening slightly as her mind worked out that if they didn't know who she was, they couldn't be MacNaughton's people. Maybe. Rather than answer the question, she turned to the woman and asked anxiously, "Where am I?"

"Kilcairn," the man said, drawing her gaze back his way.

"Kilcairn," Allissaid echoed. The name sounded vaguely familiar, though she couldn't place it just then. But it wasn't Fraoch Eilean, the castle MacNaughton inhabited and had dragged her to. That was something.

"I'm Inghinn Campbell," the woman said now. "And the big oaf presently pinning ye down is me brother, Calan Campbell, Laird o' Kilcairn." She smiled gently and explained, "He's only holding ye down like this because ye were thrashin' while I was tryin' to clean yer wound."

"Oh," Allissaid breathed, her body shuddering with relief and relaxing a little under his weight.

"If ye promise no' to move while I stitch ye up, he'll get off ye," the blonde offered gently.

"Aye," Allissaid said at once. "I'll stay still."

When the blonde nodded and then turned an expectant gaze to the man on top of her, Allissaid shifted her gaze to him too and watched as he released his hold on her arms, sat up and then climbed off her. It was only then she realized that there were furs piled on top of her. He'd been on top of them. She'd been so upset to find herself pinned down that she hadn't noticed that.

"I hope ye did no' add to her bruises," Inghinn said wryly as her brother settled in a chair on the opposite side of the bed.

"Nay," the man rumbled, crossing his arms over his chest. "I was careful."

Allissaid glanced to the blonde with confusion. "Bruises?"

"Aye. Ye've bruises everywhere," she explained slowly, a frown crossing her face, followed closely by deepening concern. "Do ye no' remember anything at all?"

Allissaid hesitated. She remembered quite a lot, actually. But the last thing she recalled was trying to pilfer the plaid of a warrior swimming in the loch, being chased, getting knocked down from behind, and pain slamming through her head as she tumbled to the forest floor. She hardly wanted to admit to these people that she'd tried to rob some poor man of his plaid. As for what had happened before that . . . Allissaid didn't even want to think about what MacNaughton had tried to do, let alone talk about it.

Taking her silence as an answer, the blonde sighed

and then forced a smile. "Well, do no' worry. Yer memories will probably return with a little time."

Happy to let them think that she'd lost her memory, Allissaid merely closed her eyes.

"I'm going to finish cleaning yer wound now," the blonde told her.

Allissaid blinked her eyes open to see that Inghinn was dipping the bloody cloth in a bowl of water on a small table next to the bed. As she then wrung it out, the woman warned, "'Twill sting something awful, but I need ye to stay still. If ye can no' do that, I'll ha'e to ha'e me brother hold ye down again." She started to lean over, and then paused to offer, "I can give ye some uisge beatha. It may help."

Allissaid almost said "aye" at once, but then stopped to consider it. She truly wasn't a fan of pain, and dulling it with the harsh alcohol held some attraction. Except that she was afraid the liquid might loosen her tongue and have her saying something to reveal that she hadn't lost her memory at all. That didn't seem a good idea, so she let her breath out on a small unhappy puff of air, and shook her head. "Nay. Thank ye. I'd rather no'."

Inghinn looked as disappointed as she felt at this decision, but nodded and leaned over her again.

There must have been some kind of medicinal in the bowl of liquid the woman had dipped the cloth into, because it stung like a bugger when she began to dab at her forehead. Allissaid sucked in a breath at the first shock of pain, and noticed the way the Campbells both tensed at the sound. She didn't move, however. She made herself remain completely still as the woman worked, but it was hard. Her entire focus was on the pain . . . until a warm hand claimed hers and squeezed gently.

Allissaid's gaze flickered down toward her hand. She couldn't see it from that angle, but she could see Calan Campbell's arm stretching toward it, and knew it was he holding her hand. The touch was both soothing and distracting, his skin rough and incredibly warm against her colder hand. Wanting more of that warmth, she instinctively turned her hand over and laced her fingers through his.

"Squeeze if ye need to, lass," Calan Campbell said gruffly. "As hard as ye need. It may help."

Allissaid considered saying "thank ye" but was afraid if she opened her mouth, she might cry out in pain, so merely clutched his hand harder as his sister continued to work.

She was more than a little relieved when, what felt like an eternity later, Inghinn pronounced herself satisfied that the wound was thoroughly cleaned. That relief only lasted until she saw her pick up a needle and some thread and realized it was time to stitch the wound closed.

Swallowing, Allissaid asked anxiously, "Do ye really need to—?"

"I'm afraid so," Inghinn interrupted her gently. "Yer wound is still bleeding, and will till 'tis closed."

Allissaid nodded solemnly, and the woman bent over her again. She closed her eyes then and tried to brace herself, but there was just no way to prepare for the pain that screamed through her as Inghinn squeezed the wound closed and began to press the needle through her flesh. Dear God it hurt . . . and took so long. Mayhap if the woman had worked quickly, she could have taken it longer, but—probably in an effort to minimize any scarring there would be afterward—the woman was as slow and cautious as an old woman.

Allissaid felt Calan squeeze her hand in what she thought might be encouragement, but this time his touch didn't work as well as a distraction. It felt to her like she couldn't get any air into her body despite the short, shallow huffs of breath she was taking. Or perhaps because of them. She needed to take deeper breaths, Allissaid told herself, but couldn't seem to stop panting. She felt sweat break out on her body as she fought a primal urge to struggle and end the pain, and then she was going hot and cold. A fuzzy buzzing began in her ears, followed by her vision blurring and Allissaid felt unconsciousness rising up to claim her. She didn't fight it.

"YE CAN LET GO O' HER HAND, SHE'S NO' CONscious anymore."

Calan tore his gaze from Allissaid's face and glanced at his sister at those words. He then reluctantly let go of the small delicate hand he'd been clasping. Sitting back in his chair, he watched silently as Inghinn put in another stitch and then asked, "Will she get her memory back?"

Inghinn's mouth twitched unhappily to one side and then she sighed and sat back to stare at the lass. "I hope so. It depends on what has caused the memory loss, I suppose."

Calan raised his eyebrows at the comment. "Would it no' be caused by one o' the head wounds?"

"It could be," she allowed and smiled wryly. "She certainly has enough o' them at the moment."

"Aye," he agreed grimly.

"But she's also suffered a horrible attack o' some kind," Inghinn continued. "It could be her upset o'er that causing the memory loss. Perhaps she just does no' want to remember," she suggested and bent back to her work again, muttering, "And who could blame her?"

Calan scowled and shifted his gaze back to the lass. Her eyes were closed now, but in his mind, he could still see the vivid blue that had stared back at him earlier when she'd first woken. The lass had beautiful eyes, and when awake and animated, she was quite pretty despite the swelling and bruising presently marring her face. She was also incredibly brave. It was obvious she'd fought off an attack of some sort, and escaped. It was hard for him to see any other explanation for her being naked in the woods with so many wounds. She'd also shown her strength as Inghinn had cleaned and sewn her forehead. The lass had gone deathly pale, sweat had broken out on her upper lip, and her whole body had trembled, but she hadn't uttered a word. He'd seen warriors handle similar situations with less fortitude. She'd impressed him.

"If she does no' recall her name, we should give her one," Inghinn said suddenly as she tied off the stitches and cut the thread with her sgian dubh. "We can no' just call her lass."

Calan grunted at the suggestion. They did need a name for her, but he wasn't comfortable just assigning her one. "We'll let her pick a name when she wakes up then."

"Good idea," Inghinn decided as she began to wrap linen bandaging around the lass's head. "Mayhap she'll e'en pick her own true name without kenning it, and we'll be able to figure out who she is."

"Aye," Calan rumbled, and asked, "How long do ye think she'll remain asleep this time?"

Inghinn considered the girl's peaceful face as she continued to wrap the linen around her head, but finally said, "I do no' ken. It could be minutes or hours. Why?"

"I was thinkin' on going below and givin' me orders fer the day if ye thought 'twould be long enough before she woke," he admitted.

"No' 'til I restitch yer chest, ye'll no'," Inghinn told him firmly. "But I'll sit with her after that while ye give orders, do ye like."

Calan grimaced. He'd forgotten all about that. Now he pulled his shirt away from his chest and glanced inside hoping the wound had stopped bleeding and he could convince his sister not to bother. Unfortunately, there was a steady drip of blood slipping out. It would have to be tended to. Sighing, he let his shirt drop back into place and resigned himself to letting his sister tend him.

ALLISSAID AWOKE ABRUPTLY FROM A NIGHT-mare of Maldouen MacNaughton trying to force himself on her. Her eyes shot open on a cry of fear that turned into one of pain as her body reminded her of the multiple injuries she'd gained in MacNaughton's care. Squeezing her eyes closed, she instinctively raised a hand to her forehead, which seemed to be where the worst of the pain was coming from. Encountering cloth, she felt gingerly around, slowly realizing that the head wound Inghinn had been working on when she'd fainted was now bandaged.

"Are ye all right, lass?"

Opening her eyes, Allissaid stared at the man sitting in the chair next to the bed. Calan Campbell, Laird of Kilcairn, she recalled. It was obvious from his drowsy expression that he'd either been sleeping, or just dozing off in the chair as he'd watched over her.

"Are ye all right?" he repeated now, looking a little more alert. "Is it yer head painin' ye?"

She felt her eyebrows rise slightly at the question, and said, "Aye. How did ye ken I was in pain?"

He smiled faintly at her raspy voice, and reached out to run one large finger over the skin between her eyes. She stilled at the gentle touch, her eyes wide and confused until he said, "Ye've a furrow right here that was no' there before."

Retrieving his hand, he turned to the table next to the bed and picked up a pewter tankard. "Inghinn left this fer ye. She said yer head would probably ache when ye woke up and this would help."

He started to offer her the tankard, and then paused and frowned. "'Twould be easier fer ye to drink did ye sit up. Can ye manage on yer own or do ye need help?"

"I can manage," she said, and flushed when her voice came out a rusty croak again. Grimacing at herself, she started to struggle to a sitting position, surprised when it was more of an effort than she'd expected. She was equally surprised, but also embarrassed, when he set the drink aside and was suddenly kneeling on one knee on the bed. Catching her under the arms, he lifted and shifted her back in the bed, then held her shoulder with one hand in what she assumed was an effort to help support her, while with the other he grabbed the top fur and stuffed it behind her, bundling it into something she could lean back on.

"Thank ye," she murmured, a little embarrassed at being fussed over. It wasn't something she was used to. Her mother had died four years earlier after a prolonged illness, and while her older sister, Claray, had stepped up and tried to take her place, with there being five younger sisters besides Allissaid herself and one young brother for Claray to look after, there had been little time for fussing over any of them. Not that Allissaid would have wanted to be fussed over. In fact, she'd done what she could to help her sister with the others since their mother's death.

"Me pleasure." Calan's response recalled her to what was taking place, and Allissaid raised her gaze to him as he picked up the pewter tankard again. Turning back, he warned her, "'Twill taste foul, but Inghinn's tonics work. She learned them from our mother."

Allissaid nodded silently. She would rather have taken the tankard in her own hands to drink, but Calan didn't give her the chance. Instead, he pressed it to her lips himself. Biting back her protest, she simply opened her mouth to take the liquid in.

It was godawful! Allissaid didn't think she'd ever tasted anything so horrid. But she drank without protest. She had never been a big fan of pain and was happy to drink the tonic if it would help rid her of the throbbing ache in her head. At least, she was until she had the sudden thought that the tonic might make her sleep again. She couldn't afford to sleep any longer. She needed to leave here and make her way to MacFarlane to warn her family and find out what she could do about the situation she found herself in with MacNaughton. Her father would know how to handle this mess. He was the smartest man she knew and would find some way out of this predicament, she was sure.

That thought in mind, she raised a hand to clasp his around the tankard and tried to urge it away, but he ignored her and tipped it farther. Her choice was to swallow the liquid or choke. Allissaid swallowed. She gulped mouthful after mouthful, letting it run over her tongue and straight down her throat in an attempt to get it over with quickly. She managed to down the whole tankard, but was a bit breathless when he took it away and gulped in breaths of air, even as she shuddered and grimaced at the foul taste the tincture had left in her mouth.

"Here. This may help wash away the taste." He held another tankard to her lips now, and Allissaid almost pushed it away until she smelled the sweet scent wafting from it and recognized that it was apple cider.

She took a mouthful of the liquid, but this time didn't swallow right away. Instead, she swished it around first, hoping to wash away the tonic that had preceded it. When he offered the drink again after she swallowed, Allissaid took a moment to be sure she'd eradicated the flavor of the tonic, and then shook her head.

"Thank ye, nay. I'm good now," she said sagging against the collection of fur and whatever else was bunched up behind her back. Her gaze then moved over the room as he turned to set the apple cider back on the table. It was a large room, and well outfitted. The bed she was in was huge, with dark blue curtains that were presently open allowing a clear view of several chests against the walls with weapons and shields hanging above them. Rush mats covered the floor everywhere, and a large fur had been laid out on top of them between the fire and a table missing one of its chairs. The one he was sitting in, she supposed, and guessed that this was the laird's room. The thought made her frown and glance nervously at Calan Campbell. "Where am I?"

The question made his eyebrows pull together with concern. "Do ye no' remember, lass? Ye're at Kilcairn. Me sister told ye that the last time ye woke."

"Aye, but whose bedchamber is this?" she specified a bit tensely.

His eyebrows rose slightly at her tone, but he admitted, "Mine."

Allissaid sucked in a quick breath, and then threw the linens and furs aside, ignoring the pain it caused, and scrambled to get out of bed. Much to her surprise, her legs weren't up to taking her weight just then, and she would have tumbled to the rush-covered floor when they gave out under her if he hadn't reacted quickly and caught her.

"Whist, lass," he said his voice surprisingly gentle as he eased her to sit on the bed. "What are ye fashin' about?"

"I should no' be in yer bed," she said stiffly, crossing her arms over her chest and pressing her legs tight together when she saw that all she was wearing was a man's shirt that, large as it was, didn't reach her knees sitting. It was probably his, she guessed, and was suddenly sure she could smell his scent on it. Panicking a bit, she asked, "What am I wearing?"

"Me shirt," he answered as if it were the most natural thing in the world. "Ye had naught on but yer skin, lass. I could hardly bring ye back to Kilcairn like that."

"So ye brought me back in naught but yer shirt fer all to see?" she asked in a strangled voice, horror roaring through her. Dear God, her reputation would be in ruins.

"Nay. I would hardly parade a lass in desperate difficulties through the bailey in naught but me shirt," he assured her. "I brought ye in through the secret passage, straight here to me room. I thought it best to keep yer presence a secret until ye woke and we discovered what exactly the trouble is ye're in." He frowned slightly and added, "But now I'm thinkin' we should keep it that way until ye regain yer memories and we can sort out yer problem, or get ye back to yer clan."

"Oh." Allissaid lowered her head to avoid his gaze, guilt coursing through her for lying about not remembering. Part of her wanted to correct that issue now and tell him everything, but another part of her was more cautious. She didn't know the Campbell Laird, his sister, or anyone else at Kilcairn. She had no idea if she could trust these people. Would he take her straight home to MacFarlane if she told him who she was? Or would he hand her over to MacNaughton? For all she knew, he could be friends with the man.

Allissaid was aware that MacNaughton was bordered by Campbell land on both the north and the south. Her father had speculated that Maldouen was concerned about the Campbells perhaps wanting to absorb, or eradicate his clan and make MacNaughton part of Campbell territory. But which Campbell? They were two separate lairds, each with their own clans and people, and while they were cousins, that didn't necessarily mean they were friendly. Perhaps there were jealousies and issues between them and one Campbell wanted the larger sweep of land to be more powerful than the other, and hoped to take over MacNaughton to manage that. Calan Campbell could hope to take over MacNaughton, or he could have sided with MacNaughton to prevent his cousin from taking it over. She just didn't know enough yet to risk revealing who she was.

And, truthfully, in the end it didn't really matter. She needed to get home to MacFarlane. She had to tell her father what MacNaughton had done and hope he could fix it. She also had to warn him of MacNaughton's plans. Her father knew that the bastard planned to kill off all but one female member of her family who he intended to marry so he could claim MacFarlane and increase his own power base. Her father even probably suspected MacNaughton had her right now. For her absence surely would not have gone unnoticed and no one else was a threat. But there were other things MacNaughton planned that could hurt the people in their lives, and she had to warn someone so it could be prevented . . . If it wasn't too late, she thought unhappily, and lifted her head to look at Calan again.

"How long have I been here?" she asked abruptly.

"Dawn was breaking when ye tried to thieve me plaid this morning," he answered. "I brought ye directly back, and 'tis now late afternoon."

Allissaid felt herself flush. She abhorred thieves, but she'd been naked and desperate. Still, she wasn't sure if God would think that was a good enough excuse for trying to steal something that didn't belong to her. She could have asked for help. Although that could have been risky considering her unclothed state at the time. But . . .

Guilt pinching her, Allissaid opened her mouth to apologize for the attempted theft, only to snap it closed as she recalled that she wasn't supposed to remember any of this. If she really didn't remember, she'd probably be horrified at the very suggestion that she might do any such thing, Allissaid realized and tried for a dismayed expression instead. "I would never steal anything from anyone. I'm no' a thief."

"I'm sure ye would no'," he said soothingly. "Normally. But ye were in a desperate situation, lass."

"Mayhap, but I was raised properly, me laird. Theft is abhorrent. If I was making off with yer plaid, I was probably just borrowing it," Allissaid assured him, because that was what she'd told herself when she'd crept up to lay claim to the plaid. She'd just borrow it to get home and have her father send it back with one of his men to find and return it to its owner.

Calan did not look convinced. "Borrowing usually means permission was gained to take an item, lass. Ye did no' ask, and I did no' give permission."

"Well, I . . ." Allissaid floundered for what to say. She wasn't supposed to remember anything, so could hardly tell him the part about planning to have it returned to him. Besides, he was right; she hadn't asked, and he hadn't given permission. She had been stealing.

"Do no' fash yerself o'er it," he said, bending to cover her hands to stop the wringing they'd begun in her lap. Her hands stilled under his, and he squeezed gently. When she lifted her head uncertainly, he added, "Ye were in a damnable position and I understood in the end. I'd ha'e given permission fer ye to borrow it given the chance. Besides, ye more than paid fer the attempt when I tackled ye to the ground and ye banged yer head. I'm sorry fer that, lass."

"'Twas no' yer fault," Allissaid said with an uncomfortable shrug and straightened her shoulders determinedly. "I should leave and let ye ha'e yer room back."

"Nay."

She scowled at him for the blunt refusal. "Am I a prisoner here then, m'laird? To be locked in yer room like some poor Sabine lass ye can jest—" Much to her amazement, he covered her mouth with his hand, bringing her words to a halt. She was about to bite his hand and make him remove it when she noted his expression. He was glowering at her most unpleasantly. The man was obviously furious at her for her words, which she supposed might have been insulting if his intentions were good.

"Ye're no' a Sabine lass, and I'm no' some Roman bastard set on rapin' ye," he growled after a moment where she eyed him warily and he glared back. He took a deep breath and then said more calmly, "I brought ye here to tend yer wounds and keep ye safe. Ye're under me protection now, and that includes yer virtue and reputation."

Allissaid nodded slowly to let him know she understood. Much to her relief he then removed his hand. Taking a moment to gather her thoughts and what argument she could make, she said in a much more reasonable tone, "But do ye no' think 'twould be better fer me reputation were I no' sleeping in yer bed?"

"Aye, 'twould," he acknowledged. "But there is too much chance o' yer being seen by one o' the servants do we move ye now, and I'll no' risk that until we ken who ye are, who attacked ye and what danger ye're in."

"Ye do no' trust yer clan members?" Allissaid asked with surprise. There wasn't a person at Mac-Farlane she did not trust. She'd grown up with the clan members, knew and loved them all as extended family. She couldn't imagine not trusting her own people.

"Aye, o' course I trust me clan," Calan said impatiently. "But some o' them ha'e married lasses and men from other nearby clans, and while they've pledged their fealty to me, they still ha'e family among those other clans. A slip o' the tongue while visiting with kin, or e'en in front o' one o' the merchants who come here daily, and yer presence could be revealed to the wrong person."

His mouth twisted with displeasure before he added with frustration, "And the hell o' it is, without kenning who ye are and what landed ye naked and so badly abused down by the loch, I would no' e'en ken who that wrong person might be." He shook his head firmly. "Nay. Fer now 'tis just smarter to keep ye here."

"Oh," Allissaid breathed on a sigh. What he said made sense. There probably was a MacNaughton lass or two among his clan now, or even a Mac-Naughton male who had married and been folded into the Campbell clan. There could even be a Mac-Farlane or two here. She supposed that might make it risky for her to be seen and possibly recognized. If word got out that she was here and the MacNaughton heard . . .

"But that does no' mean I planned to take advantage o' ye," Calan added grimly. "Ye can ha'e the bed, and I'll take a pallet on the floor until ye regain yer memories."

Allissaid bit her lip, struggling again with the urge to just tell him who she was and what had befallen her. The only thing that held her back was not knowing what his relationship was with MacNaughton. She was trying to think of some way to get him to tell her without asking straight out when Calan spoke again.

"Are ye hungry?" he asked, his voice gruff and a little short. He was obviously still put out at her for the Sabine bit.

"Nay," Allissaid lied huskily, only to flush with embarrassment when her stomach rumbled.

Calan relaxed then, a faint smile curving his lips. "I fetched up some food from the noonin' meal fer ye. It should yet be warm. Ye can eat at the table, or in bed if ye'd feel better getting back under the furs."

Allissaid glanced down at her bare legs and flushed with embarrassment. She then ground her teeth against the pain it caused her as she scrambled back to sit in bed with the furs pulled up almost to her throat.

Calan stood and walked to the table by the fireplace again.

Allissaid watched him, but her mind was on the fact that the food was from the nooning meal. That meant she'd slept the morning away. A good seven hours by her guess, since the sun rose early in the summer. She was fretting over that when he returned with a trencher of something that smelled delicious.

It couldn't hurt to eat before she left, Allissaid decided as her stomach rumbled again. She needed her strength to make the journey home to Mac-Farlane anyway if she was to walk the entire way there.

That thought made her frown as she accepted the trencher he offered. Her gaze dropped to the food he'd brought and she looked over an assortment of cheese, fish, beef and neeps.

"I was no' sure what ye'd like," Calan said quietly, reclaiming his seat. "So, I brought a little o' e'erything."

Allissaid nodded, but then simply stared at the food in the trencher as she realized she didn't have her sgian dubh to eat with. It had been missing when she'd woken up after being knocked out at MacFarlane.

"Here, lass."

Lifting her head, she saw that Calan was holding out his own sgian dubh, and accepted it with a murmured, "Thank ye."

"So," Calan said as she speared a bit of fish with the sgian dubh. "How is yer head feeling now?"

"Sore," Allissaid murmured, and then raised the bit of fish on the knife to her mouth to taste. It was good, moist, tasty, not at all fishy, which was nice.

"Are ye sore anywhere else?"

Allissaid merely shrugged and concentrated on eating rather than stop to give a long list of her aches and pains, and it *was* a long list. But there was nothing that could be done about any of them. They just had to heal, which would take time. Aside from that, now that the food was there before her, there was no denying her hunger. She was starved, and as Allissaid ate, she tried to sort out how long it had been since she'd last eaten. It had been mid-morning when she'd gone in search of her brother, Eachann. So, a full day and a couple of hours ago was when she'd been knocked out and dragged to MacNaughton.

It was longer than that since she'd eaten though. Her father had passed on the news of her sister Cla-ray's rescue, marriage and the threat MacNaughton now was to the rest of them the moment they'd ar-rived at the table to break their fast that morning. Allissaid had found herself with little in the way of an appetite after the news he'd imparted and hadn't eaten. She'd merely pushed the food around in her trencher as she'd listened and considered all he'd said.

It was no wonder she was hungry then, Allissaid supposed as she finished the last of the meat and cheese and even broke off a bit of the trencher where the bread had soaked up the beef juices and ate that as well.

"Aye, ye were hungry," Calan said with amuse-ment, taking the remains of the trencher from her when she glanced around uncertainly for someplace to set it. He carried it back to the table where he'd got it from. "Inghinn left these fer ye."

As she watched, he now collected a pure white chemise and a dark blue gown that she hadn't no-ticed hanging over the chair. Carrying them back, he set them on the bed next to her and added, "She wanted me to let her ken when ye woke up so ye could don it and she could pin the gown fer takin' in. She did no' think 'twould be a good idea fer ye to be up and about until tomorrow at least, but wants to take it in so 'twill be ready fer ye when she feels ye can leave yer sickbed."

"Thank ye," Allissaid breathed, reaching out to touch the soft cloth of the gown as relief coursed through her. Having a proper gown on again would go a long way toward making her feel less vulnerable just now.

"I'll go fetch Inghinn and send her up. With yer being unsteady on yer feet just now, ye should wait fer her to come up before trying to don the gown. The last thing ye need is to fall and give yerself another head wound."

Allissaid glanced up at those words, but he apparently wasn't expecting a response. Calan was already slipping out of the room.

Chapter 4

ALLISSAID WATCHED THE DOOR CLOSE BE-
hind Calan Campbell, and then looked down at the
clothing he'd given her. She had no doubt he just expected her to obey his last edict and wait for Inghinn
before dressing, but . . .

Pushing aside the furs and linens covering her,
she shifted carefully out of bed, gasping at the pain
that rippled through her stomach as she got to her
feet and straightened. Swallowing the moan that
wanted to slip out, she paused then, waiting to be
sure her legs didn't give out again. Fortunately,
while they were still a bit shaky, they didn't col-
lapse this time. Even so, she took a couple of deep
breaths to try to ease the trembling that seemed to
have infested her muscles the moment she moved,
but then she set to work removing the borrowed
shirt. It was a ridiculously arduous activity for her.
Every movement took more energy than it should
have and caused her a great deal of pain. So much

that she had to wonder how she'd managed to leap from the bed earlier.

Her panic must have overridden the pain at the time, Allissaid decided when she got the shirt off and paused to inspect her poor abused body. This was the first chance she'd had to see the damage the struggle with MacNaughton had wrought. It was really quite distressing. Allissaid didn't remember getting half the bruises now painting her body. They were everywhere, her legs, breasts, arms, wrists, and especially her stomach were mottled red with blue and black starting to appear. She imagined there were more on her back and face that she just couldn't see, but frankly didn't want to.

If she'd doubted Calan's claim that her virtue was safe before, Allissaid didn't now. It was hard to imagine any man would want her looking like this. Except MacNaughton, of course. But he had never wanted her for herself. He wanted MacFarlane, and she was merely the key to his getting it.

Mouth tightening, Allissaid picked up the chemise and slowly pulled it on over her head, wincing as her arms, stomach and shoulders complained at the movements.

Despite the pain it caused her, she felt better once it was on. The linen gown was a little long, pooling on the floor around her, and the bodice was quite roomy, but at least it covered her all the way down to the floor. Allissaid hadn't felt at all comfortable with her calves and ankles on display in the borrowed shirt. Ladies simply didn't walk around with so much skin showing.

Picking up the dark blue gown next, Allissaid held it up for an inspection, noting that it was well-made with a pale blue undercoat and lovely bead-work on the neckline. Not that she supposed that mattered. She was not trying to impress anyone. Grimacing at that thought, she began to don it too, but with all the added material the gown had, it was a lot more work to get on. Allissaid was breathless, sweaty and shaky again by the time she tugged it down into place. But she managed it.

Sighing her relief, Allissaid glanced down at herself, noting that whoever owned the gown was obviously not only taller than her, but had larger bosoms. She could have rolled up the shirt she'd just taken off and stuffed it inside the top there was so much room. It made her cast her mind back to the brief memory she had of Inghinn leaning over her, but their positions and the bloody cloth the woman had held before her made it impossible for Allissaid to guess if this was her gown. Not that she really cared whose gown it was. She was just grateful to have something to wear.

Allissaid dropped wearily to sit on the side of the bed again, acknowledging to herself that she really wasn't ready to be out of bed yet if just dressing left her shaky and exhausted. She was actually consid-ering going back to sleep when the door suddenly opened. Tensing, she glanced swiftly toward it, re-laxing a little when she saw the tall blonde woman entering and recognized her as Calan's sister . . . And, yes, the gown was probably hers, Allissaid decided as she looked her over. Inghinn was tall, with an ample bosom that could easily fill the gown she was wearing. The lass also looked younger than she'd thought, Allissaid noted. About her own age, or perhaps even a year or two younger.

"Oh, ye're already dressed," Inghinn said with surprise once she'd closed the door. Worry pinching her face, she crossed the room and set several items on the small bedside table, then reached out to feel Allissaid's forehead, commenting, "Ye're terribly flush."

"I do no' think I ha'e a fever," Allissaid murmured, knowing that was what the girl was checking for. "I fear, dressing was just more work than it would normally be."

Apparently satisfied that she wasn't ailing, Inghinn nodded and let her hand drop away. "And no doubt painful. Ye should ha'e waited fer me to help ye."

"Aye, I should ha'e," Allissaid agreed quietly.

Inghinn eyed her with concern. "Do ye feel up to standing so I can pin it? We can wait and try again later if ye've worn yerself out."

"Nay. Let's get it done," Allissaid said with weary determination. She'd need to wear something to leave here, which she intended to do the first chance she got. She had to get home. She also needed strength in case it turned out these Campbells were friends to MacNaughton and she had to flee. Taking a deep breath, she forced herself to stand. Much to her relief she managed it, though her legs were shaking a little again once she was upright.

Inghinn eyed her briefly, but then nodded and promised, "I'll be quick."

"Thank ye fer doing this at all," Allissaid murmured as she watched the blonde gather pins from the table where she'd put them.

"Me pleasure," Inghinn said lightly as she turned back and knelt to start to work on the hem of the gown. "I could hardly leave ye running about in me brother's shirt."

Allissaid merely nodded in agreement.

"What should we call ye?" Inghinn asked suddenly.

Allissaid blinked in confusion at the question. "What?"

"Well, ye do no' remember yer name, and we ha'e to address ye as something," she pointed out, and then peered up from the hem she was pinning and asked, "What name would ye like 'til ye remember yer own?"

"Oh." Allissaid looked away guiltily and gave a helpless shrug. "I'm no' sure."

"Just say the first name that comes to mind," Inghinn suggested. "It may e'en end up being yer true name, though we'll no' ken 'til ye get yer memories back."

"Eara," Allissaid said abruptly. It was the first name to come to mind that wasn't her own.

Inghinn's eyebrows rose and then she smiled, and announced, "I like it."

Allissaid forced a smile of her own even as she wondered why she hadn't stopped to think before blurting that name. Eara meant woman from the east, and MacFarlane was east of Campbell. Good Lord! She'd just given them a clue as to her real identity.

Well, she reasoned, trying to calm herself. In truth, MacFarlane was southeast of Campbell, not straight east, so perhaps it would be fine. Besides, few people knew the meanings behind most names, she told herself. Still, it had been a stupid mistake. She really needed to learn whether the Campbells of Kilcairn considered themselves friend or foe to MacNaughton. The problem was how to find out without just asking that and giving away something that might endanger her.

Unfortunately, she hadn't come up with anything by the time Inghinn straightened and began to fuss with the front and sides of the gown, pulling the material tight over her chest and releasing it again.

Surprised at the woman's attention shifting to the bodice, Allissaid tilted her head to peer down at the bottom of the gown to see that the girl had finished hemming it already. "Ye're very fast at this."

"Well, I do no' want ye to ha'e to stand any longer than necessary," Inghinn murmured, gathering a handful of cloth on either side of her breasts and pulling tight again. She released it once more, and then instead gathered a larger section in the center, right over her chest, commenting, "Ye're much smaller in the bosom than me."

A snort slipping out, Allissaid assured her, "I'm much smaller in the bosom than everyone."

"Nay," Inghinn said at once.

Positive the other woman was just trying to make her feel better, Allissaid waved her reassurance away and said, "Aye, I am. In fact, all me sisters are better endowed than me. The only sibling in me family with smaller bosoms is me little brother."

It wasn't until Inghinn stiffened and turned excited eyes her way that Allissaid realized her mistake. For one minute she froze as panic overtook her, and then she forced her eyes wide and tried to infuse some excitement in her voice as she exclaimed, "I ha'e a little brother," as if it were news to her.

"And several sisters from the sounds of it," Inghinn said, beaming at her. "Can ye remember how many, or any o' their names?"

"I . . ." She tried a confused expression, wasn't sure that was the right reaction for someone who wasn't just feigning memory loss, and then let her shoulders sag and unhappiness cover her face as she shook her head.

Apparently, that was the right reaction, or at least, Inghinn thought it was, and patted her shoulder sympathetically. "'Tis all right. This is good news. It means yer memories were no' knocked out o' yer head by the injuries and are still there. Ye'll most like get them back. 'Twill just take some time."

Allissaid merely nodded unhappily, not having to feign the emotion this time. She *was* unhappy. She felt stupid for the mistake she'd just made, and awful for lying to Inghinn. To Calan too. Both of them had been nothing but kind, and were trying to help her, yet she was repaying them by withholding information and flat out lying. She felt awful, but she didn't know what else to do until she found out how friendly they were with MacNaughton and whether they were friend or foe.

"Oh, I forgot about this stain," Inghinn said suddenly.

"Stain?" Allissaid glanced down at the front of the gown where Inghinn was scratching at a small, dark spot in the center of the neckline. It was barely noticeable against the dark blue cloth.

"Aye. Wine," Inghinn explained with a grimace. "Maldouen jostled me arm at table a couple weeks back and I spilled a bit o' wine on meself."

"Maldouen?" Allissaid breathed, feeling like her insides had suddenly frozen.

"Maldouen MacNaughton. He's our neighbor to the south," Inghinn explained distractedly, continuing to scratch at the spot. "And 'twas no' the first time he's made me spill something on meself either. I swear he's clumsier than me, and I can be terribly clumsy," she assured her.

"Oh," Allissaid murmured weakly.

"Ah, well," she said, giving up on removing the spot. "'Tis fine. I was thinking the easiest thing to do would be to cut out the center panel here and sew the two sides together anyway. That would remove the stain altogether," she said brightly. "Now stand still and I'll just pin it."

Inghinn needn't have made the request, Allissaid felt as if she'd frozen solid. She'd just got her answer to her worries about whether MacNaughton was a friend to the Campbells or not. He was a good enough friend to dine here regularly. She had jumped out of the fire into the neighboring fire, she thought faintly.

"Are ye all right? Ye're swaying on yer feet, lass."

Inghinn's concerned voice drew her back to the situation at hand, and she forced a smile. "I'm fine."

"Nay. Ye're no'," Inghinn said, eyeing her unhappily. "Ye've gone terrible pale. Here, I ha'e this pinned enough to ken what I need to do. Let's just get this off ye and ye can sit down."

Allissaid didn't argue, she helped her remove the gown, careful to avoid the many needles pinning the places that needed stitching, and then dropped to sit on the side of the bed when it was off over her head.

"Get under the linens and furs there, lass," Inghinn suggested as she carried the gown over to the table by the fire. "Rest is the best thing fer healing, and ye're looking like ye need it."

Allissaid lay down and pulled the linens and furs over herself, then turned on her side and closed her eyes, hoping that if she feigned sleep, Inghinn would leave her be. She needed to think on ways to get out of this room, and this keep, before Maldouen or one of his men came to Campbell to see if anyone had encountered her. She was amazed someone hadn't already come here.

Dear God in heaven, Allissaid thought with sudden panic, for all she knew, Maldouen or one of his men could be below right now talking to Calan. While she may not have given them her name, it wasn't like he wouldn't recognize the description they would give. How many naked, dark-haired women could be running around Scotland just now?

CALAN EASED HIS DOOR OPEN, PEERED CAU-
tiously inside and then relaxed and entered. While he'd been gone for a couple of hours, and had thought it was surely long enough for his sister to take in one gown, as he'd approached the room he'd worried that he may have misjudged and might be returning just as the lass was donning it to check the fit, or removing it to get back in bed. He needn't have worried though. Their guest was apparently fast asleep, while Inghinn was seated by the fire, bent over the gown in her lap as her needle flashed.

Pushing the door closed, he walked to the bed to peer down at the lass in it. She was curled up in a protective ball under the furs, only her closed eyes and bandaged head poking out from under them. Calan watched her for a minute and then picked up the chair he'd sat in earlier at the bedside, and carried it to the table to join his sister.

"How goes it?" he asked as he settled in the chair.

"Almost done," Inghinn said with a brief smile his way before ducking her head back to what she was doing.

Calan nodded, but frowned and said, "Ye should ha'e had one o' the maids do the sewing."

"And how would I explain why I wanted one o' me gowns made smaller when ye said 'twas no' safe to reveal the lass's presence here until we kenned what happened to her?" Inghinn asked archly.

Calan grimaced at the question and shook his head, knowing she was right. He glanced toward the bed. "Did she pick a name?"

"Aye." His sister smiled as she announced, "Eara."

"Woman from the east," Calan murmured, and when Inghinn looked perplexed, explained, "'Tis the meaning behind the name."

"Oh." She shrugged and then her smile widened as she told him, "She also had a memory return to her."

Calan stilled. "Did she?"

"Aye. She recalled that she has several sisters and a little brother."

Calan waited, but when his sister just continued to smile at him as if this was grand news, he couldn't hide his disappointment. "That's it?"

Inghinn's smile was replaced with a scowl. "It may no' seem like much, but 'tis very encouraging. It means she still has the memories in her, they just need to work their way out."

Calan supposed that was good news. Better news would have been her remembering everything now though. His gaze slid to the bed again and he wondered who she was, and if she was betrothed. She couldn't be married since Inghinn said her maiden's veil was still intact.

Unless the attack she'd suffered had been on her wedding night by her new husband attempting to consummate the wedding and her fighting him off, he thought suddenly. The very idea was an abhorrent one to him. If it was a new husband who had abused her so horribly . . . Calan didn't even want to think on that. He could not return her to such a brute.

"I wonder who her clan is," Inghinn murmured suddenly.

Calan glanced to his sister.

"I hope 'tis no' one we are at war with," she added with concern, and admitted, "I like her."

His sister's words made Calan stiffen as he realized he had no idea who he had under his roof and that she could be an enemy.

"Yer chest wound's painin' ye."

Calan stilled at those words and let his hand drop away from where he'd been absently rubbing the bandaged wound. "'Tis fine."

"'Tis been two weeks since ye took the arrow and the wound has no' fully closed yet," she said quietly. "It ne'er will, either, do ye keep reopening it ere it heals, brother. If ye'd just take four or five days to rest and did no' insist on wielding yer sword or carting lasses about, ye'd heal and be done with it."

"I'm resting now," he pointed out.

"Aye, after ripping it open again this morning trying to carry the lass," Inghinn said dryly.

Calan narrowed his eyes. "Did Gille tell ye that?"

"Nay. He did no' ha'e to," she said with exasperation. "The lass was unconscious when I first saw her here in yer bed, and yer wound had to be restitched. E'en a fool could ha'e sorted out what happened."

"Well, ye sorted it wrong," he informed her with satisfaction. "Gille carried the lass back here."

Inghinn narrowed her eyes. "No doubt because ye ripped yer stitches trying yerself."

When he glowered at her, but didn't deny it, she gave a little "harrumph" and lowered her head back to her sewing. Calan scowled at her, and then turned his gaze back to the lass in his bed. She apparently had no trouble sleeping and healing. He almost envied her that. Anytime he tried to rest or relax, guilt assailed him. It had been that way since his father died and he found himself laird of his clan. There was much to do as laird, and his people depended on him to get it done. Aside from seeing to their safety, he had to ensure there was enough food and clothing for all. He had to see that the keep and wall were in good repair, that the men kept up their training in battle so that they were ready to serve at their king's whim, or fight any battles that came up. He had to see to trade and ensure they had the taxes the king demanded. He had to hold court among his people and solve any disputes. The list of chores was endless. Not that he minded. He'd been born to the duty and had been well trained for the position as laird. But it meant he wasn't the sort to find it easy to lounge about "healing" and had a tendency to work himself to the point of exhaustion even when ill or injured.

In truth, Calan supposed Inghinn was right. Perhaps he'd try to relax a bit for the next few days. Guarding the lass in his bed should help with that since he felt she should remain hidden here in his room until they sorted out who she was. He wanted to be here when she recalled, so that he could send news to her family and help with whatever situation had befallen her and seen her so badly treated.

"There. All done," Inghinn said with a sigh, drawing Calan's attention as she set her needle aside and shook out the gown. She then held it up for a brief inspection.

"Ye should go eat," he said when she—apparently satisfied with her efforts—stood to lay the dress over the back of the chair she'd been seated in.

"Aye. I'm hungry," Inghinn said, bracing a hand against her back and stretching to ease the strain bending over her sewing had caused in her muscles.

"Ye'll ha'e to take the passage down to the bailey and come in through the great hall doors though. Mother thinks ye've been down at the village all this time."

When Inghinn raised her eyebrows in surprise, he shrugged. "She was fretting o'er where ye were. I said ye were tending the blacksmith's wife."

Guilt crossed Inghinn's face at the mention of the woman. "I should have gone down there today to check on both the innkeeper's wife and the black-smith's wife who's with child."

"I'm sure word would ha'e been sent if ye'd been needed," Calan said soothingly as he stood and walked to the bed to check on the lass and be sure she was still asleep. She looked like she was, but it was the soft snore she emitted that convinced him. A smile crossed his face briefly at the indelicate sound, and then he moved to the mantel to open the passage for his sister while she gathered her things and retrieved a candle off the mantel. She lit it by the fire before crossing to where he waited.

"Thank ye, sister," he rumbled as she slipped past him into the dark passage.

"I'll come check on her ere I retire," Inghinn assured him as she headed away.

Calan watched until she started down the stairs that wound around the tower, then closed the panel of wall and shook his head. He knew his sister. She wouldn't just come to check on the lass, she'd insist on staying in here with them for the night in a misguided attempt to protect the girl's virtue and reputation. It really wasn't necessary, "Eara" was safe with him, but he wouldn't protest. It might make the chit more comfortable to have another woman there with her.

Settling back in his chair by the fire, Calan eyed the lass in his bed and pondered who she might be. She'd chosen the name Eara, and he had to wonder why. He didn't consider it a very pretty name, so doubted she'd chosen it because she especially liked it. Had she given her true name without realizing it? Or was it just one pulled willy-nilly from her memory? Or mayhap even one that belonged to a sister or aunt? He considered all three possibilities, but only knew one clan with a woman with that name, and the lady in question was in her dotage.

Letting go of the name she'd chosen as a possible lead to her clan, Calan next considered which clans had several daughters and one younger son. The first that came to mind was the MacFarlane clan. Which, incidentally, lay to the east, though it was more southeast he supposed. Still, the MacFarlane laird had six or seven daughters and one son who was the youngest of the brood. Then too, MacFarlane wasn't far from Campbell. It was right next to MacNaughton which was why Maldouen had wanted to marry Claray MacFarlane and—

Calan's head whipped around toward the woman in his bed as he recalled that the MacNaughton men who had been caught on Campbell land last night had claimed they were looking for their laird's lost bride. He hadn't believed the claim because he'd heard that the Wolf had rescued Claray, prevented the wedding and got her safely home to MacFarlane. But what if that bastard had managed to get his hands on her again?

Calan knew MacNaughton was determined to marry Claray MacFarlane. But it wasn't lust driving that determination. He felt sure it had been purely to make an alliance with her father. He suspected Maldouen was hoping that such an alliance would offer him some protection from Calan himself, and his cousin Finlay Campbell, who was laird over the Campbells at Ardchonnel to the south. MacNaughton knew the Campbells were both growing tired of his antics, and that it wouldn't take much to urge them into removing him as a problem whether that was by war with the MacNaughton clans or trial by combat. No doubt MacNaughton was scrambling for a way to save himself, and hoped that marrying Claray would do the trick.

Although, how he could imagine that would work

was beyond Calan. Gannon MacFarlane would hardly align himself with a man who kidnapped and forced his daughter to marry him . . . unless Maldouen used the lass as a bargaining chip, he thought with a scowl. A threat like, "Form an alliance with me or I'll abuse your daughter horribly," might work with a father who loved his children as Calan knew the MacFarlane did.

Aye, Calan could see Maldouen doing that. He was a sneaky, greedy bastard who had no qualms about taking what he wanted. Calan was pretty sure the bastard had been doing that ever since inheriting the title from his father ten years ago. He believed the man had been mounting raids on both Kilcairn's outlying farms and those of Ardchonnel to the south of MacNaughton for years, and probably others, although he couldn't say for sure. In truth, he couldn't prove that it was MacNaughton's men running the raids on Kilcairn and Ardchonnel either, else he and Finlay would have done something about it before now. But recently Calan and his cousin had begun meeting together to try to come up with a way to prove MacNaughton was behind the raids and put a stop to them.

Calan had heard whispers for a while that MacNaughton had approached MacFarlane, trying to convince the man to let him marry his eldest daughter, Claray. Then two and a half weeks ago, shortly after Calan's first meeting with his cousin, MacNaughton had shown up at Kilcairn. Not yet having proof that he was behind the raids they'd suffered, Calan had felt forced to offer the hospitality Scots expected from each other and had invited him to dinner. He hadn't been pleased to have the man and his first at his table, but had been even less pleased when MacNaughton had tried to convince him to let him marry Inghinn. Aside from the fact that he wouldn't marry a dog to the bastard, Inghinn's betrothed had only died two days earlier, shot by a stray arrow while on a hunt. Calan had thought it grotesque that the man would approach him so soon after the death. He'd refused to even consider the marriage, and sent him on his way. The very next day Calan himself was hit by a "stray arrow" while out hunting with his men.

Calan was sure MacNaughton was behind both hunting accidents. The timing just could not be coincidental. But again, he had no proof. That hadn't stopped him from riding to MacNaughton the moment he could rise from his bed to tell the bastard that he was done with the clan, and that any MacNaughton fool enough to cross onto Campbell land should know they'd be forfeiting their life. MacNaughtons would be killed on sight if they trespassed. Last night was the first time any of them had tested his stance on the matter, and while his men hadn't killed all of them, he felt the point had been made.

Calan glanced toward the bed and then stood and walked over to peer at the girl. She'd turned over in her sleep and pushed the furs down. They no longer covered her face at all, and while her eyes were closed, he could still picture what she had looked like when awake. The lass had beautiful blue eyes, a heart-shaped face and long dark chestnut hair. If he recalled correctly, other than the dark hair, she looked a good deal like the late Lady Merraid MacFarlane, Claray MacFarlane's mother. His own mother had been a friend to her and he'd met the lady on a few occasions over the years while she'd still lived.

Aye, this lass could very well be a younger version of the woman, he thought. Although, he couldn't be sure. He hadn't accompanied his mother on her visits to her friend, he'd merely ridden with his father to collect her a time or two when she was ready to return.

But, he recalled now, Inghinn had often accompanied their mother on those visits, and had been friends with one of the younger daughters. Annabel or Arabella or something had been her name, he thought. Yet Inghinn didn't seem to recognize the girl. Wouldn't she recognize one of her friend's older sisters?

Calan wasn't sure. It had been four years since Lady Merraid had died, and at least five since she'd fallen ill and stopped taking visitors. Between that and the bruises on the lass's face, he supposed it wouldn't be surprising if his sister didn't recognize her.

Good Christ, he might have Claray MacFarlane in his bed, Calan thought with dismay. If his mother found out, she'd skin him alive. As he recalled, she'd loved Merraid MacFarlane like a sister, and had always been fond of the woman's daughters.

Mind you, she'd be even more upset if it turned

out the poor lass was Claray and had been kidnapped and forced into marriage to MacNaughton.
So would he for that matter. He really needed to
help the lass get her memory back so they could
handle her situation. If what he suspected was true,
he'd kill Maldouen MacNaughton himself.

Chapter 5

$\mathcal{I}$T WAS DARK IN THE ROOM WHEN ALLISSAID opened her eyes again. Not full dark. The dying embers of a fire in the fireplace did cast some light into the room. But it was obviously nighttime now. That was the only reason she knew she'd fallen asleep. To her it seemed like just moments ago that she'd closed her eyes to feign sleep. Apparently, she'd dozed off for real though and slept for hours. Unfortunately, that meant that the effects of Inghinn's tonic had worn off and her head, as well as most of her body were now paining her.

Sitting up slowly, she looked toward the chair where Calan had been when she woke up the last time. He wasn't there, and a quick survey of the bedchamber showed that it was empty. Inghinn wasn't there either. She was alone.

Pushing the furs and linens aside, Allissaid eased to sit on the edge of the bed, moving slowly in an effort not to aggravate her aches and pains. She stood up carefully, unhappy to find the pain was worse than it had been earlier. Her muscles had stiffened while she'd slept, but at least the trembling she'd suffered before seemed milder this time.

Sighing, Allissaid peered down at herself in the overlarge chemise she hadn't removed after Inghinn had helped her out of the equally large gown. The blonde had planned to hem and take in the dress for her while she slept. Now Allissaid wondered if she'd managed to finish the task.

She peered around the room again, this time in search of the gown. Relief rushed through her when she spotted it hanging over the back of the chair by the fire. Allissaid made her way over to it as quickly as her body would allow, and then examined the gown. A sigh of relief slipped from her when she saw that all the pins were gone, and the hem and bodice were both newly stitched.

"Thank ye, Inghinn," Allissaid breathed, and then considered the overlarge chemise she was wearing. They hadn't pinned it for taking in, but it didn't matter really. She didn't care about that. In truth, she didn't care much about the gown being taken in either. Being fashionably attired just was not on her priority list at that moment.

Like the first time Allissaid had donned the gown, it was a lot of work to get it on, but this time it was also absolute agony. It had been easier when it was too large and roomy than now that it was smaller. Tears were streaming down her cheeks, and Allissaid was nearly sobbing with the effort by the time she finished dressing.

She had to lean against the chair briefly afterward while she regained her strength. As she did, Allissaid considered how she would get out of Kilcairn keep. She suspected simply walking out might be a problem. Even if Calan hadn't ordered that she be kept here, the guards on the wall would probably have questions when a lass they'd never seen before suddenly exited the castle, crossed the bailey and sauntered out of the gates. Aside from that, though, she didn't even have her sgian dubh with her, let alone any kind of weapon to defend herself with as she made her way to MacFarlane. Not that she thought she could successfully fight off attackers if she ran into bandits or MacNaughton men. She had never been trained with the sword. But having any kind of weapon would make her feel better.

The thought made her look toward the chests she'd noticed on first waking in the room, and after a hesitation, she moved to them and opened the first to consider the contents. It was full of weapons. Two swords, a bow, a quiver full of arrows and a selection of knives filled the chest. The swords were too heavy for her to handle with any competency, but she was good with a bow and arrow, and she could certainly manage a knife. She pulled out the bow and quiver, then grabbed two of the knives before turning her attention to the second chest and opening it to explore inside.

This chest held clothing; fine white linen shirts, plaids, a strip of leather, some lengths of rope, and what was obviously a spare sporran. Allissaid selected one of the smaller bits of rope which was still quite large, and then pulled out the top plaid. She quietly closed the chest, then straightened and quickly arranged the plaid into an arisaid over the gown she was wearing, using the length of rope as a belt. Allissaid then turned her attention to the weapons she'd collected.

She slid the first knife under the rope, but paused and considered the second knife as her conscience pricked her. She could almost hear Calan calling her a thief for taking them. Her gaze slid over the two knives and the bow and arrow uncertainly. She was good with a bow, but did she really need it? She wasn't likely to stop to hunt for food on the way home. It would take too much time. She'd more likely be scavenging for berries and mushrooms in the woods along the path. And if she was attacked, the bow and quiver of arrows would most likely do her little good against a party of men. Hiding and waiting for any groups of travelers to pass would be her better option to avoid capture or a skirmish.

Muttering impatiently under her breath, Allissaid quickly put the bow and quiver back in the first chest, and started to return the knives as well, only to change her mind and only put one back. The finer, more expensive-looking one went back into the chest and she kept the other. Allissaid then considered the plaid she'd transformed into an arisaid. She debated the issue briefly, but then decided she did need it. The nights could be cold, and pulling the back over her head like a cloak would help conceal her identity should she run into anyone. Aye, it was better to keep the plaid. She'd just make sure her father sent it and the knife back with a soldier once she reached MacFarlane, Allissaid assured herself as she closed both chests.

Straightening then, she turned to peer toward the fireplace and slowly walked over to it. Leaving through the secret passage that Calan had mentioned would make things a lot easier. She could take it all the way out to the last entrance, find the loch and follow that south for a bit, then turn east and travel around MacNaughton to MacFarlane. It meant possibly crossing into MacGregor territory, but the MacGregors were friends to the Buchanans who were cousins to her through her mother. She doubted they would do her harm if she mentioned her cousin Aulay. They might even see her the rest of the way home if she were lucky.

But only if she could find the entrance to the secret passage, Allissaid thought grimly. At Mac-Farlane it was in the mantel, and she suspected the same would be true here. There it was a simple matter of turning one stone and pushing another to get the panel to open. It could be the same thing here, but which stone did she push and which to turn? Or was it just push a stone or pull another? It could be a combination of anything and any two stones. Or perhaps three or just one. There were a lot of stones in the mantel surrounding the fireplace.

Mouth tightening, Allissaid ran her hands over the stones, pushing one here and another there, but nothing happened and she acknowledged to herself that it could take years to sort out how to open the passage. She didn't have years. Allissaid wasn't sure she even had minutes to try. Calan might have just slipped out to use the garderobe or fetch a drink. He could return at any moment. Something she really should have considered before this, Allissaid acknowledged and turned reluctantly away from the mantel. She'd have to try to slip out of the keep the way most people left it.

Pulling the spare material of the arisaid over her head as a cloak, she crept to the door and eased it open to peer out. Relief coursed through her when she saw that the hallway was empty and took note of how quiet it was. It was late enough that everyone had retired for the night.

She surveyed the hallway nervously, noting that most of the torches in the sconces along the hall were extinguished with just one on either end lit. It left a lot of dark shadows to hide in if necessary between the door of the bedchamber she was in and the stairs she could see at the other end.

Holding her breath, Allissaid slipped from the room and started to creep up the hall, wincing at every creak and whisper of sound she caused. She didn't breathe again until she reached the top of the stairs. Pausing there, she scanned the great hall anxiously. The only light below was a dim glow that came from the large fireplace at one end of the room. It was enough though for her to see that, as expected, the floor was awash with bodies. Servants and soldiers alike were curled up on pallets wherever they could find space, though they'd left two clear paths on the floor; one from the stairs to a door she suspected led to the kitchens, and another path that led to a set of large double doors that could only lead out to the bailey. She supposed the pathways had been left to avoid anyone being trampled should someone arrive late or leave early.

Her gaze moved over the bodies below again. Everyone appeared to be sleeping, and they probably were, she assured herself. It was like that at Mac-Farlane. The people worked hard, and generally fell asleep as soon as they laid their heads down.

Biting her lip, Allissaid quickly crept down the stairs, staying close to the wall and the shadows there. At the bottom, she paused briefly to eye the people on either side of the path leading to the doors to the bailey, but when no one moved and she didn't see any open eyes, she caught her skirts and drew them close to avoid their brushing across anyone and waking them, then moved quickly forward. Moments later she was cracking one of the entry doors open just wide enough to slip out into the bailey.

Easing the door closed again, Allissaid sagged briefly with relief, and then turned to survey the bailey. It was empty of activity. The only movement was on the wall where soldiers walked or stood, watching for trouble. Not one of them was watching the bailey itself though. They were all looking for trouble coming from outside the castle walls. Relief coursing through her, Allissaid rushed down the stone steps. She then scurried toward the wall and gasped in shock when a heavy hand landed on her shoulder and spun her around.

Allissaid's mouth opened on an alarmed cry that died in her throat when she found herself staring

up at Calan's grim face. The man looked angry.
Very angry, she noted, and then—without saying
a word—he simply caught her by one hand and
turned to head back to the keep, towing her behind
like a recalcitrant horse.

Allissaid went, but not willingly. She dragged
her feet and tugged at her arm, trying to free herself, but his grip was like iron and Calan didn't slow
down for her. She had to give up the foot dragging,
or risk falling on her face. But she scowled at the
back of his head and continued to tug furiously at
her arm all the way back into the keep, along the
path through the sleeping castle inhabitants, and up
the stairs.

Allissaid was so distracted with her efforts to
break free that she didn't at first notice when he
suddenly stopped halfway up the hall to his room.
She simply continued to tug at her arm and dig her
heels in and pull. Not that it did her any good. It
wasn't until he started to move again and she was
yanked forward, that Allissaid glanced up to scowl
at him and noted the older woman standing at the
end of the hall, gaping at them with amazement. It
was all she saw before Calan dragged her into his
bedchamber.

THE MOMENT HE'D CLOSED THE DOOR, CALAN
released his hold on the lass who'd chosen the name
Eara, but who he suspected was Claray MacFarlane,
and turned to scowl at her with a combination of irritation and exasperation. Honestly, to his mind, the
lass must be witless to try to sneak out of the keep

in the middle of the night like this. And alone, for heaven's sake. After all he'd done for her too; seeing her injuries tended to, giving her food, his protection and a bed to recuperate in. His bed, in fact, he thought and glowered at her.

Calan had sat watching over her after Inghinn had finished with her gown and left. But after his disrupted sleep the night before, it hadn't been long before he'd dozed off in the chair. He'd slept for hours, only to wake up with a stiff neck, a terrible thirst and a rumbling belly for his trouble. After assuring himself that the lass still slept soundly, he'd slipped from the room planning to fetch some food and drink for them both in case she woke up. But she must have woken up the moment he'd left, he decided now, for he'd come back out of the kitchen with said food and drink just in time to see her slipping out of the keep.

The sight had so shocked him, Calan had just stood there watching her go, but then he'd given his head a shake and quickly returned to the kitchens to set down everything he'd gathered. Calan had then headed back out to chase after her.

Eara/Claray had been halfway to the wall when he stepped out of the keep, and much to his alarm, not a single one of his men had seemed to have noticed the dark wraith slipping through the bailey. Even worse, he suspected they might not have noticed her leaving even once she reached the wall and slid into the darkness beyond. Their attention was on the distance and any sign of trouble approaching, not on one slim lass leaving.

It was as he'd chased after her that it had occurred to him to wonder where she thought she was going? She had no memories, had no idea of who her clan were, where her home was, or even what her name was. Where in Scotland did she plan to go if she left Kilcairn? On foot?

That was when he'd realized that this wasn't right at all. You generally had a destination in mind when you set out on a journey. The lass had to know who she was and where her home was, else he was sure she wouldn't be trying to leave. Or she was a mad-woman. The possibility that she had her memories, and had simply been lying to them since waking had infuriated him. Truly, Calan couldn't recall ever be-ing so furious at a woman before in his life and he didn't like feeling that way now.

He'd clenched his teeth to keep from bellow-ing at the wench, and merely reached out to clasp her shoulder when he caught up to her. It had been enough to bring her to a halt, and rather than berate her as he'd wanted to do, he'd simply dragged her back here. Mostly because in that moment he'd been so mad, he'd feared that if he'd done anything else at all, he might have wound up taking her over his knee and paddling her bottom to ease some of the rage he was feeling at her for lying to him and try-ing to flee. So, he'd simply escorted her back to his room for the discussion that needed to happen.

Calan had rather hoped that the worst of his tem-per would have passed by the time they got to his room, but he was still hungry, thirsty, his neck still had a kink in it from sleeping sitting up, and he was still mad as hell. The fact that his mother had witnessed his dragging the lass into his chamber didn't help either. He knew she'd probably assume it was one of the maids that he intended to dally with, but since Eara/Claray had obviously been trying to break free, she'd think she was an unwilling lass. That just didn't sit well with him either.

He needed to sort things out with the lass, so that he could reveal her presence to his mother and correct the impression she'd just got that he dragged unwilling servants to his bedchamber for nefarious purposes.

"I'm thinking 'tis time ye told the truth, lass," he said finally and grimaced when his voice came out an angry snarl. So much for his temper cooling, he thought unhappily, and said more calmly, "Ye obviously ha'e yer memories, and I ken who ye are, and we both ken it's no' safe fer ye to be wandering about the countryside alone. Hell, even if ye were no' who ye are, ye're a woman, and 'tis no' safe fer a lone woman to be traveling without an escort. And ye were going without even a horse," he added with exasperation. "Did ye plan to walk all the way to MacFarlane?"

The lass had started to scowl back at him as he spoke, but at the mention of her clan name the scowl disappeared and her jaw dropped in amazement.

"Aye," he told her solemnly. "I've sorted out that ye're Claray MacFarlane."

"Oh, fer heaven's sake, Calan. The lass is no' Claray MacFarlane."

Calan jerked around at those exasperated words,

his eyes widening at the sight of his mother standing in his now-open door, a torch from the hall in hand.

"Mother," Calan began, uncertain what to say as he rushed across the room to close the open door behind his mother. In the end, he didn't have to figure it out.

"Lady Fiona?" Eara/Claray's words and uncertain tone brought his head around to see confused recognition on her expression as she squinted at his mother's face by torchlight.

"Aye, Allissaid, dear." Smiling now, his mother shoved the torch at Calan, barely waiting for him to take it before she let go and rushed across the room to draw the lass into an encompassing embrace. "My goodness, child, 'tis good to see ye. How long has it been?"

"The summer before mother fell ill, I think," the lass he'd thought was Claray MacFarlane, but who was instead someone named Allissaid, mumbled on what sounded like a sob. She was also hugging his mother as if she were a lifeline.

As Calan gaped at the pair of them, his mother rubbed the lass's back soothingly and murmured, "Aye." She then leaned back to peer solemnly down at the chit as she said, "Yer mother did no' feel much up to visiting after she became ill."

"Nay. She did no' want anyone to see her like that," Allissaid told her apologetically.

"I understood," his mother assured her, and then smiled sadly. "I missed her though. I still do."

"So do I," Allissaid admitted, her voice breaking and eyes pooling with tears.

Lady Fiona nodded, hugged her again and then slid her arm around the lass's waist, and turned to survey him with narrowed eyes and pursed lips. "Now, son, why were ye dragging this lovely young *lady* into yer bedchamber against her will?"

Ignoring the question, Calan asked, "Allissaid who?"

"MacFarlane," his mother responded grimly.

Well, he'd had the right clan, at least, Calan thought. But didn't remember a daughter named Allissaid. There'd been several girls with names starting with *A* though. Besides, while he knew that Lady MacFarlane used to be a dear friend to his mother, it wasn't something he'd been involved with. It had been a woman's thing, and honestly, the visits had been a rare occurrence while his father had lived. They'd become more frequent after his da's death, but at that point, Calan had been enmeshed in taking over as laird of the clan and all the new duties it meant taking on. Knowing the friendship and visits were helping both his mother and sister cope with the death of his father, he'd encouraged them.

"What made ye think I was me sister Claray?" Allissaid asked with curiosity, drawing him from his thoughts.

Calan shrugged. "Ye look like yer mother . . . other than the hair," he added, his gaze sliding over the dark chestnut waves around her face. "And last night me soldiers had an encounter with Mac-Naughton's men when they crossed the border onto our land. They claimed they were looking fer their laird's lost bride. I knew the MacNaughton had tried to force Claray MacFarlane to marry him, so I just assumed—"

"I thought he failed at that," his mother interrupted with a frown. "Ye said the Wolf was sent to rescue her and brought her home."

"Aye, and he did. But I thought mayhap our neighbor had caught her again," Calan admitted.

"Nay. Claray is safe," Allissaid assured them. "Father arranged for her to be married the night she returned to MacFarlane and her husband took her away to his home as soon as the wedding was consummated." She hesitated briefly, and then said, "Da says MacNaughton'll no' go after her again now that there's a chance she may already be carrying her husband's child." Her mouth tightened then and she added, "Except to kill her and possibly her new husband."

"Kill?" Lady Fiona turned to the girl with amazement. "Why on earth would he kill them?"

"Because he was no' really after Claray," Allissaid told her grimly. "He only tried to force her to marry him as part of some plot to gain MacFarlane that included killing our father and the rest o' us so only Claray was left to take the title." Mouth twisting bitterly, she added, "But now she's married and Da thinks MacNaughton is more likely to try to kill the pair o' them."

"But what would that gain him?" Lady Fiona asked with confusion.

When the lass hesitated to respond, Calan answered for her, even as he realized what the answer was. "He would still gain MacFarlane if he married one o' the younger sisters and killed the rest o' the siblings and her father."

"Aye," Allissaid said wearily.

"Oh, no," his mother murmured, her expression troubled, and then her eyes widened suddenly and she turned to Calan. "Ye said MacNaughton's men claimed they were looking fer his lost bride?"

Calan nodded and then shifted his gaze to Allissaid and growled, "He came after you."

"Oh, dear God, no child, ye're no' married to the MacNaughton?" Lady Fiona breathed with horror.

"Nay!" Allissaid assured her quickly, and relief had just started to pour through Calan when she frowned and added, "At least, I do no' think so."

Calan stiffened at once.

"What do ye mean ye do no' think so, lass?" his mother asked. "Either ye are, or ye're no'."

"Aye, and I do no' think I can be, but . . ."

When Allissaid paused and began to wring her hands agitatedly, Calan said quietly, "I think ye'd best tell us what happened, lass."

Chapter 6

𝕸UCH TO CALAN'S FRUSTRATION HE DIDN'T get the answers he was looking for right away. His mother insisted on everyone "settling comfortably" for the telling. Which meant he had to light several candles from the torch he was still carrying, and then return it to its sconce in the hall.

Once back in the room, he found his mother had got Allissaid settled on the edge of his bed, and had sat down beside her. Calan reclaimed the chair he'd set beside the bed earlier to watch over the lass as she slept, mentally braced himself for hearing something he didn't want to, and then nodded. "Go ahead. Tell us what happened."

Allissaid swallowed, and lowered her gaze to her hands as they wrestled with each other in her lap. She then sighed, stopped their anxious movements and said, "Well, ye ken MacNaughton went after our Claray—" She paused and glanced up to ask, "Did ye ken he convinced our uncle Gilchrist to help him with his plot?"

"Aye," his mother said. "The story we heard was that MacNaughton had yer uncle get his daughter, Mairin, to invite Claray to Kerr fer a stay. The plan was for yer uncle to help force her to marry Mac-Naughton. But yer father got wind o' the matter and sent the Wolf to rescue her."

"Aye, and the Wolf *did* rescue her," Allissaid assured them. "He also married her."

"The Wolf forced her to marry him?" his mother gasped with surprise.

Calan held his tongue but was sure that couldn't be the case. He'd always heard the man was an honorable sort despite being a mercenary.

"Oh, nay," Allissaid told his mother quickly. "She was no' forced, and it was with me father's blessing. They married at MacFarlane once he got her back," she told them, and explained, "The Wolf is really Bryson MacDonald, Claray's betrothed, who we'd always been told had died as a boy, but apparently had no'."

Calan's eyebrows climbed up his forehead at this, but he was more interested in getting to the part where Allissaid may, or may not be married to MacNaughton, and asked, "What happened then?"

"Well, Claray and her husband left MacFarlane yestermorn before most o' the castle was even awake. The MacKays were at MacFarlane as well. Laird MacKay is Bryson's—"

"Uncle," Lady Fiona finished for her. "Aye. I ken."

Allissaid nodded. "They apparently attended the wedding along with my cousins and father, and then left with Claray and Bryson to ensure they reached Deagh Fhortan safely," she explained, and then continued. "We—me and me other siblings—found out all o' this when we got up and went below to break our fast. Da explained all that had happened and their suspicions about MacNaughton's plans and warned us all no' to leave the keep until MacNaughton was taken care o'."

"But ye did," Lady Fiona guessed mournfully.

"Nay," Allissaid assured her, and then grimaced and admitted, "Well, aye. But only to fetch Eachann back."

"Who is Eachann?" Calan asked at once, his voice sharper than he'd intended.

"Her little brother," Lady Fiona muttered, before asking Allissaid, "Why did he go out?"

"Moire said he wanted to go to the river."

"Moire?" Calan asked.

"A maid at MacFarlane," she explained. "She caught him trying to slip out o' the keep earlier that morn and reminded him doing that was no' allowed just now. She said he went to his room, but when she went to check on him after, he was gone." Allissaid hesitated and then admitted, "We ha'e secret passages at MacFarlane too."

"Ye thought he used them to leave the keep and ye went out after him," Lady Fiona guessed, and when Allissaid nodded an admission, asked with exasperation, "Why did ye no' tell yer father and let him send men after him?"

Allissaid shrugged helplessly. "Moire was worried that Da would be angry at her fer no' going to him and telling him that Eachann had tried to slip out. I felt bad fer her. Besides, Da had said that MacNaughton was still at Kerr, so I thought if I was quick . . ." She didn't bother finishing telling them what she'd hoped would happen, and instead she said wearily, "Da was wrong. MacNaughton was no' still at Kerr."

"What happened to Eachann?" his mother asked solemnly.

"I do no' ken," Allissaid said unhappily. "When I got to the river there was no sign o' him. I turned to head back to the castle, thinking I'd ha'e to tell Da now, and he'd ha'e to send men out to search. But I was suddenly surrounded by MacNaughton and his men."

"Oh, no," his mother moaned, sounding as pained as Calan felt at this news.

"Aye," Allissaid breathed the word miserably, and then continued, "I had barely recognized the man when someone hit me on the back o' the head, knocking me out." She reached up to rub the back of her head where Inghinn had found a swollen lump while looking her over earlier. Letting her hand drop after a moment, she said, "When I woke up, I was on a horse with one o' Maldouen's warriors and we were approaching MacNaughton. The soldier carrying me had no' noticed I'd woken, so I pretended to still be unconscious. I thought surely Maldouen would just lock me away somewhere until I woke up. I thought it would give me time to think o' a way out o' the trouble I was in." Her shoulders sagged. "But it did no' go that way."

"What happened?" Calan asked when she fell silent, her expression troubled.

"He had the warrior carry me into the great hall," she continued reluctantly. "A priest was waiting there as if 'twas all planned."

"It probably was," Calan said grimly. "Maldouen's a sneaky bastard. He probably intended to kidnap ye or the first one o' yer sisters he came across and bring ye back to wed."

"Aye. That would be me guess too," Allissaid admitted unhappily.

"So, what happened next, lass?" Calan prompted when she sat there miserable and silent as she contemplated MacNaughton's machinations. "Did he pour water o'er ye? Or slap yer face in an effort to wake ye, or—?"

"Nay," Allissaid said grimly. "He did no' bother to wake me. He just told the priest to go ahead and marry us, and he did! The priest just started in with the marriage ceremony," she told them, her eyes wide and shocked as if she still could not believe it. "I was no' e'en conscious!" Blinking then, she frowned and said, "Well, I was, but they did no' ken that."

"Are ye sure the priest thought ye unconscious?" his mother asked with a troubled expression.

"Aye. He had to. He asked did I take Maldouen to husband, and I just lay there, feigning being senseless," she assured her. "But MacNaughton said, '*She says aye, and I do too. Finish it, Father.*' And then the priest just said, '*I pronounce ye man and wife*' and that was it," she told them with amazement.

"I mean, there's more to the ceremony than that, is there no'? And it could no' be a valid wedding when I was no' e'en conscious and did no' speak me vows. Could it? Well, I mean I was, but they did no' ken that."

Calan exchanged a glance with his mother, knowing she was thinking what he was. That the priest was obviously MacNaughton's man, bought and paid for, and if he lied and claimed she'd been conscious and willing and spoke her vows . . . On top of that, he had no doubt every one of MacNaughton's men would back up any lie he told them to. Calan's gaze shifted to Allissaid and he could tell from her expression that she was thinking exactly what they were.

Sighing wearily, Allissaid peered down at her tangled fingers and continued quietly, "I wanted to shout at them that 'nay, I did no' take him to husband.' But I was still sure that feigning being unconscious was the best course to keep me safe and get me out in the end. So, I just lay there in his soldier's arms when MacNaughton ordered the man to carry me to the tower. I expected they'd dump me in a room and leave me alone until later that night, or the next morn and then check to see if I'd woken up before trying to move forward with . . . anything."

Allissaid swallowed, and then added painfully, "But he did no' wait. He tried to—I was unconscious. Well, I was no' really, but he thought I was and he just tried to . . ."

"Consummate the wedding," his mother said gently when she flushed and fell silent.

She nodded jerkily, her face paling, and then flushing again. "I could no' let him. I gave up pretending to be unconscious then. We struggled. Violently. He was most free with his fists, and things got a little blurry at one point. One minute I was on the floor and he was kicking me in the stomach, and the next I was on me back on the bed with him throwing me skirts up and forcing me legs open," she whispered, her face flushing again and shame covering her face. "I reached out to try to push him away and me hand landed on his sgian dubh."

She paused and bowed her head, not continuing for long enough that Calan was beginning to wonder if sgian dubh was some sort of euphemism for MacNaughton's cock. Then she lifted her chin and continued grimly, "I pulled it from his belt and stabbed him."

Not his cock then, Calan thought wryly, and noted the way Allissaid's mouth twitched with disappointment as she added, "I was aiming for his stomach, but he got his arm up in time to block the knife. I ended up stabbing him there instead, just above his wrist."

She rubbed the spot just above her own wrist, and then her mouth twisted slightly as she told them, "He was no' happy, but he did give up trying to rape me. He merely punched and kicked me a time or two more, said something about mayhap I'd be more amenable after a week without food, and stormed out." Her hand dropped away from her arm, and she sighed. "I think I fainted then. I'm no' sure fer how long, but it was late afternoon when we arrived at

MacNaughton and full night when I next opened me eyes. I could hear men outside me door talking. Guards. I checked the window and the shutters opened. He had no' bothered to nail them shut or anything. I suppose with the room being in the top o' the tower, he did no' think I would try to escape."

"But ye did, and succeeded," his mother said with obvious pride.

Allissaid nodded. "Me first plan was to make a rope out o' the bed linens to escape out the window and climb down the wall. But once I'd tied together every strip o' cloth I could find, then attached one end to the foot o' the bed in the chamber and dropped the other end out the window, the makeshift rope only stretched about halfway to the grassy strip o' land below the window." She hesitated, and then blushed brightly as she admitted, "I even used me own gown and chemise tryin' to make it as long as I could, but I simply did no' ha'e enough material."

That explained her being naked when he encountered her, Calan thought. But he wasn't surprised that even with that sacrifice the rope hadn't been long enough. The towers of MacNaughton's keep were near forty feet high on the side overlooking the loch. It would take more than a gown, a chemise and a couple of ripped-up linens to make a rope that would reach as far as she'd have needed to reach from a bed probably across half the length of the room, out the window and to the ground below a tower wall.

"What did ye do then, dear?" his mother asked.

Allissaid shrugged unhappily. "I considered

climbing down to the end and dropping from there, but was no' sure I'd survive the drop." Grimacing, she added, "I did no' mind that so much. The dyin' I mean. I'd ha'e chosen that o'er being married to the MacNaughton. However, the ground below the window was soft. There was too great a risk that I might survive, but in no shape to try to escape again."

Allissaid paused and swallowed, before continuing. "So, I examined me options and noted that together the strip o' land and the rocks that separated it from the loch were still very narrow. At least, it looked narrow from the window by moonlight," she added wryly and then shrugged. "So, then I thought mayhap if I climbed down to the end o' the linens and pushed meself away from the tower wall so that I swung outward on the cloth rope, and then let go, mayhap I'd get lucky and hit the water rather than the rocks."

"Oh, dear God, child," his mother breathed with horror. "Ye could ha'e died on the rocks or drowned. How could ye take such a chance?"

Calan understood his mother's distress. He found himself rather upset too at the risk Allissaid had taken. But the lass raised her chin defensively and said, "Because trying was better than no' trying. I thought if I tried and failed, I'd definitely die, but me family would be safe. MacNaughton could no' kill them all and claim MacFarlane if I was dead," she pointed out. "But no' trying meant remaining in Maldouen's clutches and the death o' me entire family if his plan succeeded."

Calan couldn't fault her reasoning. In fact, in her

place he probably would have done the same. And it had worked, he reminded himself. Her being here in his room was proof of that, so he said, "Obviously, yer plan succeeded and ye hit the water rather than the rocks."

"Aye," she agreed, and then grimaced and told them, "Though, I did no' think so at first. I felt sure I'd hit the rocks when me back slammed into the water. It felt that hard."

Which explained the dark red stain on her back that Inghinn had mentioned. His sister had been right. She'd landed hard in water, back first, from a height.

"But then the water closed o'er me head and I kenned I'd missed the rocks," Allissaid continued. "Jumping from such a height, I plummeted deep in the loch. The water was so cold . . ."

"Aye, the loch is deep and grows colder the deeper ye go," his mother murmured, eyeing Allissaid with concern when she shuddered as if just the memory chilled her.

Managing a crooked smile, Allissaid nodded. "The moment I stopped sinking, and swam fer the surface. The water was a bit warmer there, but still very cold. I wanted to climb out at once, but I was right next to the keep and feared being seen, so I swam until I could no' bear the cold anymore before getting out. Then I slipped into the trees and followed the shoreline for hours."

She met Calan's gaze, and smiled crookedly. "Until I came across a man who had left his plaid on shore while he took a swim."

Calan found his own mouth tipping up with a smile in response, until he noted the way his mother's eyes slid from her to him with interest and then growing suspicion. He wasn't terribly surprised when she asked Allissaid, "Would I be right in guessing this man *swimming* was me son?"

"Aye," Allissaid admitted and didn't seem to notice the scowl Lady Fiona then sent his way.

Calan sighed inwardly at the look, knowing she'd berate him later for going swimming while still recovering from his wound.

"What happened next, dear?" she finally asked while still glaring at him.

"Ashamed as I am to admit it, I fear I stole his plaid," Allissaid confessed with a guilty grimace.

"Borrowed it," Calan countered at once with a faint smile, and then noting the interest on his mother's face as she looked at him, he killed the smile and finished the tale for Allissaid. "I spotted what I thought was a lad making off with me plaid and rushed out o' the water to give chase. I ran him down in the woods, and tackled him from behind, knocking him to the ground. Unfortunately, he hit his head as he fell and was knocked unconscious. It was no' quite dawn yet, and dark in the trees. It was no' until I carried him out o' the woods and back to the beach that I realized he was a woman."

"And carrying her is how ye split yer stitches again," his mother said with much more understanding than she'd shown that morning when she'd noticed that he'd burst another stitch. Apparently, she didn't mind so much if it was to save this lass.

"Aye," he admitted without regret. "I probably would ha'e lost a couple more had I had to get her up on me horse and carry her back here. Fortunately, Gille arrived in search o' me after I'd finished putting me shirt on her, and donning me plaid. He helped me with her, and he is the one who carried her up here to me room."

"I ne'er saw—" his mother began with a frown, and then paused and guessed, "The passage."

Calan nodded. "I'd noted the ring she wears, so I kenned she was a lady. But she was wet, unconscious and wearing only me shirt. Bringing her through the bailey and great hall fer everyone to see did no' seem a good idea."

"Definitely no'. That would ha'e ruined the poor lass," his mother said grimly, and then turned back to Allissaid to ask, "But ye said ye'd walked fer hours between leaving the loch and encountering me son. Why were ye wet still? Surely ye should ha'e dried off by the time ye stumbled on Calan?"

"Well, the first time I got out o' the water and started to walk, I'd no' gone ten feet when I heard horses approaching. Kenning it would be Mac-Naughton's men looking fer me, I rushed back to the water and submerged meself, leaving only me face on the surface until they passed. That decided me to stick close to the water and walk the shoreline afterward. It was harder to walk on the sand and shingle than walking in the woods would ha'e been, but it seemed safer. That way I could slip into the water anytime I heard horses approaching," she explained.

Calan stared at the lass, amazed at her cleverness. Her pale, naked body would have been like a beacon in the woods. But no one, including his warriors on patrol, would have paid much attention to the loch other than a quick scan in search of boats in the water, and men or warriors on horseback on the beach. They wouldn't even have noticed a face that had probably barely been an inch above the surface of the water.

"I had to get back in the water just minutes before I spotted Calan swimming, and tried to take his plaid," Allissaid added. "Thinking on it now, it was probably him and this Gille he mentioned who rode by that time."

"Most like," Calan agreed.

"Who tended yer wounds, love?" his mother asked now, reaching up to brush her fingers over the bandage on her head.

"Inghinn," she answered before Calan could intervene, and he sighed when his mother frowned at this news.

Turning another scowl his way, she asked, "Ye told yer sister that Allissaid was here and ye did no' tell me?"

"I did no' tell Inghinn," he said calmly. "She walked into me bedchamber and saw her."

That only brought a deeper scowl from his mother and the question, "Why did ye no' tell me?"

Calan shrugged. "I did no' ken what kind o' trouble she was in and who had done this to her. It seemed best no' to let anyone ken she was here until she remembered who she was and what had happened so I would ken where the threat lay."

"Well, I was no threat!" his mother snapped.

"Nay. But ye were in the great hall, and the hall is always busy and full o' people. I did no' want anyone to overhear."

His mother's eyes narrowed. "I see. So it had naught to do with the worry that I might make ye remove her from yer room and—" She stopped abruptly, and frowned before suddenly asking, "What do ye mean until she remembered? Did she no' remember anything when she first woke up?"

"Good question," Calan said dryly, and turned arched eyebrows to Allissaid. "Lass?"

The guilty flush that covered her face gave him the answer before she admitted to his mother, "Aye, I remembered everything. But I let yer son and daughter think I did no' because I was no' sure who they were and whether they were friendly with MacNaughton and therefore a threat to me."

"Well, surely once ye realized they were me son and daughter, ye kenned ye'd be safe here," his mother said with amazement.

"Aye, but I did no' realize ye were their mother until I saw ye standing in the door to this room just minutes ago," she explained. "I did no' recognize Inghinn as the wee lass, Ginny, who used to come with me mother's dear friend to visit and always disappeared to play with me little sister, Arabella." She looked uncertain and then asked, "Inghinn is wee Ginny is she no'?"

"Aye," his mother assured her with a smile.

Smiling wryly in return, Allissaid nodded and told her, "I do no' think I e'er heard her called Inghinn. She was always just called Ginny at Mac-Farlane."

"Aye. She preferred Ginny as a child, but once she got older, she felt her full name, Inghinn, was more dignified," his mother explained.

"I still find it hard to believe Inghinn is Ginny," Allissaid said wryly. "She's grown so."

"Oh, aye," his mother said with a faint smile. "She used to be such a skinny little waif, and still was the last time we visited. She shot up a good six inches the year yer dear mother fell ill and we had to stop going to MacFarlane." Shaking her head, she added, "Inghinn got Eve's curse then too, and gained her figure as well. Her bosoms seemed to sprout out nearly overnight, and goodness, she was so uncomfortable with them at first."

Calan found himself sinking into horror as his mother shared these fond reminiscences. He suddenly wanted to stick a sgian dubh in each ear to deafen himself so he wouldn't have to listen. He had no desire to hear about his sister's breasts sprouting or her getting her courses. As far as he was concerned, she didn't have either. Which even he had to acknowledge was ridiculous. Of course, he'd noticed that she'd gained curves, and he supposed he'd known in some part of his mind that she must menstruate as all women did, but Inghinn wasn't a woman to him. She was his sister.

"Calan."

Blinking, he forced his attention warily back to his mother. "Aye?"

"We must send a message to Allissaid's father reassuring him that she's here and telling him what happened. He'll probably want to petition the king to annul the wedding, or simply render it null and void since it was no' a true wedding anyway. I'm sure Gannon is already keeping a close eye on everything else to prevent MacNaughton from killing them all, but something has to be done to ensure Allissaid is safe from MacNaughton and he can no' try to claim they are truly married and force the issue."

He nodded, but was a bit confused on how the conversation had changed so quickly. If it had. How long had he been lost in his horror at the discussion of women's bodily functions?

"Messages need to be sent to the MacLaren and MacLean clans as well," Allissaid said anxiously. "Immediately, else it may be too late . . . if 'tisn't already," she added cryptically.

Calan shifted his gaze to the lass. "Warn the MacLaren and the MacLean about what?"

"That Maldouen intends to kill them."

A moment of silence passed as Calan and his mother tried to absorb that, but it was hard to understand. He, at least, had no clue what the two men had to do with anything, and finally asked, "Why would MacNaughton kill the MacLaren and the MacLean?"

"So, they'd no' marry Annis and Arabella," she told him, and apparently reading the confusion on his face, explained, "Our parents arranged betrothals fer all o' us as children. Annis is to marry the MacLaren, Arabella the MacLean, and they betrothed me to Alban Graham."

Calan found himself displeased by the news that she was already betrothed to someone. He didn't know why, and frankly, he should have expected it. It was a common practice for parents to arrange betrothals while their children were young. His own parents had arranged one for him while he was still a bairn. However, his betrothed had died of a childhood ailment long before he could have claimed her. Noting that his mother was eyeing him with some curiosity, he tried to school his face into an expressionless mask as Allissaid continued speaking.

"Well, Da has been delaying allowing any o' the betrothal contracts to be fulfilled and the marriages to take place. He felt that Claray, as the eldest daughter, should marry first."

"But now that Claray is married, he decided to allow the rest o' ye to marry?" Calan suggested, ignoring his mother's steady gaze.

"Mayhap," Allissaid agreed. "But really I think it has more to do with MacNaughton's plans to kill us all. I think he believed we'd all be safer if several o' us were away from MacFarlane with our new husbands and their clans. It might even have put an end to MacNaughton's plans altogether. It would certainly make managing all o' our deaths that much harder than if we were all together at MacFarlane," she pointed out. "So, Da apparently sent messengers to all three men, telling them to come claim us."

"Apparently?" Calan asked before she could continue.

"Aye, well he did no' tell us. Me sister, Cairstane, says she overheard Da talking about it with our cousins Aulay and Alick Buchanan. 'Tis the only reason I kenned anything about it, and was no' completely taken by surprise when we arrived at MacNaughton and I overheard Maldouen sending men out to watch fer the two men to cross onto MacFarlane land and kill them ere they got near the keep."

"Nay," his mother said with disbelief, finally tearing her watchful gaze from him to eye Allissaid with amazement. "That would be mad! It would pit all three clans against him alongside MacFarlane."

"Only do they find out," Calan pointed out to her and then shifted his attention back to Allissaid. "But ye said the two men, no' three?"

"Aye." Allissaid lowered her head and whispered, "He's already killed me betrothed, Alban Graham."

"Nay," his mother gasped.

Allissaid nodded and raised her head again as she admitted, "I saw his body when I opened me eyes on first awaking on the journey back to MacNaughton. He was hanging o'er the horse next to the one I was on with the soldier. Once we reached the castle and were in the bailey, Maldouen ordered his men to '*weigh Graham down and put him in the deep.*'"

"The loch," Calan growled, refusing to examine the mixture of emotions that assailed him at the news that the lass's betrothed was no longer in the picture.

"Aye," Allissaid said sadly, and then her voice sounding stronger, she said, "'Tis too late fer Alban, but we ha'e to warn Annis and Arabella's betrotheds. Da thought it would take them longer to get to MacFarlane. They may yet live."

"Ye need to send men out to warn them, son," his mother said, turning on him with concern clear on her face.

"Aye. I'll send men out at once." He stood, but then paused to tell Allissaid gently, "While I do that, ye should write a letter to yer da. Tell him everything that has happened so he can decide what to do about this supposed wedding to MacNaughton. And tell him ye're safe here, and we'll ensure ye remain so, does he wish it. Point out, it may be safer fer ye to remain here where no one kens ye are, rather than to return ye to MacFarlane where there's obviously a spy who will tell MacNaughton ye've returned. If Maldouen kens ye're there, he may try to claim the marriage was legitimate, ha'e the priest back him up on that, and demand ye be returned to him."

"Ye think there's a spy at MacFarlane?" Allissaid asked with alarm.

"How else do ye think MacNaughton kenned yer father sent messages to the men who were betrothed to ye and yer sisters?" he asked solemnly. "If he'd found out by stopping the messengers themselves, he would ha'e just killed them and taken the messages and there would be no need to kill yer Alban Graham and the MacLaren and the MacLean, because they'd no' ha'e set out fer MacFarlane." His mouth compressed grimly. "There must be a spy."

When Allissaid paled at the suggestion, he said

more gently, "Write the letter to yer da, lass, and I'll see it gets to him. In the meantime, I'll see me men find the MacLaren and the MacLean, warn them o' what MacNaughton is up to, and join their parties fer the journey. If 'tis no' already too late, they'll see they get safely to MacFarlane."

Calan didn't wait for her response, but left the room to go rouse his finest soldiers for this task. He didn't know the MacLean well, but Allistair Mac-Laren was a friend. He just hoped he wasn't too late to save the man's life and the MacLaren wasn't already "weighted down in the deep."

Calan shuddered at the thought, and wondered how many bodies lay a hundred or three hundred feet down in the loch, compliments of the Mac-Naughton bastard. It made him wish he'd killed him after the arrow he took. Or even years ago when the raids on his people had started and he'd suspected the MacNaughton. The bastard had pushed too far this time.

Chapter 7

"Ye can stop fretting now," Lady Fiona assured her, drawing Allissaid's gaze from the closed door. "Calan'll take care o' warning the Mac-Laren and the MacLean and seeing to their safety. Meanwhile, ye're safe here, and we'll write to yer father so he can take care o' this ridiculous fiction o' a marriage MacNaughton would try to force. All will be well."

Allissaid managed a weak smile, but the words didn't ease the anxiety clawing at her as she knew the lady had hoped they would. She suspected nothing was going to do that until she knew for sure that she would not be forced into this sham of a marriage to the MacNaughton. Allissaid knew that she couldn't possibly be married to the man. But she was no fool. If it came to her word against MacNaughton's and a priest's, she would be the loser.

In truth, the wedding itself was not the main problem. Her father could petition the king to have it annulled, and probably would the moment he found out what had happened.

If he lived long enough to find out.

That was the real worry. MacNaughton would know that was a risk if she made it to MacFarlane. What if her escaping didn't succeed in throwing a wrench in Maldouen's plans after all, but instead moved him to kill her father at once? And her entire family with him? It might be a risky move on his part. He would be gambling on the chance that she didn't die before he caught up and recaptured her, but he could always keep one of her sisters alive to marry in case that happened.

The thought of all the ways the MacNaughton could still ensure his plan succeeded was frightening and exhausting. Allissaid could feel her thoughts and worries dragging at her, so wasn't surprised when Lady Fiona said, "Ye seem tired, child."

"I am," she admitted and then shook her head. "I should no' be. I slept all day and a good portion o' the evening."

"Aye but ye've had a hard two days," she said sympathetically. "Knocked out, kidnapped and then beaten within an inch o' yer life from the looks o' it," she added, frowning as her gaze slid over her.

Allissaid shifted uncomfortably under her eyes, aware that the woman was examining the bruises that were visible.

"Yer body needs to heal, and bed rest is the best thing to aid with that," Lady Fiona announced firmly. Standing suddenly, she moved to the head of the bed to pull back the linens and furs. "Now, come, let's remove yer gown and get ye tucked up in bed."

"But I ha'e to write a letter to Da," Allissaid protested as Lady Fiona moved back to stand in front of her.

"Ye can lie in bed and tell me what to say, and I can do the actual writing fer ye," Lady Fiona said soothingly, urging her to her feet and toward the top of the bed. "Now come along, dear, and let's get yer gown off."

Allissaid removed the borrowed sgian dubh first and set it on the table next to the bed, but when Lady Fiona began to work at her stays, she frowned and asked, "Should I no' move to another room? This is yer son's bedchamber."

Much to her surprise, the lady shook her head at once. "Nay. We can no' risk ye being seen about the castle."

"But everyone is sleeping," she pointed out.

"Aye, and yet I got up to use the garderobe, finished me business and came out to see me son draggin' ye into his chamber, did I no'?" She shook her head firmly. "Nay. I'll no' let ye risk being seen by another. There could as easily be spies here as at MacFarlane. In fact, MacNaughton's just crafty enough to place spies wherever he can."

Allissaid murmured agreement, but was now fretting over the possibility of there being a spy at MacFarlane. The very idea horrified her. She loved and trusted her people. But Calan was right, MacNaughton *had* somehow found out about the messengers her father had sent out, as well as the contents of the messages. A spy was the most likely answer. She needed to put that in the letter she wrote to her da. She needed to warn him that someone at MacFarlane may be a spy for MacNaughton.

"Let's get this gown off ye then," Lady Fiona said, drawing her back to what was happening.

Allissaid tried to hide the pain the simple act of removing the now-fitted gown caused her. She suspected she didn't do a very good job of it, though, because Lady Fiona kept apologizing and murmuring soothingly as she worked to help her get it off. She also went extremely slowly, and carefully as if Allissaid might shatter at any moment. It was a relief to both of them when it was finally removed.

"I hope Inghinn is no' upset that I did no' recognize her when she learns who I am," Allissaid commented when she noticed the concerned way Lady Fiona was eyeing her as she helped her into bed. It was an effort to distract them both from the ordeal that simply getting into bed was causing her. While Allissaid seemed to hurt everywhere, her stomach muscles definitely pained her the most as she climbed into the bed.

"I would no' worry too much. She did no' recognize you either," Calan's mother reminded her.

"Oh, aye, she did no', did she," Allissaid agreed, feeling a little better about not recognizing the lass.

"Nay. Although, yer face is badly swollen and bruised, so mayhap that excuses her," the lady muttered before saying with concern, "Ye're in a lot o' pain, child."

"Nay. I'm fine," Allissaid lied, and again tried to

distract her, this time by saying, "Inghinn's grown up so since the two o' ye used to visit us at MacFarlane. She and Arabella were wild little things when young. Now she's a proper lady."

"Well, it has been six years," Lady Fiona pointed out, an audible sigh of relief slipping from her lips once Allissaid was reclined in the bed. As she began pulling the linens and furs up to cover her, she added, "She was only eleven the last time ye saw her. A child. She's seventeen now. A woman."

"Aye," Allissaid agreed, and then shook her head. "I wish I'd realized where I was sooner. It would ha'e saved me a lot o' frettin'. But I ne'er thought o' ye as a Campbell. I'm no' e'en sure I kenned that was yer clan or that ye were from Kilcairn back then. Ye were always just me mother's friend, Lady Fiona, in me mind."

"I'm no' surprised," Calan's mother said mildly as she picked up the gown she'd laid on the foot of the bed after they'd removed it. "Like Inghinn, ye were young too when yer mother fell ill and the visits stopped. And as I said, it has been six years since last we saw each other."

"True," Allissaid murmured. Although, she'd been thirteen at the time and had felt like a grown woman.

"Now, ye just rest fer a heartbeat while I go fetch a quill, some ink and a scroll to write that letter," Lady Fiona said as she laid the gown over the back of the chair Calan had sat in. "I'll no' be a moment."

"Thank ye," Allissaid murmured.

Lady Fiona nodded and smiled down at her affectionately. "I hope ye ken yer mother would be proud o' how ye handled MacNaughton and got out o' the fix he put ye in."

Allissaid swallowed a sudden lump in her throat at those words. She really had missed her mother these last years, and hoped that she would have been proud of her as Lady Fiona suggested.

"I'll return directly," Lady Fiona assured her as she slipped from the room.

CALAN WATCHED THE MEN RIDE OUT OF Kilcairn, and then turned to cross the bailey toward the keep. He'd sent out three different groups. One was headed to Graham with a quick letter he'd written imparting what Allissaid had witnessed. Alban Graham's clan deserved to know the son of their laird was dead. The second group had been sent to MacLaren and the third to MacLean, both with letters warning them of what the MacNaughton was up to. Hopefully, his men wouldn't arrive too late, but it was the best he could do for now. That and sending a warning to Allissaid's father. He had a fourth group of men waiting on the letter Allissaid was hopefully even now writing.

That thought made Calan frown as he entered the keep and started along the path through his sleeping people. He fully expected when Laird MacFarlane learned where his daughter was, he would either ride for Campbell or send someone in his place with a return message. Probably one requesting Allissaid be escorted home, Calan thought, and didn't like the idea at all. In his opinion, she would be safer at Kilcairn. Aside from the fact that MacNaughton didn't know she was here, the bastard would be expecting her to return home, and probably had men spread out between MacNaughton and MacFarlane watching for her. If the bastard got his hands on the lass and *did* force a consummation of that sham of a wedding he'd instigated . . . well, there would be little hope of annulling it. She'd most like be stuck with the bastard, and that was the very last thing he wanted.

Calan didn't know Allissaid well, but he already respected her. She'd shown both intelligence and courage escaping MacNaughton. He couldn't bear the idea of her having suffered everything she had, only to land back in the bastard's clutches. That was one of the reasons why he'd also written a letter to include with Allissaid's to be taken to Gannon MacFarlane.

In the letter, Calan had explained his thoughts on her being safer at Kilcairn for now, and assuring her father that he would do everything in his power to keep her safe and out of MacNaughton's clutches. He'd also offered to help deal with the MacNaughton. However, Calan had also written down every bit of what Allissaid had revealed about being kidnapped from MacFarlane's, the wedding, MacNaughton's attack on her in the tower and her eventual escape. He'd done it because he suspected the lass wouldn't tell her father everything in her own letter. The attempt to force a consummation, for instance. He feared she'd gloss over that, or skip it altogether, and simply say she was locked in a room in the tower and escaped.

Calan understood, of course. No lass wished to tell their father that they had been brutalized and nearly raped. But he felt her father needed to know all the facts to decide how best to handle the situation.

If he was wrong, and Allissaid had told all in her own letter, then her father would just get to read about it twice. But if she hadn't, at least he'd know what—

Calan was drawn from his thoughts when he reached the top of the stairs and found his mother in his path.

"Have ye selected men to go to MacFarlane?" she asked, backing up to let him off the steps.

"Aye, and I already sent men to MacLaren, Mac-Lean and Graham. They'll scout fer bodies, or traveling parties on the way," Calan told her solemnly, his gaze dropping to the scroll she held in her hand. "Is that Allissaid's letter?"

"Oh, aye," she murmured glancing down at it with a small frown, before holding it out. "She left out quite a bit o' what happened."

"Ye read it?" he asked with surprise, noting the wax seal on it.

"I wrote it," she corrected. "She's in a lot o' pain. I wanted her to rest, so offered to write down whatever she wished, but she skipped from her feigning being senseless at the wedding, to escaping from a locked room in the tower. She said there was no sense upsetting her father with more detail."

"'Tis all right," Calan assured her. "I feared she would leave much out, so wrote a letter o' me own to accompany it. I included everything she told us."

"Oh. Good," Lady Fiona said, relaxing a little. "She's exhausted after all her misadventures, and tucked up in yer bed. She'll probably sleep the night through."

"Most like," Calan agreed, waiting for the other boot to drop.

While his mother had relaxed a little at the news that he'd written a letter to include with Allissaid's, her tension hadn't completely disappeared. He knew there was something else on her mind, and suspected it had to do with the fact that Allissaid was presently in his room, and in his bed. He had no doubt she'd insist he sleep in the barracks, or that they make up one of the beds in the unoccupied bedchambers along the hall. But he was prepared for that and had a list of arguments against it, so was surprised when she said, "I arranged a pallet and furs on the floor fer ye."

Calan stared at his mother for a minute, and then asked uncertainly, "On the floor where?"

"In yer bedchamber, o' course," she said as if that should be obvious.

"Ye want me to sleep in me bedchamber with the lass?" he asked slowly, finding that hard to believe. He'd expected to have a battle on his hands over the subject.

"Do no' be difficult, son," his mother said with exasperation. "We can no' risk movin' her to another chamber. And ye can no' sleep in one o' the empty chambers, or the barracks with the men without raising questions we do no' wish to answer."

"Aye," he agreed slowly, amazed that she was throwing out the very same arguments he'd intended to use to convince her that he should sleep in his room. Now he found himself bringing up what he'd expected to be her response. "But she's a lady. Her reputation—"

"Will be safe so long as no one kens she's here," his mother interrupted. "And 'tis sure I am that her virtue is too. I trust ye to behave with the lass," she told him sternly, and then continued, "Besides, we can no' be sure everyone in the great hall was sleeping and someone did no' see ye dragging her through the hall and up here. I did after all," she pointed out and then shook her head. "Nay. She's in terrible danger and under our protection. Ye're the laird here. 'Tis yer duty to guard her. I expect ye to stay in that chamber with her night and day until this matter is resolved."

She smiled brightly and added, "We'll just say that ye've decided to rest after this latest incident bursting yer stitches. That ye've agreed to it finally, in the hopes o' yer wound healing at last. That way, Inghinn can use the excuse o' checking yer wound to come up and check Allissaid's head wound as well. And I'll help by bringing up meals fer ye both. Though bringing up two trenchers would raise questions," she said thoughtfully, and then shrugged. "I'll just pile one high with food fer the two o' ye to

share. Ye'll ha'e to share drinking vessels as well."
She focused her gaze on him again and said, "Do ye
no' think ye should give Allissaid's letter to yer men
and send them on their way? Gannon must be mad
with worry fer her."

"I—" he began with confusion, and then simply
sighed, "Aye."

Nodding, she leaned up to kiss his cheek. "Good
sleep, son. I'll check in on the pair o' ye in the
morning." She then hurried away down the hall to
her room.

Calan stared after her with a perplexed frown,
unsure how the conversation he'd expected to have
had been turned on its head like that. Scratching the
back of his neck with bewilderment, he turned to
start back down the stairs to take Allissaid's letter
to the men waiting at the stables.

ALLISSAID SHIFTED RESTLESSLY, AND THEN
gave up trying to sleep and eased up slowly and
painfully into a sitting position. While she'd been
exhausted when Lady Fiona had tucked her into
bed, dictating the letter to her father and the realization that Lady Fiona expected her to sleep in here
with Calan had shaken off any weariness she'd been
experiencing.

In truth, she supposed it was mostly sharing a
room with Calan that had truly made her exhaustion flee. She'd been confused when Lady Fiona
had left after finishing with her letter, only to return moments later with a pallet and extra furs. But
she'd been positively shocked when the lady had ex-

plained they were for her son to sleep on . . . there on the floor in the same chamber as her.

Allissaid was sure she'd just lain there gaping as the older woman had explained her reasoning for why this was a necessity. Every point had been a valid one, really. But there were several equally valid arguments against it in her opinion, such as her reputation. All right, that was only one point, but it was a huge one in her mind. However, Lady Fiona had waved it away as unimportant and assured her Calan would protect her reputation as well as keep her safe. Besides, no one knew she was there, the woman had pointed out. She'd then paused and asked if she was afraid of Calan and felt physically unsafe with him.

Allissaid had answered, nay, without even having to think about it, and it was true. She wasn't afraid of Calan now that she knew he was Lady Fiona's son. She hadn't even really been afraid of him before she'd realized who his mother was. The only reason she'd tried to leave Kilcairn earlier that night was because she'd thought he was a friend of MacNaughton's. Even then, she'd only feared he might hand her over to the man, not that he'd actually hurt her himself. Allissaid didn't know why she trusted him that way. She just did, and realizing that had left her frowning as Lady Fiona had smiled brightly and said that in that case, all would be well . . . and that really this would be good for her son. That, so long as Calan was here in the chamber protecting her, he wouldn't be out in the bailey, practicing with his men or doing any of

the other dozen things likely to make him split his
stitches . . . again.

Apparently, bursting his stitches was a repetitive
occurrence since Calan had gained some unknown
wound to his chest that hadn't yet been explained
to her. This propensity was one that was worrying
Lady Fiona horribly, and so to her mind, this ar-
rangement all worked out nicely. Allissaid would
be safe, and her son would have to rest and heal.
Perfect, Lady Fiona had pronounced brightly, and
then had wished her "good sleep" and departed the
room, leaving Allissaid staring after her, feeling
slightly lost.

Sighing, she glanced toward the door, wondering
where Calan was and when he'd return. Allissaid
knew Lady Fiona had taken the letter for her father
to give to him, so she supposed he was passing it
on to the men he'd chosen to ride to MacFarlane,
and giving them any last-minute orders. But it felt
like it had been quite a while since Lady Fiona had
left. Surely, he should have been back by now? Not
that she really wanted him here. She was sure she'd
be uncomfortable being alone with him in his bedchamber, but waiting for him to arrive was making
her anxious and—

"Oh, good Lord," Allissaid muttered, pushing
the bed linens and furs aside. Now she had to relieve herself. Perfect. Shifting her legs off the bed,
she stood up cautiously, grinding her teeth when her
damaged stomach muscles protested the movement.
Dear God in heaven, using them was becoming
more of an agony with every passing hour, and she

stood panting briefly as she waited for the pain to pass. That was when she noticed that while her legs were still a bit shaky, they were a little better than the last time she'd stood up.

That had to be a good sign, Allissaid told herself, and then rolled her eyes as she began to make her way cautiously toward the door. As she shuffled forward, she tried to sort out why her legs were shaky at all. It wasn't like she was recovering from some terrible illness, or something that included strength-stealing fevers and such.

Allissaid supposed she'd have to ask Inghinn about that. While she knew the basics of healing, she was not as well trained as the younger girl and knew it. Her mother had just started in on training her in healing, and had barely covered the basics when she'd fallen ill. Allissaid supposed she could have asked Claray to continue her training in the matter. But directly after their mother's death, her sister had been struggling with taking over all of the things their mother used to handle. Allissaid hadn't wanted to trouble her with it then, and later . . . Well, she just had never really got around to it.

Pausing at the door, she eased it open and peered out. As it had been the last time she'd tried to leave this chamber, the hall was empty and mostly dark with only two torches lit, one at either end. Allissaid glanced first one way along the hall, and then the other before slipping out and easing the door closed. She didn't know this castle, but at MacFarlane the garderobe was through a door at the end of the hall where an overhang was built to allow the waste to drop straight into the moat. She suspected it would be the same here, and headed silently toward the end of the hall with a door in it.

CALAN ADDED A PAIR OF PLUMS, AND A HANDful of cherries to the bag of food he'd collected, paused, and then added a couple of pears too. He wasn't keen on pears. He didn't care for their gritty texture, but Allissaid might like them. He had no idea. In fact, he had no idea what her preferences were when it came to eating. It was causing a bit of a problem for him as he collected food for the both of them. Did she prefer mutton or beef? He didn't know, so he'd grabbed a good amount of both. Which cheese would she like? The soft crowdie, or the harder, sharper cheddar he'd purchased off a traveling merchant several days ago? He put a bit of both in. Cider or mead? He'd fetched a pitcher of each and two tankards.

Now he had to get it all upstairs. Calan considered the two pitchers of liquid, two empty tankards, and the sack of food briefly and then simply dumped the empty tankards into the sack, tied it to his belt and picked up a pitcher in each hand. His gaze slid to the doors to the bailey as he shouldered his way through the door between the kitchens and the great hall, but this time there was no little slip of a lass making her grand escape.

Calan shook his head at the memory of Allissaid's earlier attempt to leave as he followed the path through the bodies in the great hall to the stairs to the upper chambers. He could still recall his shock on seeing her slipping out of the keep. He'd never imagined she'd do something like that, not in the shape she was in. Between her head wounds, and the beating she'd taken, he was sure every movement must've been an agony for the lass. But that hadn't stopped her. Apparently, she was a determined little thing when she set her mind to something, Calan thought as he mounted the stairs.

Heading out on her own like that showed she was brave too, he acknowledged, and then grimaced as he decided she was too brave, really. Trying to leave on her own in the middle of the night had just been madness. She hadn't even tried to steal a horse to make the journey. Which would have been the smarter move. Certainly smarter than setting out to walk all the way to MacFarlane . . . and with Mac-Naughton soldiers searching for her too.

Calan shook his head at what might have befallen the lass had he not come out of the kitchen just when he had the last time and spotted her trying to sneak away. She could have been caught by Mac-Naughton, not to mention there were other dangers out there: bandits, wolves and so on.

Madness, he thought again. But fortunately, they no longer had to worry about her trying to slip away again. The lass knew his mother, and Inghinn too, though she hadn't, at first, recognized her. Allissaid knew they were on her side, and were doing all they could to help in this situation.

Aye, Calan thought as he reached the door to his bedchamber and shifted both pitchers to one hand so that he could open the door, the only thing he'd have to worry about was finding a way to entertain the lass while she was stuck in his room for who knew how long. She wouldn't be trying to escape again he was sure . . . right up until he pushed the door open and stepped inside to see that his bed-chamber was empty.

Chapter 8

$\mathcal{A}$LLISSAID HAD TO LEAN AGAINST THE DOOR of the garderobe briefly before trying to leave. Walking caused terrible pain in her stomach and back, but settling on the garderobe and getting up again were worse. She'd actually had to bite her hand to hold back the cry of pain that had tried to push out of her mouth during both actions, and now felt shaky and weak again.

Silently cursing MacNaughton for the bastard he was, she took a couple of deep breaths and then made herself straighten and push the garderobe door open a crack to peer out to be sure no one was in the hall. She then slipped out and made her way back to Calan's bedchamber. She'd just reached out to open the door, when it was yanked away from her grasping hand, and Calan Campbell nearly trampled her in his rush to get out of the room.

Gasping, Allissaid stumbled back and nearly fell in her effort to get out of the way, but then found her elbows caught in strong hands that prevented her fall as Calan came to a halt almost on top of her. For a minute they both stood frozen, chest to chest, and then Allissaid, lifted her head and hissed, "Ye're hurtin' me."

The hold on her arms eased at once, but he didn't let her go. Instead, Calan propelled her into his room and closed the door. Only then did he release her.

Rubbing one arm and then the other where she suspected she'd have new bruises to add to her collection, Allissaid turned warily to face her host.

"Sorry, lass," he said, frowning over her expression. "I did no' mean to grab ye so hard. It looked like ye were going to fall and I just meant to prevent it."

"Aye. I mean, thank ye," Allissaid said huskily, relaxing a little.

He nodded, but asked, "Where were ye?"

Flushing with embarrassment, she turned away to head toward the bed, mumbling, "Garderobe."

"Ah."

The word oozed with a relief that startled her, and had Allissaid pausing to glance back in question.

Shifting uncomfortably, he admitted, "When I found the chamber empty, I worried ye'd tried to run off again."

Her eyebrows rose at the suggestion, and his obvious discomfort made a smile curve her lips that she quickly stifled before pointing out, "I'd hardly go without the gown Inghinn lent me, and at least a sgian dubh fer protection."

When his gaze immediately dropped to the thin chemise she wore, Allissaid wished she'd kept her mouth shut and turned to scamper to the bed. She was flat on her back in it and under the linens and furs so fast that the pain of moving, when it struck her, felt like an afterthought. It didn't make it any less unpleasant though, and she closed her eyes briefly as she rode it out. The rustle of movement caught her ear, but since the sound was drifting away from her, she ignored it until Calan asked, "Are ye hungry?"

Allissaid's eyes blinked open.

"After I sent the men off with yer letter, I stopped in the kitchens to fetch some food."

She lifted her head to see that he was standing by the table next to the fire.

"I thought ye might be hungry too, so brought enough fer us both," Calan announced turning back just in time to see her nose begin to twitch as the scent of roasted meat reached her in the bed.

It smelled heavenly, and Allissaid *was* hungry now that the option of food was on the table, so to speak. But the pain was just beginning to recede and she wasn't eager to bring it about again by sitting up, getting out of bed and walking to the table. Sighing unhappily, she let her head drop back on the bed and closed her eyes again. "Nay, thank ye. I'm no' hungry."

"Ye're a terrible liar, lass." Calan's voice sounded amused when he said that, but was more sympathetic when he added, "If ye do no' think ye can manage sitting at the table, I could always bring the food to ye and ye could eat in bed."

Allissaid opened her eyes again as she inhaled

another breath of the delicious-smelling scents filling the air.

"I'll take that as an aye," Calan said sounding amused again. "Would ye prefer cider or mead? I brought both."

"Mead please," Allissaid answered, giving in to her rumbling stomach and starting the miserable job of hefting herself upright.

"Wait, lass. I'll help ye," Calan ordered, appearing at the bedside. He set a pitcher and two tankards on the small table beside the bed, and then leaned over Allissaid to catch her under the arms and raise and shift her back on the bed. "Ye should rest yer stomach muscles. They took a lot o' abuse and need to heal. Ye should no' use them fer a bit."

Allissaid remained silent and simply gritted her teeth against the pain as he quickly built a wall behind her consisting of a bolster, pillows and a couple of furs.

"Thank ye," Allissaid breathed once he'd eased her back against them.

"Me pleasure." His breath brushed her cheek as he spoke, and then he straightened. Turning to the table, he poured some of the mead in one of the pewter tankards, and then handed it to her, before returning to the table by the fire to collect a bag lying there.

Allissaid eyed it with interest as he carried it back. Her gaze remained focused on that bag until he climbed onto the bed next to her to sit crosslegged and set it down between them. Only then did she let her gaze actually flicker uncertainly to him.

It made her uncomfortable that they were now abed together. But while she was still debating whether she should say anything, he opened the bag and pulled out two plums and offered her one.

Allissaid just managed not to pounce on it, but to take it politely and murmur "thank ye" as she lifted it before her nose and inhaled. She loved plums.

"Pear?"

She tore her gaze from the plum to the pear he was now holding out, and shook her head. "Nay. Thank ye."

"Ye do no' care fer pears?" he asked with interest.

Allissaid grimaced apologetically. "The flavor is fine, but I do no' care fer the gritty texture."

Much to her surprise he smiled at this as if she'd said something particularly clever. She didn't understand until he set both pears on the small bedside table on his side and said, "I do no' care fer the grittiness either. I ne'er eat them, but thought mayhap ye'd like them."

"Oh." She smiled faintly, and then her eyes widened as he next pulled a handful of cherries from the bag. "Ooooh, cherries!"

"I'm guessing from that ye like cherries," he said with amusement as he set them on the bed and reached into the bag to retrieve more.

"Oh, aye. God made cherries," she assured him as she peered at the plump red fruit on the bed.

Calan let one eyebrow slide up on his forehead. "I'm quite sure God made everything, lass."

"Mayhap," she said with a shrug. "But cherries

are one of his more glorious creations . . . He did have a few failures in me opinion."

"Such as?" he asked with interest.

"Such as midges," she said with distaste. "And fleas. And spiders."

"No' a large fan o' the wee beasties, I'd guess?" he commented, digging into the bag and pulling out something wrapped in linen.

Allissaid's nose twitched, her body stiffened, and her gaze focused on the item with interest. "Is that cheese?"

"Cheddar I bought off a traveling merchant who stopped by here," he told her, setting the cheese on the bed next to the cherries. "And," he added, digging into the bag again. Pulling out a second cloth-wrapped item, he said, "Crowdie. Again, I did no' ken which ye'd prefer."

"Both," she told him with a grin. "I love all cheese. God made that too."

"Actually, a farmer here at Campbell made the crowdie, and I'm quite sure the cheddar was made in the village o' Cheddar in England. At least the traveling merchant I bought it from claimed it was."

Allissaid merely nodded and watched as he reached into the bag again. Another linen-wrapped item came out.

"I brought up both beef and mutton," Calan said as he set this package on the bed and reached in to retrieve another.

"Because ye were no' sure which I'd like," she said softly, and wasn't surprised when he nodded.

Allissaid shifted her gaze down to the food, but her mind was on Calan's thoughtfulness. He'd brought two different kinds of everything to ensure she would have something she enjoyed to eat. It was unexpectedly sweet and considerate. Or perhaps not unexpected at all, since it appeared to be his nature. After all, she'd tried to rob him of his plaid, yet he'd dressed her, brought her back here, given her his bed and seen her stitched up and tended to. All before even knowing who she was and her connection to his family through their mothers' friendship. Another laird might have had her punished for thieving his plaid. She'd heard of a case where a thief had his ears cut off, and then was whipped, before being hung for the crime. That easily could have happened to her. Or worse. She was very fortunate that Calan was the man who she'd tried to rob.

"Eat up. Ye need yer strength to heal."

Allissaid glanced up at those words from Calan and managed a smile before reaching out to take some of the cheese he was cutting. She ate silently at first, her thoughts still on what could have been done to her, but as she reached for some beef, Allissaid finally said, "Thank ye."

Calan gave an uncomfortable shrug. "'Tis little enough to feed ye, lass."

"Nay. I mean, thank ye fer the food too, but I was thankin' ye fer takin' care o' me as ye ha'e, and no' simply seeing me in yer dungeon, or otherwise punished fer trying to thieve yer plaid."

"Ye were borrowin' it," he reminded her with

amusement, and then added more seriously, "And I'd no' see a naked lass in me dungeon fer trying to cover her nakedness."

"Aye, but this night I was wearing the dress yer sister took in fer me. I did no' need the plaid to cover up . . . and I took it. I took yer sgian dubh too," she pointed out, and wondered what kind of idiot she was to do so, even as she said the words.

Calan was silent for a minute, his gaze on the mutton as he cut it into small chunks on the linen it had been wrapped in, but finally, he lifted his eyes to her to ask solemnly, "Why were ye trying to run tonight?"

Allissaid hesitated, but then admitted, "Kenning ye were friends to the MacNaughton, I was afraid ye'd hand me over to him once ye kenned who I was."

"Friends to the MacNaughton?" he asked with surprise. "Wherever did ye get that idea?"

"Inghinn," she told him. "While she was pinning the dress she took in fer me, she started to fret o'er a stain on the bodice. She said that MacNaughton had bumped her arm and made her spill wine on herself. She said he was clumsier than her, and it was no' the first time he'd caused such an accident. It sounded like he was a frequent visitor and friend. So, I thought it best if I left ere he showed up here and ye mentioned me to him."

"Maldouen is no' a friend, nor a frequent visitor at Kilcairn anymore," Calan said firmly, his expression grim.

"Anymore?" she queried gently.

Calan grimaced at the word, but then sighed and admitted, "His father, Gordain, the old laird o' MacNaughton, was an ally and friend to me da. When I was young, Gordain came often to visit . . . and he usually brought Maldouen with him." He paused, his gaze turning inward as he thought of that, and then said, "I once heard him tell me da that he was trying to teach Maldouen how to be a man, that his wife coddled the boy, spoiled him rotten. He felt he was becoming a sneaky, sniveling little shite and wanted to get him away from her influence as much as possible, so always made him accompany him on his travels."

Allissaid's eyebrows rose slightly, but not because she couldn't see Maldouen as a sneaky, sniveling little shite as a boy. She could believe that quite easily. She was, however, a little surprised that the father was unable to train him out of it, which was obviously the case. As an adult, the man was a sneaky, sniveling bastard despite his father's efforts.

Calan shook his head as if removing a memory from his mind and told her, "Maldouen was a pain in the arse e'en back then. He started out trying to bully me. He was a year older, seven to me six, and he was taller, but had no muscle to speak o' so that did no' go o'er well when I would no' be bullied and fought back. The first time he tried it, I came out swingin' and got in more than one good blow. He ran to his da with a bloody nose and tried to claim that I and several other lads had jumped him. But there had been witnesses to what happened and the truth came out. His da was disgusted, first with his thinkin' to bully a smaller lad, and then with his running crying to tattle and lie about it. He took him home right then, but brought him again the next time he visited and every time after."

"Did Maldouen ever try to bully ye again?" Allissaid asked with curiosity, quite sure she knew the answer.

"Nay," he said, confirming what she'd suspected. "He steered well clear o' me after that. A few months later I turned seven and went to be a page fer the MacAllister and did no' ha'e to deal with him unless they came around while I was visiting. But that rarely happened, so I had no more trouble with him until I was about eighteen," Calan admitted.

"What happened when ye were eighteen?" Allissaid asked with curiosity, and then added, "Ye would ha'e been a squire rather than a page by then, would ye no'?"

"Aye, I was a squire by fifteen," Calan said. "But as to what happened, I had come home fer a visit. Inghinn was just three, close to four years old then, I think," he added, squinting as if trying to work it out in his mind, but then said, "Anyway, she was just a wee lass, and the sweetest little thing with her big eyes and blond hair," he added with an affectionate smile. But it faded quickly to be replaced with a scowl as he announced, "Apparently, she'd taken a liking to Maldouen, which none o' us could understand at all. At any rate, I gather she had a tendency to follow him about when he came with his da to visit. Something he obviously found quite annoyin' because on that visit I happened upon them in the bailey just as he shoved Inghinn face-first into a huge puddle."

"What?" Allissaid exclaimed with dismay. Inghinn had just been a child while Maldouen MacNaughton must have been at least nineteen at the time. What grown man would treat a child like that?

"Aye," Calan said with disgust, and admitted, "I saw red. I could no' believe e'en he'd treat a wee lass so callously. I confronted him. Pushed him into the same puddle. Put him there face-first, and warned him if I ever saw him mistreat me sister like that again, I'd beat the hell out o' him."

"Good," Allissaid said staunchly. The bastard deserved that and more in her opinion.

Calan smiled faintly at her, and picked up some mutton, but simply held it as he said, "Anyway, I had to go back to MacAllister to finish me training and earn me spurs, but for the next two and a half years Gille kept an eye on Maldouen for me when he visited, to be sure he left Inghinn alone."

"And did he?"

Calan scowled. "According to Gille, while Maldouen ne'er outright attacked Inghinn again, he instead resorted to 'accidents' such as bumping her elbow at table so she spilled her drink or food on herself, and other petty little things that could no' be proved to be deliberate."

Allissaid shook her head as she popped some more beef into her mouth and chewed. The man was just so vile. He probably kicked puppies and tortured wee kittens too, she thought with disgust.

"Unfortunately, he refrained from having any o' those little 'accidents' when I was home on visits else I would ha'e warned him to be less careless, and told him o' the consequences did it continue." Calan ate a bite of mutton, before finishing with, "And then the visits stopped."

"Do ye mean Maldouen stopped accompanying his da, or they both stopped coming?" Allissaid asked with interest.

"They both stopped comin'," Calan answered. "Gordain fell ill with the sweating sickness. He was a strong man, so we were all surprised when he lost his battle with it, and died," Calan admitted with a troubled expression that suggested he was still bothered by the outcome. But then he shook his head and continued, "O' course, me da invited Maldouen as the new MacNaughton laird to come visit to reaffirm our alliance. But Maldouen begged off saying he was busy taking on the mantel o' laird now his father was dead and could no' spare the time. Me da gave him the benefit o' the doubt, and decided to give him half a year or more and then invite him again."

"And he refused again?" Allissaid guessed.

"I suspect he would ha'e, but Da ne'er got the chance to extend the invitation. Six months later he fell ill. A lung complaint. Struck him hard, it did. A month later he was dead."

"I'm sorry," she said solemnly.

"So am I," Calan assured her.

"Were ye able to come home to be with him when he passed?" she asked, thinking that being away when it happened would have made it all that much harder.

"Aye," Calan smiled faintly. "I wanted to leave and head home at once when I got me mother's message. O' course, she'd written that me father had insisted she include in the letter that he wanted me to stay at MacAllister until I'd had me dubbing. But that was no' to take place for another month at Easter."

Allissaid nodded. She knew the dubbing ceremony was often planned to occur during feast days; Easter, Christmas, and so on. The soon-to-be knight would have a ritual bath the night before, be dressed all in white and then spend the night in prayer at the altar where the ceremony would take place. The next day he would swear his oath, and the laird who had trained him, or in some cases a master of ceremony, would dub them on the shoulders with a sword, knighting him. He would then don his armor, receive his sword and participate in various displays to demonstrate the skills that he'd learned, before the feasting would commence.

"Fortunately, MacAllister was a good man," Calan told her. "He kenned I was more concerned with me father than a feast, and he kenned me father would be fair wroth if I returned ere gaining me spurs, so he held the ceremony a month early. There was no large feast, and little fanfare, but everything else followed the usual path. I bathed, dressed in white, held me prayer vigil through the night and was dubbed in the morning. MacAllister then insisted I take to me bed fer a rest ere leaving.

I woke fer the nooning, ate me last meal as part o' the MacAllister household, and then headed home. I got to spend one night and one day with Da before he passed."

"I'm sorry," Allissaid said sincerely.

Calan nodded, but sat a little straighter. "Aye. Well, it was a long time ago. Anyway, I became laird and as I kenned me da would want, I invited Maldouen to Kilcairn to reaffirm our alliance. He again put it off, claiming he could no' leave Mac-Naughton just then, and since I had me own hands full taking o'er as laird here, I simply told him to send word when he was ready fer such a meeting, and concentrated on Kilcairn."

"And how long did it take fer him to be ready?" Allissaid asked with interest.

"I'm still waiting," he said with dry amusement.

When Allissaid's eyebrows rose, he shrugged.

"I was no' going to chase him, and I do ha'e enough here to keep me busy. Time slipped by quickly as it does, and then a little more than two weeks ago he arrived at our gate with his first and half a dozen men. I thought he'd finally decided to ha'e the meeting to renew the alliance," he added grimly. "And frankly, after all the trouble he's caused the last ten years, I was debating whether to accept an alliance, or just run the bastard through."

Allissaid's eyebrows rose at the depth of the fury in Calan's expression, but said, "I'm guessing by yer comment that an alliance was no' the reason fer his arrival?"

"Nay," he agreed grimly. "Though I did no' ken

that at first." He popped a bit of meat in his mouth and chewed viciously. She got the idea he was wishing it was part of Maldouen's hide he was gnawing on, but waited patiently for him to continue.

"O' course, I had to invite him in and offer him food and drink as hospitality demands."

Allissaid nodded silently. Hospitality was important in Scotland, even demanded. The English might be rude bastards who could turn away one and all, but Scots were expected to offer hospitality to every guest. Including enemies in certain circumstances.

"Mother and Inghinn joined us and we'd barely seated ourselves when Maldouen accidentally bumped me sister's arm and made her spill her wine," he added, obviously still angry about it. "O' course, she was embarrassed. She rushed off to change and mother went with her to help. I was about to blast him fer the trick when he spoke first and I was suddenly glad they were both no' there to hear the reason for his visit."

Allissaid leaned forward with interest. "What was the reason?"

"He wanted to contract fer Inghinn's hand in marriage."

She blinked several times at this news and then shook her head with confusion. "Nay."

"Aye," Calan assured her, his mouth twisting with disgust. "I could no' believe the bastard had the gall to e'en suggest it."

Allissaid didn't know why *he'd* been surprised at it, but she couldn't believe Maldouen had made the suggestion after two years of pestering her father to marry Claray, and just two weeks ere trying to force Claray to marry him. A plot that had to have been planned ere he'd ever proposed a marriage to Inghinn. Her uncle had suggested Mairin invite Claray to Kerr a week or so before Maldouen had proposed a marriage between him and Inghinn. Had that only been a backup plan in case Calan refused to agree to Inghinn marrying Maldouen? She considered that briefly, but then another thought disturbed her, and she asked, "Did yer parents no' arrange a betrothal fer Inghinn when she was young?"

"Aye. O' course they did," Calan said at once. "She was to marry the son o' the Cameron laird. But he died in a hunting accident. Took a stray arrow just two days ere Maldouen showed up here."

Allissaid's eyes widened incredulously. "Two days?"

"Aye. The messenger only arrived with the news an hour before the MacNaughton rode into Campbell. I had no e'en had the time to sort out how to tell her yet, and here he was, trying to push a contract fer them to marry?" He snorted with disgust. "The bastard must suffer under delusions to think I'd want him married to me sister to begin with, but to e'en broach the subject so close on the heels o' the death o' her betrothed? It was sickening."

"Aye," Allissaid murmured.

Calan's breath came out on an irritated huff, and then he said, "I told him nay in no uncertain terms, and invited him to leave . . . and the next day I rode out with the men to hunt up some meat and took a stray arrow meself."

"Nay!" she gasped, her gaze shooting to his chest where his hand had moved.

"Fortunately, it missed me heart," he said quietly, and then admitted, "No' by much. But it missed."

Allissaid lifted her gaze from his chest, back up to his face and said slowly, "So Inghinn's betrothed took a stray arrow in a hunt, Maldouen showed up two days later to try to convince ye to let him marry her, you refused, and the next day ye were shot while ye were hunting." She tilted her head slightly. "Maldouen?"

"I've no proof, but aye, that's what I suspect," he said grimly.

"All in an effort to marry Inghinn?" she asked.

"I'm sure had I succumbed to me wound, Maldouen would ha'e ridden here intending to force the marriage."

"Surely your people would ha'e stepped in and prevented it," Allissaid protested.

"Aye. If necessary. But most like they would no' ha'e been needed. 'Tis sure I am me mother would ha'e handled Maldouen herself."

"Lady Fiona?" she asked with surprise.

"Aye." A smile suddenly pulled his lips tight, one tinged with viciousness. "The man obviously has no clue what me mother can be like, but trust me, he'd rather deal with me than her. I'd ha'e just killed him had he tried to force the issue. Mother would ha'e cut out his heart and fed it to him. She's as protective as a mother badger with her young when it comes to Inghinn and me."

Allissaid was sure her eyes were as wide as pitchers at these words. They were just so unbelievable. Lady Fiona was sweet and kind. At least, that was her memory of her from years ago, and she didn't seem any different now. She certainly didn't seem like someone who would cut out a man's heart and make him eat it. Although, Allissaid suspected she herself might do that to save a loved one. After all, she'd stabbed Maldouen. She'd got him in the arm, but had been trying for the stomach, not the heart. But mostly because she'd grabbed the knife from his belt and the stomach had been closest. She may have gone for the heart had the situation allowed. She wouldn't have made him eat it though. That was just disgusting.

"Fortunately, I did no' succumb to me wound," Calan said now, "and soon as I could mount a horse, I rode to MacNaughton to ensure he kenned I was alive and well."

"Did ye accuse him o' loosing the arrow on ye?"

"Nay. I had no proof he had. 'Sides, he would no' ha'e done it himself. He'd ha'e sent one o' his men to do it. Then too, when I got there he pretended to be relieved to see me up and about when he'd *heard I'd suffered a terrible accident.*" Calan rolled his eyes. "In the end, I just assured him I was fine, and told him that as he had no' seen fit to renew the alliance between our clans, and as we'd had a lot o' troubles with raiders the last ten years, MacNaughtons were no longer welcome on Campbell land and would be killed if found there."

Allissaid stiffened. "Troubles with raiders the last ten years?"

Calan nodded. "It started shortly after Da died. Small raiding parties attacking me people's farms close to the border with MacNaughton, stealing their livestock and such. It was just one raid every few months at first with only a few animals taken. It always happened at night, and the men carrying out the raids were ne'er seen except from a distance in the dark, so were unrecognizable.

"A year after it started, I took some men and rode to MacNaughton, but Maldouen denied it was his people and I had no proof so there was little that could be done except to step up the number o' men on patrol and suchlike. That usually ended the raids fer a while at least, but then the minute I relaxed the patrols, they'd start up again." His mouth twisted with irritation. "It was a nuisance, but no one was hurt and there was little loss at first. Still, I tried to set traps, alternated the routes o' the men on patrol and such, trying to catch them out, but since it happened so rarely . . ." He shrugged helplessly.

"It was MacNaughton," Allissaid said with certainty.

"Aye. 'Tis sure I am 'twas. But as I said, I ha'e no proof he's behind them."

"'Tis still happening," she said with certainty.

"Oh, aye. But they've grown worse the last few years. The raids occur more frequently, and more animals are taken, along with anything o' value. A couple o' me people ha'e e'en been injured while trying to defend their property. But again, there would be large breaks between each grouping o' attacks."

Sighing, he reached for the mead he'd poured for himself and took a drink before continuing. "And then, six months ago me cousin Finlay Campbell came to Kilcairn. He is laird at Innis Chonnel on the south end of Loch Awe," he explained, and when Allissaid nodded, went on, "He's actually a second cousin. His grandfather and mine were brothers, but ne'er got along, so the families were no' close. I'm no' e'en sure if his da and mine e'er met in person," he admitted. "At any rate, it seems Finlay was ha'ing a similar issue with raiders at Innis Chonnel. He came here after a fruitless meeting with MacNaughton who denied his people ha'ing anything to do with the raids. Finlay wanted to ken if I knew anything about it."

"He thought yer people were behind the raids at Innis Chonnel?" Allissaid asked with amazement.

"Nay. He just wondered if I kenned anything MacNaughton might ha'e been up to," he assured her. "After some talking, we sorted out that when the raids stopped at Kilcairn, they started at Innis Chonnel, and then when they stopped there, they began again at Kilcairn. Though there was always a small break o' a month or so between them stopping here at Kilcairn and starting at Innis Chonnel."

"We've had trouble with raiders at MacFarlane too. Along the MacNaughton border as well," Allissaid told him solemnly. "And as with what ye describe has been happening here at Kilcairn, there'd be one or two and then a goodly time between those raids and when they would strike again. At least at first," she told him. "Recently, while there were still large breaks between the attacks, the number o' attacks each time increased. They became more violent as well. The last one was quite vicious. A farmer was killed and his wife raped and beaten so bad she near died as well. Father too suspects the MacNaughtons are behind it."

Calan's mouth tightened and his brows drew together in a fierce scowl. "The bastard must ha'e worked it in a circuit. Kilcairn, MacFarlane and then Innis Chonnel, before starting the rotation again. I should ha'e thought to write to yer father to ask if he'd had similar troubles." He shook his head with disgust. "For all that he's a coward, Maldouen's a clever coward. Those breaks between attacks are why it took so long to react. The lull between them tended to steal the outrage and anger."

"I think 'tis the same fer me father," Allissaid told him.

"I should ha'e killed the bastard right after talking to Finlay," he said abruptly. "If I had, I'd no' still be waiting on a wound to heal, and he'd no' ha'e tried to force yer sister to marry him, and then kidnapped and beaten you."

"Ye had no proof he was behind the raids," she reminded him gently. "Besides, had he no' gone after Claray, she might still be at MacFarlane, thinkin' her betrothed was dead and she would ne'er marry. I'm sure she's much happier with her husband."

"She really had no idea her betrothed still lived?" Calan asked, scooping up a handful of cherries and holding them out to her.

Allissaid took several of them from him as she shook her head, and began to tell him what she knew about her sister and her new husband.

Chapter 9

CALAN OPENED SLEEPY EYES, STARTED TO let them close again, and then stiffened and opened them wide to stare at his mother and Inghinn. The pair stood at his bedside, staring down at him.

"What—?" The word died on his lips when alarm immediately filled the faces of both women and his mother quickly raised a finger in front of her lips. Recognizing the signal to remain silent, he stared at her blankly until she lowered her gaze to his chest. Letting his own eyes follow, he blinked at the sight of the small lass curled up against his side. They were both seated upright in bed, their backs braced by the bolster, pillows and furs he'd arranged last night. Well, his back was braced by them. Allissaid was curled up against his chest and right arm.

She was also still sound asleep, he noted and wasn't surprised. They'd talked long into the night with Allissaid telling him what she knew of her sister Claray's adventures. She'd been yawning by the time she was done, but Calan hadn't been ready to sleep. He enjoyed listening to her. The lass had a way of telling a story that made even the most mundane tale sound enthralling. So, he'd asked her to tell him about her other sisters.

Allissaid had fallen asleep halfway through the telling, her head nodding and body leaning into his shoulder. Calan had planned to get up and lay her down properly in bed so that she could sleep more comfortably, but he'd liked having her there and had decided to just enjoy it for a minute before stirring himself. Apparently, he'd dozed off during the enjoying.

Although, he was enjoying it all over again now, and briefly considered waving his mother and sister away so they wouldn't wake Allissaid. Unfortunately, that wasn't possible. Now that he was awake, he was becoming aware of a rather urgent need to relieve himself.

Sighing inwardly, he began to shift his position, sliding out from behind her and easing Allissaid back onto the pillows and furs as he went. The lass didn't even stir. Calan wasn't terribly surprised; they'd talked until nearly dawn. She'd probably sleep for hours more, as would he have if his mother and sister hadn't woken him up.

Standing, Calan walked around the bed, paused to kiss his mother's cheek, and then continued on to the door, unsurprised when she and Inghinn followed him out of the room. He didn't stop or slow though, but picked up speed instead.

"Calan," his mother hissed, chasing after him up the hall.

"Aye?" he asked agreeably.

"Fer heaven's sake, son," she said with exasperation. "Will ye stop?"

"Nay."

"What do ye mean, nay?" she asked with what sounded like outrage. "I would talk to ye."

"And ye will," he assured her, finally stopping. Opening the door to the garderobe, he headed in, muttering, "After."

"After wh— Oh," she ended as she realized where he was going. She sounded embarrassed as she muttered, "Well, I guess we can wait."

Calan didn't respond, he simply let the door close between them. He wasn't at all surprised when he finished his business a couple minutes later and came out to find his mother and Inghinn both pacing in front of the garderobe.

His mother looked relieved the moment he appeared; his sister though, seemed more amused than anything, he noticed as his mother rushed forward to clasp his arm. "Is she all right?"

Calan raised one eyebrow in question. "Who?"

"Allissaid," his mother said with exasperation. "The way the two o' ye were sleeping. Sitting up with ye supportin' her . . . Was she ha'ing trouble breathing, and needed to sleep that way to help, or—?"

"Nay," he interrupted reassuringly. "We were talking and dozed off."

"Talking?" she asked, seeming bewildered. "Ye were talking to Allissaid?"

"Aye." He moved around her to head back up the hall.

"Ye mean no' just grunting and such, but actual talking?" she persisted, making Inghinn chuckle as the pair followed him.

"It has been known to happen, Mother," he said with exasperation. "I'm no' mute."

"Ye may as well be fer all the talking ye do to us," Inghinn said under her breath.

Calan chose to ignore the comment.

"So, she's really all right?" his mother asked, apparently ignoring the comment as well. "She was no' ha'ing trouble breathing or anything last night?"

The question made him frown and pause. Turning to her, he asked, "Is trouble breathing a possibility?"

"Well, she has some terrible bruising on her upper stomach and e'en some on her chest," she pointed out with a sigh. "I ha'e seen cases where a broken rib does internal damage and they can no' breathe because o'—" She broke off with surprise when he turned abruptly and hurried the rest of the way to his door.

Calan didn't slow until he was in the chamber and at his bedside. His mother's words, along with the fact that Allissaid hadn't even stirred when he'd shifted her, now had him worrying that perhaps she hadn't stirred because she had stopped breathing while he slept.

Concerned, he surveyed Allissaid's face briefly, but couldn't tell if she was still breathing or not, so leaned down to press his ear to her chest and listen. Unfortunately, that positioned his other ear just inches from her mouth when she suddenly emitted a startled shriek.

Jerking upright, he rubbed his ringing ear and surveyed the lass in his bed. She was definitely awake now, and judging by the color in her cheeks and how loud her scream had been, she was definitely getting lots of air into her body.

"Sorry, lass," Calan muttered. "Mother was afraid ye'd stopped breathing."

Allissaid blinked at him before shifting her gaze to where his mother now bustled up to the bed to push him aside. "'Tis all right, love. How are ye feeling this morning? Are ye hungry? Thirsty? We'll need to check yer head wound, but Inghinn can fetch ye up something to eat and drink first if ye'd like."

Calan scowled at the words, and turned to head for the door. "I'll fetch her food."

"Calan Campbell, do no' dare leave this room," Lady Fiona barked before he'd reached the door.

He was so surprised at the sharp order that Calan paused and turned back with raised eyebrows.

"Ye're supposed to be resting abed to let yer wound heal," Inghinn reminded him gently. "'Tis the cover fer keeping the maids away, and our bringing food and such up here," she pointed out. "If ye can go below to fetch the food, why would ye need to eat it up here?"

"Oh. Aye," he muttered with a frown.

"I'll go fetch food and drink fer both o' ye," Inghinn said, patting him on the arm as she moved past him.

Calan nodded, but then said, "She likes cheese. Any kind o' cheese. And cherries and plums, but no' pears. Do no' bring pears," he ordered firmly. When Inghinn paused at the door and turned an interested gaze his way, he scowled, but then added, "She prefers mead to cider too."

Noting the way her gaze slid past his shoulder, he peered around to see that she was looking at his mother, and the pair were exchanging meaningful glances that he couldn't quite interpret. Or perhaps he just didn't want to, Calan acknowledged to himself as he ignored the pair of them and moved over to drop into one of the chairs at the table by the fire.

"Well," his mother said cheerfully as the door finally closed behind Inghinn, "let's get these bandages off ye, lass, and ha'e a look at yer head wound."

"Aye, but . . . while 'tis embarrassing to admit, I fear I ha'e a pressing need to use the garderobe first, m'lady," Allissaid admitted in a pained voice.

"Oh, dear. Well, that's no'—I mean, someone might see ye. Mayhap 'twould be better to use a bedpan," his mother said anxiously.

Calan glanced over in time to see the dismay and embarrassment that flashed across Allissaid's face at this suggestion, and stood abruptly. "I've a better idea."

Both women immediately looked his way, his mother with concern, and Allissaid with hope, he noted, as he crossed the room to the bed.

"What are ye doing Calan?" his mother asked with alarm when he reached the bed and pulled the furs and linens away to uncover Allissaid in the overlarge chemise.

"Ye said she should no' use her stomach muscles fer a bit to let 'em heal," he pointed out.

"Well, aye, but—Oh, I see," she breathed when Calan bent and scooped Allissaid out of bed, holding her in the seated position she'd been in.

The abrupt action elicited a squeak of alarm from Allissaid, which was followed by her grabbing frantically for his shoulders as if she feared he might drop her. But it was the low moan that followed that concerned him.

"Breathe, lass. Ye're clenching yer stomach muscles and causing yerself unnecessary pain. Relax and breathe. I'll keep ye safe."

Eyes wide and somewhat frantic, she met his gaze, but something in his face must have soothed her, because she let her breath out on a soft sigh, her body relaxing in his arms.

Nodding with satisfaction when she began to breathe normally, Calan turned slightly so that Allissaid's back was to the fireplace and said, "Open the passage, Mother."

She seemed shocked at the suggestion, but after an anxious glance at the girl in his arms, she moved to the mantel to open the section of wall that led to the secret passage off his room.

Calan's gaze dropped to Allissaid then, and he smiled faintly when he saw that she was peering directly at him, not looking around to try to see where his mother was and what she was doing. "Ye may want to close yer eyes, lass. There are lots o' spiders and such in there and I ken ye do no' care fer them."

He suspected Allissaid wasn't fooled at the

comment, but simply closed her eyes and lowered her head. Satisfied that she wouldn't see where exactly the entrance was, Calan headed for the opening as his mother held it ajar for him.

"Wait, let me get a candle," his mother said as he started to step in, and Calan paused to wait. A moment later she'd fetched the candle from the bedside table, lit it from the hall, and was leading him into the dark corridor. "My bedchamber is closest to the garderobe. I suppose that's what ye're thinking."

"Aye," he agreed mildly, turning to move sideways through the narrow space. There simply wasn't enough room to carry her any other way.

"I really should ha'e given ye the chamber after yer father died. 'Tis the master's chamber, and ye're laird here now," his mother said fretfully as she led him along the dark and dusty passage.

"I'm fine where I am," Calan assured her.

"Aye, but Allissaid would ha'e an easier time getting to the garderobe if—"

"Please do no' e'en think o' moving bedchambers about fer me sake," Allissaid protested quietly. "I can walk. I did it last night, and could do it now. And if being seen is such a problem, I could wear a plaid o'er me shoulders and head, then pull it forward to hide me face or some such thing. Or—"

Calan actually heard her swallow she gulped so loud before finishing, "Or I could use a bedpan."

There was such defeat in her voice at the very thought of doing that, that Calan vowed to himself that he'd be sure she never had to resort to using a bedpan. Ever.

"Here we are."

Calan paused as his mother found the correct rock and maneuvered it to open the entrance into the room his parents had shared while his father lived, and that his mother had occupied alone since his death. He followed when she led the way inside.

Curiosity had him glancing around as he crossed the room. He hadn't been inside since his father's illness and death ten years earlier. He'd forgotten how huge it was. Calan's own room was quite large as chambers went, but this room was nearly twice the size of his with colorful tapestries on the walls, a curtained bed half again bigger than his own, a table and chairs to the side of the fireplace to dine at, two large furs, one covering the rush mats before the fire and a second at the foot of the bed. There was also a wooden bench just past the fur at the foot of the bed and a round pavilion tent made up of strips of gray and red cloth in the corner, its flap presently tied back to reveal the tub large enough for two that resided inside.

He'd forgotten about that tub. His father had moaned about it when his mother had insisted on having it and the tent put in, but once done, he'd announced that she was brilliant and it was the best idea she'd ever had. Calan suspected that had had something to do with the fact that his parents had always bathed together after its installation. Purely to save the servants from having to cart water up and down more than necessary, of course.

"If we switched chambers, Allissaid could ha'e a bath."

Calan's head swung around to his mother at that comment, even as Allissaid's eyes blinked open.

"A bath?" she asked, sounding more alarmed than charmed by the idea.

"Well, the water might soothe yer aches and pains, and the pavilion would give ye privacy," his mother pointed out, gesturing to the corner.

Allissaid followed the direction his mother was pointing, her gaze finding the tub tucked away there inside its round tent with its conical top, and her eyes widened incredulously. "Ye've a pavilion in yer bedchamber, m'lady."

"Aye. I sewed it meself. It makes a nice all-around privacy curtain fer the tub," she said with a smile. "Once ye close the flap, the entire clan could march through the chamber and no' see a thing."

"Yer tub looks like half o' a rather large cask," Allissaid commented, eyeing it with fascination and Calan supposed she'd never seen a cask that was five feet across.

"That's exactly what 'tis." His mother nodded proudly. "And that was me idea too. But, good heavens, me husband moaned and complained about having it special made and havin' to collect and transport it here." She shook her head. "And the cursing when the men were trying to get it above stairs and into this chamber! Ye'd o' thought it was a whole tun cask full o' wine." She chuckled softly and then told her, "But he ended up lovin' that tub. And the pavilion too. Did he no', son?" she asked, turning to him.

"Aye, he did," Calan admitted, continuing on to the door.

"Oh, wait!" His mother rushed past him to the door and cracked it open to peer out. After a moment, she relaxed and stepped aside to hold it open for him. "'Tis clear. Go on then, be quick."

Calan carried Allissaid out of the room and straight to the door of the garderobe.

"Nay, Calan. Ye can no' carry that chest, ye'll split yer stitches again."

Allissaid turned her gaze from where Inghinn and Lady Fiona were making up the bed with fresh linens to the large ginger-haired man named Gille as he set down the chest he'd just carried to the door, and rushed back across the room to take away the one Calan had picked up.

When Calan scowled at him, the other man clucked with irritation and pointed out, "'Sides, someone might see ye, and yer need to rest and heal is the reason no one's supposed to be enterin' yer room to see the lass here." When Gille nodded in her direction as he said this and Calan looked her way, Allissaid flushed with embarrassment and turned quickly away.

"Very well. I'll no' carry anything heavy," Calan said with resignation and Allissaid glanced back in time to see the scowl slide off his face.

The other man nodded. "Good." He headed for the door with the chest, and then swung back. "Can ye get the—?"

"Aye," Calan interrupted dryly. "I'll get the door since that's all I'm good fer at the moment."

"Thank ye."

"I suppose I'd best come with ye to open the other door as well," Calan offered.

"Aye," Gille said and then hesitated before adding, "But try to look sickly and weak while in the hall."

"Sickly and weak?" Calan asked with amazement.

"Aye. I ken that'll be hard fer a big brute like you, but do yer best anyway," Gille teased cheerfully and sailed out with the heavy chest, leaving a scowling Calan to follow.

Allissaid shook her head as the door closed behind the pair, and turned a concerned gaze to Lady Fiona and Inghinn.

"M'lady, this is really unnecessary," she protested again, simply unable to help herself. "There's no need fer ye to give up yer bedchamber to Calan just to put me closer to the garderobe. I can walk there easily on me own. I did it last night and could ha'e done it again this last time. I'll be fine."

Allissaid didn't miss the glance Lady Fiona exchanged with her daughter before she set down the linens they'd been stretching over the bed, and crossed the room to her. She didn't understand that look, but didn't get the chance to sort it out. She was distracted when Calan's mother took her hands and squeezed them gently. "Ye may be able to walk, child, but ye should no' be doing it. Or at least, ye should no' be sitting up and lying back down under yer own power. The MacNaughton gave ye a terrible beating. I suspect the muscles in yer stomach were damaged by it. Resting them for a week, or e'en more, is the best thing to help them recover, and that means no' using them. Which means Calan'll ha'e to carry ye to the garderobe repeatedly, day and night. 'Twill definitely be easier on him from here. 'Tis much closer to the garderobe."

"Calan should no' be carrying me. He'll burst his stitches," she reminded her, unsure why Lady Fiona no longer seemed to be concerned about that. "I can walk. And, honestly, the distance is no' a problem. As I said, I walked there from his chamber last night and had no issue making it on me own two feet," Allissaid pointed out with exasperation. "Besides, I can no' stay lying down for a day, let alone a week. I'll need the garderobe several times a day."

"Aye, but if ye stay sitting up during the day, sleep in a sitting position at night, and let Calan carry ye to the garderobe and back in that same position, ye'll no' be using yer stomach muscles."

Allissaid rolled her eyes at the comment, and assured her, "I'll be using them. I had to straighten up and stand after he set me down in the garderobe and left to wait in the hall with ye. I was sitting on me chemise, I could no' use the garderobe that way," she explained. "And then I had to stand again when I finished me business. There is just no way around ha'ing to use me stomach muscles on occasion."

"Oh." She scowled slightly at this news.

"There's also the issue o' yer being seen," Inghinn put in when Lady Fiona seemed dumbfounded. "Being in this chamber reduces the likelihood o' someone seeing ye from the great hall. Calan's bedchamber is easily visible from there, while this one is no'. 'Tis safer."

"Exactly!" Lady Fiona said with obvious relief. "Being seen would be bad. We may ha'e Mac-Naughton spies here too."

Allissaid narrowed her gaze as she peered from Calan's mother to his sister. It wasn't that she doubted that they were right about the reduced risk of her being seen slipping to the garderobe from the master's chamber. That was true enough, but the exchanged glances, and odd relief and such were making her terribly suspicious that there was more to this sudden desire to see her and Calan in this room rather than his.

Lady Fiona took in her expression, and grimaced. "Very well, there are other reasons too. For one, yer presence here at Kilcairn and his need to protect ye is the only way we're likely to get Calan to sit in one spot long enough fer his wound to heal properly, and it really needs to heal. I fear if he does no' do this, it'll eventually get infected and perhaps take his life."

Allissaid relaxed a little at this explanation. She could understand her concern. The risk of infection was no joke, and the longer it took to heal, the longer the risk of infection remained. Still . . . "I understand that, m'lady, but he can heal in his bedchamber as easily as here in yer chamber."

"Aye, but—I was thinkin' mayhap a nice warm bath may help yer aches and pains, and here the pavilion offers ye more privacy fer a bath than it would in his chamber where we'd just ha'e to trust in his keeping his back turned," she pointed out.

Allissaid's eyes widened and shifted to the tub inside its pavilion. She would certainly be more comfortable taking a bath inside there rather than in a tub brought up and set in a corner of Calan's chamber where she had to trust that he wouldn't peek. Not that she thought he would, but she would be anxious the whole time that he might unthinkingly glance over or something.

"Besides," Lady Fiona said now, "whether he carries ye or ye walk, it really is much more convenient to get to the garderobe from here. I'd feel horrible if the MacNaughton got wind o' yer presence here because the wrong person saw ye leaving Calan's chamber to make yer way to the garderobe. Being in this chamber'll much reduce the risk o' that happening."

Pausing, she slid her gaze around the room, and then murmured, "I really should ha'e moved out o' this chamber when me husband died and Calan became laird. 'Tis his right to ha'e it. I just was no' ready at the time and he was no' bothered about it, so I stayed. But I shall ha'e to move out eventually and give it o'er to him. This seems as good a time as any." Turning back, she smiled softly and added, "I'm ready."

The last word had barely left her mouth when the door opened and Calan led Gille into the room. Calan was still scowling as he held the door for Gille to carry in one of his own chests from the other room. He obviously wasn't pleased to be delegated to door opener while his friend did the heavy lifting, but he probably would have lost another stitch to the endeavor were he to be lugging the heavy chests about. Besides, she knew the only reason they'd been able to convince him not to help with moving his mother's things to his old chamber, and his to this one was because of her presence and the need to act like he had agreed to rest as an excuse for him to be up here all the day long with her without servants or soldiers coming to see him.

"Thank ye," Gille said as Calan closed the door behind him. "But that scowl ye're wearing really does no' make ye look the weak, ailing man at death's door we were hoping fer. Ye should work on that."

Calan's responding growl could barely be heard over the other man's laughter as he set down the chest.

The removal of Lady Fiona's hands from hers brought her attention back around to see the two women returning to the bed to continue making it, and Allissaid sighed with resignation. It seemed they were switching rooms.

Chapter 10

"Is Gille yer first?"

Calan glanced up from the chessboard at that question from Allissaid, his gaze sliding over her face. The poor lass looked like hell. The bruising under her eye and along her chin had darkened, with blue and black appearing amongst the deep red, and the swelling was worse now too. He imagined the same would be true of the rest of the red markings he'd noticed on her body the morning before, but knew they would probably darken and swell even further this next day before the bruising began to fade and the swelling to ease. It was the usual process with injuries like she'd sustained, and he'd expected it. Still, it angered him to see it.

"I'm sorry, I did no' mean to make ye angry. Ye do no' ha'e to answer that question do ye no' wish. I was just curious," Allissaid said quietly, her gaze dropping to the chessboard.

"I'm no' angry at ye," Calan said at once with surprise.

"Well, ye look like ye are," she told him, glancing back up again. "Ye're scowlin' at me."

Calan sighed at the announcement and tried to school his expression into a smile as he said, "I'm no' angry. I just— Well mayhap I am, but no' at you," he assured her. "'Tis the MacNaughton I'm angry at. E'ery time I see what he did to ye, I just want to . . ." Calan shook his head rather than admit he wanted to throttle the bastard and then run a sword through him. Repeatedly.

"Oh," Allissaid breathed the word, her head dropping self-consciously as if to hide her face.

Silently cursing himself for making her uncomfortable, Calan decided a change of topic was needed and sought about for something to say. He then recalled her question and supposed he shouldn't be surprised by it, since his cousin had spent a good deal of time with them that morning, helping to shift rooms before leaving with the assurance that he would check on the men for him. "Gille is no' me first."

Allissaid lifted her head again at that, her eyebrows rising. "Nay?"

"Nay. He's me second and me cousin," Calan explained.

That seemed to surprise her, and he understood why when she murmured, "He looks nothing like ye."

"Aye, well, he got his looks and ginger hair from his mother," Calan explained. "While I look very like me da and uncle."

Allissaid nodded at this explanation, moved her knight on the board and asked, "Did his parents die when he was young? Is that why he was raised here?".

"Nay. He was no' really raised here. At least, no' until he turned seven. Then he came here to be a page and then a squire fer me da. That was two years ere I turned seven and went to MacAllister."

"He's the older o' the two o' ye?" she asked with surprise.

"Aye," he admitted, and then smiled faintly and asked, "Ye thought he was younger?"

Allissaid nodded and then grimaced. "Though mayhap that is just because o' how he acts. He does seem to like to tease ye."

"Ye noticed that, did ye?" Calan asked dryly, and then said, "'Tis no' only me he teases. Inghinn gets a fair bit o' it too. Probably more than me if I'm honest."

"Really?" she asked with interest.

"Aye. Gille drives her wild sometimes with his teasing. Gets her so mad I think she's like to hit him, but she just walks away most times. Or stomps away," he corrected himself wryly.

Allissaid smiled faintly, but asked, "Why did he train here and no' at MacAllister like you?"

Calan paused to make his own move on the chessboard, before explaining, "His da was me father's younger brother. He had a small holding on the edge o' Kilcairn that he inherited from their mother. Just a tower and a bit o' land really. Nothing grand. Da knew none o' the other lairds were like to offer a fostering to Gille, so he offered himself," he said with a shrug. "Gille trained as a page and then a squire under me da and earned his spurs a year and a half ere I did."

"Yet he did no' return to his father's holding to help run it once he'd earned his spurs?" she asked with interest.

"There was nothing to run by that time," Calan said quietly. "When Gille first came to us, he visited home frequently since it was so close. But those visits got a little sparser when his mother died. That happened when he was sixteen. After that, he only visited once a year, but his da came to Campbell three or four times each year as well."

Calan paused to watch her make her next move on the board, before considering his own as he went on, "But then almost two years ere Gille earned his spurs, me uncle stopped visiting. Da thought little o' it at first because that winter was a hard one. We got snow like we'd ne'er seen before, and 'twas uncommon cold too. There was ice everywhere. Traveling, e'en short distances, was nigh on impossible for a while. And then when the spring came, it seemed to rain all the time. But when summer came, me uncle apparently still did no' start with visiting again. He simply sent letters to Gille, asking after his training and telling him all was well, but busy there at the holding."

"Me da had Gille write a couple o' times the next year, inviting him to visit, but me uncle just put him off and gave excuses fer why he could no' come to Kilcairn, and when me da suggested Gille write and ask about going home to visit him instead, his father put that off too, saying it was no' a good time,"

Calan told her solemnly. "However when the next spring came and went without a visit and only letters, Da became concerned enough that he wrote me uncle himself telling him that he was coming to see him to be sure all was well. 'Twas then me uncle finally admitted that he'd been ill. He did no' say what the illness was though, but assured him he was recovered now and just trying to catch up on all that he had let fall by the wayside while bedridden for an extended period. And that a visit at that juncture would be most inconvenient and unwelcome, but he would be there for Gille's dubbing in the fall.

"Da let it go then, but when Gille earned his spurs that fall and me uncle did no' show up for the dubbing ceremony as promised, Da was done. He insisted on accompanying Gille home so he could see his brother and find out what the hell was happening."

Calan sighed and ran one hand around the back of his neck with agitation, before telling her, "Da said it was hell on earth there. The holding was a shambles, and me uncle was on the brink o' death. The illness he'd had was Saint Anthony's fire."

He wasn't surprised when Allissaid's eyes widened with dismay at this news. Saint Anthony's fire was a terrible ailment to suffer. The victim had horrible hallucinations, convulsions, agitation, cramps, nausea, and suffered an inability to sleep as well as a burning pain in their extremities that often led to their limbs turning black and simply falling off at one joint or another, without a drop of blood shed.

"Some say Saint Anthony's fire is a judgment by God on a sinner," Allissaid said quietly.

Calan was just stiffening when she added, "But me mother always suspected it was from something the people had eaten."

"Really?" he asked with interest. His own mother was of that opinion too.

"Aye," Allissaid said. "Though she never sorted out what that could be ere she died. Even so, while she said it was a tragic and terrible ailment for anyone to suffer, she insisted it was no' God's judgment o' the person ailing like everyone seems to think."

"Me mother believes the same," he acknowledged. "And considering e'eryone at the holdin' had suffered it, I think they're both probably right."

"E'eryone?" Allissaid asked with dismay.

"E'ery man, woman and child," he said sadly.

"Oh, no," she breathed unhappily, and then asked, "What happened?"

Calan grimaced. "A lot o' me uncle's people had died or fled the year before when the ailment first struck. By the time Da and Gille got there, those left behind had either lost limbs to it and could no' flee, or had been so weak fer so long that—" He shook his head. "The fields had gone fallow, the tower was a wreck, they'd gone through all their stores, coin and animals, and those remaining were all half-starved and barely alive when me da and Gille arrived."

"Why did the messenger no' tell yer father what was going on when he returned to Kilcairn all those times he was sent carrying messages?"

"That's exactly what me da wanted to ken when

he realized what had happened," Calan said grimly. "It turns out the same young clansman had ridden out with the message each time. He'd volunteered fer the job, and since me da kenned the man had family near there and would probably take the opportunity to visit his kin, he allowed it. But it turned out, he did no' go to me uncle's holding, nor e'en his own family's small farm. He was in love with a lass on the neighboring farm to his family's. He went there e'ery time, to flirt and lift the skirts o' the lass . . . after givin' her little brother a coin to take the message to the tower and wait fer a response."

"Oh, dear," Allissaid breathed, and then frowned and asked, "Well, surely the lad noticed—Nay?" she interrupted herself to ask when he started to shake his head.

"Nay," Calan said grimly. "The lad ne'er got close enough to the tower or bailey to notice anything. Someone always rode out to meet him as soon as he was spotted leaving the trees. They took the message, bade him wait there fer a response, and rode back to the tower. He'd nap in the grass until someone returned with me uncle's answering message, and then would ride home to give the message to his sister's lover to bring back to Kilcairn."

"Yer uncle made sure the boy, and probably e'eryone else, did no' get close enough to see the state o' the place," Allissaid said with quiet realization. "But why? Surely he did no' believe Saint Anthony's fire is God's judgment like some say. Surely, he did no' think yer da would believe . . ."

"Aye, he did," Calan assured her. "It seems me

uncle had been jealous o' me father since they were lads. That me da would become laird o' Kilcairn, while he would be left with the tower, a much smaller holding. I gather that jealousy only grew when his wife, who he loved dearly, died while his brother's wife, me mother, still lived." Calan sighed unhappily. "Me uncle thought getting the ailment was God's judgment on him fer his envy, and he did no' want me da to ken his shameful secret."

"How awful," Allissaid breathed sadly.

They were both silent for a minute, and then Calan told her, "Me uncle was one o' the ones who'd lost his limbs. He was abed and at death's door from starvation when they found him. Da sent to Kilcairn fer our priest at once, hoping he could help, but while they tried to get him to eat, or drink and rally, me uncle could no' keep food down. All they could do was sit with him while he passed, bury him and the others who did no' make it, and then bring the few survivors back to Kilcairn."

He glanced down at the chessboard before continuing, "Gille had planned to return to his home to live there now he'd earned his spurs, but there was really nothing to return to. While his da had at first survived the illness, losing his legs and hands had sapped his spirit. Then too, many o' his people had also been ravaged by the ailment, while others had fled rather than risk getting it. There was no one to work the fields or run the holding, and me uncle himself could no'. He felt useless, but was too stubborn to tell me da or anyone who could help that he'd e'en been ill. He let the whole place go to rot and ruin and had just been waiting to die."

Calan shook his head at the memory of the change in his father after that. "I do no' think Da e'er forgave himself fer no' checking on me uncle sooner to be sure all truly was well. He suffered a lot o' guilt o'er it."

"Is that why Gille did no' stay at his holding?" Allissaid asked. "Because being there made him feel guilty?"

Calan's eyebrows rose at the suggestion. "I ne'er thought o' that," he admitted with surprise. "I always assumed it was just because it reminded him o' his father's sad state at the end, and because the job o' refurbishing it to its former state would be a herculean task. But aye, mayhap guilt was a large part o' it too," he said thoughtfully, and then shook his head. "Anyway, me da was the one who suggested he should return to Kilcairn with him and stay on a while longer. He promised Gille that when he was ready, he'd send men, seeds and coin with him to help him clean and repair the tower and get the fields growing again. I gather it took some convincing, but eventually Gille gave in and returned to Kilcairn. Me father gave him a position as his second, and life went on."

"He was ne'er ready to return?" Allissaid asked with a small frown.

Calan shook his head. "Da ne'er pushed it, and when he died and I took o'er, I offered to uphold me da's promise and help Gille set it to rights did he wish, but he said he'd wait. He was happy

where he was here with the clan, and would no'
bother to fix it until he was ready to take a wife
and start his own family." Calan shrugged. "He's
yet to show an interest in any lass, so I kept him
on as second and here he stays."

Allissaid nodded with apparent understanding,
and made another move on the board, before saying softly, "I'm sorry about yer uncle. It must ha'e
been awful fer him, and fer Gille to see him that
way too."

"Aye," Calan murmured, surveying the board and
the moves open to him. But then he stopped and met
her gaze as he admitted, "To be honest, I'm glad I
was no' here when they went to check on him." He
shook his head. "Me uncle was always a big burly
man, strong like me da. To e'en imagine him left
limbless and starved in a bed . . ." Calan fell silent
as his imagination provided a picture of his uncle
in that condition, one that briefly tormented him
before it disappeared like smoke in the wind when
Allissaid reached across the table and covered his
hand with her own.

Meeting her gaze again, he asked sadly, "How
could he let it happen? Mother said it takes several
weeks fer it to get to the point where the limbs rot off.
If he'd just sent fer help, we might ha'e saved him."

"From what ye said it sounds as though he believed those superstitions about Saint Anthony's fire
being God's judgment for his sins. He thought he
was being punished by God for his envy o' yer da,"
she pointed out solemnly. "If he truly believed that,

mayhap he did no' think it could be stopped and he could be saved."

"Aye," Calan said quietly, but his gaze was on her hand covering his. It was warm, and soft, and one of the few spots on her that wasn't bruised. He was somewhat surprised when his hand turned over under hers to clasp it. He didn't consciously give his hand the order to do so, it just happened. But Allissaid didn't pull away until the door to the chamber suddenly opened. Then she snatched her hand away even as he did and they both turned guiltily toward Inghinn who had paused several steps into the room, her sharp gaze on where their hands had been moments ago.

"Well?" Calan asked when a full moment passed with everyone unmoving. "I'm guessin' ye did no' come here to gawk at us like a lackwit. What's about?"

Inghinn blinked at his raspy voice, and then gave herself a little shake. "Aye. Oh, aye. Ye ha'e to leave."

"What?" Calan asked with disbelief.

"Ye ha'e to take Allissaid to yer room. Well, Mother's room now. Ye ha'e to take her there and wait fer me to fetch ye back."

"Why the devil would I do that?" Calan asked with disbelief.

"Because mother mentioned wanting a bath fer Allissaid, I mean you, to the servants this morn. She told them it was fer you, but 'twas really fer Allissaid," she explained and then clucked with exasperation at her own stumbling words, and said more firmly, "Apparently, they started heating the water at once, so when I went down to ask them to warm water fer a bath fer ye, I was informed 'tis already done, and they'd bring it up at once. So ye need to get Allissaid out o' here so she's no' seen. Take her through the passage to yer old chamber and wait there. I'll fetch ye back when they've finished filling the bath and left."

Calan was on his feet and at Allissaid's side before Inghinn had finished her explanation. He now scooped Allissaid into his arms, careful to keep her in her sitting position, and was much impressed when he noted that Allissaid closed her eyes the moment he'd finished lifting her. Calan knew it was an effort to ensure she didn't see where the entrance to the secret passage was in this room, and appreciated her doing it without his having to ask. She was a sharp lass, with a fine, considerate mind, and she smelled good.

Calan grimaced at that last thought as he carried Allissaid to the entrance to the hidden corridor even as his sister opened it. The fact that the lass smelled good was truly irrelevant other than it meant she wasn't really in need of a bath, he thought, but then recalled his mother saying that a bath might soothe some of her aches and pains. That definitely meant she needed it. Allissaid was doing her best to hide it, but it wasn't just her stomach muscles causing her pain. He'd watched her as they'd played chess and from the small grimaces and flinches that had crossed her face each time she'd moved one of her chess pieces, he'd wager her one shoulder was stiff and sore. He also suspected her lower back and hip were as well, because she'd occasionally shifted in the seat he'd set her in as if uncomfortable.

"I'll come fetch ye when they leave," Inghinn reminded him as he stepped past her to maneuver sideways into the narrow passage.

"Aye," Calan growled just as a knock sounded on the chamber door.

Releasing a little alarmed squeak, Inghinn didn't respond, but closed the entrance at once, leaving him in stygian darkness. Without a candle or any light at all to lead the way.

"Damn," he breathed and felt Allissaid's hair brush against his cheek as she lifted her head.

"'Tis dark," she whispered, obviously having opened her eyes.

"Aye," he agreed, and then said reassuringly, "But 'tis fine. 'Tis a straight shot to me old chamber."

Calan didn't mention that while it was right along the passage, he had no idea how far, and with her in his arms he couldn't feel his way along the wall for the slightly protruding rock that was the lever to open it. There was no sense in worrying her.

Rolling his eyes at himself, Calan started sidling down the passageway, trying to guess how far he had to go to reach the entrance. He was about to stop and admit that he wasn't sure and ask her to feel along the wall for the protruding stone when the silence that cloaked him now that he wasn't moving allowed him to hear muffled voices. Stiffening, he tilted his head, trying to tell where the sound was coming from, and then moved several more steps the way he'd been going before stopping again.

"That's yer mother, but who is the other voice?" Allissaid asked in a whisper.

"Her maid," Calan breathed with a small frown.

"They're probably arranging yer room to her liking," Allissaid murmured.

"Aye." Calan hesitated briefly, and then began moving back the way they'd just come. He waited until he'd gone several steps, far enough he hoped they wouldn't be overheard, before saying quietly, "We'll just wait out here until Inghinn comes fer us."

"Mayhap ye should put me down then," Allissaid suggested. "Ye can no' just hold me like this until they're done. I must be heavy."

Calan couldn't stop the snort of laughter that slipped from his lips at that worry, and was glad he'd moved away from where his mother and her maid could be heard. "Lass, ye're a wisp o' a thing. No' heavy at all. Holding ye is me pleasure."

He felt her hair brush his cheek as she turned her face toward him, and instinctively turned his own head to face her as well, but froze when his lips brushed against her soft skin. "Sorry," he whispered, but hadn't turned his head and his lips moved against her skin as he spoke.

"'Tis fine." Just those two little words on a puff of air, but her lips brushed his chin just to one side of and under his mouth, and he couldn't resist turning his head and lowering it the fraction necessary to claim her lips. He meant it to be a soft brushing of his mouth over hers, just a taste of her. But when she didn't pull away, or push at him to warn him off, Calan found himself rubbing his mouth against hers more firmly. When Allissaid sighed shakily against his mouth, he followed that up with a proper kiss, pressing his mouth firmly to hers and letting his tongue slide out to urge her lips apart.

Much to his relief, she hesitantly gave in to the demand and opened to him and . . . God in heaven! Kissing Allissaid was like getting a taste of heaven. She was warm, and sweet, her body softening and leaning into him. When he felt her arms creep around his shoulders and one hand cup the back of his neck, he let loose and deepened the kiss, drawing a moan from her that sent a charge of excitement whipping through his entire body . . . and then he lost himself in her. His tongue was thrusting, his lips demanding her response, and she gave it to him. Allissaid kissed him back with little skill at first, but an enthusiasm that did his heart good. However, she was a quick learner, and they were soon lost in a tangle of tongues and lips and need that died an abrupt death when the whoosh of the entrance being opened and light spilling into the passageway had them breaking apart.

Turning toward the opening, Calan saw Inghinn framed in the light spilling through the entrance, her head tilted as she eyed them.

"Ye can come back in now," she said softly.

Calan released a small resigned breath and nodded, then began sidling toward her. But he was thinking that he wished they hadn't been interrupted, that the servants had taken their time and he'd been able to . . . Well, actually, with Allissaid in his arms as she was, there wasn't much more he could have done other than keep kissing her. He could have stood there holding and kissing her forever though.

"Why did ye no' go in yer old bedchamber?" Inghinn asked as he slipped past her into the room with his burden.

"Yer mother and her maid were in there," Allissaid explained, and Calan glanced down to see that she'd closed her eyes on her own. It made him smile faintly as he carried her to the chair she'd been sitting in earlier and set her down.

"Oh, dear," Inghinn muttered as she closed the passage. "I forgot they were going to make up the bed. Sorry."

"'Tis fine," Calan said as he straightened and moved to reclaim his own seat.

"Well." Inghinn crossed back to the table and eyed Allissaid uncertainly before saying, "I'm no' sure if we should wait fer mother to join us, or get ye in the tub right away while 'tis warm."

Allissaid's answer was to stand at once, straightening completely. She truly did her best to hide the pain it caused her, Calan would give her that, but the way she gasped in a breath, paled, flushed and then paled again as she clutched the edge of the table so tightly that he was sure she was leaving grooves in the wood, gave her away. He had to clench his own fingers into fists to keep from reaching for her, and shook his head at Inghinn to stop her when she started to move toward her as well. They simply had to watch helplessly as Allissaid rode out the pain. There was really nothing else they could do. He would have happily stripped her while she sat in the chair and then carried her naked to the tub, and set her into it, but despite the situation they were in, he knew that was definitely one step too far. If Allissaid was to get in the tub, she'd have to manage it on her own, so he waited.

After what seemed like forever to him, but was probably only a moment, she let out a shaky breath, swallowed and then forced a smile. Her voice, however, was a little high and strained when she said, "There's no need to wait on yer mother. I can manage."

"Can I help?" Inghinn asked anxiously, trailing behind Allissaid as she began to walk stiffly to the pavilion. His sister was so close on her heels she was nearly treading on them. Calan watched until they reached the tub, and then turned in his chair to face the fireplace as Inghinn began to help her undress.

Chapter 11

𝒜 LONG SIGH FROM HIS SISTER HAD CALAN glancing up from the chessboard between them, and he raised an eyebrow in question. "What?"

Inghinn shrugged and looked behind him toward the pavilion where the splashing of water and soft murmur of Allissaid and his mother's voices could be heard. "I just feel so bad fer Allissaid. She's in terrible pain, and there's naught we can do about it. Except perhaps give her a draught to make her sleep through the next few days until it improves." She paused before adding, "But she refused that suggestion. I suspect she's afraid o' MacNaughton getting his hands on her while she sleeps or some such thing."

Calan merely grunted. He wouldn't let the bastard within a mile of the lass, but selfish as it might be, he was glad she'd be awake. He enjoyed talking to her and listening to her tales of her family . . . and maybe he'd be able to sneak another kiss or two. No more than that, of course. The lass was a lady and in terrible shape at the moment. He had no desire to hurt her, or damage her reputation. But he found himself terribly hungry for more of her kisses.

A soft laugh drew his head around to peer at the pavilion, but the tent flap was down and there was nothing to see. He could hear his mother's amused voice saying something and Allissaid laughed again.

"I'm glad mother came in time to help. I do no' think I could ha'e got Allissaid in the tub without her aid," Inghinn admitted solemnly. "Getting her out o' her gown caused her terrible pain, but settling in the tub was absolute agony fer her. I do no' ken how she bore it," she added. "It hurt me just to watch, and dear God the bruises are black and angry now, and seem to be everywhere on her."

Calan frowned at this news as he turned back to the chessboard. His mother had entered just moments after Allissaid and Inghinn had reached the tub. She'd rushed forward at once to help disrobe her, and get her into the water. With his back to them, Calan hadn't been able to see, but he'd heard every gasped breath and pained moan Allissaid had tried to cut off or stifle. Calan had sat with his hands clenched and teeth grinding, wanting to tell them to let her be, not do anything to hurt her, including the bath if it was causing such agony. But he knew the benefits might outweigh the temporary pain, so he'd held his tongue and simply waited. It had been something of a relief when Inghinn had left their mother to assist Allissaid in washing her hair and joined him at the table suggesting a game of chess. He'd thought the distraction might be good, but it wasn't really much of a distraction. While he was making his moves and trying for some level of strategy, he was also listening intently for any sound of trouble from the tub.

"I like Allissaid," Inghinn said suddenly, her voice barely above a whisper. "I hope you do too."

Calan glanced at her sharply, giving her a quelling scowl. He had no interest in talking about such things with his younger sister.

Inghinn, however, scowled right back and hissed, "She's been through a lot, Calan, and does no' need ye to put her through more. If ye do no' like her and are no' thinkin' seriously o' a future with her, ye should let her be."

"Shut it," Calan growled. "'Tis none o' yer affair."

"I saw ye holdin' hands earlier, and kissin' her in the passage," Inghinn said quietly. "If I catch ye doin' more than that, 'twill be me affair, and I'll tell mother," she warned him. "And her father, and they'll force a wedding. I'll no' let ye dally with Lady Allissaid and cause her more troubles and heartache."

Calan opened his mouth to snap back, but shut it and jerked his head toward the pavilion when a cry of pain rent the air. It was accompanied by some violent splashing that had him getting abruptly to his feet, but then he hesitated and barked, "Is all well?"

"Just a minute," his mother called back. She sounded upset and Calan shifted his feet, fighting the urge to rush over and whip open the pavilion's flap to see what was happening as he listened to his mother's anxious whispers from inside.

"Nay!" That gasped cry from Allissaid was definitely not whispered, and he had to wonder about it as his mother's murmurs became more insistent. A moment of silence followed and then his mother called, "Inghinn, bring me a drying linen, please."

His sister rushed forward at once to snatch up the linen lying over a chest beside the pavilion and crack the flap of the tent open enough to pass it through.

"Is all well?" he heard her ask.

"Nay. She can no' get out on her own, and I can no' help. She's wet and slippery and the pain is too great. Calan is going to have to lift her out."

His eyes widened at those words, but his feet started forward, taking him to the pavilion.

"Cal—Oh!" Inghinn said with surprise when she turned to find him right beside her. Managing an anxious smile, she said, "Mother needs yer help."

Inghinn stepped back as she spoke, and his mother stuck her head out of the tent to eye him with concern. "Ye should no' be lifting her. Ye'll probably pop yer stitches again havin' to lift her from the tub. I'm surprised ye ha'e no' burst 'em already today with ye carrying her into the passage and back." She paused to scowl at Inghinn for letting him do that, but then turned her gaze back to him and said, "Close yer eyes and come lift her out o' the tub, please."

Calan blinked. "Close me eyes?"

"Aye. Well, I've put the linen o'er her, but it's soaked through, o' course, and ye can see right through it. So ye'll ha'e to close yer eyes."

"Close me eyes and what?" he asked dryly. "Feel me way?"

His mother gave him a perturbed look, and then released a frustrated sigh. "Oh, very well. Ye can look, but just enough to see where ye're puttin' yer hands. Then close yer eyes and I'll lead ye to the bed to set her down."

Calan gave a disbelieving huff of amusement, but moved forward when she stepped to the side, pulling the flap open. He honestly didn't intend to ogle the lass. He thought he'd just get a quick look at the situation, scoop Allissaid up and carry her to the bed, keeping his gaze trained on where he was going and not on her. But his first sight of her was a shock. The last time he'd seen her fully naked, her body had angry red markings in various spots. That was not the case now. While the linen covered her from neck to knees, as his mother had said, the water had made it transparent. It did nothing to hide the dark blue and black bruising that now covered her body nearly everywhere from mid-thigh up to her face. There were the two bruises on her face, the choke marks around her throat, the hand- and finger-shaped marks on her shoulders, arms and wrists, the bruises on her breasts and an ocean of black and blue from her breasts down to her groin and then on her upper thighs. It was obvious Mac-Naughton had brutalized the lass terribly, and he knew she must be in absolute agony. In fact, he was in awe that she had not been weeping every minute of the day since she'd awoken.

"Calan."

His mother's voice drew him out of his shocked silence, and Calan muttered an apology even as he bent to scoop up the lass out of the water, careful to ensure he kept her in a seated position.

"The bed?" he asked, as he turned to step out of the pavilion, and then glanced at his mother in question when she hesitated.

"I'm no' sure," she said on a sigh. "Hot baths are good for easing muscle aches and such, but cold is better to help reduce the swelling. Mayhap just put her in the chair fer now while I try to come up with a way to make the bath water cold enough to do some good and—What are ye doing?" she interrupted herself with surprise when he moved toward the fireplace.

"Taking her to the loch," Calan growled. "The water there is cold enough to help the swelling I'd think."

"Aye, 'tis," she agreed. "But—"

"Close yer eyes, lass," Calan ordered, and then glanced to his sister and nodded toward the entrance. When she rushed forward at once to open it for him, he turned to his mother and said, "Have more hot water brought up. She'll want to warm up after the loch."

Much to his surprise, his mother merely nodded and didn't try to protest his taking the lass, naked with just a scrap of damp linen covering her, down to the loch for a dip. She didn't even protest about him possibly ripping his stitches.

Not really caring whether she protested or not at that point, Calan turned and made his way into the passage.

ALLISSAID KEPT BOTH HER EYES AND MOUTH shut as Calan carried her into the secret passage. She wanted to protest that she didn't need to go to the loch, and insist he set her down in the bed where she could pull the linens and furs over her head, and pretend she hadn't seen the horror and disgust on his face when he'd looked down at her in the tub. His expression was burned into her memory, and made it a certainty in her mind that her virtue was not under threat despite being completely naked in the man's arms. He was probably even regretting the kisses they'd shared in the dark passage before Inghinn had interrupted him.

That thought made her shiver in his arms as the memory of that interlude filled her mind. His kisses had been . . . Dear Lord, she'd never experienced anything like them, and they'd made her aches and pains fade as other sensations overwhelmed her. The taste, the smell, the feel . . . Her entire body had tingled and trembled and she'd wanted it never to end. Now, Allissaid suspected it would never happen again. It had been dark after all. He hadn't been able to see her swollen and bruised face, and had perhaps briefly forgotten how awful she presently looked. She didn't think he'd forget again after his expression when he'd looked down on her in the bath. But ashamed as she was to admit it, Allissaid wished he would. She wished he'd kiss her again as he had then, make her feel all those delightful tingles and that warm heat that was even now coursing through her body and making her shiver again at just the memory.

"Ye're shiverin', lass. Are ye cold? Should I go back fer a dry linen to wrap round ye?" Calan asked with concern.

"Nay. I'm fine," Allissaid murmured, and pushed the memories causing her shivering from her mind. Once she did, she became more aware of their surroundings. Her thoughts had distracted her long enough that they now appeared to be descending stairs, and it seemed they were wider than the passage had been, allowing him to walk normally rather than having to sidle sideways. At least, it seemed to her he was. She couldn't be sure. It was inky dark and she had no idea how Calan was navigating his way. She presumed it was because he used the passage often and knew it well. Although it did seem to her that he was moving more slowly and cautiously than she suspected he did when he could actually see.

"I'm sorry, lass."

Allissaid turned to try to look at him, but of course, couldn't see a thing, not even a dark outline of his head. Everything was just black. "What for?"

"Fer gawkin' at ye like I did," he rumbled. "Yer bruisin' is just . . . more than it seemed when I first saw ye. It took me aback a bit."

"'Tis ugly," she muttered with embarrassment.

"Aye. 'Tis," he agreed mildly. "But they'll fade. I'm more concerned with the amount o' pain ye must be in."

Touched by his concern, but not liking how grim and serious he sounded, Allissaid assured him lightly, "Do no' concern yerself. It only hurts when I move . . . or breathe."

"Oh, is that all?" he asked with dry amusement, and she relaxed a little in his arms, feeling she'd lightened the mood. At least she hoped she had.

Wanting to remove his thoughts from her aches and pains and such, she searched her mind briefly for a change of topic, and grabbed at the first to pop into her mind, saying, "Ye ne'er told me, how did Inghinn take the news that her betrothed had died?"

Calan hesitated for a moment as the stairs ended and the passage floor became flat once more, and then said, "I'm no' sure. I told me mother first, and she insisted on telling her herself. Inghinn's no' broached the subject with me. But I imagine she's . . ." He paused briefly and then confessed, "I'm no' sure how she would feel. They'd ne'er met, so she did no' ken him as a person, and yet his name has been linked with hers since shortly after her birth, and she was raised thinking she'd marry him."

"Oh," Allissaid murmured.

"How do you feel about yer betrothed's death?" Calan asked.

The question made her blink in surprise, because she'd quite forgot about Alban Graham since waking up here in Kilcairn. A rather shocking realization since the man had been her intended husband. Now, she considered the question and was ashamed to realize she wasn't feeling much of anything at all. Or, perhaps she was feeling too much. Allissaid couldn't be sure and tried to explain that.

"I think I'm mostly confused," she said slowly. "I was horrified when I recognized 'twas him hanging o'er that horse and realized he was dead. I was outraged too, and furious that MacNaughton had murdered him like that, and then I felt . . . guilty."

"Why guilty?" Calan asked, sounding surprised.

"Because, had his parents no' arranged a wedding contract between us, he'd still live," she pointed out solemnly. "He is only dead because o' me."

"Nay," Calan said at once. "He's dead because o' MacNaughton. Ye can no' be takin' responsibility fer his sins onto yerself, lass."

"But—"

"Do ye think Inghinn is responsible fer the death o' her betrothed?" he interrupted.

"Well, nay, o' course no'," she said. "But that may ha'e been an accident."

"Oh, aye," Calan said dryly. "He had an accident and then days later I had the exact same accident."

Allissaid grimaced, but admitted—if only to herself—that it didn't seem likely.

"Had ye met yer betrothed?" Calan asked after a moment.

"Aye," she said quietly. "He's come to MacFarlane twice a year fer three years, e'er since I turned sixteen."

"To see you or yer da?" Calan asked.

"To see Da, and ask that our marriage take place," she said. "But he talked to me each time as well ere leaving."

"And what were those talks like?" he asked. "Did ye like him?"

Allissaid shrugged, and then grimaced and stilled the movement as her shoulder pained her. Finally, she said, "I do no' much recall what we talked about. Mostly the weather, I think. He seemed nice enough. A decent man."

"Did he kiss ye?" Calan's voice sounded different this time, tense and gruff and her eyes shot to where she thought his face was, but she still couldn't see anything.

"Nay," she admitted and was grateful for the darkness surrounding them. The question reminded her of the kisses they'd shared and Allissaid suspected she was probably blushing now. At least, her face felt incredibly warm.

"Did ye want him too?"

"Nay!" she gasped with amazement, shocked at both the question and that he'd ask it. Allissaid was quite sure proper ladies did not flounce about imagining the men they were betrothed to kissing them. Did they? Maybe they did. She had no idea, but she hadn't. Allissaid hadn't even realized that there was such a thing as kissing. Well, of course, she'd kissed her mother's and father's cheeks, and seen her parents do the same to each other. She'd even come upon soldiers and lasses indulging in kisses more like the ones Calan had given her in the passage, or at least she'd glimpsed them and now assumed that's what she'd witnessed. She'd never stuck around to watch or anything. Embarrassment at intruding had always sent her scampering on to wherever she'd been headed at the time.

"Did ye like me kissin' ye?"

Allissaid stopped breathing at that question and suddenly felt like she was walking on uneven ground, despite the fact that she wasn't walking at all.

"'Tis a simple question, lass," Calan said gently, and then told her, "Ye seemed to like me kisses, but if ye did no', I'd no' do it again."

"I liked them," Allissaid blurted, her face suddenly as hot as a pot over the fire as she realized she probably should have kept that to herself. It felt like she'd as good as asked him to kiss her again.

If Calan took it that way too, he didn't accept the invitation, but continued to walk in silence. Allissaid bit her lip, wondering what he was thinking, and how big a blunder she'd just made. Had she just made a complete fool of herself? Or perhaps she'd shamed herself with the admission. She didn't know, and frankly was suddenly too depressed and exhausted to care. It was not as if she did not have enough on her plate at the moment. MacNaughton and his machinations, the threat to her family, her injuries, being all alone so far from home . . . and why had her father not responded yet to her letter? Surely an answer should have arrived by now?

Before she could voice that concern, Calan stopped walking and did something. She wasn't sure what, but suspected he kicked out at something with his foot since his hands were busy holding her

at the moment. Whatever the case, a grinding sound
started and a crack of light appeared before them.
Just a sliver, and not bright light but after so long in
utter darkness even the dimmest light would seem
bright.

"Should I close me eyes?" she asked quietly.

"If ye would no' mind," he responded, and Allissaid closed them to avoid seeing where this entrance
came out. She then listened as a sliding sound filled
her ears before Calan began to move again. He
stopped briefly after a couple of steps and she heard
the sliding sound followed by a slight thud, and then
he was walking again.

"Ye can open them now," Calan said after a
moment.

Allissaid blinked her eyes open and then peered
around. He was carrying her through dark woods
and she supposed it was near or just after sunset.
There was enough light to make out the trees and
bushes surrounding them, but that was about it. It
was brighter once the woods fell away and they
started across a beach, but definitely sunset. The
light was waning fast.

She wasn't sure what she'd expected when he'd
carried her out of the bedchamber heading for "the
loch." Allissaid supposed she'd thought he'd set her
down on the beach and let her walk in by herself. He
didn't. Calan carried her down to the shoreline and
then just kept going.

"Ye'll get yer plaid wet!" she protested with
amazement as he strode into the water, and then
gasped a moment later when cold water flowed over

her toes and then her feet. Allissaid found herself stiffening and tightening her arms around his shoulders as that cold moved up her lower legs. When it hit her bottom and thighs, she gasped at the shock of it, and then bit her tongue and merely suffered through it as the water closed over more of her body.

Calan didn't stop until the water covered her to her neck. By then, Allissaid was stiff as a board, eyes squeezed closed and holding her breath, which she'd been doing since the first touch of water. It was cold. Not as cold as the deeper water she'd fallen into when she'd jumped out of the MacNaughton tower, but cold enough that she was half tempted to try to crawl Calan like a tree to escape it. It was for her own good though, so she didn't. She simply tightened her grip on his shoulders and held her breath, waiting for the water to cover her completely.

"Breathe," Calan said gently.

Allissaid blinked one eye open and peered about uncertainly before opening the other and letting her breath out. Smiling at him with chagrin, she explained, "I was expecting a sudden dunking. The shore did no' go out this far in most o' the spots where I went in. It seemed to drop off sharply o' a sudden."

"Aye. There are some areas like that along the shore, including where I was swimming the day we encountered each other," he admitted. "But here the water deepens more gradually for a bit further ere dropping off. 'Tis why I picked this spot."

"Oh." She smiled weakly and resisted the urge to huddle against his chest. His body was hot, warming hers where they touched. Trying to ignore the cold for now, she let her gaze move over his shadowed face in the dying light. He was a handsome man, his cheekbones high, eyes a deep green and kind, nose straight, chin strong and his lips . . . the upper was thinner than the lower, but they were nice. They'd felt both firm and soft against her own when he'd kissed her.

"I like talkin' to ye, lass," Calan said suddenly. "I remember e'ery word o' what ye've told me since we've met."

Allissaid's eyes shot to his with surprise, unsure where that comment had come from, and then she recalled his asking if she'd enjoyed talking to Alban and her saying it was fine or some such thing, though she hadn't recalled what they'd talked about. She'd thought it might have been the weather. She and Calan had never once discussed the weather, and she too liked talking to him and recalled everything he'd told her, so she confessed, "'Tis the same fer me."

He smiled faintly, and then the smile faded as his eyes focused on her lips and he said softly, "And I liked kissin' ye too."

Allissaid swallowed, her own gaze dropping to his mouth. She was so focused on it that it took her a minute to realize that it was drawing nearer to her. Once she did recognize that, she simply closed her eyes and waited. She was hoping for the same passionate kisses as they'd shared in the passage, but instead, Calan merely brushed his lips over hers, once, softly. When he then withdrew, she opened her eyes uncertainly.

"We're alone, lass," he pointed out gently. "And ye're less than properly dressed. 'Twould no' be a good idea fer me to lose me head with ye here, and I very easily could, ye excite me so. Besides, ye've so many bruises and pains . . . I'd no' like to hurt ye. So 'tis just better do we no' indulge in proper kissin' here."

Allissaid swallowed, nodded and turned her head away. But she was wondering if it was that he did not want to hurt her, or that he did not want to kiss her as much now that he'd seen the ugly bruises and swelling marking her body. And they *were* ugly. She could barely stand to look at them herself since waking. They were also an outward sign of what Maldouen had tried to do, his shameful attack on her. They made her feel marked and dirty despite having just bathed and being in water now.

His warm breath on her ear distracted Allissaid from her unpleasant thoughts, and she drew in a hitching breath and stilled as his lips claimed her ear lobe, sucked and then tugged gently. It was an odd thing to do, but had an even odder effect on her body, making her straighten slightly in response to the warm wave of something she didn't understand rolling from her ear down.

"Are ye cold?" His voice was a husky growl by her ear before he nipped at it.

"Mmmm," was all Allissaid could manage in response as his lips began a slow trail down the side of her injured throat. She kept waiting for it to hurt, but he was being so gentle it didn't. In fact, she liked it and tilted her head, stretching her neck to give him more access. She then gasped when he took advantage of the move to nibble and lick lower to the base of her throat.

"Loosen yer hold, lass. I want to raise ye a bit," he said in a raspy voice before pressing a kiss to the hollow at the base of her throat.

Allissaid loosened her grip on his shoulders, and bit her lip as he moved further out into the water, raising her at the same time as he trailed kisses down the slope of one breast as it emerged from the water. When he then closed his lips over her nipple when it made its appearance above the water's surface, she cried out at the shock of pleasure it sent through her.

Calan immediately paused to ask with concern, "Are ye tender? Does me sucklin' ye hurt?"

"Nay," Allissaid managed in a choked voice, excitement warring with embarrassment at his blunt question. Much to her relief, he didn't ask anything else, but lashed the hardening nipple with his tongue and then claimed it again, nursing the excited bud to grow harder still until she almost could not bear it anymore. Despite that, she couldn't prevent the moan of disappointment that slid from her lips when he suddenly let her nipple slip from his mouth and began to lower her in the water again. But he silenced the sound of discontent by covering her mouth with his and kissing her the way he hadn't at first. This was no soft brushing of lips, it was a hungry pillaging, his tongue thrusting past her lips and demanding a response she was more than eager to give him.

Calan kissed her until her head was swimming with need and her body was beginning to stretch and twist in search of something she didn't quite understand. The movement caused her some pain, and she moaned from a combination of need and pain, but gasped a protest when he suddenly broke the kiss.

"Hush," he muttered, trailing his lips from her mouth to her ear. "Ye'll hurt yerself fashin' about like this." He lashed her lobe with his tongue, and then muttered, "I knew I should no' kiss ye. I just wanted so bad to taste ye."

"I'm sorry. I'll try no' to move," Allissaid panted, desperate for more kissing. "Please don't stop."

That brought a short laugh, and then his mouth returned to hers and he gave her what she wanted, deep hungry kisses that made her forget all her troubles, and that they shouldn't be doing this, that she was an untried lass, as good as naked, in water with a man who was neither her betrothed nor her husband. Allissaid couldn't even feel the cold anymore as she kissed him back, or perhaps it just wasn't cold anymore. Perhaps their bodies were warming the water around them. She didn't know, and didn't care, she just never wanted this to end.

Allissaid was vaguely aware of the hand at her back shifting downward, and merely tightened her hold around his shoulders to make up for it. She then groaned into his mouth when that same hand reached her bottom and squeezed gently before splaying under both cheeks to support her position as the hand under her knees was removed. Her legs didn't drop fully, but remained buoyed by the water, drifting open of their own accord. Something Allissaid didn't realize until his hand slid up one inner leg, grazing the tender bruises briefly before continuing upward.

The small bit of pain from the brief contact with her bruised thigh was forgotten entirely when he palmed her core and pressed gently. Allissaid gasped in shock, and then began to suck on his tongue as the heel of his palm moved against her in slow circles, ratcheting up her excitement and need to heretofore unknown levels. It was shocking, and overwhelming and—Good God, she hadn't even known this was a thing people did! Her mother had died ere ever getting the chance to explain congress between men and women, and Claray, well, frankly Allissaid doubted her sister knew about it either. If she did though, it was very unkind of her not to share that knowledge with her, she decided as his hand shifted to allow his fingers to work over the excited flesh he was whipping into a frenzy.

The problem was, the more excited Allissaid got, the more her body clenched, including her stomach muscles, and she couldn't seem to stop them doing it. Pain was now beginning to push against the pleasure he was giving her. It was suddenly as if a war was being waged in her body. It was causing confusion and making her want him to stop and not at the same time, and then she felt something pushing into her even as he continued caressing her, and the issue was moot. Allissaid screamed into his mouth as her body convulsed, pleasure and pain roaring through her like charging horses as she writhed in his arms. When it finally ended, she collapsed against him, weak and weeping in his embrace.

"Are ye all right, Allissaid?" Calan asked with concern, shifting his hands to hold her properly as he peered down into her face in the darkening night.

Unable to manage more than a small moan, she turned her face into his shoulder and closed her eyes, unwilling to deal with the various emotions trying to well up within her. Especially the shame that was trying to lay claim to her now that the excitement was past.

Chapter 12

CALAN STOOD STILL FOR A MOMENT, PEER-
ing down at Allissaid. He was afraid he'd hurt her. He
was quite sure she'd enjoyed it at first, but suspected
at the end there had been pain mixed with the pleasure and that had not been his intention. Although,
frankly, Calan couldn't say what his intention had
been. At first, he'd just wanted so badly to kiss and
taste her . . . He'd been grateful when she'd asked him
not to stop. Then, as his excitement had built, he'd
wanted to touch and caress and suckle and . . .

Hell, he'd wanted to do everything to her, Calan acknowledged to himself, and knew that if he
weren't so conscious of all the bruising on her and
the pain it would have caused, he probably would
have taken her innocence right there in the water, or
perhaps on the beach. But he *had* been conscious of
it, so he'd had to be satisfied with just the kissing,
touching and caressing.

Calan had been a little surprised when giving
her pleasure had given him enough to make him

hard as a dead hen. He could even now recall the taste of her as he'd suckled her breast, and the feel of her warm body closing around his finger. At the time, he'd imagined it was his cock sliding into her and getting the benefit of the warm, wet heat. Still caught up in that fantasy when she'd begun to convulse, her muscles tightening and sucking at his finger, he'd nearly spilled himself on the spot like an inexperienced youth.

But there had been more than pleasure in Allissaid's cry when she'd found her release, and now that he was again thinking with something other than his cock, Calan was realizing that the excitement would have made her muscles clench everywhere, including her stomach. What had been intended to give her pleasure had probably ended in pain, he recognized unhappily.

Sighing, Calan glanced around at the quiet shoreline, wondering how long they'd been there and how long she should remain in the cold water to help reduce the swelling of her various injuries. His mother hadn't told him the length of time needed to do her good. In fact, his mother hadn't said much at all, and he was surprised she hadn't protested his walking off with Allissaid with nothing but a wet and transparent linen for covering.

The thought drew his gaze down to her again, and his eyes skimmed over her body. The linen had shifted in the water and was gathered around her groin with the ends floating to the side as if trying to swim away. It left her mostly on display. He noted that she was a little thing, body slim, and her breasts much less than a handful. But her legs were shapely and there was a nice curve to her hips. It made him wonder how she'd bear up in the birthing of bairns. Which led to him imagining her cradling his child in her arms as it suckled at her breast.

The image gave him a warm fuzzy feeling and brought a smile to his face, which widened when she made a sleepy little snuffling sound very close to a snore. The lass was asleep, or at least on the verge of it.

Raising his head, Calan peered around again and then decided Allissaid had probably been in the water long enough if it felt warm enough to her that she could sleep, so he turned and carried her out of the loch. His soaking plaid slapped wetly against his legs as he left the water and crossed the open beach to the trees. It was the only sound to accompany them as he carried her through the woods to the cave where the entrance to the secret passage lay hidden.

Calan didn't have a candle or torch, but then he didn't have a free hand to carry it anyway. It didn't really matter though. He could navigate the passage in the dark easily enough. He knew the route pretty well. He'd just have to shuffle his feet a bit to be sure he didn't get off path as well as to find and mount the stairs. Of course, finding the correct room in the dark once he reached the passage along the bedchambers might be another issue. At least that's what he thought until he reached the upper corridor and saw that the entrance to one of the rooms was open. Turning sideways, he stepped up into the narrow passage and sidled along until he reached it and saw the master chamber through the opening.

Inghinn was no longer there, but his mother was seated at the table, attending some darning. She set it aside and stood quickly when he entered. Her mouth opened as she rushed toward him, but closed again when Calan quickly shook his head and nodded down to the woman in his arms.

Lady Fiona followed the gesture, her eyes widening in surprise when she saw that the girl was sound asleep. He supposed the fact that the linen was only covering her groin could have added to that surprise, but it wasn't like he had a free hand to cover her.

Rather than carry her to the tub he'd asked to be warmed, and risk waking the lass by setting her in it, Calan headed straight for the bed. Apparently, realizing what he intended, his mother rushed around him to pull the linens and furs back, and then quickly stepped out of the way so that he could lay Allissaid in it. She waited for him to remove the wet linen, and then helped him cover her back up with the bedding.

Calan eyed the girl briefly as his mother used her fingers to brush a stray hair away from the lass's face. He then turned to head for the tub inside the open pavilion, his hand reaching to undo the pin at his shoulder as he went. The sodden plaid hit the floor with a slap as he stopped next to the steaming tub. His shirt followed, and then he eased into the tub with a sigh of pleasure.

The loch had been cold. He'd quickly adjusted to it, and would have said it was even comfortable by the time he'd left it, but the cold water running down his body from his soaked plaid on the return walk had been unpleasant and left him chilled. Calan shifted in the tub to lie back and dunk his head under the surface, having to bend his knees and allow them to protrude out of the water to do so. He remained like that for a moment, on his back with his raised knees poking out of the water, and holding his breath as he allowed the steaming liquid to warm his head, face and torso, and then sat up and leaned back against the tub to relax.

Calan only realized his mother had followed him to the tub when she said, "I'll wash yer hair."

It was more an announcement than an offer, and his mother didn't wait for him to agree, but gathered his long hair behind his head and began to soap it. The chore was one she hadn't performed since he was a boy, but Calan didn't protest. He simply closed his eyes as she worked.

"How was the loch?"

The question was mild, but Calan wasn't fooled. All he said though was, "Cold."

"And Allissaid?"

He felt his mouth twitch with irritation at what he suspected was the beginning of a grilling, but merely asked, "What o' her?"

"Was she all right? Did the cold bother her? Did she fall asleep in it, or on the way back? Did ye talk?" The questions shot out one after the other and he sighed inwardly.

"She was fine. The cold did no' seem to bother her unduly. We talked at first. She fell asleep in the loch ere I carried her back," he answered and heard his mother huff with vexation.

"What do ye think o' her?" she tried next.

Calan's eyes opened then and he turned his head to meet her gaze. "What do ye really want to ken, Mother?"

Fiona Campbell scowled at him briefly, and then said, "Allissaid is the daughter o' a woman who was a dear friend o' mine. I ken who raised her and how. She's a good lass and ye seem to like her. I was just wonderin' . . ." She paused when he raised his eyebrows, and then blurted, "Little Beth Ross. Yer betrothed," she added apparently thinking he might have forgotten who the lass was. "She—"

"Died years ago o' a childhood ailment," he finished for her.

"Aye," she agreed. "And ye're laird here now. Ye should be thinkin' on contracting a new betrothal and supplying an heir. I was thinkin' that Allissaid would make a fine Lady Campbell."

Calan eyed his mother briefly, and then turned to face forward and relaxed in the water again. "Aye."

His mother froze, her hands clenching in his hair, which he could tell because he was quite sure she yanked out several strands with the action. She then released the wet, soapy mane and moved up beside the tub. Her eyes were wide with a combination of uncertainty and excitement. "Aye?"

"Aye," Calan repeated, hiding his amusement at her reaction. "Once we've cleared up this trouble with MacNaughton, I'll broach the subject with her father."

A wide beaming smile burst across his mother's full lips, and she moved back behind him to continue with his hair before murmuring, "I kenned ye liked her."

Calan didn't say anything to that. What could he say? In truth, he hardly knew the lass. But what he did know, he liked. And he certainly had a hunger for her, one that couldn't be assuaged any other way than through marriage. Truth be told, he really had to marry her after his behavior down by the loch. His honor demanded it. The kissing wasn't so bad, but touching her as intimately as he had was really unacceptable. She'd be ruined if anyone knew that he had. Worse than that though, he knew he'd do it again. And more.

If it wouldn't hurt her, Calan thought suddenly and frowned.

"I mixed up both a lotion and a tonic fer Allissaid while ye were gone."

Calan stilled, his eyes blinking open. His mother had been chattering away ever since he'd agreed about Allissaid making a good Lady Campbell, but he hadn't been paying attention until she said that.

"The lotion should numb her skin so her bruises are no' so painful. She's no' said a word about it, but I ken it hurts just to have the weight o' the furs on them and I hate to see her in such pain," she muttered unhappily. "I'm a little concerned about the tonic though. I mixed some willow bark, henbane and belladonna amongst other things in wine. I'm hoping 'twill ease her pain, and relax her muscles, but if I'm no' here when she wakes up and ye give it to her, only give her a little at first to see how she handles it. Then more if she needs it. Do no' let her just gulp the whole mixture down," she said firmly, urging him forward in the tub.

"Aye," Calan murmured, shifting as his mother directed and waiting for her to collect a pail of fresh water from a handful of them that sat next to the pavilion. When she returned with it, he tilted his head back and closed his eyes for her to pour the water over him and rinse the soap from his hair. The water was a bit cool, but Calan barely noticed. His mind was on what his mother had just said. A lotion to numb Allissaid's pain, and a tonic that would also do that as well as relax her muscles. Perhaps he could show the lass some proper pleasure with the aid of those to prevent her enduring any pain.

ALLISSAID STIRRED SLEEPILY AND THEN WINCED as she became aware of pain in her shoulder. Grimacing, she instinctively turned onto her back to ease it and nearly moaned as the movement made her stomach muscles hurt instead from being used. Squeezing her eyes tightly closed, she silently cursed Maldouen MacNaughton to hell while she waited for the pain to pass, and then released a relieved little sigh when it ended.

She opened her eyes then and stiffened, making her muscles start squawking again as she took in the dark red bed curtains overhead. This was not Calan's bed. Where—Oh aye, she thought, her body relaxing. His mother's chamber. Well, his now, she supposed, recalling that the two had switched rooms so that she could safely use the garderobe.

And that thought made her realize that she was presently in need of using the facility. Allissaid grimaced at the thought of all the pain she would have to endure to manage the task, but then heaved out another sigh, took a determined breath, and forced herself to sit up. It was as painful as she'd expected, and ended with her just sitting there for several minutes, holding her breath and trying not to scream. When the worst of the pain passed, she let her breath out slowly and opened her eyes.

The room was pretty dark with light only coming from the flames in the fireplace. But it was enough to see that the room was empty. Allissaid was a little surprised by this, but was then distracted by the pewter tankard on the bedside table. Picking it up, she eyed it with curiosity and then gave it a sniff. Her nose wrinkled at the bitter scent, as she recalled Lady Fiona mentioning she'd make her a tonic for her pain. Realizing this must be it, and knowing how unpleasant it would probably be, she plugged her nose with the thumb and finger of one hand and raised the tankard to her mouth.

Hoping to ease her suffering for the trip to the garderobe, and eager to be done with it quickly, Allissaid downed the liquid in one long series of gulps. The tonic was as bad as she'd expected, and she couldn't prevent the shudder of distaste that went through her as she set the empty tankard back on the table. It did seem to her that things that were supposed to be good for you, or assist you, were the most awful tasting.

Biting her lip, Allissaid glanced toward the door, wondering how long she dared to wait before making her way to the garderobe. She would rather wait long enough for the tonic to start taking effect, but she really had to make use of the garderobe quite desperately. Sighing in resignation at the knowledge that she couldn't wait, Allissaid pushed the linens and furs off and then stilled at a snore from beside her. When a second snore sounded, her head whipped around to find Calan asleep next to her in the bed. Well, not really in it so much as on it. He was above the linens and furs she'd been lying under. She peered at him silently for a moment, watching him sleep, and then shifted and turned on the bed to slip her feet to the floor. It hurt, but she'd expected that and merely ground her teeth against it. Allissaid was surprised she didn't snap her teeth when she then pushed herself to her feet, it hurt that bad . . . or perhaps not quite as bad as she'd expected. Not as much as sitting up had. But surely the tonic couldn't be working this quickly?

Allissaid considered that briefly as she stood waiting for the pain to pass. But then let the matter go for more urgent considerations and began to search for her chemise, or dress, or basically anything to cover herself with before Calan woke up and saw her standing there naked as the day she'd been born. Not that it wouldn't be something he'd already seen, she thought grimly. She was naked the morning they'd met, and more recently, he'd carried her down to the loch with little more than a scrap of linen on her. Presumably he'd carried her back the same way.

Spotting her chemise lying over one of the chairs at the table by the fire, Allissaid moved as quickly as she could to it, and set about the painful task of donning the soft shift. However, it didn't seem quite as painful a task as it had the last time she'd had to pull on clothes. Perhaps the tonic was beginning to work after all, she thought hopefully as she let the thin gown settle around her body.

Letting out the breath she hadn't realized she was holding, Allissaid next headed for the door and the hallway beyond. Finding the hall silent, empty and dark, she scampered to the garderobe and slipped inside to tend her business. Everything was fine until she was done and tried to regain her feet to leave the garderobe. It wasn't pain that was the problem by then. She did suffer a bit with the effort, but it was a far-off pain, or muffled. She couldn't think how to describe it except that it felt somewhat removed from her. The real problem was a sudden lack of balance that had her stumbling against the door and nearly tumbling out of the small room before she caught herself on the door frame. Clutching at it, Allissaid paused to take a couple of deep breaths, trying to steady herself before she attempted the return journey to the chamber where Calan slept.

CALAN WASN'T SURE WHAT HAD WOKEN HIM. One minute he was sound asleep, and the next some small sound was drawing him back to consciousness. He woke up fully alert and prepared for battle, body suddenly stiff and ready to leap up if necessary, but the sight of the master chamber and the bed he lay in had him relaxing at once. Until he realized the bed beside him was empty. Calan was out of bed a heartbeat later and turning abruptly, his gaze scanning the room, but there was no sign of Allissaid.

Cursing, he headed for the door, opening it just in time to catch Allissaid as she stumbled through the doorway on unsteady feet.

"Allissaid? What's happened? Are ye hurt, lass?" Calan asked with concern, scooping her up and giving her a cursory once-over as he carried her to the bed. He didn't see blood anywhere, or any other sign of a new injury on her, but there was definitely something wrong. Her head was lolling drunkenly and her body growing limper by the moment.

"What's happened?" he asked, as he laid her in the bed and began to run his hands over her body in search of a possible wound.

"Tonic." Allissaid slurred the word, making it sound more like "stonic," and Calan glanced at her face sharply. He then shifted his gaze to the tankard of tonic that his mother had left on the table. The drinking vessel was empty. God in heaven she'd drunk the entire thing! Exactly what his mother had told him not to let her do.

"All right," he muttered a bit frantically. "'Tis all right. I'm sure 'twill no' harm ye. 'Twill most like just—" Calan broke off there. He had no idea what effect it would have. And, really, he wasn't completely positive that it wouldn't harm her. Cursing, he straightened abruptly and headed for the door, intending to fetch his mother back to be sure all would be well. He'd barely taken a couple of steps when Allissaid slurred his name. At least, he thought it was his name. It was close enough that he stopped and turned back with concern.

"Don' leave me," she muttered now, trying to lift her head. Or perhaps she was trying to raise herself into a sitting position. He couldn't really tell, but whatever the case, she was failing at both miserably.

Frowning, Calan moved back to the bed, and lifted her into a sitting position, taking a moment to stuff the bolster, pillows and a couple of furs behind her before easing her back against them. "How are ye feelin'? Are yer muscles painin' ye?"

"'s good," Allissaid told him almost drunkenly. "Feel better than e'er."

At least that's what he thought she said. It was hard to tell. Her speech seemed to grow worse by the minute.

"I really think I need to get me mother to ha'e her check on ye," Calan told her, his concerned gaze sliding from her to the door. "She said ye should no' drink the whole tonic in one go, but it looks like ye ha'e, and ye seem plum fou, lass. Did I no' ken better I'd think ye'd been drinkin'."

"Aye. Drink stonic," she muttered, her head rolling on the furs and pillow. Once her eyes landed on him, Allissaid smiled and then frowned, and then asked, "Are ye goin' to kissmeagain?"

Calan blinked at the question. In truth, that had been his intention. Give her a dose or two of the tonic, massage the numbing lotion into her naked flesh, and then touch and kiss and caress her the way he'd wanted to and hadn't been able to in the loch. But that plan was blown all to hell now. He couldn't do any of that with her in this condition. He'd be an ass even considering it.

Sighing, Calan leaned forward to press a kiss to her forehead and then stood again. "I'll be right back. I'm just fetching Mother."

"Mother," Allissaid muttered with a frown. "Me mother's dead."

"Aye. I ken, lass. Just rest a bit and I'll fetch mine to help ye."

"Yer's is snice," she told him with a crooked smile. "I like yer mudder. Yer sishter too." She paused to yawn indelicately and then closed her eyes. "I could shleep ferever."

"Nay, ye can no'," Calan said with immediate concern. Dropping to sit on the side of the bed again, he caressed her cheek to try to get her to open her eyes once more. "I think it best ye stay awake, lass. At least until Mother has a look at ye."

"Aye," she said agreeably, opening her eyes.

"That's me lass," Calan said with relief as he stood again. "Now, ye stay awake and I'll fetch Mother back. Right?"

"Right," Allissaid assured him brightly.

Nodding, Calan turned and hurried from the room.

It was exceedingly strange approaching his old

chamber knowing it was no longer his. Calan stopped, frowned at the door, started to raise his hand to knock and then paused again. He then glanced over his shoulder toward the great hall where his people were all long asleep, before turning back to the door and simply opening it. He only opened it a few inches though, just wide enough to get his hand in and knock on the inside of the door lightly. He wanted to wake his mother, not the entire keep.

"Calan?"

He stuck his head through the breach at that soft, questioning voice to find his mother up, sitting by the fire with some mending. Apparently, the women in his life were like to stay up of a night, he thought with irritation as he slid into the room.

"Is something wrong?" Lady Fiona asked with concern as he hurried across the room.

"Aye. Ye'd best come check on Allissaid. She drank the tonic. All o' it," he rushed out as he reached her.

"All o' it?" his mother asked with dismay, and then scowled at him as she set her sewing aside. "Calan, I told ye no' to let her—"

"I did no' let her," he said impatiently. "She woke while I was asleep and drank it down herself."

"Oh, dear," his mother muttered. Getting up, she led the way to the door at a steady gait that he found far too slow.

Calan followed silently, half tempted to pick her up and carry her back to the other chamber. He was worried sick about Allissaid and wanted to get back as quickly as possible, but his mother, despite her words, wasn't showing the same urgency.

Calan managed to restrain himself until they reached the other room. Once inside the door though he rushed around her to hurry to the side of the bed when he saw that Allissaid had fallen asleep again while he was gone. Sure that couldn't be a good thing, he was reaching out to shake her awake, when his mother caught his arm to stop him.

"Let her sleep," she ordered, urging his hand away.

"Should we no' rouse her and keep her awake to fight the effects o' the tonic? She drank the whole damned thing," he reminded her, and then frowned. "Will it kill her?"

"What?" his mother gasped with amazement, and then scowled at him for the question. "O' course no'! I'd no' poison the dear lass. She's going to be me daughter by law when ye marry. What on earth would make ye think I'd gi'e her anything that could harm her?"

"Well, ye said ye put belladonna in it and no' to let her drink the whole thing at once," he pointed out with a little irritation of his own. "I thought . . ."

"Oh, Calan," she said with exasperation when he let his voice trail off. "I just did no' ken how it would sit in her stomach. I did no' want her bringing it back up," she explained, and turned to survey Allissaid as she added wryly, "But that does no' appear to be an issue."

"Nay," he agreed with a scowl. He'd had such

high hopes for taking advantage of the effects of the tonic to explore more intimacy with Allissaid. It didn't look like that was going to happen now. Probably. Unless—"How long is she like to sleep?"

His mother considered the lass for a moment and then asked, "How was she when ye woke up?"

"Stumblin' about and slurrin'," he told her.

"Hmm." His mother bent to lift one of Allissaid's eyelids to peer at the eye revealed and then shook her head. "That's probably the result o' the wine I mixed the tonic in."

"It was only one—"

"Very large tankard o' wine," she finished for him dryly, and then added, "On an empty stomach. She did no' ha'e the sup."

"Oh. Aye," Calan muttered, peering at the lass now himself as she made a little snuffling snort of sound and smacked her lips without waking. Her sleep was sound, but her cheeks had more color to them than he'd seen since meeting her.

"She'll no doubt sleep through the night," his mother said now, releasing her eyelid and straightening. "And hopefully a peaceful one without pain to plague her. A good thing too. She needs rest and plenty o' it to heal."

"Aye," Calan muttered, feeling guilty for his disappointment at a lost opportunity. Allissaid had taken a terrible beating. Sleep was the best thing for her.

"Well, ye may as well get some rest yerself. I suspect we'll ha'e a message from her father by first light if no' sooner. In fact, I'm surprised he's no' already here pounding on our gate."

"I had the messengers ride up through MacNab territory on their way to MacFarlane," Calan murmured, his gaze on Allissaid's peaceful face. "I did no' want MacNaughton or his men catching wind o' their journey."

"Oh. Well, that explains the delay then, and 'twas very clever, son," she complimented him.

Calan grunted in response and then ran one weary hand through his hair.

"Ye're tired." His mother patted his shoulder as she turned to head to the door. "Ye'd best get some sleep then. I'll see ye come the morn."

"Aye." Calan walked her to the door, wished her "good sleep," and then closed it and returned to the bed to stare down at Allissaid. After a moment, he glanced toward the pallet set up on the floor by the door, but merely grimaced at it. He'd slept sitting up in bed with Allissaid the night before, and had been asleep on top of the furs next to her tonight when she'd woken up, drank the tonic and made her way to the garderobe. Sleeping on the pallet now seemed ridiculous. Besides, it would be uncomfortable.

Nodding to himself, Calan moved around to the empty side of the bed, unpinned his plaid, and bedded down next to her again, wrapped in the plaid for warmth.

Chapter 13

"DAMN ME, YE WON AGAIN!" GILLE SAID with disbelief. Throwing his cards down he then accused, "Ye said ye'd ne'er played Poch before, lass, but I swear ye ken the card game well and were cheatin' all the way through."

When the smile that had been blooming on Allissaid's face died abruptly and was replaced with dismay at those words, Calan leaned toward her. But before he could reassure her that his cousin was just teasing and didn't really believe she was cheating, Inghinn chirped in.

"Do no' pay Gille any mind, Allissaid. He accuses me o' cheatin' e'ery time I beat him too, whether at chess, Nine Men's Morris or Poch." His sister beamed at the girl. "Fer all yer head wounds, 'tis obvious yer thinkin' is still fine. Ye played well."

"Aye, ye did," Gille assured Allissaid before turning on Inghinn to tease, "But you, Ginny Campbell, do cheat, and ye do it e'ery game we play."

The taunt brought an immediate scowl to Inghinn's face that Calan knew had more to do with Gille's using her childhood nickname than for the accusation itself. Calling her Ginny was a surefire way to annoy his sister, something Gille knew and used liberally when wanting to get under her skin.

Shaking his head as the two began to squabble, Calan told Allissaid, "Ye do play well, lass, and me cousin does no' really think ye were cheating. He was just teasin' ye."

"Oh." Allissaid relaxed a little, a small smile gracing her lips before she commented, "He does seem to like to tease."

"Aye, he does that," Calan agreed, eyeing the other couple still sniping at each other, and thinking that teasing wasn't so bad, except that Gille's favorite target was Inghinn, and his sister was not one to enjoy it, or put up with it. It always ended in a shouting match, or Inghinn stomping off with annoyance and ignoring Gille for ages. Calan was about to intervene when he heard a hailing shout coming from outside.

Standing, he crossed to the nearer window to peer out, his gaze narrowing on the lone rider stopped at the gate, shouting up to the men on the wall. When they then let him ride in, Calan watched the man cross the bailey toward the keep on his horse, but even when he was close enough to see well, Calan didn't recognize him.

"Do ye think 'tis a messenger with an answer from the gel's da?" Gille asked, drawing Calan's

attention to the fact that his cousin had given up his
battle with Inghinn to join him at the window to see
what was going on.

"Mayhap," he allowed, and actually hoped that
was true. It was late afternoon now and he'd expected a response to arrive by midmorning. The
lack of one had begun to worry him. Now he was
worrying over what had taken so long and what the
response might say. Turning away from the window,
he said, "I'd best go find out."

"Nay. Yer mother would ha'e fits did ye go below
after all we've done to ensure everyone leaves ye
alone up here," Gille said with amusement.

"Oh. Aye," Calan said with a frown.

"I'll go see what's about," Gille assured him, and
headed for the door.

"Thank ye," Calan breathed, but doubted his
cousin heard him. Shaking his head, he glanced to
the table to see Allissaid and Inghinn eyeing him
with worry.

"A lone rider has arrived. Gille is going to see
what's about," he explained, moving back to the
table.

"Is it a MacNaughton?" Inghinn asked as Allissaid began to wring her hands in her lap.

Like his mother, the lass did seem to like to
mangle her fingers when worried or upset. However, she didn't try to hide it like his mother did.
He suspected that was because she wasn't aware
of the habit. Reclaiming his seat, he reached out
to cover her hands to stop their fussing, even as he
said, "Nay. At least, I do no' think so. I did no' rec-

ognize him. 'Tis most like a response to one o' the messages I sent out."

"Only Graham and MacFarlane are close enough to answer this quickly," Inghinn pointed out, and Allissaid immediately began to chew on her lower lip.

Calan was just wondering if he should cover her lips as well to prevent her abusing them, but thought that might not go over well. Certainly, if he placed his hand over her mouth both she and Inghinn would probably be upset. But what if he covered her lips with his own? He was just blinking in surprise at the wayward thought when the door to the bedchamber opened.

"He insisted on seeing the lass at once," Gille said apologetically as he led a tall dark-haired man into the room. That was all Calan got a chance to notice before Allissaid suddenly released a gasp. That was followed by a cry of pain when she thoughtlessly leapt to her feet, a move that was followed by her hunching her shoulders and grasping the edge of the table as she bent slightly forward and panted through the pain she'd caused herself.

"Lass," Calan jumped up at once to go to her, but the newcomer was quicker still and was in front of her before he could get to her side.

"Oh, Allie, love, what did that bastard do to ye?" the man moaned peering down into her ravaged face.

Much to Calan's amazement, when the newcomer then wrapped his arms carefully around her, Allissaid sagged against his chest and began to weep.

CALAN DIDN'T KNOW HOW LONG HE STOOD there staring at the pair embracing, but it was apparently long enough for his mother to enter the room and cross to his side.

When her warm hand closed over one of his, Calan glanced down to see that his mother was squeezing his clenched fist. Both his hands were fisted at his sides, he realized. Very tightly. As if they wanted to be around someone's throat, squeezing and throttling the life out of the dirty bastard touching Allis—

"That's Allissaid's cousin Alick Buchanan," his mother announced quietly.

Calan suddenly focused on her face. "Her cousin?"

She nodded solemnly. "Mayhap we should leave them alone to talk."

When Calan scowled at the suggestion, she pointed out, "It would reassure him that Allissaid is no' held here against her will."

"That's no' necessary," Allissaid said, pulling away from Alick Buchanan and quickly dashing the tears from her eyes. Flushing, she added, "Sorry. 'Twas just nice to see family after all o' this," she explained, and then turned to the younger man and said, "I'm no' being held here against me will. The Campbells ha'e been helpin' me."

"I ken," Alick said with a faint smile, brushing a stray tear away from her cheek. "Uncle Gannon said Lady Fiona was good friends with yer mother, and the Campbells are considered allies."

"Aye. We are allies," Calan agreed, moving forward to stand on Allissaid's other side and unable to resist putting a possessive hand on her back. "We'll do all we can to keep the lass safe."

Alick's eyebrows rose slightly at the move, and the way Allissaid instinctively moved closer to him at the touch, but all he said was, "I've brought several letters from Uncle Gannon."

"Several?" Allissaid asked with surprise.

"One fer you, one fer Lady Fiona and one fer Laird Campbell," he explained.

"Oh." A crooked smile tipped her lips. "Da always was most thorough like that."

"Aye." Alick grinned, but then told her, "He wanted to come fer ye at once, but Aulay—me brother," he told Calan in case he did not know who he spoke of. When Calan nodded abruptly to let him ken he did know, Alick turned back to Allissaid and continued, "Aulay did no' think that'd be a good idea. He thinks it best everyone stay exactly where they are fer now. He thinks 'tis safer than fer any o' ye to travel ere we deal with MacNaughton."

"O' course." Allissaid nodded her understanding. "I'm glad he insisted on that. If Maldouen got his hands on father, or any o' me siblings . . ." Her mouth tightened grimly at the thought, and she blurted, "He killed me betrothed, Alban Graham."

"Aye. Yer father told us what was in yer letter," Alick said quietly, his gaze again sliding between his cousin and Calan, before he offered, "I'm sorry, Allie."

She nodded, and tears again glazed her eyes, but she raised her chin determinedly and blinked them away before saying, "So am I. He did no' deserve that."

"Nay," Alick agreed. "Although it might be for the best."

"What?" Allissaid gasped with shock at the suggestion.

Alick shrugged, and explained, "Alban did no' grow up as well as yer parents hoped. He took to gambling, drink and whoring and the whispers were he had the great pox."

Allissaid's mouth had dropped open as her cousin spoke, but now snapped closed. Her voice was strident with shock and horror when she said, "The French disease?"

"Aye. Why do ye think yer father was delaying letting ye wed?" her cousin asked with faint amusement.

"He said 'twas because Claray had to marry first," she told him with a frown.

Alick Buchanan shook his head. "That was an excuse to put off the wedding until he could decide how best to break the betrothal without making enemies o' the Grahams," he explained. "O' course, once he said that, he could no' allow the MacLaren and MacLean to claim Annis and Arabella, so he had to put them off as well."

"Oh," Allissaid said weakly, and then asked again, this time with a wince, "The French disease?"

Alick nodded apologetically.

"But Da sent word to Alban to come claim me just ere I was kidnapped," she pointed out.

Alick nodded and explained, "With MacNaughton's plans to kill ye all, Alban began to seem the lesser o' two evils. Besides, while the gambling, drinking to excess and whoring were verified, his havin' the great pox was mostly gossip. But yer da and Aulay planned to find out if he really did ha'e the pox ere letting him wed ye. If he did, yer da planned to break the betrothal and damn the consequences. But if he did no' have it, it seemed better fer ye to be safely wed to a man o' lesser character than to be dead at the hands o' MacNaughton. He was doing his best to keep ye all safe."

Allissaid merely nodded at the words, and then sighed and leaned into Calan's side in a search for comfort that he suspected she wasn't even aware of. Ignoring the way Alick Buchanan was eyeing them both, Calan rubbed her back soothingly as he thought that Allissaid had made a lucky escape there. The very idea of her being trapped in a marriage with a husband who gambled, drank to excess and whored was bad enough, but a husband who gave her the great pox . . . His mouth thinned at the very idea. The French disease, or great pox, was a nasty ailment. Aside from being terribly painful, it disfigured its victims and ended in an agonizing death. The lass deserved better.

"Ye said ye had a letter fer me amongst those ye brought?" his mother said now.

"Aye." Alick reached into his plaid and retrieved three scrolls. He examined the seal on each, and then passed one to Calan's mother, before offering another to him and the last to Allissaid. When Calan peered at the scroll himself, he saw a small *C.C.*

scratched into the edge of the MacFarlane wax seal. He assumed that stood for Calan Campbell and that Allissaid and his mother's messages would have their own initials on each.

"Thank ye," his mother murmured and then gestured toward the table. "Please sit down. I'll send fer drinks fer ye. Are ye hungry?"

"Alick is always hungry," Allissaid said with a faint smile, clutching the scroll he'd handed her.

"Me cousin is no' wrong there," Alick said apologetically.

Lady Fiona chuckled at the admission, and said, "Well, then I'll be sure to ha'e lots o' food brought up. Please sit and rest. Ye must be weary after yer journey."

"Thank ye." Alick gave a slight bow, and then turned toward the table Lady Fiona was gesturing to, only to freeze, his entire body going still.

Unable to see the man's expression, Calan glanced toward the table with curiosity to see what had caused that reaction. His eyebrows rose when he saw that his sister was getting slowly to her feet, her cheeks turning a bright pink as she stared back at the man.

"Oh, dear, I'm so sorry," Lady Fiona said, rushing around Alick to reach her daughter's side. "In all the excitement, we forgot to introduce ye. Alick, this is me daughter, Inghinn."

"A pleasure to meet ye, Lady Inghinn," Alick said in greeting. Stepping forward to take her hand when her mother nudged her to hold it out, he then bowed low over it and pressed a kiss to the top. He continued to clasp her hand as he straightened, and Calan saw the younger man rub his thumb across her knuckles before finally releasing it. More interesting to him was his sister's reaction to the familiar caress. The pink in her cheeks turned to a brilliant crimson he would bet went all the way down to her toes in response, and she clasped the hand he'd touched as if protecting the spot he'd caressed.

"Well," his mother said suddenly, a satisfied smile curving her lips. "Why don't the four o' ye no' all sit down? Inghinn, I fear 'twill fall to you to entertain Alick while Calan and Allissaid read their letters and I go arrange fer food and drink."

Inghinn's eyes widened with something like alarm, but she sounded calm enough when she said, "Mayhap I should come help ye collect food and drink, Mother."

"Aye," Gille agreed, reminding them all of his presence. "Ye'd best let Inghinn help ye, Aunt Fiona. Ye can no' ha'e servants bring it up else they'll see Allissaid."

"Oh, I forgot," Lady Fiona said with a small frown and then brightened and walked over to slide her arm through Gille's. "But you can help me with that while Inghinn takes o'er me hostessin' duties. We'll be back directly," she called over her shoulder as she urged an obviously reluctant Gille from the room.

Calan shook his head as he watched the door close behind the pair. He had no doubts about what his mother was up to. Now that he'd admitted he was interested in Allissaid and intended to talk to her father about a betrothal after this MacNaughton business was over, she was looking to arrange a betrothal for his sister. And it appeared to him that she'd set her sights on Alick Buchanan as her future son-in-law.

Not that he minded, Calan decided as he watched Alick hold out Inghinn's chair for her to reclaim her seat. The Buchanans were a powerful family, and from what he'd heard the siblings were all close, loved and supported each other, and the brothers were all said to treat their wives extremely well. His sister could do a lot worse, he decided as he urged Allissaid back to her own seat.

Once she was seated, he reclaimed his own chair and immediately broke the seal on the scroll Alick had given him. Inghinn's and Alick's voices became a quiet murmur in the background as he unrolled and began to read it.

Gannon MacFarlane first thanked him for the aid he'd already given to his daughter. He also appreciated that he'd imparted absolutely everything his daughter had endured. As Calan had expected, and his mother had verified, Allissaid hadn't told him everything in her own letter, and he was grateful that Calan had filled in the holes she'd left in the tale. It just proved how urgent the issue was. The man also appreciated his offer to keep her safe there, and feared he would have to take him up on it. Gannon and his nephew Aulay Buchanan thought it was far too dangerous for her to travel anywhere until they'd handled things with the king and ensured MacNaughton couldn't claim this fake marriage as real. He did not wish to risk her landing in the man's hands again before that.

The letter also said two other Buchanan nephews, Dougall and Niels, had been dispatched to speak to King James about the forced wedding and see that it was decreed null and void. Meanwhile the other Buchanan siblings had gathered their armies and descended on MacFarlane to guard Gannon and his remaining children from any possible attack by MacNaughton until this was all resolved.

Gannon had no idea how long it would take and apologized for that, but promised to keep him informed. He'd sent Alick at Aulay's suggestion. The youngest Buchanan son was to help guard Allissaid, and to assist in any way he could, whether it be carrying messages back and forth, or answering any further questions he had.

Calan was just finishing his own letter when Allissaid said, "Father says he and all me siblings, including Eachann, are safe at home, and MacFarlane is presently surrounded by an impenetrable wall o' Buchanan, MacDonnell, Carmichael, Drummond and Innes warriors."

"Sinclair warriors too will be there soon to add to their number," Alick announced, and told Calan, "They're friends from the north. They ha'e farther to travel, else they would ha'e been there already."

Calan nodded at this news. He was well aware of the connections the Buchanans had. Pretty much everyone in Scotland did. The clan was growing in strength and influence. He suspected that alone would ensure the king sided with them on this matter and voided this sham of a marriage MacNaughton had tried to force.

"He says I'm to stay here," Allissaid said apologetically, lifting her gaze from the message she was reading to cast a troubled look his way.

"I suggested it in me letter to yer da," Calan said reassuringly, and explained, "'Tis no' safe fer ye to travel until MacNaughton is dealt with. If he got his hands on ye and forced a consummation o' the sham wedding he instigated—" He paused, silently cursing himself when Allissaid blanched at the thought and dropped her scroll to the table. Covering her hand with his own, he said firmly, "Ye're safe here. I'll no' let him anywhere near ye."

Much to his relief, Allissaid relaxed a little at that and nodded.

Sighing, he released her hand and sat back, asking, "What else does he say?"

Allissaid picked up the scroll again and continued to read. "That I'll ha'e to be patient. It may take a week or mayhap even several for Dougall and Niels to get to speak with the king."

Calan nodded, not at all surprised at the information. The king was a busy man. He also tended to travel around a lot. They'd probably waste several days just trying to find him. Then they'd have to wait to be given an audience, and then the man might take his time coming to a decision. Everything took time when it came to the king. To avoid insult, he would have to consult his advisors and they would take their time, Calan thought and then noticed that Allissaid had begun to frown and asked, "What is it, lass?"

"Moire has gone missing," she said with concern.

"Moire?" Calan asked, his eyebrows knitting together at the name. It sounded familiar, but he couldn't place where he'd heard it.

"She's the maid who wouldn't let Eachann go down to the loch," Allissaid explained.

"She went missing the same time you did," Alick announced. "She was last seen leaving the bailey, hurrying in the direction o' the river. It seems she found Eachann in the gardens behind the kitchen, climbing the fruit trees with a couple o' clan lads. She gave him hell and sent him inside, then rushed off. Yer da thinks she must ha'e headed out to tell ye he was at the keep and fine, so ye did no' risk being outside the walls any longer than necessary and—"

"Encountered MacNaughton and his men," Allissaid breathed with horror.

"Did ye see her when ye woke up on the MacNaughton soldier's horse?" Calan asked.

Biting her lip, Allissaid shook her head unhappily. "Nay, but I could no' see much without raisin' me head to look around, and I did no' want to do that and risk them kenning I'd woken up. I only saw Alban because the horse he was hanging o'er was next to the one I was on."

They were all silent for a minute, and then a loud bang at the door had every one of them jumping in surprise. Standing, Calan rushed to open it, arriving just in time to prevent his cousin from kicking the door again. Pulling it wider, he stepped back for Gille and his mother to enter. Both of them were carrying long wooden trays. The one Gille carried was heavy with food, while his mother's had two pitchers and several tankards on it. Calan closed the door behind them and then hurried to take the tray his mother carried and conveyed it the rest of the way to the table.

"There are only four tankards," he pointed out as he set the tray on the table.

"Aye. Well, there are only four chairs in here. Besides, they are setting up for the sup below and I thought Gille and I should make a showing at table so our clan does no' think they've been abandoned," his mother explained, smiling around at them. "But you four go on and enjoy yer meal. I shall return after I've eaten below." Lady Fiona turned for the door. "Come along, Gille. Cook will no' let the serving lasses bring the food out until we're there, and we do no' want our meal to go cold."

Gille nodded at them, and then followed her from the room again.

"This all looks good," Alick commented as the door closed behind Lady Fiona and Gille.

Calan turned back to the table and nodded, but his concerned gaze was on Allissaid as he sat down again. She was still looking troubled and he knew she was worrying about the maid who had gone missing. He didn't blame her. If the lass had rushed down to the river to tell her Eachann had been found, and encountered MacNaughton and his men . . . Well, her prospects were not good. If she was not dead, she had probably been taken back to MacNaughton and was now a prisoner there. Judging by how Allissaid had been treated by Maldouen, the maid probably wouldn't fair well.

"Aye," Inghinn said now, responding to Alick when Calan didn't. "We are fortunate to ha'e a good cook."

That set the tune for the meal. Allissaid was silent, a troubled look on her face as she mostly picked at the food he placed before her. Calan ate, but he too said little, and spent most of the meal casting worried glances at Allissaid. It left Inghinn and Alick to carry the conversation on their own, which they managed well enough, he supposed, briefly tuning in to hear they were talking about dogs one of Alick's brothers apparently trained. Leaving them to it, Calan eyed Allissaid again and wished the meal was over, the other couple was gone, and he could distract and soothe Allissaid.

"ALLISSAID IS SPENDING A LOT O' TIME SLEEPING."

Calan eyed the man walking through the dark woods beside him. Alick Buchanan. It had been ten days since the younger man had arrived at Campbell with the letters from Gannon MacFarlane, and ten days since Calan had been alone with Allissaid. Much to his distress, Alick took the chore of protecting his cousin very seriously. Except for brief excursions to the garderobe, the man hadn't left the master chamber since entering it. He'd eaten his meals there, and spent the hours from dawn 'til dusk there; talking, laughing, and playing games such as Poch with Calan, Inghinn, Allissaid—when she wasn't sleeping—and even

Gille the few times he'd joined them. Alick had even slept there.

The last part was what upset Calan. Rather than using the room that had been prepared for him, Alick had insisted on sleeping on a pallet in the master chamber to help guard Allissaid. It had eliminated any possibility of Calan finding even a moment alone with Allissaid to attempt some of those intimacies he'd been hoping to explore. It had also forced Calan to sleep on a pallet as well. He would hardly risk embarrassing Allissaid, or offending a member of her family, by taking up his position on the bed as he had those first nights of her presence in the keep before the youngest Buchanan's arrival.

The only time Alick had even taken his sharp gaze off Allissaid over the last ten days was when she went into the pavilion to bathe, or when Alick himself took his turn in the tub. Until tonight. Tonight, when Calan had mentioned going down to the loch to swim, Alick had asked if Gille, who had joined them for several rounds of Poch that night, could guard the door so that he could accompany Calan to the loch rather than bathing in the tub. Which was how Calan found himself accompanied by Allissaid's cousin for this outing.

"Aye," Calan said finally, as the trees they'd been walking through gave way to the head of the beach. "The extra sleep seems to ha'e helped though. Her injuries appear to be paining her less e'ery day."

"True," Alick agreed quietly as they both began to strip down. "But I'm concerned about her humors."

Calan glanced to Alick sharply as his plaid hit the ground. "Her humors?"

Alick nodded, and pointed out, "She seems to be sleepin' more e'ery day."

"Aye, she does," Calan agreed with the beginnings of a frown. Allissaid had seemed fine at first, waking early and laughing and chatting the day through until they'd all been ready to retire. But after a week in the room with everyone, Calan had begun slipping away to check on his men and the state of things at Campbell. This despite his mother's protests, and mainly because he'd started to feel incredibly restless and just needed some air and time alone. But every time he returned these last three days, he'd found Allissaid asleep in bed and Inghinn and Alick talking quietly by the fire. She was sleeping quite a bit, he realized with concern.

"I'm afraid she's suffering melancholy from being locked up in the room so long," Alick said solemnly. "I ken ye're trying to keep her presence here a secret lest MacNaughton find out where she is, but I'm beginnin' to worry her being locked up in the room day and night is doin' her humors harm. That's why I wanted to join ye tonight," he admitted. "I wanted to discuss it with ye. I was hopin' mayhap we could think o' some kind o' safe outing that we could—"

"I ha'e an idea that may help," Calan interrupted. He didn't then explain, but tugged his shirt off over his head, let it drop to the sand and shingle beach, and strode into the cold water.

"This must be drivin' ye mad, Allie," Inghinn said, using the nickname Alick and most of her other relatives called her.

Allissaid blinked her eyes open, and quickly closed them again as Inghinn tipped the pail of water over her head to rinse away the soap in her hair. Fortunately, she was quick enough to avoid getting any in her eyes, and she waited until Inghinn had emptied the pail before asking, "What must be drivin' me mad?"

"Bein' locked up in here night and day fer so long," Inghinn explained. "Ye must be restless and bored to tears."

Allissaid opened her eyes again to see the lass, who she considered a friend after these past weeks spent with her, setting down the now empty pail and picking up another. When she turned back with the fresh water, Allissaid asked, "Are you restless and bored to tears?"

"Well, nay. But I get to escape to me own bedchamber e'ery night fer some privacy and a change o' scenery. While ye've been stuck in here without a moment to yerself," she pointed out, and then began to raise the pail she'd collected over her head.

Allissaid quickly closed her eyes, but considered her words. The truth was she hadn't minded at all. At least, not when Calan was there. She had enjoyed all the talking and laughing, and repeatedly beating the men at Poch had delighted her too. It had been a bit less fun since Calan had started to slip away to check on his people and keep. She enjoyed it more when he was there. But she had also taken to napping while he was gone in an effort to encourage what Allissaid suspected was a blooming romance between Inghinn and Alick.

"I've been rackin' me brain tryin' to come up with an outing the men would allow," Inghinn admitted. "There must be some safe way fer us to get ye out o' here to enjoy some fresh air, e'en if just fer a little while. Somewhere we could go."

"There is."

Allissaid's eyes blinked open in surprise at the sound of Calan's voice from outside the pavilion, and then she squealed and threw herself to the side in the tub as the pail of water came crashing down toward her head. Inghinn had just begun to tip the pail when her brother's words had apparently startled her enough that she'd dropped it. Fortunately, Allissaid was quick enough to elude getting hit directly, and merely suffered a good soaking as the pail sent bathwater splashing everywhere.

"Oh, my dear heavens! Allissaid, are ye all right? Did I get ye?" Inghinn cried with dismay, dropping to her knees and grabbing her head to begin feeling for a new lump.

"Nay," Allissaid said on a laugh as she caught at her hands. "I'm fine. The pail missed me."

"Oh, thank ye, God," Inghinn breathed, sagging against the side of the cask tub with relief.

"If ye two are done tryin' to give us both apoplexy with all yer squealin' and splashin', ye might want to quit muckin' about in there and get dressed," Alick said, sounding annoyed. "We ha'e a plan to get Allissaid out o' this room fer a bit."

"Yer cousin sounds angry," Inghinn said, her eyes sparkling with delight.

"Ye do no' seem too concerned by it," Allissaid pointed out with amusement.

"Oh, nay. I'm no'," she said with a grin, and then called out, "And what's this grand plan the two o' ye ha'e come up with?"

"A picnic," Alick announced.

Allissaid and Inghinn exchanged surprised glances and then both asked at once with uncertainty, "A picnic?"

"Aye, a moonlight picnic." Alick hesitated, and then added, "'Twas Calan's idea."

"Oh, my heavens," Inghinn breathed. "That's so sweet. Calan's ne'er troubled himself to be sweet with any other female that I ken o'. He must really like ye."

Allissaid felt her face heat up at the claim, and just sat there tongue-tied.

"Come," Inghinn urged, standing up and grabbing another pail of water. "We need to finish rinsin' the soap from yer hair, get ye out, dried and dressed. We're goin' on a moonlight picnic."

Chapter 14

"WHAT A LOVELY NIGHT," ALLISSAID BREATHED, leaning back to look up at the night sky, and glad she could with barely more than a twinge of pain. Her healing had been slow, but was progressing. Two weeks had seen her head wound healed enough that wrapping was no longer needed, and most of her bruises had faded away. In fact, the only bruises that yet remained were on her stomach, and there they were much smaller than they had been at first and were now a pale yellow-green.

"Aye, 'tis a beautiful night. Perfect fer our picnic," Inghinn agreed, raising her own eyes to the star-filled sky as she added, "And 'tis nice to be out o' Calan's chamber fer a change too."

When Allissaid merely smiled faintly at the words, Inghinn added, "Ye should take advantage o' our outing and go fer a walk while ye ha'e the chance, Allissaid. It might be good fer ye to stretch yer legs a bit."

Allissaid wasn't sure she'd be allowed to actually

go for a walk, so merely offered a silent smile that
was replaced with a startled gasp when Calan suddenly lunged up from his reclining position on the
plaid, and was at her side, lifting her to her feet with a
gruff, "Aye. A walk. Keep Inghinn company, Alick."

Eyes wide, Allissaid glanced over her shoulder as
Calan urged her away, and saw Alick frowning and
Inghinn grinning at her as if to say "I told ye so."
Of course, Allissaid knew that was exactly what the
younger girl was thinking. The girl was positive that
Calan liked her, and had made sure to tell her as
much the last two times she'd helped her rinse her
hair in the bath.

The only response Allissaid gave her now was a
roll of the eyes and a shake of the head, before she
turned to watch where she was stepping.

They walked in silence at first, Allissaid's distracted attention half on negotiating the uneven
ground, as the other half played over the picnic
she'd just enjoyed.

The men had arranged everything before coming above stairs to collect them. Once Allissaid had
dried off, and dressed, she and Inghinn had left the
pavilion to find both men holding fresh plaids. She
hadn't understood the purpose of them until Calan
had stepped forward to drape the heavy cloth across
her shoulders even as Alick had done the same to
Inghinn. They'd then both been instructed to draw
the cloth over their heads like a cloak for the walk
through the great hall. Once they'd done as asked,
Calan had taken her arm to lead her out of the room,
leaving Alick to escort Inghinn. The four of them

had then crept up the hall, down the stairs and along the path through the sleeping bodies in the great hall, to the kitchens.

Allissaid had expected that they'd have to stop to collect food for their picnic then, so had been surprised when Calan hadn't stopped, or even slowed, but had led them through the warm, dark kitchens and out through another door at the back that opened into the gardens. They'd walked down a path between an herb garden and a vegetable garden, not stopping until they were a good ten feet into the rows of fruit trees that filled the rest of this area. It was only when Calan had then stopped and stepped to the side that she'd spotted several large sacks lying on a plaid already spread out and waiting for them.

Allissaid had been smiling ever since. She couldn't help it. Calan had packed all of her favorite foods in those sacks, as well as a skin of mead, which she knew he didn't like as much as he did ale. Yet he'd brought the mead because she liked it. He'd also been making an effort to speak to her. She'd noticed these last ten days that he didn't join the conversation as much when others were around. He usually just gave yes and no answers, or grunted in response to other people's comments. It had led her to believe that the Campbell laird might be a touch shy. But tonight, Calan had been more like the man who had sat up all night talking with her before Alick's arrival. He'd joined in the conversation, and laughed along with the rest of them. It had been lovely so far.

"Ye look pretty in yer new gown."

Allissaid glanced toward him with surprise at those words, and then mumbled, "thank ye," as she peered down at the forest green gown she was wearing. It was another of Inghinn's dresses. They'd been taking it in that day to give her something to wear besides the blue gown Inghinn had taken in for her during her first days at Campbell. Allissaid thought they'd done a fine job of it. It also suited her coloring well, and she thought the embroidered neckline was gorgeous, so was pleased he liked it too.

"The cousins yer da sent to the king should ha'e reached him by now," Calan commented.

"Alick's brothers Dougall and Niels," Allissaid murmured with a nod, and then voiced the concerns she'd been having the last few days. "Surely they should ha'e reached him long ago? I ha'e been worrying o'er our no' havin' heard anything yet."

Calan shook his head and let his hand drop from her elbow, down to clasp her hand. Giving a gentle squeeze of reassurance, he said, "Our king likes to travel a good deal and seems e'er to be moving from place to place tryin' to drum up coin and support. I'd no' be surprised to hear yer cousins ha'e been chasin' after him from clan to clan tryin' to catch him up. I expect we'll hear news soon though."

"Oh," Allissaid breathed, relaxing a little. She'd begun to worry more as the days had passed, and Calan's words made her feel a little better.

"Once we get word all is well and the king has voided the fiction o' a marriage MacNaughton tried to force, I'll escort ye to MacFarlane and ask yer father to contract a marriage between us."

Allissaid was so startled by the words that she stopped walking to gape at him.

Feeling the tug of resistance on his hand, Calan stopped to turn back. Concern crossed his features at her expression, and he glanced around briefly before suddenly clasping her at the waist, picking her up and carrying her to a low stone wall that surrounded the fruit trees. He set her on it, and then stood in front of her and said, "I've come to think highly o' ye, lass. Ye've proven yerself smart, and brave . . . and I think ye ken I find ye lovely to look on."

"Ye do?" Allissaid asked wide-eyed, for surely, she had never been less attractive in her life than she had been on meeting Calan after MacNaughton's beating. Of course, the worst of the swelling and bruising that had marred her face and body had faded and gone away for the most part now. But Allissaid had never considered herself more than average in looks even before that. Looking at herself dispassionately, she'd always thought she and her older sister, Claray, had been rather cheated when it came to attractiveness, while their younger sisters, Annis, Arabella, Cairstane and Cristane, seemed to all be one more lovely than the other.

"Oh, lass," Calan said with a sad shake of the head at her obvious surprise that he might find her attractive, and then as if to prove he liked the way she looked, he kissed her.

Caught by surprise when his head suddenly

swooped down and his mouth claimed hers, Allissaid gasped in surprise. He immediately took advantage of the action to slip his tongue past her lips to fully taste her and she sighed into his mouth and relaxed against him as his arms closed around her. It was mere seconds before all those lovely feelings he'd stirred in her down at the loch came rushing back to life inside of Allissaid. It had been so long since that night that she'd begun to think she'd imagined the whole thing. Of course, the fact that he hadn't kissed or touched her again since then hadn't helped. She knew that the constant presence of her cousin and Inghinn might have forestalled him, but he hadn't tried to get her alone either, so Allissaid had begun to worry that perhaps it hadn't been as passionate and exciting as she'd recalled it to be. Or, at least, perhaps it hadn't been for him. But that passion was back and burning between them as he ravished her mouth, and surely he wouldn't kiss her so fervently if he weren't also feeling the passion?

It was the last coherent thought Allissaid managed before Calan's kisses overwhelmed her ability to think clearly. When his hands then began roaming over her, she stopped thinking at all and began to arch and moan and whimper instead as he caressed here and then there. His hands slid down her back, up her arms, and then around to find and cup her breasts, and she gasped and shivered and then cried out softly into his mouth when he pinched her nipples through the cloth of her gown. Allissaid was vaguely aware of his tugging at the neckline of her dress, and then felt the cool night air slide over her excited flesh as it was exposed, before his warm hands covered her breasts without the cloth's interference.

It was only then that she truly joined the foray. Up until that point, Allissaid had been acquiescent, accepting his kisses and caresses. Enjoying them but not truly responding. But now she let her hands creep up around his neck and began to kiss him back with the passion he was stirring in her. She wasn't sure if she was doing it right, and didn't really care. Allissaid just did what her body urged her to, alternately sucking at his tongue and letting her own wrestle with his, while her hands pulled at him, and her body struggled to get closer until she was perched on the very edge of the stone wall he'd set her on.

Her eagerness seemed to unleash something in Calan, and what Allissaid now realized had been a deliberately banked fire that he'd been showing her, turned into a flagrant inferno. His kisses became more demanding, his caresses more possessive as he stepped closer, moving between her legs until his groin pressed against her.

When Allissaid broke their kiss on a desperate cry at the excitement that move sent through her, and instinctively pushed her feet against the face of the wall to thrust her hips forward to rub herself tighter against him, all hell seemed to break loose. Dropping his head to suck at one excited nipple, Calan clasped her bottom in his large hands to urge her tighter still, and thrust, rubbing against her through the cloth of her gown and his plaid so that she couldn't mistake the hardness between them.

Allissaid knew she was muttering and mumbling nonsensical pleas, but couldn't have said what she was begging for. All she knew was she didn't want this to stop, and was desperate for something more. Her body was trembling with a need for it.

A gentle breeze creeping up her legs was followed by his warm hand gliding up her thigh and then he found her core and Allissaid jerked and arched, her mouth opening on a cry that he stifled with his own covering hers. Beyond the ability to realize she needed to be quiet, she groaned and cried out into his mouth as he began to caress her, her hips moving into his ministrations as he drove her mad with need. This time there was no pain when her body began to clench, or at least so little that it was overwhelmed by the pleasure. Allissaid clung to him, her body dancing to some unheard tune until she was nearly sobbing into his mouth with her desperation, and she nearly bit his tongue before she caught herself when he began to push a finger into her. Afraid she might yet bite him unintentionally in her fervor, Allissaid broke their kiss then and gasped for air as her body tightened even further and fought for its release.

So caught up in trying to control herself and keep from crying out again, she didn't notice him shift position until the caressing stopped and she felt his hands clasp her thighs and urge them wider. Blinking her eyes open, she found he was no longer in front of her, and then glanced down just as he pressed his face between her legs and began to caress her again, but now with his mouth.

Shock had her open her mouth on a protest, but

the feel of his tongue rasping over her excited flesh stole her voice and had her gasping and grabbing for his head to help keep her balance as her entire body responded to the caress and nearly sent her tumbling backward off the low wall. Seeming to sense the problem, Calan moved one hand from her thigh to splay it on her lower back to help keep her in place, but his lips and tongue never stopped their work. When his other hand left her thigh and she felt him pushing into her again, even as his tongue swirled the core of her excitement, Allissaid's poor body could not take any more and she cried out as the night exploded around her.

CALAN STRAIGHTENED AND WRAPPED HIS arms around Allissaid, holding her as she shuddered and shook in the throes of her release. But it was hard. His body wanted to be thrusting into her wet heat, driving her back to that pinnacle again, but with his cock . . . and with him joining her there. But there was one thing stopping him . . . well, two, really, he acknowledged grimly. The first and most obvious one was her reputation. Allissaid was a lady. He shouldn't have even been kissing and touching her as he had. He could have sullied her reputation had they been caught.

But the second reason was that while Calan had been with a lot of women in his years of life, he'd made it a practice to never dally with a virgin. That was a problem now. Because never having dealt with one before, he wasn't at all sure how to go about it without hurting her terribly and possibly putting her off the marital bed. And that would be a terrible crime to his mind. He didn't know if it was purely because of her innocence or if it was her nature, but the lass was the most passionate creature he'd ever encountered. She responded to his touch with such speed and fire that it made him instantly hard just to think of it. And her cries and moans and mewls of pleasure as he'd touched and caressed her had nearly driven him wild. He didn't want to mess up the first time he bedded her, and possibly kill all that fire and passion in her.

Calan was thinking he might need to have a chat with one of the older clan members he trusted for advice on how to handle a virgin the first time ere they married. But there was plenty of time for that, he assured himself, sliding his hands soothingly up and down Allissaid's back. They had to wait to hear from her cousins, and then he had to escort her back to MacFarlane and negotiate a contract with her father. He was sure they would want some time to prepare for a wedding and such, so he had plenty of time to worry about gaining the knowledge he needed to make her first time as pleasurable as possible.

"Well now, I'm thinking this means I need to fetch the priest."

Calan stiffened, and turned his head slowly to see Alick Buchanan not ten feet away, eyeing him and Allissaid with raised eyebrows and a mouth pursed with disapproval. Calan scowled at the man, and then glanced back to Allissaid when she gasped and pushed at him to be released. It was only as she struggled to pull her neckline up to cover the bosoms he'd bared, and at the same time tried to brush the front of her skirt back down from where it remained gathered around her waist, that he recalled her state of deshabille.

Cursing, he helped tuck her breasts back into her gown, leaving Allissaid to handle her skirts as he did, but mentally, he was debating how to handle this situation. He'd planned to marry Allissaid, but had expected to have some time before that happened. Not a lot. He'd been thinking a week or so to get her back to MacFarlane, depending on when news arrived about the cousins' transactions with the king, and then perhaps a couple of weeks to cover both the contract negotiations with her father, and for the wedding arrangements for the feast to be made and any family who wished to attend to arrive. Calan had been hoping to have her to wife in no more than a month. In fact, he'd been thinking he'd make that part of the marriage contract. Calan was not interested in a long, drawn-out affair. He was too eager to bed her to wish to wait months to claim her to wife. But by the same token, he hadn't expected it to have to be a rushed affair to save her reputation either. Besides, Alick was not Allissaid's father and had no right to—

"So, shall I fetch the priest, or do you wish to do it?" Alick asked, intruding on his thoughts.

"Oh, do be quiet, Alick," Allissaid growled, sounding cross for the first time since he'd encountered her. She was also flushed with obvious embarrassment at being caught out as they had as she slid off the low wall he'd set her on, and scowled at her cousin. "Calan has already made his intentions clear. He intends to speak to father about contracting a wedding as soon as we hear from Dougall and Niels on the king's decision."

"Aye, well, that will no' do at all now he's compromised ye," Alick said firmly. "A wedding'll ha'e to be takin' place right away, and proof o' consummation shown."

"It would probably be fer the best," Inghinn said gently, stepping out of the shadows next to Alick to make her presence known. She then pointed out, "'Twould also be a protection fer ye, Allissaid. In case the king's decision does no' go in yer favor and he decides to uphold MacNaughton's marriage claims. We can counter with that 'tis too late as ye've married Calan, the consummation has taken place, and hold up the bloody sheet as proof that ye came to him untried. 'Twould prove MacNaughton's attempt to force ye into marriage was no' completed and he has no claim."

Calan was just thinking that his sister was right about that, when Allissaid said anxiously, "The king would no' decide against me, would he? No' when he hears the true tale o' what happened."

When she turned an alarmed gaze his way, he grimaced and then gave a reluctant nod. "'Tis possible. Maldouen's father was a dear friend to the king ere his death. He may feel he owes his son some—"

"Nay!" Allissaid cried with alarm, shaking her

head frantically. "He can no' make me marry that animal. I'd flee to the abbey and take the veil first, or take me own life, if necessary, to avoid it."

Calan was scowling at the very thought of either outcome when Alick said easily, "Then 'tis a good thing Uncle Gannon gave me guardianship o' ye while I'm here and I'm demanding the two o' you marry to save yer reputation. That way, at least we have an argument to present to the king if he tries to enforce the first sham o' a wedding Maldouen is trying to pass off as real."

"Da gave ye guardianship o' me?" Allissaid asked with surprise.

"He said I was to see to yer well-being and safety and do whate'er was necessary to ensure it," Alick said solemnly. "I'm thinkin' that includes demanding Calan marry ye after ruinin' ye so." He then grinned at Calan and added, "'Tis just good fortune he wants to marry ye anyway."

"Aye," Calan agreed, and caught Allissaid by the elbow to begin urging her back toward the keep. He'd negotiate the contract with Alick, and do so quickly, and then fetch the priest from his bed to perform the ceremony at once, he thought. Concern immediately began to pull his eyebrows together as he realized that would mean bedding her this night. He could hardly go drag one of the older clansmen from their sleep to question them on the bedding of virgins at this hour without causing a lot of questions. But he damn well wasn't going to attempt it without some advice to help him ensure he caused her the least pain possible to avoid ruining her enjoyment of the marriage bed. Which meant . . . Dear God, he'd have to ask his mother!

The horror of that thought was enough to make him silent and grim faced all the way back to the keep and up to his chamber.

"WHAT?"

Calan grimaced at his mother's stunned and somewhat horrified expression. He and Alick had hammered out the contract quickly. Mostly because he'd basically just agreed to everything the other man had demanded he put in the contract. Not that the young Buchanan had been ridiculously demanding on Allissaid's behalf. In fact, the contract seemed very fair to him. But at any rate, they'd finished the task quickly, both had signed it, and then he'd come to wake and warn his mother. She'd at first been alarmed at being woken in the middle of the night, thinking that something was amiss. But once he'd explained that he was waking her because he intended to marry Allissaid at once and thought she might like to witness it, she'd been surprisingly good about it all. His mother hadn't even protested at the wedding taking place at once and at this hour. But then he suspected she was just relieved that he was taking a wife, and happy at the prospect of soon having grandbabies to spoil and coddle.

The woman had been nagging him for years about finding a new young woman to replace the lass he'd been betrothed to as a child, and he'd been ignoring her for just as long. He supposed she'd begun to fear he'd never marry, and while she'd suggested he marry Allissaid and he'd agreed to it, she probably wouldn't stop worrying that it would never happen until it actually did. Now it would . . . Once he had this most uncomfortable conversation with his mother and fetched the priest.

"I asked fer yer advice in bedding Allissaid after the ceremony," he repeated quietly, quite sure his face was flushing with the embarrassment he was feeling. Dear God, he was asking his mother for advice on bedding his soon-to-be bride. Who the hell did that? He was probably the only man in history to do it, he was sure. And even he wouldn't be doing it if he could have asked anyone else. But aside from the men guarding the wall, the only man awake right now was Alick Buchanan, and he doubted the younger man had any more experience of virgins than he did. At least, he hoped not. Calan would lose all respect for the young man if he ran around despoiling virgins.

Shaking that thought from his mind, he focused on his mother and scowled when he saw that repeating the question did not seem to have cleared up things for her. She was still sitting in bed, blinking at him as if he was a stranger who'd just wandered into her room.

"Mother?" he asked impatiently.

"I'm sorry," she said at once, sitting a little straighter in bed. "I just—Ha'e ye ne'er been with a lass, son?"

"What?" he gasped with horror.

"Well, I mean if ye do no' ken how to go about the consummation—"

"I ken that part," he barked with exasperation. "I've bedded lots o' women, Mother."

"Well . . ." She shrugged. "There ye are then."

"Nay. There I'm no'," Calan countered grimly. "I've bedded lots o' camp followers and such, Mother. Allissaid is untried, and the first time will be painful. How do I make it less so fer her so she does no' come to fear or dislike the marriage bed?"

"Oh," she said with sudden understanding and some relief. "I see. Aye, well—" She paused suddenly, to smile at him affectionately, and reached out to caress his cheek. "Ye're so like yer father. Considerate and kind. Allissaid is lucky to ha'e ye fer husband, son."

Calan silently ordered his body not to dare blush, and simply waited for her to give him the advice he was asking for. Much to his relief, she didn't make him wait long. In fact, she threw back the linens and furs covering her, climbed out of bed in her nightshift and moved to one of her chests to begin pulling out clothing as she said, "Well, there's really nothin' ye can do to prevent her feeling pain. Although, no' all lasses suffer a great deal o' pain the first time. Some feel no pain at all."

Calan was just brightening at the possibility that this might be the case for Allissaid, when she continued.

"By the same token, some feel terrible pain. The best ye can do is make sure she is well prepared fer it." Pausing, she cast a frown at him over her shoulder. "Ye ken what I mean by well prepared, do ye no'? I do no' have to explain that bit to ye, do I?"

"I understand," he assured her dryly.

Nodding, she turned back to rummaging through her clothes, pulling out a clean chemise and then sorting through her gowns as she continued. "Well, make sure ye ha'e her good and worked up ere ye breach her, and then, afterward, I'd say make sure ye give her lots more pleasure to make her forget whatever pain the breachin' might ha'e caused. That's the best ye can do."

Calan felt some of the tension that had been knotting his body since realizing he would soon be bedding Allissaid ease, and stood up. "Thank ye, Mother. I'll leave ye to ready yerself and go fetch the priest."

"Aye. I'll head to yer room as soon as I'm dressed," she responded distractedly, holding up a gown for consideration.

He was just opening the door when she said, "And son?"

Pausing, he glanced back. "Aye."

"I ken she'll make ye a good wife. The two o' ye will ha'e a happy marriage."

Calan merely nodded. He was pretty sure of that himself.

Chapter 15

MARRIAGE WAS HELL, ALLISSAID THOUGHT unhappily. Or, at least, the getting married part was. After depositing her and Inghinn in the room to "ready her for the ceremony," Calan and Alick had gone off to "hammer out the marriage contract" in one of the spare chambers along the hall. The men had apparently roused Gille from his bed to guard them while they were gone, because he'd shown up not long after the other two men had left, and had, at first, insisted on being in the room with them. At least, until Inghinn had chased him out, claiming Allissaid had to have another bath and change her clothes.

It was only once the man had left the room that Inghinn had admitted that she didn't really need to bathe again and they really didn't have anything else to dress her in. The blue gown had been taken below to be cleaned and the forest green gown she was wearing was the only other gown in the castle that would fit her at present. The best they could do was fix her hair and pinch her cheeks to add color. Both actions had ended up being hellishly painful. Inghinn had done her hair up in some fancy and very tight knot on her head that had started causing her a headache before the girl had even finished with her handiwork. As for the cheek pinching, Allissaid had begun to think she'd have bruised cheeks rather than rosy red ones by the time the girl had announced herself satisfied.

Unfortunately, that had been followed by the arrival of Calan's mother. Allissaid had always liked Lady Fiona when she used to visit her mother, but the two of them had grown quite close these last weeks since her arrival. In fact, she would go so far as to admit that she had begun to see her as something of a mother figure and grown quite fond of her. But that didn't make it any easier or less embarrassing for her when the dear lady had asked if her mother had ever had the chance to have a discussion with her about what to expect from the consummation. Even more distressing had been that when Allissaid had admitted that "nay, the subject had never come up ere her dying," Calan's mother had decided to take on the task herself.

That conversation had left Allissaid positively squirming with discomfort and embarrassment as Lady Fiona had laid out the bare facts for her. She was sure that by the end she was blushing so hard that Inghinn's efforts to give her rosy cheeks had been a completely unnecessary torture. Still, at least she now knew what to expect. Although, frankly it had sounded quite awful when explained, and nothing like the beautiful, exciting and passionate things she'd encountered so far with Calan when it came to kissing and such. In fact, much to her concern, the lady hadn't mentioned anything about kissing, touching and the things Calan had done with his mouth. She'd basically said he'd put his sword in her scabbard and there'd be blood and pain, but it would be better after that. Of course, Lady Fiona had used a lot more words than that, and she'd spoken gently and tried to be reassuring, but frankly that was the gist Allissaid had got from it. Sword. Scabbard. Blood. Pain.

Their talk had barely ended when Calan, Alick and Gille had entered with a somewhat cranky and disheveled old man with the bald head and scrunched up face of a bairn about to burst into squalling. Father MacMillan was apparently the clan priest at present, and was obviously not pleased to have been rousted from his bed, nagged into his vestment and dragged up to the master chamber to perform a wedding at that hour. He'd been terse, suspicious and full of questions as to the unusual request until he'd ascertained that Alick was her guardian at present, a contract had been negotiated and that both Allissaid and Calan wished the wedding to go forward.

Allissaid suspected it was the fact that Alick was a Buchanan that had finally made the man stop dragging his feet and proceed with the wedding. Her cousins were becoming known as a powerhouse in Scotland what with all the alliances forged by their advantageous marriages. It was probably enough to scare any priest into submission. No one wanted to bring the wrath of their combined clans down on them.

The ceremony itself had been fine if long. Or perhaps it had just seemed long because of her increasing headache from having her hair so tightly restrained. Although, it was certainly much longer than the farce of a ceremony Maldouen had instigated at MacNaughton. It had started with the traditional handfasting, with Father MacMillan having them join hands so that he could tie a bit of cloth loosely around their wrists and hands, and then he'd read a passage from the Bible that Allissaid, frankly, hadn't caught much of. She'd been too aware of the feel of Calan's hand enclosing her own, and too busy reliving what those hands had already done to her and then fretting over the "*Sword. Scabbard. Blood. Pain.*" bit Lady Fiona had explained was coming, to pay attention to Father MacMillan's droning voice. After that had come the exchange of vows where she'd promised to love, honor and cherish him and he her. It had ended with Father MacMillan reciting a blessing over them before removing the cloth from around their clasped hands and pronouncing them man and wife.

Much different than her experience at MacNaughton, Allissaid thought as Calan walked the priest to the door, thanking him for his service.

"Allie?"

Pulling her gaze away from Calan and the priest, Allissaid turned to Alick as he caught her hand and drew her a little away from the others before stopping to peer down into her face with concern. "Are ye all right, cousin? Ye did want to marry him, did ye no'?"

"Aye, o' course," Allissaid assured him quickly, and it was true. Well, she thought it was probably true. She hadn't really had much time to think on the subject. She'd been so worried about what might be happening at MacFarlane, and what the king's decision might be that she hadn't ever even considered marrying Calan until he'd announced he intended to broach her father on contracting a marriage between them. But her initial response had been a happy one at the thought, so she supposed she was glad to be married to him.

Certainly, she liked Calan, enjoyed talking to him, beating him at chess, and was grateful to him for the help he'd given her. Allissaid was also most definitely attracted to him and enjoyed the things he'd done to or with her so far, which was a sharp contrast to her experience with Alban Graham.

When Calan had asked if Alban had ever kissed her, she hadn't been completely honest with him. While they had never kissed, it wasn't for lack of his trying. Allissaid had been the one to avoid the contact each time he'd made the attempt. Something, she hadn't once even thought to do with Calan. The, admittedly few, times Calan had kissed her, she hadn't even considered turning her head away, or slipping out of his reach to avoid contact. If anything, Allissaid had spent the last ten days since that experience at the loch trying to figure out how to get the man to kiss and caress her again. So, other than the whole "*Sword. Scabbard. Blood.*

Pain." thing, which would be an issue with any man she took to husband, yes, she was definitely fine being married to Calan and had great hopes it would turn out all right. Certainly, higher hopes than she would have had for marriage to either the gambling, drinking, whoring and possibly diseased Alban Graham, or the treacherous and murderous Maldouen MacNaughton.

"Are ye sure?" Alick asked with concern. "Ye do no' look happy. In fact, ye're startin' to look peaked."

Allissaid grimaced at the claim and reached up to rub her forehead, muttering, "'Tis just that I ha'e an aching head. I'm fine and happy. Truly."

Relaxing a bit, he nodded, and then they both turned to Lady Fiona as she approached.

"Welcome to the family, dear girl," Lady Fiona said happily, drawing her into a quick, tight embrace. She then released her and stepped back to make room for Inghinn to offer her own congratulations and hug.

"Well," Lady Fiona said cheerfully as Inghinn and Allissaid separated. "That's Calan taken care of, now there's just our Inghinn." Turning to Alick, she added, "Her betrothed died recently, ye ken."

"Mother!" Inghinn said with dismay.

"Well, he did," she pointed out with a shrug. "And the Buchanans know a lot o' people. Mayhap Alick kens o' an unbetrothed male or two he thinks may be interested in meeting ye with the possibility o' arranging a new betrothal contract." Smiling sweetly at Alick, Lady Fiona asked, "Do ye ken any unmarried second, third or even sixth or seventh sons o' a good family, such as yer own, in search o' a bride?"

"No' a first son?" Alick asked with amusement.

"Oh, nay," Lady Fiona said at once. "Inghinn comes with Gordon castle. I'm a Gordon by birth, ye see, and while I had an older brother expected to be laird, he died without issue, so it passed to me. A cousin o' mine is presently running it with the understanding that Inghinn's husband will take o'er when she marries. So, a first son, likely to become laird o'er his own family castle, would no' be very helpful. He could no' give Gordon and its people the attention they deserve. A son unlikely to inherit a title and castle would be better," she pointed out, and then tilted her head. "Gordon sits along Innis's southern border. Did yer brother, Geordie, no' marry Dwynn Innis a couple years ago?"

"Mother!" Inghinn's voice was tinged with horror now, her face flaming red. When Lady Fiona ignored her and continued to smile expectantly at Alick, the younger woman shook her head and turned toward the door, muttering, "I'm to bed. Good sleep all."

"Good sleep," Lady Fiona called cheerfully, and then told Alick, "She's such a good lass."

Allissaid's cousin nodded with amusement and said, "Lovely too."

"Do ye think so?" Lady Fiona asked with interest.

"Aye, I do," he assured her, and then added, "In fact, if I were ready fer marriage meself, I'd be putting meself forward as a possible husband. Unfortunately, I ha'e responsibilities and promises to keep, and can no' e'en think to marry fer a couple more years at least."

"Oh well, do no' consider yerself out o' the runnin' on that account," Lady Fiona said breezily. "Inghinn just turned seventeen and I'd be pleased to keep her here with me fer a few more years ere givin' her up to a husband."

"Good to ken," Alick said solemnly.

Eyes wide, Allissaid glanced from her cousin to her new mother-in-law, and then turned when Calan appeared beside her and placed his hand on her back.

"Gille and Father MacMillan have gone to find their beds," he announced. "The priest promised to return early."

Allissaid bit her lip at his words. She knew exactly what Father MacMillan would be returning early for. Proof of consummation of the wedding. In other words, he would expect to find a bloodstained sheet, she thought unhappily and recalled Lady Fiona's lecture. *Sword. Scabbard. Blood. Pain.*

Oh, dear, Allissaid thought weakly and then glanced around with surprise as she realized everyone was suddenly moving.

"I'll head to bed meself then." Lady Fiona squeezed Allissaid's arm in passing and wished her "Good sleep."

"Good sleep," Allissaid whispered.

"I'll be on a pallet in the hall if ye need me," Alick announced, following the older woman.

Allissaid nodded silently. Of course, Alick would be sleeping on a pallet in the hall from now on.

Because she and Calan were married. And her husband would want privacy to consummate that, Allissaid thought as she turned to stare at the bed with mounting worry. *Sword. Scabbard. Blood. Pain.*

"What are ye thinkin', lass?" Calan asked, his voice husky as he returned from closing the door.

"Nothing," Allissaid managed to get out in a voice little more than a squeak.

"Well, stop thinkin' about nothin' then. 'Tis givin' ye worry wrinkles," he said in a teasing voice as he paused behind her and settled his hands on her shoulders.

Allissaid went still at his touch, her heart rate picking up with anxiety. "*Sword. Scabbard. Blood. Pain.*" ran through her mind, and she tried to swallow around a sudden lump in her throat. Allissaid was not a huge fan of pain. In truth, when it got right down to it, she was a terrible coward when it came to pain. Anytime she had a sliver that might need digging out, or any kind of wound that might need stitching . . . well, frankly, she'd rather let a limb rot off than suffer the pain of the treatment needed to heal it. Or, at least, that's what she always thought even while enduring whatever painful treatment was needed.

"Yer hair looks lovely like this, but I like it better down," Calan murmured, pressing a kiss to the side of her neck even as his fingers began undoing all the effort his sister had put into her hair.

Allissaid did not protest the action. If anything, she was grateful for it and released a breath of relief as the tight knot was undone, the pressure eased, and her hair fell around her shoulders in soft waves.

"I love yer hair, lass," he murmured, tangling his fingers in the heavy mass. He then used that hold to tug her head back so that he could claim her mouth. This kiss was soft and questing, a slow seduction that had the tension slowly ebbing from her body. When his tongue finally slid out to request entrance, the last of it slipped away on a little sigh and she welcomed him and responded. Allissaid kissed him back tentatively at first and then with more passion as the kiss deepened and he slid his arms around her stomach.

When his hands then slid up to cover her breasts through her gown, she moaned and leaned into him. Her head twisted further to keep kissing him back as he palmed and cupped her mounds and then squeezed, before he concentrated on the nipples pebbling under the cloth. Allissaid gasped and groaned by turn as he pinched and flicked the sensitive nubs, and then cried out into his mouth when one hand dropped away and down to slide between her legs.

Pushing the cloth of her gown against this sensitive spot, he rubbed gently, and then more firmly until she no longer had the presence of mind to kiss him back. She was merely panting into his mouth, her hips moving into his caress and her back arched almost painfully to thrust her breast into his hand as well.

Allissaid couldn't stop her groan of disappointment when his hand slid from between her legs and he broke their kiss. Her legs were trembling and weak, and she leaned against him, her eyes closing as he began to nuzzle her ear and neck. She was vaguely aware of his hands moving over the stays of her gown, but it wasn't until they loosened and the gown began to slip off her shoulders that she realized what he was doing.

Blinking her eyes open, Allissaid glanced down to watch the dark green material drift down her body to land in a heap around her feet. She was blinking at it when Calan caught her by the shoulders and turned her to face him. Catching her gaze, he held it as his hands next began to tug her chemise off. Swallowing, Allissaid stared back and then shivered as the thin cloth began to slither off her body to join the dress. A protest rose on her lips when his eyes released hers to travel down her body, but she bit it back and suffered his looking in silence until he raised a hand and ran his knuckles over one nipple. She simply couldn't hold back the gasp that slipped from her lips then.

"Do ye like that, lass?" Calan asked. He didn't wait for an answer, but leaned her back over one arm slightly and bent his head to claim the nipple he'd teased. He drew it into his mouth and began suckling eagerly until she moaned and closed her arms around his head, hugging him to her.

Calan's free hand then ran down her side to her hip before sliding around to cup and squeeze one soft cheek of her behind and urge her against him so that she could feel the hardness beneath his plaid. His sword, she thought vaguely and then gasped and moaned when he rubbed it against her core, setting off an explosion of excitement and need inside of her.

When his hand shifted below her bottom to grasp her upper thigh and urge her leg around him, Allissaid grabbed for his shoulders to help maintain her balance. This time when he rubbed against her, it was directly on the sensitive spot he'd found in the loch and again in the garden, and Allissaid cried out at the rush of sensation this caused.

"Aye, ye like that," he growled around her nipple, and thrust against her again, then suddenly released her nipple and leg and straightened to kiss her almost violently.

Allissaid responded in kind, pouring all the need and passion he was awakening into that kiss, her hands moving now and roving over his strong chest and plucking at the material of his shirt, wanting him to remove it. But when her hand crept down toward the hardness that she wanted against her again, Calan caught her hand, broke their kiss and suddenly strode to the bed, pulling her behind him.

Afraid she'd offended him somehow, Allissaid opened her mouth to apologize, but bit off the words on a gasp as Calan suddenly used his hold to spin her and push her down on the bed. She blinked up at him from her prone position, and then her eyes grew round as he quickly removed his plaid and shirt. Her gaze slid over his strong, wide chest, and then dropped to his "sword," and she stared at it with concern and more than a little fear. *Sword. Scabbard. Blood. Pain.* The words ran through her head as she tried to imagine him sheathing his sword in her scabbard. It didn't sound the least bit enjoyable to her. Kissing and rubbing and touching was one thing, but . . .

Allissaid's thoughts scattered to the four winds when Calan suddenly knelt on the floor at the foot of the bed. She'd landed on it with her knees hanging off the end, and he now urged them farther apart and then lifted one and turned his head to inspect it briefly, before pressing a kiss to the arch of her foot.

A nervous giggle slid from her lips in response to the tickle that feathered through her skin, and then his lips began to move up her leg, grazing her ankle, her calf, the spot behind her knee.

"Ahh," Allissaid breathed, arching on the bed and twisting her head as the tickling turned to fire and suddenly raced ahead of his lips toward her core. When his mouth finally made it to that spot, she nearly bucked off the bed altogether, and was sure she would have had he not placed his hands on her upper thighs to hold her down.

Allissaid was aware that she was making little unintelligible sounds of need and pleading as he pleasured her with his mouth, but couldn't seem to stop them any more than she could prevent her head from twisting on the bed, and her back from arching and falling. She couldn't even seem to catch her breath and was soon panting like a well-ridden horse. Allissaid tried to control it, and stop the sounds she was making, but it was impossible. Even the knowledge that her cousin was on a pallet outside the door and was no doubt hearing every sound couldn't move her to silence. It also didn't prevent the scream that ripped from her throat when the pleasure her new husband had been lavishing on her suddenly exploded through her body like a burning arrow, setting every nerve ending in her body alight.

It was only Calan's mouth coming down on hers that brought an end to her cry, and then the feel of something pushing into her. His sword, Allissaid realized, as he thrust forward and she felt a sharp pinch that stole some, but not all of her pleasure. It was the oddness of feeling him inside her that did that. It was just . . . new and unusual, and her body went quiet and still even as he froze fully in her.

"Are ye all right, lass?" Calan asked after a moment, sounding breathless and grim.

Allissaid opened her eyes to peer up at him with confusion. Lady Fiona had not mentioned that the man would also suffer pain with the joining. Yet it certainly didn't sound like her husband was experiencing pleasure. His expression looked pained too, she noted, and said uncertainly, "Aye. Are you? Is it too painful?"

Much to her surprise, a little huff of a laugh slipped from Calan's lips at the question, and then his expression softened, some of the sharpness leaving his face as he bent to press a kiss to her forehead, then her nose and finally her lips. He stayed there though, and the gentle benediction of a kiss deepened. His mouth slanted over hers again and again, until her uncertainty and the oddness of the feel of him inside her was forgotten and she began to kiss him back. Only then did Calan move again, slowly withdrawing his sword from her sheath, before easing back in once more at an angle that allowed for rubbing against the tightening nub he'd first stirred to such an excited state with his lips and tongue.

Allissaid moaned into his mouth as her excitement began to reawaken inside of her. When he did it again with the same result, she found herself bracing her feet and pushing back, silently urging him on. Calan responded with a steady, rhythmic thrusting that soon had her panting and making little pleading mewls of sound again as she struggled toward that release he'd already given her once. This time when she tumbled over into that abyss of pleasure, Calan joined her with a shout that she was sure drowned out her own cry. He then collapsed half on top of her, before rolling in the bed and taking her with him so that he lay on his back with her resting on his chest, their bodies still joined.

Allissaid lay there for several moments, waiting for her breathing and heart to return to normal. When they finally did, she didn't move, but now because she was feeling ridiculously shy. She was searching her mind for something to say, when he suddenly murmured, "Eara."

Allissaid tilted her head up to peer at his face in question. "Eara?"

"When we thought ye did no' remember yer name, and Inghinn told ye to pick one, she said ye picked Eara," he reminded her.

"Oh. Aye, I did," she agreed.

Calan nodded, but then asked, "I was just wondering why ye picked Eara?"

Allissaid stared at him blankly, completely bewildered as to how that would pop into his head at this moment. But, finally, she had to tip her head back down to ease the strain to her neck muscles. Once she was no longer looking at him, Allissaid considered his question and then admitted, "I do no' ken. Inghinn said to just pick the first name I thought o', and that was the first to come to mind."

"Woman from the east," he said now.

Allissaid jerked her head back up.

"That's what the name Eara means," Calan explained, apparently taking her stunned expression as confusion. "When Inghinn said 'twas the name ye picked, I thought to meself that while 'twas a nice enough name, 'tis no' the one I would ha'e picked fer you."

"Oh?" Allissaid asked with interest. "And what name would ye ha'e picked fer me then?"

Calan smiled faintly, and reached out to brush several strands of hair behind her ear as his gaze slid over her features. "I'm thinkin' Bonnie or Alana would suit ye more."

She could feel her face heat up at the suggestion. Both names meant *lovely*. But, surely, he didn't know that, Allissaid told herself.

"Or mayhap Bridget fer yer strength," he added. "Although, Eilean would suit ye as well, and is a pretty name too."

"And what does Eilean mean?" Allissaid asked huskily, amazed that he actually did know the meaning behind the names he was listing off. She had always been fascinated with names and their meanings, and she did know what Eilean meant, but was interested to see if he did.

"Ray o' sunshine," Calan said and shrugged. "I always liked the name."

"So do I," she admitted solemnly, and was being honest now. It was one of the names she'd selected as a possible name for a future daughter if she had one.

Allissaid had barely had the thought when he said, "Eilean would be a good name fer any bonnie wee lass we may ha'e, do ye no' think?"

"Aye," she agreed huskily, wondering how he'd plucked the thought from her mind like that. But then she'd often been left with that question these last few weeks they'd spent together. Calan frequently seemed to say things she was thinking. He also enjoyed the same foods she did, preferred Poch and chess over other games like herself, and had a similar sense of humor to her own. Of course, there were differences too. He preferred ale while she liked mead more, but both of them disliked wine.

From what she knew of Calan so far, they seemed to have more in common than not. Allissaid was now hoping that might make for a happy and harmonious marriage.

"Mayhap there's already a little Eilean growin' inside ye e'en now," Calan pointed out.

Allissaid blinked at the suggestion and lowered her head to peer down at her stomach with awe at the possibility. Could he have planted a bairn in her? Might she be carrying their child already? She wondered about it, and then gasped in surprise, when Calan suddenly shifted, rolling her onto her back on the bed.

"Would that make ye happy, lass?" he asked as he settled between her thighs and Allissaid felt his hardness there. He'd slipped out as they moved, but felt just as hard as he'd been earlier as he pressed against her. "Would ye like to carry me bairn?"

"Aye," Allissaid breathed as he rubbed himself against her, sending excitement charging through her body.

"I would too," Calan told her and then shifted down her body to flick his tongue over one hardening nipple.

Allissaid licked her lips and watched as he toyed with the sensitive tip, licking, flicking, nipping and finally suckling, at first gently and then more firmly until she gasped and tangled her hands in his hair.

Releasing the first nipple, Calan then shifted to the second one, but rather than subject it to the same treatment, he glanced up her body and asked, "Are ye tender, love?"

"Tender?" she echoed with confusion, unable to think of anything but her desire for him to suckle that nipple too.

"Here?" he asked, shifting a bit and sliding one hand down her body to allow his fingers to glide between her legs.

"Nay," Allissaid gasped, not sure if that were true or not, just knowing that she didn't want him to stop what he was doing as his fingers began to circle and rub in a most exciting manner. Aware that Calan was watching her face as he caressed her, Allissaid tried to keep her expression serene, but it was impossible with him doing what he was and she began to bite her lip, her neck stretching and legs shifting restlessly. She only released that lip when he finally lowered his head to claim her second nipple and began to suckle at it even as he continued to stroke and touch her.

Mouth open now, Allissaid gasped and panted, her fingers tangling in the linens they lay on and tugging almost viciously as he drove her to the edge of release and then eased back, allowing her passion to wane a bit. He did that several times, until Allissaid thought she might scream with frustration, and then he left off his playing, rose up on his knees, caught her by the hips to lift her behind off the bed and thrust into her.

Allissaid groaned, a long "ahh" of sound as he filled her. This time it did not feel as strange. This time her body welcomed and clung to him, and her legs wrapped around his hips, urging him on as he began to move. Unlike the first time, while Calan started slow and steady, he didn't stay there, but picked up the pace, his hands shifting to squeeze her bottom as he slammed into her.

Allissaid was positive she was on the verge of finding her release, when Calan suddenly stopped, withdrew and urged her to turn and shift to her knees. Confused, she did as he wanted and then gasped with surprise when he entered her from behind.

At first, Allissaid wasn't sure she liked this position, but then he leaned down and slid a hand around and under her to find that secret spot that ached for his touch. When Calan began to caress her, even as he withdrew and thrust in again, she curled her fingers into the bed linens and began a long ululating moan as he quickly pushed her over that edge into the pleasure-filled heavens again.

Calan didn't join her this time though, and didn't stop either. Even as she was struggling to recover from the overwhelming sensations pouring over her, he continued to caress and love her until Allissaid found her release again . . . and again. The fourth and final time he gave her that pleasure, her cries were finally drowned out once more by his own voice as he too found his pleasure.

Chapter 16

To CALAN, IT FELT LIKE HE'D BARELY DRIFTED off to sleep when knocking at the door startled him back awake. Scowling, he turned his head toward the door, his mouth opening to tell whoever was banging on it to bugger off. But the words died in his throat when his gaze landed on the lass in bed beside him. Allissaid. His wife.

Memory pushing his sleepiness away, Calan lunged from the bed and strode to the door to answer it before the pounding woke her. He'd kept his wee wife awake most of the night with his lust. He didn't want her awoken unnecessarily. Besides, Calan didn't want the whole castle being roused from sleep either. He and Allissaid might be married, but that didn't mean he wanted anyone to know she was there yet. Until they heard from her father on what the king had decided to do, it wasn't safe to let her presence be known. Not that he really cared what the king decided. The wedding MacNaughton had tried to force hadn't been real. His had been. He wasn't giving the lass up. So if the king didn't proclaim Maldouen MacNaughton's farcical wedding null and void, he'd just have to kill the bastard, Calan thought grimly.

Although, frankly, he was beginning to think he'd have to do that anyway. Maldouen wanted to kill Allissaid's entire family and claim MacFarlane through marriage. On losing out on the eldest sister, Claray, he'd simply turned his lascivious eye onto the next daughter, Allissaid. Doubtless the moment MacNaughton realized he'd lost out on claiming her to wife, he'd simply turn his nefarious attentions onto the third eldest daughter of the MacFarlane household. Which meant everyone in the family was still under threat. There was no doubt in Calan's mind that if the bastard did manage to force one of the girls into a real marriage, he'd kill the rest, including Allissaid and any other sisters who ended up wed. There was no way Calan would allow that to happen. Nay. MacNaughton was a thorn in his side that needed plucking.

But that was an issue for later, Calan told himself grimly. Right now, he was more concerned with the man waiting outside his bedchamber door.

Three men and two ladies, Calan corrected when he cracked the door open to find not just Father MacMillan, but also his mother, Gille, Alick and Inghinn all on the other side.

"We've come fer the—" Father MacMillan began.

"Wait," Calan interrupted and closed the door. He then turned to stride toward the bed, intending to scoop up his sleeping wife and move her, furs and all. But he paused after just a couple of steps when he realized the bed was empty.

Movement caught out of the corner of his eye had him glancing toward the fireplace in time to catch just a glimpse of his wife's shapely derriere before her chemise dropped to cover it as she scampered to the table and chairs by the fireplace. It seemed he hadn't silenced the knocking quick enough to prevent her being woken, and she'd managed to slip out of bed and don her gown while his back was turned.

Shaking his head, Calan continued on to the bed to snatch up his plaid, wrapped it around his waist so that he was at least covered from there down, and then peered toward his wife as he returned to the door.

Allissaid was sitting primly in one of the chairs at the table, wringing her hands anxiously. The sight was enough to almost make him detour to the table to reassure her, but in the end, Calan decided the only thing likely to make her feel better was getting this business done and over with. So, he continued to the door and opened it again, but this time he pulled it wide to allow their unwanted guests to enter.

Calan closed the door behind the group as they headed for the bed. He then walked over to stand by Allissaid as he waited for the priest and the others to inspect the bottom bed linen. But when the priest began to strip the linen off the bed and the others glanced his way with concern, he heaved a sigh and strode forward. "Ye can take the sheet and keep it somewhere safe if ye like, Father. But, at the moment, ye can no' hang it from the railing or anywhere else it might be seen."

"What?" the priest turned to him with surprise, the stained cloth in his hands. "But yer people ha'e the right to see this proof that the marriage was consummated and that their new lady came to ye an innocent."

"Aye," he agreed mildly, his gaze flickering to where his mother and Inghinn were remaking the bed with fresh linens the younger woman had carried in with her. Turning his full attention back to the priest then, he said, "Me people will learn about the wedding and their new lady, but no' 'til 'tis safe fer them to know."

The man blinked at him owlishly. "I do no' understand. What do ye mean by safe?"

Calan's mouth compressed, but then he quickly explained the situation. It was only as he noted the change on the man's face when he explained about the faux wedding the MacNaughton had tried to force on Allissaid that he realized the man might take issue with the situation.

"Ye had me perform a sacrament when the lass is already married to another?" the priest interrupted with dismay.

"Nay, o' course no'," Calan said with irritation, and then scowled and glanced toward the window when shouts from the bailey distracted him. After a hesitation, he gave in with a curse and strode to the window to look out over the bailey, his gaze narrowing when he saw one of his men from the night patrol riding up to the keep with a limp woman in his arms.

"Moire," Allissaid breathed with dismay, making him aware that she, along with everyone else had followed his lead and moved to the windows as well.

"Yer maid?" Calan asked, recognizing the name.

"She was no' me maid, but one o' the bedchamber maids," Allissaid told him, her gaze locked on the unconscious woman below. "She is the one who told me what Eachann had got up to."

"She does no' look to be in very good shape," Gille commented from his other side.

Calan nodded grimly. Even from there he could see that the maid's gown was torn and that bruises were peeking out through the cloth. But it wasn't until the man carrying her shifted her to dismount that he saw her face and the bruises there.

"I should go to her," Allissaid muttered, rushing away to find the gown he'd stripped off her last night. It still lay in the crumpled heap it had landed in at the time.

"Ye're no' going below, lass," Calan said firmly and then turned to Gille. "Fetch the maid up here."

When Gille nodded, and turned to head out of the room, Calan moved through the others to search out a clean shirt from one of his chests and set about getting dressed.

"M'laird," Father MacMillan said firmly, following on his heals. "We ha'e to discuss—"

"I've no time fer discussin' anything just now, Father," Calan interrupted grimly, dragging a clean shirt on over his head. Grabbing a fresh plaid next, he dropped to his knees to quickly pleat it.

"But this is important," Father MacMillan protested.

"Then ye'll ha'e to hang about and wait until I've handled this to talk," Calan growled.

Much to his relief, the man didn't protest further. He didn't leave though either. Instead, he stood and watched, his expression disapproving as Calan finished working on his plaid and then donned it.

Calan had barely finished dressing when someone banged on the door. Moving quickly to open it, he let Gille in, his gaze moving over the woman in his arms as he walked past.

Up close, the bruising the girl suffered was even worse than it had appeared when she was below, but it still wasn't as bad as Allissaid's had been. It was bad enough though, and mostly concentrated on her face from what he could see. That was so swollen and bruised it was hard to tell what she'd looked like ere the beating. But the bruises he could see on her body didn't appear as dark, large or all-encompassing as Allissaid's had been when she'd first arrived.

"Moire!" Allissaid rushed forward to meet Gille as soon as the door was closed and then hovered at his side as he carried the maid to the bed. Calan was actually impressed that she had managed to wait for the door to close before rushing to Gille's side to check on the lass, but supposed after nearly two weeks of hiding from the other inhabitants of the castle, it had become second nature for her to avoid open doors or anything that might allow someone to see her.

"Why someone's beat this lass near to death," Father MacMillan said with concern, joining the other men when they circled the bed as Allissaid moved to stand at the top of the bed to watch anxiously as his mother and Inghinn began to check Moire over.

"While her face is a muckle mess, she's no' near as bad as Allissaid was when she first arrived after escaping MacNaughton," Calan told him grimly. "At least she does no' ha'e bleeding head wounds, or bruising on the throat from being choked."

"What?" Father MacMillan asked with shock.

Calan opened his mouth to respond, but paused when his mother straightened from running her hands over the maid's head and upper body and announced, "I've found no broken bones. Inghinn?"

His sister straightened from performing the same examination of the unconscious woman's lower body and shook her head. "Nay. No broken bones."

Lady Fiona nodded and then bent to lift the maid's head and examine it as well, before saying, "She's no lumps, bumps or cuts on her head either."

"Then why is she unconscious?" Allissaid asked with concern, settling on the top corner of the bed, and taking the lass's hand in her own. "Is it from her facial injuries?"

"Most like," his mother said on a sigh as she set the woman's head back down.

Calan eyed the maid's face and felt his hands clench. Moire had two black eyes, her lip was split, and one side of her face was more than half covered with a swollen bruise, while the other was fully bruised and misshapen with swelling. It looked to him like the only place she hadn't been punched in the face was her nose. A good thing, he supposed, otherwise it would probably be broken. It reminded him of the sad state Allissaid had been in when he found her, and all the pain she'd gone through while healing, and it just infuriated him.

"Moire? Ye're awake?"

Calan's gaze shifted to Allissaid when she leaned closer to the lass, and then back to the maid to see that one of her eyes had opened a slit.

"Can ye tell us what happened?" Allissaid asked, brushing the hair back from the young woman's forehead, the only place the maid wasn't bruised. "Did MacNaughton do this to ye?"

"Aye," the woman answered, her voice a raspy whisper. "He was upset ye escaped."

"So, he did kidnap ye the same time as me?" Allissaid said sadly. "I'm sorry."

When Moire merely grunted and let the one eye she could open close again, Allissaid looked anxiously to his mother. "Can we give her the tonic ye made fer me? She must be in terrible pain."

"I'll mix it right away," his mother assured her. "In the meantime, I think we should move the lass to the guest chamber we prepared fer Alick. She'll be more comfortable there while healing."

"Gille," Calan said turning to his cousin, "could ye carry her there while Allissaid and I talk to Father MacMillan?"

His cousin nodded and immediately moved to the bed to again scoop up the lass. Allissaid tried to follow when he headed for the door, but Calan caught her arm as she made to pass and drew her to a halt. She looked to him and opened her mouth to protest, but then her gaze landed on Father Mac-Millan beside him, and she nodded on a sigh and relented.

They remained silent until Gille carried the lass out and his mother followed. Only once she'd pulled the door closed behind them did Calan turn to survey the people remaining. In a silent show of support, Alick and Inghinn had moved to take up position on either side of him and Allissaid. Inghinn was on his wife's right and Alick on his own left as Father MacMillan moved in front of them to start his attack.

"I think ye'd best explain," Father MacMillan said solemnly. "Obviously, there is much here I do no' understand. But I do no' appreciate yer tricking me into marryin' the two o' ye when Lady Allissaid is already married to Laird MacNaughton, and—"

"Nay, Father!" Allissaid protested at once. "I'm no' married to MacNaughton. I can no' be. I ne'er spoke a vow. I feigned unconsciousness throughout the wedding, and it was no' e'en a ceremony. Certainly not one as lovely and reverent as the one ye performed last night. There was no binding o' our hands, no lovely recitation as ye gave, and while the priest asked did I promise to love, honor and cherish Maldouen, I was feigning unconsciousness and said naught. It was Maldouen who said, *'She says aye, and I do too. Finish it, Father,'*" she told him grimly, and then added, "The priest, who sadly is no' as good and faithful to our father the Lord as ye obviously are, then did no' e'en pretend to finish the ceremony, he merely said, 'I pronounce ye man and wife' and walked away."

Pausing, she lowered her head and swallowed, before continuing, "'Twas only when Maldouen tried to force a consummation that I gave up pretending to be unconscious and fought. He beat me viciously fer it."

"Most viciously," Inghinn said, speaking up then. "I stitched up her head wounds and saw the bruises, Father. Her injuries were ten times worse than the maid ye saw today."

"They would ha'e been worse still, and would ha'e included takin' me against me will had I no' stabbed him," Allissaid said solemnly. "He left me after that, leaving me locked up in a room in the tower. The window was me only escape, and 'twas risky, but I kenned we were no' really married and would no' let him force a consummation o' a marriage that was no' e'en real. So, I jumped into the loch from the tower to either escape or die. I survived and swam fer a bit, then walked following the loch, and ended up here."

Raising her chin, she finished grimly. "There is no way I can be married to Maldouen MacNaughton. The ceremony ye performed was a true one. I'm married to Calan Campbell, and as that sheet proves," Allissaid said blushing even as she gestured to the crumpled, bloodstained sheet he still held, "the marriage has been consummated. It can no' be undone. I came to him with me innocence intact."

"Aye," Alick put in when she fell silent. "Calan only wants ye to hold off on announcing their wedding and her presence here to keep me cousin safe until we are sure MacNaughton can no' come after her, steal her away again and hurt her. Me own brothers, Dougall and Niels Buchanan, rode to the king to ensure MacNaughton could no' get away with his wicked efforts to force Allissaid into marriage."

While Calan was sure Inghinn's and Alick's words had only reaffirmed the priest's decision, he knew it was really Allissaid's words that had swayed the man fully to their side. It was her calling Father MacMillan's recitation lovely, and the bit about his obviously being faithful to their Lord. The man had puffed up a bit more with each compliment, and Calan was quite sure that by the time she'd finished, the priest was wholly on their side, so wasn't terribly surprised when the man nodded solemnly.

"Very well. We will no' hang the linen fer now," Father MacMillan decided. "In fact, I think 'twould be best that before we do hang it, we ha'e another ceremony, one at the steps o' the church fer all to witness."

"A good idea, Father," Allissaid murmured when Calan merely grunted at the suggestion.

Father MacMillan nodded, and said, "If we are doing that, we may as well just forego mentioning the first ceremony, and hang the sheet the morning after the next one as if it were the first and only wedding."

"Aye," Calan agreed, just glad the man was co-operating.

"Thank ye, Father," Allissaid breathed, her lips curving into the first real smile since the priest had begun to squawk about sacraments and her possibly being married to MacNaughton.

"Then ye may as well keep this here, in yer chest or somewhere safe, m'laird," he suggested, holding out the crumpled sheet.

Calan took it with a nod.

"Very good." Father MacMillan turned to cross to the door, but then paused to say, "I suppose ye'll no' be able to attend mass until this is resolved?"

"Nay," Calan said before Allissaid could respond.

The priest nodded thoughtfully, and then said, "Well, then I shall come up here to hold a separate mass fer the two o' ye until this situation is over."

Before Calan could respond, the priest opened the door and departed the room.

"Lucky you," Alick said with amusement after the door had closed.

"Aye," Calan said dryly, and then scowled at Allissaid and caught her arm when she headed for the door. "Where do ye think ye're goin'?"

"I want to go check on Moire and be sure she's all right," Allissaid said, tugging at her arm.

"Nay," he said at once, urging her toward the bed instead. "Ye need yer rest. Ye've had hardly any sleep at all."

"But—"

"Besides, if Mother has given her a tonic, the lass'll sleep all day," Calan pointed out reasonably, and when she looked fretful, promised, "I'll take ye to check on her later, through the passage, so no one sees ye. Now get back into bed. I do no' want ye sick from lack o' sleep."

"Oh, very well," Allissaid said with resignation, and turned to walk toward the bed, but complained, "But I'll no' sleep long fretting o'er Moire. Besides, I'm hungry."

Calan had turned to head for the door, but stopped walking at once at her words. Now that she'd mentioned food, he was aware that his own belly was complaining at being empty. He was also thirsty.

"Get into bed," he said after a pause to consider the matter. "I'll fetch us both a snack and drink."

Calan didn't wait for her response, but then turned toward the door again. All it took was a glance for Inghinn and Alick to join him.

"I'd appreciate it did ye stay here to guard the room until I return with food and drink," he said to Alick as he stepped out into the hall. "But ye can go below to break yer fast once I'm back. I'll keep Allissaid safe while ye're below."

"O' course," Alick said at once.

Nodding, Calan escorted his sister below stairs to the trestle tables, and then hurried into the kitchens to see if Cook had any sweet pasties. He was having a hankering for them and knew Allissaid enjoyed them as well.

ALLISSAID SHIFTED RESTLESSLY IN THE BED, her gaze moving to the door and away as she waited impatiently for Calan to return. She was hungry, and thirsty, but now that she was in bed and no longer distracted by the priest with his concerns, and Moire and her injuries, she was quickly growing tired. She'd yawned so wide and so many times since Calan had left, her eyes had begun to water. Her husband hadn't been lying when he'd said she'd had little sleep last night. They'd spent hours in the bed, but with precious little sleep to show for it. Her husband had appeared insatiable their first night as man and wife. Worse yet, his hunger had raised a powerful one in her as well and she'd behaved most . . . well, truthfully, she'd been shameless in her need for him.

Calan may have started the loving, but in the end, Allissaid was pretty sure she'd reached for him as often as he'd reached for her in the night. The pleasure he'd shown her was truly addictive and she hadn't been able to stop, even when she'd grown tender where they joined from all the activity. Allissaid had never experienced anything like the need he raised in her and wondered if that would continue. Even now, she couldn't help wondering if he'd bed her again before they rested.

She shook her head at her own sudden compulsion for loving . . . at least when it was with Calan. She didn't think she'd want anyone else to do the things he had to her. That was something, at least, she supposed. Although, Allissaid suspected some of her enthusiasm for the marriage bed might be tempered by whatever penance Father MacMillan gave her after her next confession.

Grimacing at the thought, Allissaid shifted restlessly again and decided to think of something else. Her mind immediately turned to Moire and her poor battered face. The maid was normally a pretty little thing. So pretty in fact, that she was quite popular with the soldiers at MacFarlane. Not that any of them had got anywhere with her. As far as Allissaid knew, Moire had rejected every one of her father's men who had approached her, which had led to some of them claiming Moire thought she was "too good for her own sort." Whatever that meant. Allissaid just supposed the lass was choosey about who she kept company with. In her opinion, there was nothing wrong with that. In fact, Allissaid felt the maid was lucky to have the choice. She herself hadn't been given one. Her parents had hammered out the marriage contract with Alban Graham's parents when they were both still bairns.

Of course, that hadn't turned out in the end, and really, when it came right down to it, while circumstances had led to her marriage to Calan, Allissaid did sort of pick him herself by responding so shamelessly to his advances in the garden. She was just fortunate that he was good, and kind, and considerate and made her toes curl in the marriage bed.

Finding herself back thinking on that, Allissaid shifted her mind determinedly back to Moire and briefly debated trying to talk her way around Alick to go check on the maid. But she knew that wasn't likely; Alick could be as stubborn as his older brothers when it came to duty, and he would no doubt consider it his job to keep her safely in the bedchamber until Calan returned. Now, if she knew how to open the secret entrance to the hidden passage here, she could slip out that way to go look in on the maid.

That thought had her looking toward the fireplace and the large stone mantel around it. That of course would be where it was. At least, she suspected it must be, and the next thing Allissaid knew, she'd tossed the linens and furs aside and climbed out of bed to go examine the stone surrounding the fireplace. There were no strangely shaped, or slightly protruding stones to give away how to open the passage, but with nothing better to do, she began running her hands over the cool, smooth rocks, pushing here and tugging, then trying to turn others. She was so caught up in the hunt that she didn't hear the door open, and didn't realize her husband had returned until he said, "Ye'll ne'er find it on yer own."

Gasping, Allissaid whirled guiltily away from the wall and clasped her hands in front of herself as she watched him carry a tray of food and drink to the table and set it down. "I was just . . ."

"Hoping to sort out how to open the passage to go check on Moire while I was away?" he suggested.

"Aye," she admitted quietly and swallowed nervously when he walked toward her. Calan didn't seem angry, still she actually flinched when he raised his hand toward her.

The action made him stop at once, and for a moment she saw anger flash across his face. But then he rested his hands lightly on her shoulders and said solemnly, "Pay attention, love. I'm no' like Mac-Naughton. I do no' hit women, and will definitely ne'er hit you. That's a vow I'm makin'. I will ne'er hit ye. Do ye understand?"

When Allissaid nodded silently, he used his hold on her shoulders to turn her toward the stones she'd been examining just moments ago. "Count three stones o'er from the mantel and three down."

Allissaid hesitated, and then placed her hand on the stone three over and three down from the mantel.

"Now, turn it from left to right and then push on it," he instructed.

Allissaid turned the stone as far as it would from left to right and then pushed and felt the click rather than heard it before the wall shifted and popped open a few inches toward her.

"There," Calan said, and then reached over her shoulder to push the wall back into place and turn the stone in the opposite direction. "Now ye ken."

"Thank ye," Allissaid whispered, turning to face him.

Calan shrugged, and caught her hand to lead her to the table where the food waited. "Ye're me wife. Ye should ken how to open the passage. Now come and let's eat. I've another thing or two I'd like to show ye ere we sleep."

"Another thing or two?" she asked with curiosity as he stopped next to the table.

"Aye," Calan said easily, pulling a chair out for her to sit on. As he pushed it closer to the table, he leaned down and whispered by her ear, "Things ye need to be naked for."

Allissaid's eyes widened, as much from the words as from the way they made her body start to hum. She couldn't wait to see what these "things" were.

Chapter 17

$\mathcal{A}$LLISSAID FOUND HERSELF ALONE IN BED the next time she woke up. Stifling a yawn, she sat up and peered around the room for her husband, but he wasn't there. A little disappointed by his absence, she hesitated briefly, and then climbed out of bed and began to look for her clothes. Now that she was awake, again, Allissaid had to use the garde-robe, and quite desperately.

That concern paramount in her mind, she dressed quickly, and then hurried to the door and cracked it open. Allissaid wasn't at all surprised to find Alick on the other side of it. She was a little surprised, though, to see Inghinn there, laughing at something he'd said. The girl's laughter died, her eyes going wide when she spotted Allissaid.

"Ye're awake," she proclaimed as if it were a grand surprise.

Allissaid did not have time for niceties. Nodding, she looked up the hall to be sure no one else was about, and then slid out of the room.

"Where do ye think ye're—Oh." Alick ended his question when she reached the door to the garderobe and pulled it open.

Ignoring him, Allissaid simply slipped inside to tend her business and was more than a little relieved to be able to do so.

"Where is Calan?" she asked when she stepped back out into the hall a couple of minutes later.

"Down in the bailey with his men," Alick answered, opening the bedchamber door for her as she approached. "He did no' think ye'd be awake anytime soon. I'm sure he'll return shortly though."

Allissaid nodded, but slowed as she approached the door, and glanced past the couple to the other rooms up the hall. "How is Moire doing?"

"She's sleeping still," Inghinn answered. "Though mother thinks she will wake soon."

"Really?" Allissaid asked, buoyed by this news. She really wanted to talk to the girl, find out what had happened and if she had any news on what MacNaughton was getting up to and what he planned to do next.

"Aye," Inghinn assured her.

"Which room is she in?"

"The next one up the hall between the master chamber and Calan's old room," Inghinn answered helpfully.

"Ye're no' going to see Moire, so get that out o' yer woolly head right now," Alick said at once, his eyes narrowing on her.

Allissaid scowled at her cousin, opened her mouth to argue, and then closed it again just as quickly. In the end, she just shrugged and walked through the door he was holding open, saying, "Then I suppose I might as well go back to sleep fer a bit. I only woke because I had to use the garderobe."

Much to her relief, Alick and Inghinn took her at her word, and wished her good sleep before Alick pulled the door closed.

Smiling to herself when she glanced back to see that the door actually was closed and that her cousin and new sister by law had not followed her into the room, Allissaid immediately changed direction and headed for the mantel. Alick might be able to stop her going next door via the hall, but she had another way she could go now, Allissaid thought. She'd just pop next door, check on Moire, and be back before Calan or anyone else discovered she was missing.

CALAN WAS WALKING BACK TO THE KEEP FROM the practice field when a group of his men escorted a pair of riders into the bailey. His eyes narrowed briefly on the two newcomers, and then widened as he recognized that they were Buchanans. At least, that was his guess. They both looked a lot like older versions of Alick Buchanan, just a little bigger and grimmer.

It was that grimness that set his teeth on edge, and had him picking up his pace as he hurried to catch them before they entered the keep. On foot as he was, Calan wouldn't have managed the task had one of his men not seen him coming and pointed him out to the two newcomers. It was enough to make the men wait for him after dismounting.

"M'laird, this is Dougall and Niels Buchanan," Hamish, one of his better men and head of the day patrol, announced as he reached them. "We came across them on our patrol, so escorted them back."

Calan nodded at the man, and then shifted his gaze to the brothers, but his heart was suddenly pounding something fierce. These were the two men who had ridden out in search of the king to put Allissaid's plight before him and ask him to invalidate or annul the wedding MacNaughton had tried, but failed, to force. The fact that they had come to Campbell, and looked so grim, suggested something had gone awry. Either they'd returned to find everyone at MacFarlane dead, murdered at the hands of MacNaughton, or the king had decided to uphold the sham marriage. Neither outcome was one he wanted to even consider, but truth be told he'd prefer the second option. If that were the case, he'd simply kill the bastard, making Allissaid a widow, and then marry her all over again, which he'd planned to do anyway. But if the first option was what had happened, while he'd still kill the MacNaughton, he'd also have to break the news to his wife that her entire family was dead. He didn't think he had it in him to do that.

Calan was trying to mentally prepare himself for either outcome, when the slightly smaller of the two men, Niels, Hamish had said, suddenly smiled and announced, "The king decreed the wedding MacNaughton tried to force a sham. We're here to escort Allissaid home."

Calan let his breath out slowly as those words

flowed over him, and took a moment to savor the victory. His gaze then flickered to Hamish and he gave him a nod of dismissal. The moment his men started to ride away, Calan turned to start up the stairs, saying, "Thank ye. This is good news. But ye'll no' be escorting me wife anywhere without me."

"Yer wife?" Niels barked.

"Ye ruddy bastard," the other man, Dougall, growled, rushing up the steps after him and jerking him around. "Ye promised to keep our cousin safe and then forced her to marry ye?"

"I would ne'er force a woman to do anything," Calan assured him calmly. "Allissaid was no' forced." The words had barely left his lips, when he frowned and reluctantly added, "Well, at least, if she was, it was no' me doing the forcing."

"Well, then who the hell did?" Niels asked, knocking Dougall's hold off Calan's arm and moving in front of him himself.

"Yer brother. Alick," Calan responded and then left them gaping after him and continued up the stairs. But his mind was on what he'd just said, and it wasn't really true. But was. Alick had insisted they marry right away, but neither he nor Allissaid had protested, and he had already told her that he planned to approach her father about marriage before that and she'd seemed amenable. Or, actually, she hadn't really responded at all other than to stare at him wide-eyed . . . and then he'd started in kissing and touching her. Alick had caught them at it and said they should marry at once.

While Allissaid hadn't argued, she hadn't really

said anything at all, Calan realized, and now wished she had. At least then he'd know how she felt about their wedding. He hoped she had wanted it and was glad for it. He certainly was. She was an amazing woman and he enjoyed every minute with her. Not just the bedding, which was, frankly, the most enjoyable he'd ever experienced. Calan had had many lovers in his life, all more experienced than Allissaid, and still he preferred her true passion and innocent exuberance over the tricks and expertise of more skilled women. But that was not all he liked about her. He enjoyed talking to her too. In fact, she was one of a very few people he felt comfortable discussing anything with so far. She was proving to be very smart and he liked that about her too. Calan also admired her courage and determination. He respected her, and he wanted her to feel all those things for him too. But he wasn't sure she did.

Now that he was thinking about it, Calan realized that Allissaid hadn't really been given a choice over marrying him. Once Alick had caught them in the gardens, marriage had been necessary to save her reputation. Did she want to be married to him? Had he forced her into marriage with his actions? The lass had seemed to like him, and showed every evidence of enjoying his attentions in bed, but perhaps he was no better than MacNaughton. Whether forced into marriage by brute force, or seduction, she'd still been forced and that idea troubled him.

"Alick forced Allissaid to marry ye?" Niels asked with what sounded like disbelief a moment later as Calan opened the door to the keep and strode in.

The words made him pause and he turned to
scowl at the pair. "I'd appreciate it did ye no' discuss this where others might hear. For safety's
sake, we've been keeping Allissaid's presence here
a secret since her arrival. I'd rather it no' get out
this way," he said grimly. "If ye'll follow me, we'll
go tell Allissaid and Alick the good news and ye
can talk to them yerselves."

"Very well," Niels agreed grimly. "We'll ha'e a
nice long talk with the pair o' them."

"Aye," Dougall grunted the word and glowered at
him, but Calan just turned to lead the way upstairs.

Alick was sitting on the floor in the hall outside
the master bedchamber. Inghinn sat beside him and
the pair were playing Poch and chatting idly. Calan
had no idea what they were discussing, but noted
with a bit of irritation that he made it all the way
to stand next to them before either of them noticed
his approach. So much for guarding Allissaid, he
thought grimly, and merely gestured to the new ar-
rivals following him and then walked around the
couple to get to the door.

He heard Alick's exclamation of surprise as he
spotted his brothers, and was vaguely aware of him
leaping to his feet and helping Inghinn up, but Calan
left them to it and entered the bedchamber to rouse
his wife from sleep to meet her cousins. At least,
that was his intention. He'd assumed because Alick
and Inghinn were in the hall, his wife was still abed.
But he paused a step into the room when he saw
that not only was Allissaid not in bed, but the room
was empty. Swinging around, he stepped back into

the hall and interrupted Alick's explanation to his brothers of the events that had taken place here by barking, "Where's me wife?"

Alick turned a blank expression his way, and then frowned and said, "In bed."

"Nay. She's not," Calan growled.

"Aye. She—" Alick broke off as he stepped up to the door and saw the empty room. Expression turning grim, he explained, "She came out to visit the garderobe, and then wanted to go visit Moire after."

"Moire the maid that went missing from Mac-Farlane at the same time as Allissaid?" Niels asked, joining them at the door.

"Aye. One o' me patrols found the lass on our property this morn. She was badly beaten. When Allissaid asked if MacNaughton did it, she said, aye, and that he was angry she'd escaped. I had her put in a room," Calan explained quickly, and then asked Alick, "What happened after she visited Moire?"

"She did no'. I would no' let her," he admitted. "I did no' want to risk anyone seeing her from the great hall. She said she would get more sleep then and went into the master bedchamber. She has no' come back out since."

Calan turned to peer at the spot where the entrance to the secret passage was, the entrance he'd shown her how to open just that morning, and then cursed under his breath. Pulling the door closed, he started up the hall, aware the others were following him.

Ignoring them, Calan strode straight to the room Moire had been placed in, thrust open the door and started inside. This bed, too, was unoccupied and the room empty. But there was a candle and its holder lying on the rushes on the floor near the entrance to the secret passage.

"WHY HAVE YE STOPPED?"

That question was accompanied by Moire poking Allissaid in the back with the knife she'd been holding on her ever since she'd entered the room where the maid was supposed to be resting. Instead of sleeping, Moire had been up and—Allissaid suspected—trying to find the secret entrance to the passages. Although, it was hard to imagine a way the maid could have known about the secret passage, so maybe she'd just happened to be by the fire. All Allissaid knew was that she'd lit a candle in Calan's bedchamber—and hers too now they were married, she supposed—and then opened the passage and crept along it until she'd noted a tall door-shaped section of stone that appeared recessed slightly in comparison to the other stones around it.

Stopping there, she'd quickly found the lever next to it. Allissaid hadn't hesitated to try it. She'd watched the recessed portion of wall swing inward, and had stepped inside, relieved to leave the dark cobweb-covered passage behind. Just as Allissaid had noted that Moire wasn't in bed, something sharp had pressed into her back, startling her into dropping the candle she carried. Fortunately, the flame had gone out as it fell, but Allissaid's relief at noting that had died under the shock she'd sustained on recognizing Moire's voice as she'd said, "Perfect timin', m'lady. Now turn around and step back into the passage. We're leaving."

The last several minutes before they'd reached the end of the narrow passage had passed in silence. Mostly because Allissaid was having trouble coming to grips with the fact that Moire, a maid she'd known most of her life, and trusted as she did all the people at MacFarlane, seemed to be kidnapping her. At least that's how it appeared to her. The daft woman had a knife at her back and was making her leave Kilcairn.

"Keep moving," Moire snapped, poking her more firmly with the knife.

Allissaid didn't think she'd drawn blood yet, but if the maid pressed that knife against her any harder than she was doing, she would.

"The ground drops away of a sudden here. I think it might be stairs. I'm feelin' around with me foot," Allissaid explained grimly, and then added a little sharply, "Which I surely would no' ha'e to do had ye let me relight the candle I dropped when ye first stuck me with that pig sticker ye're holdin' on me."

"Shut it and get movin' again," Moire said tensely.

Allissaid ignored the order and took another moment to make sure she knew where she was going before stepping down onto the first tread of the stairway that wound around the tower. She immediately paused again to feel for the next step, and asked, "Why are ye doing this? And what is it exactly that ye're doin'?"

"I'm takin' ye to Laird MacNaughton."

Allissaid stopped dead at this news. Turning with disbelief, she stared into the utter darkness behind her with shock. "What? Why on earth would ye e'en consider doin' that?" she asked with amazement. "Ye're safe at Kilcairn, Moire. We'd no' let Mac-Naughton hurt ye again, or get ye back. In fact, as soon as all this business is dealt with and the king decrees the marriage MacNaughton tried to force me into void, we can—"

"The king already gave his decree," Moire snapped impatiently. "Why do ye think I was sent in to get ye and bring ye out through the passage?"

"Ye kenned about the passage?" Allissaid asked with surprise.

"Aye. MacNaughton said Campbell's sister showed it to him when she was a little girl. He and his father had to stay o'er night after an unexpected storm struck while they were visiting and wee Ginny came to visit him using the passage. She thought he'd be her friend if she showed him. He explored them a bit that night, only enough to find where the tunnel exited outside the keep, then he returned to his room," she told her with grim amusement. "Unfortunately, he only knew how to open the door in the room he was staying in, which was at the far end o' the hall nearest the stairs. I was no' put in that room," she pointed out with a grimace. "I was trying to sort out where the one in the room I was in might be so that I could use it when the time came, but—handily enough—ye opened it from the passage fer me."

"Aye, I was comin' to check on ye," Allissaid admitted bitterly, and then frowned as she realized what Moire had said first. "What do ye mean the king has already given his decree?"

"Just what I said," Moire growled unhappily, and gave her a nudge to get her moving down the stairs again before saying, "One o' the king's couriers arrived at MacNaughton late last night with the news that the king has decided the marriage is no' a real one, and he wants Laird MacNaughton and that old fool priest o' his to present themselves before him at court to explain themselves."

Allissaid felt relief slide through her at this news. Despite her own belief that the wedding hadn't been valid and that she wasn't married to the Mac-Naughton, Allissaid hadn't been at all sure the king wouldn't support him and uphold it anyway. She knew Maldouen's father, the late Laird MacNaughton, used to be a close ally to King James, and had feared the man might base his decision on that connection alone. Which would have meant her marriage to Calan wasn't valid, and she could be ordered to return to MacNaughton and be his wife.

Allissaid quite simply wouldn't have done it. She'd have tied a boulder to her ankle and thrown herself into the deepest part of Loch Awe before allowing that to happen. But the king had decided on the side of right. The wedding with Maldouen was not valid, which meant her marriage to Calan was. She was definitely Lady Allissaid Campbell now. Not that she'd even admitted to herself that she was worried about that, but considering how relieved she was feeling at the moment, and that she was only now certain she could call herself Lady Campbell, Allissaid supposed she must have been. But no more. And it was wonderful. There was no longer any threat that she could be taken away from Calan by MacNaughton. She could keep him as her husband. Something that made her almost want to weep. He truly was the most wonderful man she'd ever met. The kindness and consideration he'd shown taking care of her, the laughter they often shared when talking, the passion he'd taught her . . .

Allissaid knew without a doubt that she could not have been as happy with Alban Graham. Even discounting the possibility that he'd had the French disease and would have given it to her, she had simply not found the man the least bit interesting. In any way. They hadn't even managed to fill the awkward silences between them on the few short occasions they'd been close enough to speak. Aside from that, she hadn't felt any attraction for him at all. Not like with Calan. Aye, as awful as it was to admit it, Alban's death had been a blessing for her, and she was lucky to have Calan to husband. She might even be a little in love with the man. Certainly, his smiles and approval made her feel all warm and fuzzy inside.

Smiling at the thought, Allissaid stopped on the stairs again and turned toward the other woman in the dark to say, "But do ye no' see, Moire. That is wonderful news. MacNaughton can no' hurt either o' us anymore. Ye're here and safe and we'll keep ye that way and see ye returned to MacFarlane unharmed and—"

"I do no' *want* to go back to MacFarlane!" Moire snapped with fury. "I want to stay at MacNaughton with Petey. Why do ye think I let him bruise up me face this way? 'Twas purely to get me into Campbell so that I could get ye out."

"Petey?" Allissaid asked with bewilderment.

"Me lover. We want to be together, but Mac-Naughton'll no' allow it do I no' help get ye wed to him."

Allissaid took a moment to digest that and then said dully, "Ye're workin' with MacNaughton because ye want to, no' because ye're frightened of him."

"O' course I want to!" she said with disgust. "Are ye no' listening? I want to be with Petey! And I worked hard to arrange that. Sneaking messages to him and Laird MacNaughton about what was happenin' at MacFarlane. Arrangin' with 'em to be at the river to take ye. Telling ye Eachann was out by the river so ye'd go down there. Then havin' to get away meself to meet up with 'em too."

Moire released a small growl of frustration. "But then ye ruined it. Escaped out o' the tower! Jumped right into the loch, he said. Who does that?" she cried with disbelief, pressing the knife against her side in her agitation. "Why would ye e'en do that? Laird MacNaughton's a handsome man, with his own clan and castle. His father was a friend to the king! Why could ye no' just accept him as yer husband and stay put?"

"Oh, I do no' ken, mayhap because he only wanted to marry me to claim MacFarlane and planned to kill me whole family to get it," Allissaid snapped back with some fury and frustration of her own.

"Aye, well, that's too bad," Moire growled. "E'eryone dies eventually, so what if they go a little sooner than intended? We'd be at MacNaughton and that's all that matters." She pressed the knife harder against her as she hissed, "Ye need to go to the king with MacNaughton, and tell him yer da and cousins lied. That the wedding was real and ye're happy to be his wife else all will be ruined and he'll no' let me stay at MacNaughton. I'll no' lose Petey because o' yer selfishness. I'm stayin' at MacNaughton with him if I ha'e to drag ye all the way to King James meself."

Allissaid still couldn't see the maid in the utter darkness surrounding them, but was now rather glad she couldn't. She might punch the bitch. Or choke her. Either sounded attractive to her just then as Allissaid realized that while she had trusted Moire, had always been kind to her, and had even worried about her so much that she'd left the safety of the master chamber to traipse through the nasty passage to check on her . . . Moire had been working against her from the beginning.

"Ye let this Petey beat ye to make yer way into Kilcairn purely to force me out o' where I was safe and happy and drag me back to a man who wants to kill me whole family and ye call *me* selfish?" she asked with disgust.

"Petey did no' beat me silly," Moire said with exasperation. "He slapped me around a bit is all."

Petey had done much more than slap her around a bit, but Allissaid let that go and asked, "How did ye ken I was at Kilcairn?"

She'd spent weeks stuck in one bedchamber and then another to hide her presence, only leaving for the picnic that had seen her married and—

"When ye went missing, MacNaughton sent out nearly e'ery last man he has to search fer ye. When they could no' find hide nor hair o' ye and he got word ye'd no' returned to MacFarlane either, he began to suspect ye might be either here or with the Campbells to the south. He sent his spies out to check at Innis Chonnel to the south, and had Petey find out what he could on his monthly fishin' trip with his brother."

"His brother?" Allissaid asked with confusion.

"Petey's brother married a Campbell lass, and moved here to be with her," Moire explained, and then added enviously, "He e'en switched his fealty to the Campbells to do it."

"He must ha'e loved her," Allissaid said mildly, more than happy to play on that envy in the hopes of using it against her. After all, Moire claimed to be doing this to get to stay at MacNaughton and be with Petey, whoever that was. She'd even let herself be beaten for it, and this Petey had either done it himself, or allowed it to happen. That didn't sound very loving to her, and if she could get Moire to see that, perhaps she could convince her to change sides.

"Anyway," Moire continued, "while he switched fealty, Petey's brother still visits his family on occasion, and meets up with Petey e'ery couple o' weeks to do some fishin' and visitin' too. MacNaughton told Petey to find out what he could, but no' to tip his hand and make it seem like he was fishin' fer more than trout. And he did," Moire said with satisfaction. "They got talkin' on his wife and how she's with child, and Petey's brother told him how he was worried it was makin' her a little tetched in the head. She's weepin' all the time, and then shoutin' at him, and he thinks mayhap e'en imagining things because she swears she saw a cloaked lass sneakin' out o' the keep one night when she could no' sleep, and then no' moments later, saw their laird draggin' the same cloaked lass back through the great hall and above stairs."

Moire gave a short laugh. "Petey's brother thought his wife imagined it, but MacNaughton was sure she hadn't and that the cloaked lass she saw was you."

Allissaid's mouth tightened at this news. She'd given away her own presence the first night she'd been here. Or had it been the second? she wondered. The first couple of days of her stay here were all a bit muddled in her head thanks to her injuries and Lady Fiona's tonics. As far as she could tell, she hadn't forgotten anything that had happened to her, but she wasn't sure on the timeline of some events.

"And he was right." Moire's voice was soaked in satisfaction as she said that, but then turned cold as she snapped, "Now get movin'. Petey and Laird MacNaughton are waitin'."

The words were accompanied by a sharp push that caught Allissaid unprepared and sent her stumbling back off the step she was standing on. An alarmed cry slid from her lips as she lost her balance and was suddenly falling.

Allissaid did the best she could to save herself, first reaching out for the wall, hoping to find something to grab onto. When her hand slid over smooth wall, however, she changed tactics, and threw her arms over her head in an effort to minimize the damage. They must have descended farther down the staircase than she'd realized, because her fall was over quickly, or seemed to be. Allissaid crashed through darkness, bumping off stairs and rolling down perhaps only a dozen more steps before finding herself splayed on cold stone.

A little dazed when she came to an abrupt halt, Allissaid lay still for a moment. Then she began a silent inventory of her hurts. She'd definitely gained a few new bruises, that was certain, but she'd managed to save her head from further injury, and miraculously enough, didn't think anything was broken.

She was also several steps below Moire and her knife, Allissaid realized suddenly when she heard shuffling above her as the maid started cautiously down after her.

"Where are ye?" Moire asked, sounding both angry and anxious.

Presumably it wouldn't do the maid's cause any

good if she caused her death, Allissaid supposed with disgust, and then forced herself to ignore her aches and pains and move. Trying to be as quiet as she could, she sat up. Wincing at the small, unavoidable rustling sounds she made, she then got to her feet, found the wall and began to follow it forward through the dark.

"I hear ye movin'," Moire said stridently. "Where are ye? Ye can no' get away from me. There's nowhere to go."

Ignoring her, Allissaid continued forward through the tunnel, but was searching her mind for an escape strategy. She had no idea what the plan had been. If MacNaughton was waiting at the end of the secret passage to grab her, or at some designated spot farther away. But Allissaid really didn't want to find out by ending up in his clutches again. However, she also couldn't go back the way she'd come. Blind as she was, she'd probably bump into the other woman or brush up against her. Either outcome would see her under threat of Moire's knife again. All she could do was continue forward through this new passage and hope for the best, Allissaid thought as Moire shrieked, "If ye do no' answer me, it'll be worse fer you in the end."

Allissaid grimaced at that. To her mind, worse for her would be ending up in MacNaughton's clutches again, so she stayed silent and kept moving.

"NEITHER ALLISSAID NOR MOIRE CAME OUT through the hall door," Alick said solemnly from behind Calan when he continued to stare into the empty room. "I assume ye've secret passages here?"

"Aye," Calan growled, trying to sort out why Allissaid would use them to leave.

"Where do they come out?" Alick asked, and then explained, "We'll ride out to the area while ye use the passages. Coming from both directions, we should be able to catch them between us."

"But why would Allissaid use the secret passage?" Inghinn asked with concern. "Where would they e'en be going?"

"They can no' be plannin' to go far," Alick pointed out. "Allissaid would no' just wander off for no reason, and Moire is badly beaten and can no' want to move about much."

"Nay, she's no'," Inghinn said thoughtfully and when Calan turned to her in question, she grimaced and told them, "While Moire's face looked a muckle mess when she first arrived, there were no broken bones, or permanent damage. In truth, all she had was a couple o' black eyes, a split lip, a smallish bruise on one cheek and a hand-shaped bruise on the other as if she'd been slapped sharply." Her gaze slid to the bed where the girl had been resting. "It turned out a lot o' what we thought was bruising was just dirt that washed off when we put cold cloths on the spots."

Calan's mouth tightened at this news. It sounded to him like Moire had been made to look more injured than she actually was. Now the maid was missing and Allissaid with her. The two things had to be connected, he thought, and then recalled that the only reason Allissaid had been outside of MacFarlane castle to be captured by MacNaughton was because the maid had sent her out after her brother . . . who hadn't been outside the castle walls at all.

Cursing, he turned to Alick and barked, "Fetch yer horses and find Gille. He's in the practice field with the men. He'll lead ye to where the passage comes out. Have him bring me horse too. I'll walk through the passage and meet ye all down there."

Calan didn't wait for anyone to agree with his plan, he simply stepped into the chamber where Moire had been resting, and closed the door on all of them. He then headed for the entrance to the secret passage here. He was going to find his wife.

Chapter 18

$\mathcal{A}$LLISSAID DIDN'T AT FIRST REALIZE WHAT had happened when the path ended abruptly and she walked into a solid wall. Hands rising to run over the stone surface, she figured out that it must be the end of the passage and the exit must be somewhere here.

Aware of Moire coming behind her, and that the other woman had managed to shorten the distance between them since getting off the steps, Allissaid briefly ran her hands over the surface. She was desperate to open the passage and escape, but there was no time, Moire would be on her any second.

Swallowing the curse she wanted to shout, all Allissaid could think to do was crouch down in the corner and make herself as small as possible. Maybe the maid would encounter the wall, think she'd managed to slip past her, and head back along the passage toward the castle in search of her. That would give Allissaid the time she needed to figure out how to open this door and escape. She hoped.

A soft grunt just in front of her announced that
Moire had reached the wall. Allissaid immediately
held her breath, afraid even that soft sound might
give away her position. But the woman didn't turn
and head back the way she'd come. Instead, Allissaid heard a soft sweeping sound, as if she was
brushing her hands over the stone wall.

Probably in search of the lever to release the door,
she thought, which made her panic a little. Allissaid
knew she could not hold her breath much longer
and was now sure the woman would hear even the
softest exhale and inhale. She was debating lunging
blindly upward at the woman and hopefully over-
powering her, when she recalled the night Calan
had taken her down to the loch after her bath. He'd
been carrying her, his hands full, and had seemed to
kick out at something.

Reaching out with her right hand, Allissaid felt
along the lower wall next to her until she encountered
a protruding stone. She hesitated briefly, but then—
hoping the woman would think she'd somehow
triggered a lever herself with her search—Allissaid
pushed firmly against the stone. There was a click,
and then the first bit of light since they'd entered
the passage crept through a small seam that had appeared in the wall.

Unfortunately, Moire didn't rush out as she'd
hoped. Instead, the maid pushed the stone door
further open and started to turn to look around for
her, but now with the light to aid her. The maid
didn't even manage a half turn before spotting her
crouched in the corner.

Allissaid didn't even think, reacting like any trapped animal, she launched herself up and forward. She tackled Moire around the waist with enough force and momentum that the maid stumbled back, and through the opening. Grappling now, they stumbled across a good-sized cave with an opening wide enough to make it very bright inside, but she didn't get to see much more than that before Moire lost her footing. They both crashed to the ground then, Moire on her back and Allissaid on top of her. She heard the maid grunt as the air was knocked out of her and immediately tried to take advantage of the moment to scramble up and away.

She wasn't quick enough. Before Allissaid could get more than half-upright, Moire caught her arm and then kicked at her legs, knocking them out from under her. The move sent Allissaid crashing onto her side on the hard-packed dirt next to the other woman. Moire then immediately rolled to sit on her, with her knees on either side of her waist. The maid's face was a mask of fury as she then grasped her knife in both hands, raised it over her head and brought it down swiftly, aiming for her heart. Allissaid was sure she was about to die when, halfway through the stabbing motion, Moire gasped and froze as a sword suddenly protruded from her chest.

Allissaid stared at the bloody tip of the sword, and then raised her gaze to Moire's face to see that her anger was gone. In its place was a sort of bewilderment. When it suddenly morphed into a wince, accompanied by another grunt, Allissaid automatically glanced back down to the sword tip, just in time to watch it disappear back into the maid's body.

"She's no good to me dead, ye stupid bitch," Maldouen MacNaughton snarled, suddenly coming into view next to Moire as she slumped forward. His bloody sword was now hanging at his side, Allissaid noted just before he grabbed Moire by the hair with his free hand, and dragged the woman off her. He then dropped her in the dirt with disgust, and kicked her for good measure.

Allissaid turned her head on the ground and stared at the maid, noting the short, panting breaths she was taking and the faraway look in her eyes. Moire hadn't even reacted to the kick MacNaughton had given her. While Allissaid was not well versed in medicinals and caring for the ill and injured, she was positive that Moire was dying, and despite the fact that the woman had tricked and betrayed her, she felt sorry for her and wondered where her Petey was.

"Weigh 'er down and throw her in the loch, Petey," MacNaughton ordered.

Allissaid stiffened, and then her gaze flickered to the man who moved forward into her line of vision. The dark-haired warrior's handsome face was completely uncaring as he grabbed Moire by one arm and began to drag her toward the mouth of the cave they were in. He pulled her through the dirt like she was nothing more than dross.

Cold, Allissaid thought. The bastard Moire had wanted so much to be with was as cold as MacNaughton and didn't seem to give a toss for her. She wondered if Moire had known that in some part of her heart, or if he'd lied and pretended a caring he didn't feel to convince her to do what his laird wanted.

"The rest o' ye go make sure the boat is ready," Maldouen growled next, and Allissaid turned her head to see that he was glaring at her as he spoke. He continued to do so as he waited for the three men she only now noticed to leave the cave. Only once they were gone did he approach Allissaid. Stepping up to her side, he scowled down at her where she lay and snarled, "Ye've caused a lot o' trouble, me lady wife."

That managed to free Allissaid from the shock and horror that had held her still since seeing the sword explode out of Moire's chest. Even she was somewhat surprised at the speed with which she lunged to her feet and turned on the man.

"I'm no' yer wife," Allissaid spat with disgust. "Much as ye tried to force me to be, I escaped, and the king decreed that sham o' a wedding no' valid."

"Well, ye're going to convince him 'twas a true ceremony," he assured her grimly. "That ye wanted it, and truly want to be me wife."

"I'd rather die first," she growled, her hands clenching at her sides, but knew that was a lie. Allissaid didn't want to die. Not now that she was married to Calan. She could have happily died when she made her escape from the tower. It would have been a sacrifice she'd have willingly given for her family, but now . . . Well, now she wanted to live. Allissaid wanted to be Calan's wife for as many years as she could. She wanted to experience more of the passion he'd shown her last night, and she wanted to laugh, and walk and talk with him. She wanted to bear his children, suckle them at her breast and raise them with him. She wanted a life with him, including all the joys and even sorrows that might bring.

The problem was, Allissaid wasn't sure she'd be allowed to have that. When she'd spoken to Alick, he'd said that Calan should be along soon. If that was true, he'd return to their room to find her missing, and when Alick told him she hadn't left the room via the hall, he'd have to realize she'd used the secret passages. There was not a doubt in her mind that he would come after her and then Calan would be facing four or five armed warriors and Maldouen. She couldn't bear it if that happened and her husband died. As much as she wanted to live, she'd rather die herself than watch Calan die.

"Ye're no' dying," MacNaughton assured her grimly. "But ye will be goin' to the king with me to smooth things over."

Allissaid's mouth tightened at the words, but she forced a cold smile and said, "By all means, then, take me to the king. That way I can tell him how ye planned to kill me whole clan and claim MacFarlane through the marriage ye tried to force on me. And how ye've been raiding yer neighbors fer years now. No' to mention how ye killed both Inghinn's betrothed and tried to kill Calan to force Inghinn into marriage so ye could take Kilcairn."

The man actually did a pretty good job of feigning surprise and confusion at that last accusation, but then he shrugged and sounded somewhat amused as he said, "I'll concede to the raiding and me plans fer MacFarlane. But I had naught to do with the Cameron's death or Calan's wound. Those were either true accidents or someone else's doing."

When Allissaid snorted her disbelief, he gave an uncaring shrug. "It matters little what ye think, as long as ye ken ye're in me power now. Ye'll no' mention any o' that to the king when I take ye to him, else I'll—"

"Kill me family?" Allissaid interrupted sharply. "Since that's yer plan anyway, 'tis hardly a threat fer ye to bargain with."

His gaze flickered briefly and she could almost see the cogs of his mind rethinking before he said, "Aye, well, then how about this? Ye do and say exactly what I tell ye to, and convince the king we are truly married and that ye want to be, I'll let yer younger sisters live and only kill yer father, Claray and Eachann."

A disbelieving huff of sound came from Allissaid before she could stop it. The man was unbelievable, a monster and with no shame about it.

"'Tis a good deal," Maldouen argued coldly. "Ye'd be savin' five o' yer sisters from certain death. I already have a spy in yer da's castle and others on the way to Deagh Fhortan to watch o'er Claray. They're all just waitin' on news from me on how to proceed," he informed her. "Cooperate with me and I'll spare yer younger sisters."

Allissaid's eyes narrowed on the man. She couldn't believe he was bargaining with the lives of her family members. Cooperate and he'd only kill three of them? Dear Lord! "And what if I refuse to cooperate?"

"Then I'll kill ye, kidnap and marry Annis, and kill the rest," he said coldly.

"Would that be before or after ye go before the king?"

Allissaid glanced sharply around at that question to see Calan stepping out of the open entrance behind her. His gaze found hers briefly as he walked to her side, and then shifted to Maldouen as he said, "He's sent fer ye. Do ye no' show up o' yer own accord, he'll doubtless send men out after ye. Do ye really ha'e time to dally about trying to kidnap Annis from MacFarlane and forcing yet another marriage? And what good would that do anyway since I'll no' allow ye to kill me wife."

"Yer wife?" Maldouen asked sharply, his eyes shooting to Allissaid.

"We were married last eve," she admitted, her gaze flickering anxiously to the mouth of the cave as she worried over where MacNaughton's men were. How far was the cave from the loch and the boat he'd sent his men to ready?

"Allissaid was conscious fer *our* wedding," Calan added grimly, drawing her attention back to what was happening in the cave. "She actually spoke her vows and the marriage was consummated last night."

"Nay!" Maldouen roared with fury. "I married her first. I had her fir—"

"She bled for me," Calan growled. "So do no'

e'en try to claim ye had her first. She came to me a virgin. The priest has seen the proof o' it, along with four other witnesses. She's Lady Campbell now, and'll no' be telling the king anything but that," he assured him. "Ye're on yer own with explainin' things to the king, Maldouen. Although I may come to court just to witness what happens. I'd enjoy seein' yer head on a pike fer what ye did to her. As well as for all the trouble ye've caused at Kilcairn, Innis Chonnel and MacFarlane these last years."

Maldouen's eyes widened with horror, but then—apparently hoping Calan had not heard his admission to her moments before his arrival—he said quickly, "I do no' ken what ye're talking about. I've caused no trouble anywhere."

"Nay?" Calan asked with disbelief, and then shrugged. "Well, 'tis sure I am that by now Gille and the Buchanans ha'e rounded up the men who came with ye. I doubt 'twill take much persuadin' to get one o' them to confess what ye've been up to with yer raids, and me in-laws and such," Calan said with unconcern, and then added, "And me wife herself can tell the king how ye killed her betrothed, Alban Graham, and sank his body in the loch, then ordered men to ride out and kill her sisters' intendeds the MacLaren and MacLean." He smiled suddenly. "But I should really thank ye, Maldouen. If no' fer yer ham-fisted ways when it comes to wooin' a lass, and yer incompetence in keepin' one, I may ne'er ha'e met Allissaid, and gained her fer me wife.

Aye," he said with a slowly widening smile. "I owe me happiness all to you, and I want ye to ken . . . I appreciate it."

Allissaid wasn't terribly surprised when Maldouen shrieked with fury, raised his bloody sword and charged Calan. She suspected that was what her husband had been goading him toward. She doubted he wanted to have to take the man into custody, drag him to court, listen to his lies and excuses, and wait for the king's judgment. Calan wanted this business ended here and now, and so did she really. The bastard was a snake likely to slither away at the first opportunity, only to return and raise more trouble the moment your guard was down and your back turned.

Calan had been standing loosely at her side this whole time, his sword in his belt. The moment Maldouen moved though, his sword was out. Her husband even rushed forward to meet the furious man, his sword swinging overhead in both hands. The clang of metal on metal was ear-shattering in the cave, the sound sharp, and reverberating off the stone walls.

Covering her ears with her hands, Allissaid backed up several steps to stay out of the way, and watched with her heart in her throat as her husband did battle with MacNaughton. At first, she was somewhat amazed at the way MacNaughton seemed to be holding his own. From what she knew, and all she'd heard, Allissaid never would have believed MacNaughton was very skilled with the sword. But it wasn't long before she realized that he really wasn't, and that Calan was toying with the man, drawing out the battle for some reason.

Calan was the first to draw blood, slicing Mac-Naughton's arm before withdrawing, and then moving in again and slicing an upper leg when the opportunity presented itself. Each new wound seemed to make MacNaughton more reckless, more furious. His swings became wilder with less power behind them. Eventually, though, he actually got a strike on Calan, a slice across the stomach that made Allissaid gasp in alarm. That was when her husband gave up his game and got serious. It seemed to her almost like a dance when he finally stepped in and to the side and then drove his sword into Maldouen's chest. Ironically, he struck him in almost the exact same spot that the Mac-Naughton had driven his sword through Moire's chest. Only this blow went from front to back, the sword briefly tenting the back of his plaid before Calan twisted and then withdrew it to let the other man fall.

Maldouen crashed to the ground like a stone. There was no shallow panting or slow dying as there had been with Moire. The MacNaughton was already dead before he hit the dirt. Allissaid was quite sure it was that twist her husband had given his sword before withdrawing it that had made the difference. She found herself staring at Maldouen, unable to look away.

This was the man who had tried to force her sister to marry him; killed her betrothed, Alban Graham; and then tried to force her into marriage and a consummation of it. He'd beaten her viciously to the point that death had seemed welcome, or at least not such a bad thing should her attempt to escape cause it, and yet . . . Calan was right. Without all of that, they may never have met and married. If not for Maldouen, she could even now be married to the whoring, gambling, French-disease-infected Alban Graham, never knowing what she'd missed out on with Calan. They really did owe their happiness to Maldouen MacNaughton. The thought was such a strange one, she didn't really know what to do with it, or how to handle it.

It was Calan's stepping in front of her, blocking her view of the MacNaughton, that finally pulled her from these thoughts.

"Are ye all right, love?" he asked with concern when her gaze met his.

Allissaid nodded solemnly, and then gave herself a mental shake and glanced down to the wound on his stomach, a thin line that she could just glimpse through the slice in his shirt and plaid. It wasn't bleeding copiously, so probably wasn't that deep, but even shallow wounds could get infected. "We should get ye back to the castle and tend yer wound."

"'Tis fine," Calan said, catching her hand when she reached toward it. Raising her hand to his mouth, he kissed it and then lowered it, but held on as he turned to lead her out of the cave.

Calan had mentioned while talking to Maldouen that Gille and the Buchanans had probably already rounded up the MacNaughton warriors, so she wasn't surprised when they stepped out of the cave and she saw the men and horses waiting. She was a little surprised that all of MacNaughton's men were dead however.

"We offered to take 'em peaceably, but they decided to put up a fight," Alick said with a shrug when her gaze slid over the bodies littering the clearing outside of the cave.

"Ye look upset," Gille commented with a slight frown. "We would ha'e let them live, and just taken them into custody fer judgment, but they did no' give us the choice."

Allissaid nodded in understanding, but explained, "Maldouen said he had a spy at MacFarlane and others on the way to Deagh Fhortan. I was hopin' one o' his men might ken who they were so that we could round them up."

"Oh," Alick muttered, scowling at the dead men now.

"We'll sort it out," Niels announced firmly, crossing the clearing to give her a hug that lifted her off the ground briefly. Setting her back down, he kissed her forehead and said, "Hello, cousin. Ye're lookin' all grown up and bonnier than I remember."

A real smile split her lips at that, and Allissaid patted his shoulder as he released her. "Yer eyesight is playin' ye false then. I look the same as e'er."

"Nay, ye do no'," Dougall rumbled. Stepping up for a hug of his own, he growled by her ear, "Ye look married. If ye're no' happy with that, or were forced into it, we could fix it fer ye. Mayhap make ye a widow."

"Nay!" Allissaid gasped, pulling back to meet his gaze. "I'm quite happy in me marriage, thank ye. Calan is a wonderful husband. He's considerate, and sweet and sensitive, and . . ." Her voice died when she glanced toward her husband to see him wincing as if in pain. Concern immediately claimed her. "Are ye all right, husband? Is yer wound botherin' ye?"

"Nay. Me wound is fine," he growled, looking disgruntled. "'Tis naught but a scratch."

Allissaid's eyes widened slightly at his tone, until Niels said, "Mayhap he's just feelin' *sensitive*."

Calan's sigh of resignation told her what she'd done. She had given her cousins ammunition to taunt him with. Biting her lip, she searched her mind for some way to rectify the matter, and blurted, "Aye, well he's also strong, and keeps me safe and . . . and he's shamefully good at the bedding too," Allissaid finished, her face flaming even as she said it. Pretending she wasn't presently red as a cherry, she walked to a gaping Calan and took his arm. "Ye should see me back to the castle so yer wound can be tended, husband. I'm thinkin' ye'll need bed rest to recover." Unsure if the men were getting what she was hinting at, she added, "With me o' course . . . and naked."

Eager to get away now that she'd thoroughly embarrassed herself with such brazen talk, Allissaid tried to drag him to the nearest horse, but Calan scooped her up when she reached for the saddle and carried her to another.

"Wrong horse, wife," he told her under his breath before setting her down next to a beautiful black beast and mounting. Allissaid glanced quickly toward her cousins who were still gaping after her, and then gasped in surprise when Calan caught her under the arms and lifted her into the saddle before him. In the next moment, he'd urged the horse to move, leaving Gille and her cousins to deal with the bodies of MacNaughton and his men.

"I'm sorry," Allissaid blurted as soon as they'd ridden far enough away for the other men not to hear. "I forgot me cousins like to tease, and did no' think o' what I was sayin' before sayin' it."

Calan was silent for a minute and then asked, "Which part are ye apologizing fer, wife? The sweet and sensitive part, or the good at the bedding bit?"

"Both," Allissaid muttered, squirming with embarrassment in his lap, and then not wanting him to misunderstand her, added quickly, "No' that ye're no' good at the bedding. Ye surely are. Ye near to killed me with all the pleasure ye gave me last night. But I'm sorry did I embarrass ye with such brash talk. I was just tryin' to turn me cousins' minds from the earlier things I'd said."

Much to her amazement, Calan's chest began to vibrate against her back as he laughed. Turning, she peered up at him uncertainly. "Ye're no' angry?"

"Nay," he assured her, and bent to kiss her quickly before straightening again. "It was worth the first part to see yer cousins' expressions when ye said the second," he added, and grinned as he said, "I thought Niels was goin' to swallow his tongue, he was that shocked."

"Aye, well I was a bit shocked that came out o' me mouth too," she admitted on a sigh. "Me only excuse is that 'tis yer fault."

"My fault?" he asked with surprise.

Allissaid nodded firmly and crossed her arms bel-
ligerently over her chest as she leaned back against
him. "I find it hard to think clearly sometimes when
ye're near. I start in on thinkin' about how lovely yer
kisses are, and how I'd like some and—Honestly,
husband, I could easily believe ye've visited old
Beathas and got her to make ye a tincture o' love to
make me fall in love with ye and yearn fer yer body
and attention."

"How do ye ken about old Beathas?" he asked
at once.

"Inghinn mentioned her," Allissaid admitted.
"Said some claimed she was a witch, but she's just
good with healin'."

They were both silent for a minute, the only
sound that of the horse's hooves striking the earth,
and then Calan asked, "A tincture o' love?"

Allissaid bit her lip and remained silent.

"Do ye love me, lass?"

Allissaid closed her eyes and wished herself
anywhere but there at that moment. Why did she
let her mouth run away with her like that? She really needed to think before she spoke in the future,
Allissaid lectured herself. Because her words had
led to a question that she had no idea how to answer.
Honestly, she didn't know if she loved him. She certainly liked him. A lot. But how was she to know if
she loved him or not?

Her eyes opened rapidly when Calan covered her
twisting hands with one of his own.

"Ye're wringin' yer hands somethin' awful," he
murmured, and she was quite sure her husband

pressed a kiss to the side of her head before asking a different question. "Are ye truly happy to be married to me, Allissaid? Or did ye just tell yer cousins ye were to keep them from makin' ye a widow?"

"I'm happy to ha'e ye to husband," she admitted quietly.

He was silent for a minute, and then said, "I'm glad. Because I think I love ye, lass. I ken 'tis early to say somethin' like that, but ye suit me so well, 'tis as if God made ye fer me. I meant what I said when I told Maldouen I owed me happiness to him. I ken what happened to ye was terrible, but I'm grateful it led ye to Kilcairn and me. Because I can no' imagine a life without ye, ye've become that important to me."

Allissaid's head whipped around, her eyes wide as she asked, "Truly?"

"Aye," he said solemnly. "I've ne'er been so terrified in me life as I was when I saw that candle on the floor in Moire's empty room and kenned ye'd been taken, or left through the secret passage," he admitted, and then asked, "How did ye end up in the secret passage? Moire could no' ha'e kenned about it. Did ye—?"

"She kenned," Allissaid interrupted. "She said MacNaughton told her about them. He said Inghinn showed them to him when she was a child. He and his father had been forced to stay the night during a storm, and she came to visit him through them. He explored them that night." She paused briefly and then told him, "However, while he knew about and told her how to open the one in the room he'd stayed in, Moire wasn't placed in that guest room. She was looking for the entrance in her room when I entered."

Calan's mouth tightened at this news, and then he said, "I think it best ye no' tell me sister that. Inghinn would just feel guilty did she know the part she played in Moire takin' ye."

"Nay. I'll no' tell her," Allissaid agreed, and bowed her head briefly before admitting, "I think I might be falling in love with you too." Frowning now, she added, "Well, 'tis that or I'm ailin'."

"What?" he squawked.

Allissaid shrugged helplessly. "I get all hot and shivery of a sudden when ye're near or touch me. And me thinkin' often gets muddled too when ye're close. And I ache in unusual places," she complained.

"Hmm," Calan murmured, sounding more amused than concerned. "Sounds like the ague."

"Feels like it too," she grumbled, and then admitted, "But I was scared beyond reason fer ye when ye were battling MacNaughton."

"Ye should no' ha'e been. Ye should ha'e trusted I'd keep ye safe," he said firmly. "So long as I breathe, I'll ne'er let anyone harm ye again. I vow it."

"Aye, well that was what had me scared," she said dryly. "I kenned ye'd come fer me, and that ye'd fight fer me too. I was e'en sure ye could defeat MacNaughton. But I was no' sure how far away his men were and there were several o' them. I worried they'd come running and skewer ye while ye were fighting Maldouen." She shook her head. "I did no' want that. I'd rather die than see ye die, husband. That's why I think this sickly feeling is love rather than the ague or some such thing."

"Most like," he agreed cheerfully.

Allissaid raised her head and turned to scowl at him then. "Well, ye need no' sound so pleased about it, husband."

"Why?" he asked with amusement. "I *am* pleased. I love me wife, and me wife loves me. I may just be the happiest Highlander in Scotland at this moment."

Allissaid's mouth was just curving into a soft smile when he added, "And the fact that ye told yer cousins ye think I'm shamelessly good at the bedding does no' hurt either. I've a lot to smile about."

"Hmm," Allissaid said, her eyes narrowing at this boast. "Mayhap I was wrong when I said ye were sensitive."

Calan nodded, appearing unperturbed. "Make sure ye tell yer Buchanan cousins that on the morrow."

"The morrow?" she asked with surprise. "No' at sup tonight?"

"Nay. Ye'll no' be at sup tonight," he said, and then reminded her, "We will be enjoying bed rest due to me wound." Ducking his head, he kissed her briefly, and then whispered against her lips, "Naked bed rest."

Turn the page for more
historical romance from
Lynsay Sands!

The Perfect Wife

Available May 2023

Prologue

"OH."

That soft breath of sound made Avelyn turn where she stood on the trestle table. Lady Straughton—her mother—had murmured the noise and now paused in descending the stairs to watch with watery eyes as Runilda fiddled with the hem of Avelyn's gown.

Lady Margeria Straughton had been teary-eyed a lot lately, ever since they had received notice that Paen de Gerville had finally returned from the Crusades and wished to claim his betrothed. Avelyn's mother was not taking the upcoming nuptials well. More to the point, she was not reacting well to the fact that Avelyn would be moving to Gerville soon after the nuptials were finished. Avelyn knew her mother was happy to see her married and starting on grandbabies. It was the moving-away part that Lady Straughton did not care for. But then, Avelyn and her mother were very close. So close that rather than be sent away while young, Avelyn had trained at her mother's knee, taught with patience and love.

"Oh," Lady Margeria Straughton breathed again as she crossed the great hall, her maid on her heels. Avelyn shared a smile with Runilda, then shook her head at her mother and said with fond exasperation, "Do I look so hideous that it would see you in tears, Mother?"

"Nay!" Lady Straughton gasped in denial. "You look lovely, my dear. Very lovely. The blue of the gown brings out the blue of your eyes. 'Tis very flattering."

"Then why do you appear so tragic?" Avelyn asked gently.

"Oh. 'Tis just that you look so . . . so much a lady. Oh, Gunnora! My babe is a grown woman now," she bemoaned to the servant at her side.

"Aye, milady." Gunnora smiled patiently. "And so she is. 'Tis time she married and left this home to build her own."

At the maid's gentle words, Lady Straughton's eyes filled with tears once again. They were threatening to well over her lashes and pour down her face when Lord Willham Straughton—who had been seated quietly in a chair by the fire—stood with a squeaking of leather and the jangle of mail. "No tears, my love," he chided as he moved to join the women by the trestle table. "This is a joyous occasion. Besides, we had our Avelyn longer than I had hoped. Were it not for Richard and his Crusades, we most like would have lost our girl at fourteen or shortly thereafter."

"Aye." Lady Straughton moved to lean against her husband's side as he peered approvingly up at his daughter. "And I am ever grateful that we were allowed to keep her to twenty. Howbeit I am going to miss her so."

"As will I," Lord Straughton agreed gruffly. He encircled his wife with one arm as he turned to his daughter. "You look beautiful, child. Just like your mother on the day we were wed. Paen is a lucky man. You do us proud."

For a moment, Avelyn was startled to see her father's eyes go glassy, as if he too might cry; then he cleared his throat and managed a crooked smile for his wife. "We shall just have to distract ourselves as much as possible from our loss."

"I can think of nothing that will distract me from losing our daughter," Lady Straughton said dismally.

"Nay?" A naughty look crossed Willham Straughton's face, and Avelyn was amused to see his hand drop from her mother's waist to cup her bottom through her skirts. "I may be able to come up with a thing or two," he said, then urged her away from the table and in the general direction of the stairs. "Let us to our room so we might discuss these ideas."

"Oh." Lady Straughton sounded breathy, and her next words, while a protest, were somewhat weak. "But Gunnora and I were going to count stores and see what—"

"You can do that later. Gunnora may go rest herself for a bit in the meantime," Lord Straughton announced.

The maid grinned, then slipped out of the room

even as her lady protested, "But what of Avelyn? I should like to—"

"Avelyn shall be here when we return below," he said as he urged her up the stairs. "She is not leaving yet."

"If she leaves at all."

Avelyn jerked in surprise at that softly spoken insult from behind her. She managed to keep her perch on the trestle table thanks only to her maid's quick action in grabbing her arm to steady her.

Avelyn murmured her thanks to the girl and turned carefully to face the speaker.

Eunice.

Her cousin looked as mean-tempered as ever. Her narrow face was pinched, and there was mocking amusement in the eyes that raked over Avelyn. "What do you think, Staci?"

Avelyn's gaze moved to the two young men accompanying the woman. Twin brothers to Eunice, Hugo and Stacius had matching pug-like faces that at the moment bore cruel smiles. The three of them must have entered while she had been distracted by her parents' leaving.

Grand, she thought unhappily. If Avelyn had been blessed in having loving parents, fate had made up for that kindness by cursing her with three of the most horrid cousins in existence. The trio seemed to live to make her miserable. They enjoyed nothing more than a chance to point out her flaws. They had done so ever since their arrival at Straughton some ten years earlier when their castle had been overrun and their father killed. With nowhere else to turn, their mother had brought her children to Straughton, and they had quickly become the bane of Avelyn's young existence.

"I think"—Staci's thick nose turned up as he dropped onto the bench and tipped his head back to peer over Avelyn in her gown—"once Gerville gets a look at what a bovine his betrothed has grown into, he will break the contract and flee for his very life."

"I fear Staci is correct, Avy," Eunice said with mock sympathy as Avelyn flinched under his words. "You look like a great huge blueberry in that gown. Mind you, I do not suppose the color is at fault, for in red you look like a great cherry and in brown a great lump of—"

"I believe I get the point, Eunice," Avelyn said quietly as Eunice and Hugo joined their brother on the bench seat. The warm glow that had bloomed under her parents' compliments died an abrupt death. She suddenly didn't feel lovely anymore. She felt frumpy and fat. Which she was. Only when her parents were around with their unconditional love and acceptance did she briefly forget that fact. Somehow Eunice, Hugo and Stacius were usually there to remind her otherwise.

"I have ever found blueberries lovely and luscious myself."

Avelyn turned away at those sharp words to find her brother Warin closing the door. She wasn't sure how long ago he had entered, but the way he glared at their cousins made her think it had been a while. She wasn't sorry when the trio scrambled back to their feet and made a beeline for the door to the kitchens.

Warin glared after them until they were gone, then turned to his deflated sister. "Do not let them get to you, Avy. You do not look like a blueberry. You look beautiful. Like a princess."

Avelyn forced a smile as he reached up to squeeze her hand. "Thank you, Warin."

His expression was troubled, and Avelyn knew he didn't believe he had convinced her. For a moment, she thought he would insist she was lovely, as a good brother would, but then he seemed to let it go on a resigned sigh. "Do you know where Father is?"

"He went above stairs with Mother," Avelyn told him; then some of the twinkle returned to her eyes and she added, "To discuss methods of distracting her from moping over my leave-taking."

Warin raised his eyebrows, then grinned as he turned toward the doors. "Well, if they come down anytime soon, please tell Father I need a word with him. I shall be down at the practice field."

"Aye." Avelyn watched him leave, then glanced down as her maid tugged at the material of her gown. "What think you, Runilda?"

"I think we might take it in another little bit in the shoulders, my lady. 'Tis a tad loose there."

Avelyn tucked her neck in and tried to peer at herself. Her view of her shoulders was too close and fuzzy to tell how they looked. She had a better view of her overgenerous breasts, gently rounded belly and the hips that she considered to be too wide in the blue gown. A blueberry, Eunice had said, and suddenly the cloth Avelyn had chosen with such care lost its beauty in her eyes. She imagined herself a great round blueberry, her head sticking out like a stem.

Avelyn fingered the cloth unhappily. It was lovely material. But even the loveliest material could not make a silly old round chicken into a swan.

"Milady? Shall I take in the shoulders?" Runilda asked.

"Aye." Avelyn let the material drop from her fingers and straightened her shoulders determinedly. "And the waist as well. And cut away the excess."

The maid's eyes widened. "The waist? But the waistline fits perfectly."

"It does now," Avelyn agreed. "But it shall not by the wedding, for I vow here and now that I shall lose at least a stone—hopefully two—ere the wedding day."

"Oh, my lady," Runilda began with concern, "I do not think 'tis a good idea to—"

"I do," Avelyn said firmly. Smiling with determination, she stepped down from the table to the bench, then onto the floor. "I will lose two stone ere the wedding and that is that. For once in my life I will be pretty and slender and . . . graceful. Paen de Gerville shall be proud to claim me."